FATE OF THE JEDI

# ALLIES

# By Christie Golden

# STAR WARS®

## FATE OF THE JEDI

# ALLIES

## CHRISTIE GOLDEN

DEL REY • NEW YORK

2014 Del Rey Books Mass Market Edition

Copyright © 2010 by Lucasfilm Ltd. & ® or ™ where indicated. All rights reserved. Used under authorization.

Excerpt from *Star Wars: Fate of the Jedi: Vortex* copyright © 2010 by Lucasfilm Ltd. & ® or ™ where indicated. All rights reserved. Used under authorization.

All rights reserved.

Published in the United States by Del Rey Books, an imprint of Random House, a division of Random House LLC, a Penguin Random House Company, New York.

DEL REY and the HOUSE colophon are registered trademarks of Random House LLC.

Originally published in hardcover in the United States by Del Rey Books, an imprint of Random House, a division of Random House LLC, in 2010.

This book contains an excerpt from *Star Wars: Fate of the Jedi: Vortex* by Troy Denning. This excerpt has been set for this edition only and may not reflect the final content of the finished book.

ISBN 978-0-345-50915-4
eBook ISBN 978-0-345-51956-6

Printed in the United States of America

www.starwars.com
www.fateofthejedi.com
www.delreybooks.com

Del Rey Books mass market edition: May 2011

This book is dedicated to Jeffrey R. Kirby,
for reasons as numberless as the stars

# Acknowledgments

This book did not come to be in a vacuum. The team of people contributing to this series is an outstanding collection of individuals who continue to impress me with their professionalism, talent, and good humor. Thanks must go to Shelly Shapiro, my editor, and her counterpart at Lucas Licensing Ltd., Sue Rostoni, who continue to be enthusiastic supporters of my writing. More gratitude to Leland Chee and Pablo Hidalgo, who are always so quick and helpful with any questions that arise (and special thanks to Pablo for letting me play on Klatooine, which he created). Appreciation and affection go to my two fellow authors: Aaron Allston is an inspiration in his ability to face adversity and maintain humor and good cheer, and Troy Denning has been positively Yodaesque in his advice and support. I'd be happy to buy all of you a drink at the cantina anytime. To the readers who have taken the time to write and tell me how much you enjoyed *Omen,* I am deeply appreciative and hope you continue to enjoy the series and my contributions to it. And again, as always to George Lucas, for giving us all a galaxy far, far away.

# THE STAR WARS LEGENDS NOVELS TIMELINE

 **BEFORE THE REPUBLIC**
**37,000–25,000 YEARS BEFORE**
***STAR WARS: A New Hope***

**c. 25,793** *YEARS BEFORE STAR WARS: A New Hope*

Dawn of the Jedi: Into the Void

 **OLD REPUBLIC**
**5000–67 YEARS BEFORE**
***STAR WARS: A New Hope***

Lost Tribe of the Sith: The Collected
Stories

**3954** *YEARS BEFORE STAR WARS: A New Hope*

The Old Republic: Revan

**3650** *YEARS BEFORE STAR WARS: A New Hope*

The Old Republic: Deceived
Red Harvest
The Old Republic: Fatal Alliance
The Old Republic: Annihilation

**1032** *YEARS BEFORE STAR WARS: A New Hope*

Knight Errant
Darth Bane: Path of Destruction
Darth Bane: Rule of Two
Darth Bane: Dynasty of Evil

**RISE OF THE EMPIRE**
**67–0 YEARS BEFORE**
***STAR WARS: A New Hope***

**67** *YEARS BEFORE STAR WARS: A New Hope*

Darth Plagueis

**33** *YEARS BEFORE STAR WARS: A New Hope*

Cloak of Deception
Darth Maul: Shadow Hunter
Maul: Lockdown

**32** *YEARS BEFORE STAR WARS: A New Hope*

**STAR WARS: EPISODE I**
**THE PHANTOM MENACE**

Rogue Planet
Outbound Flight
The Approaching Storm

**22** *YEARS BEFORE STAR WARS: A New Hope*

**STAR WARS: EPISODE II**
**ATTACK OF THE CLONES**

**22–19** *YEARS BEFORE STAR WARS: A New Hope*

**STAR WARS: THE CLONE**
**WARS**

The Clone Wars: Wild Space
The Clone Wars: No Prisoners

*Clone Wars Gambit*
Stealth
Siege

*Republic Commando*
Hard Contact
Triple Zero
True Colors
Order 66

Shatterpoint
The Cestus Deception
MedStar I: Battle Surgeons
MedStar II: Jedi Healer
Jedi Trial
Yoda: Dark Rendezvous
Labyrinth of Evil

**19** *YEARS BEFORE STAR WARS: A New Hope*

**STAR WARS: EPISODE III**
**REVENGE OF THE SITH**

Kenobi
Dark Lord: The Rise of Darth Vader
Imperial Commando 501st

*Coruscant Nights*
Jedi Twilight
Street of Shadows
Patterns of Force

The Last Jedi

**10** *YEARS BEFORE STAR WARS: A New Hope*

*The Han Solo Trilogy*
The Paradise Snare
The Hutt Gambit
Rebel Dawn

The Adventures of Lando Calrissian
The Force Unleashed
The Han Solo Adventures
Death Troopers
The Force Unleashed II

## REBELLION
## 0–5 YEARS AFTER
### *STAR WARS: A New Hope*

Death Star
Shadow Games

**0**

---

> **STAR WARS: EPISODE IV**
> *A NEW HOPE*

Tales from the Mos Eisley Cantina
Tales from the Empire
Tales from the New Republic
Scoundrels
Allegiance
Choices of One
Honor Among Thieves
Galaxies: The Ruins of Dantooine
Splinter of the Mind's Eye
Razor's Edge

**3** YEARS AFTER STAR WARS: A New Hope

> **STAR WARS: EPISODE V**
> *THE EMPIRE STRIKES BACK*

Tales of the Bounty Hunters
Shadows of the Empire

**4** YEARS AFTER STAR WARS: A New Hope

> **STAR WARS: EPISODE VI**
> *THE RETURN OF THE JEDI*

Tales from Jabba's Palace

*The Bounty Hunter Wars*
  The Mandalorian Armor
  Slave Ship
  Hard Merchandise

The Truce at Bakura
Luke Skywalker and the Shadows of
  Mindor

## NEW REPUBLIC
## 5–25 YEARS AFTER
### *STAR WARS: A New Hope*

*X-Wing*
  Rogue Squadron
  Wedge's Gamble
  The Krytos Trap
  The Bacta War
  Wraith Squadron
  Iron Fist
  Solo Command

The Courtship of Princess Leia
Tatooine Ghost

*The Thrawn Trilogy*
  Heir to the Empire
  Dark Force Rising
  The Last Command

X-Wing: Isard's Revenge

*The Jedi Academy Trilogy*
  Jedi Search
  Dark Apprentice
  Champions of the Force

I, Jedi
Children of the Jedi
Darksaber
Planet of Twilight
X-Wing: Starfighters of Adumar
The Crystal Star

*The Black Fleet Crisis Trilogy*
  Before the Storm
  Shield of Lies
  Tyrant's Test

The New Rebellion

*The Corellian Trilogy*
  Ambush at Corellia
  Assault at Selonia
  Showdown at Centerpoint

*The Hand of Thrawn Duology*
  Specter of the Past
  Vision of the Future

Scourge
Survivor's Quest

# THE STAR WARS LEGENDS NOVELS TIMELINE

**NEW JEDI ORDER**
**25–40 YEARS AFTER**
***STAR WARS: A New Hope***

**35** | YEARS AFTER STAR WARS: A New Hope

**LEGACY**
**40+ YEARS AFTER**
***STAR WARS: A New Hope***

**43** | YEARS AFTER STAR WARS: A New Hope

**45** | YEARS AFTER STAR WARS: A New Hope

# Dramatis Personae

Allana Solo; child (human female)
Ben Skywalker; Jedi Knight (human male)
Han Solo; captain, Millennium Falcon (human male)
Gavar Khai; Sith Saber (human male)
Jagged Fel; Head of State, Galactic Empire
   (human male)
Jaina Solo; Jedi Knight (human female)
Lando Calrissian; businessman (human male)
Leia Organa Solo; Jedi Knight (human female)
Luke Skywalker; Jedi Grand Master (human male)
Maadhi Vaandt; reporter (Devaronian female)
Natasi Daala; Galactic Alliance Chief of State
   (human female)
Sarasu Taalon; Sith High Lord (Keshiri male)
Tahiri Veila; former Jedi Knight (human female)
Vestara Khai; Sith apprentice (human female)
Wynn Dorvan; assistant to Admiral Daala (human male)

A long time ago in a galaxy far, far away. . . .

# Chapter One

ABOARD THE *JADE SHADOW*

BEN WONDERED IF HE'D BE HIS FATHER'S AGE BEFORE things started going right for him on any basis other than what appeared to be happy accidents.

Then he wondered if he'd be older than his dad.

True, he'd had a couple of uneventful years after the war. But then his father got arrested and exiled for a decade. Jedi who had spent formative years on Shelter in the Maw—and yes, Ben was among that number, how reassuring was *that* little fact—started going crazy. Ben and Luke had learned about some creepy powerful being with dark slithery mental tendrils of *need* who was probably responsible for the crazy Jedi, and had been going to pay her a visit inside the Maw when they abducted a Sith. One that was definitely easy on the eyes, but who was nonetheless a Sith, from a whole planetload of them, no less. A Sith who was still with them right now, standing and smirking at them while nearly a dozen frigates crammed with her pals surrounded them.

Yeah. He would *definitely* be older than his dad.

Luke had followed the instructions given by the unnamed, unseen Sith commander of the *Black Wave*, placing the *Shadow* in a parking orbit around Dathomir.

There was no other choice, not with eleven ChaseMaster frigates ready to open fire.

"A wise decision," Vestara said. "I'm fond of my own life, so I'm glad you're cooperating, but if you had attempted to flee they most certainly would have destroyed you."

Luke eyed her thoughtfully. Clearly, he wasn't so sure.

"So," Ben continued, "what are they going to do with us? Are we going to be the main attraction at some kind of Sith ritual party?"

"I've no idea," Vestara said. She might be lying through her teeth. She might be telling the truth. Ben simply couldn't be sure.

"Your cooperation is appreciated, Master Skywalker," came the voice that had first hailed them. Ben and Luke exchanged puzzled glances. Of course, Vestara had told them who was holding her captive, but why the courtesy and respectful title?

"I am High Lord Sarasu Taalon, commander of this force," the voice continued. "Your reputation precedes you. We have studied you, and your son, a great deal."

"I wish I could say the same," Luke said. "I know nothing about you and your people, High Lord Taalon."

"No, you don't. But I am prepared for that to change . . . somewhat. Your vessel carries a Z-95 Headhunter."

"It does," Luke said. "I presume you're about to ask me to come over to your flagship and chat over a nice glass of something."

"You and Vestara, yes," Taalon said. "You will have to turn her back over to us, of course. But there is no reason we can't be civilized about this."

"No thanks," Luke said. "Anything you have to say to me can be said at a distance. Vestara isn't the worst companion I've ever traveled with. I think I'll let her stay here with us for a while longer."

Ben looked again at the Sith girl. His father was right. She *wasn't* the worst companion he'd ever traveled with.

"Let us revisit that subject in a moment," came Taalon's reply. "As I'm sure you know by now, Apprentice Vestara Khai has done a commendable job of keeping us informed of what has transpired. We are aware that you are having . . . difficulty with certain Jedi who were fostered inside the Maw. We believe this is due to the intervention of a being known to us as Abeloth, whom Vestara encountered. Many of our own apprentices are displaying the same symptoms as your younger Jedi."

"Your younger Sith were in the Maw as well?"

"No. But such identical displays of aberrant behavior cannot be attributed to anything else."

Ben was skeptical. But there was so much they didn't know yet. His father's blue eyes met his and he shrugged slightly. It was possible.

"We are many. You are only three," Taalon continued. The third to whom he referred was Dyon Stad, a Force-sensitive human who had joined Ben and Luke on Dathomir and was currently aboard his own Suieb Soro yacht. "We have a common cause."

"Are—are you proposing a formal alliance?" Luke was so surprised he didn't even bother to hide it. Ben, too, literally gaped for a moment. Vestara seemed more shocked than any of them, judging by her expression and her feeling in the Force.

"Precisely."

Luke started to laugh. "I'm sorry, but that doesn't sound like a very Sith thing to say."

The voice was cold when Taalon spoke again. "This creature, this . . . Abeloth . . . has the audacity to reach out and harm *our* apprentices. *Our* tyros. To toy with the Tribe—the Sith. The insult cannot be borne. It *will* not be borne. We are going into the Maw and teach her a lesson."

Ben glanced at his father. "That, however, *is* a very Sith thing to say."

Luke nodded. To Taalon, he said, "It may be that we do not need to teach her a lesson, as it were. We may simply need to find out why she is doing this."

"And ask her nicely to please stop?"

Ben thought Han Solo could learn a thing or two from this Sith about infusing one's voice with sarcasm.

"You just asked me nicely to help you out. Clearly you're capable of good manners," Luke replied, unruffled. "If it accomplishes the goal with fewer or perhaps no casualties, how is that not the best solution?"

There was silence. "It is possible she may not be amenable to . . . polite conversation. What then, Master Skywalker?"

"I will do whatever is necessary to free the ill Jedi from her control," Luke said. "I assure you of that." His voice was not harsh, but there was a tone in it Ben recognized. The deed was almost as good as done when Luke Skywalker spoke like that.

"You agree, then?" Taalon asked.

Luke didn't answer at once. Ben knew what he was struggling with. And he was surprised that it was even a struggle for the Grand Master. Luke was a Jedi. These were Sith. There couldn't possibly be an alliance. Everyone would constantly be watching their own backs.

But then again . . . He glanced at Vestara. She came from an entire culture of Sith. They couldn't be backstabbing one another constantly—they'd have become extinct long ago. Somehow this flavor of Sith had learned how to cooperate. Vestara had proved it was possible. She had worked with Ben and his father before, on Dathomir, and that cooperation had saved Luke Skywalker's life.

"We do have a common goal," Luke said at last. "It would be better to work toward it together rather than getting in each other's way. But don't think that I will not be expecting treachery at every turn. There are fewer enmities more ancient than that of Sith and Jedi."

A sigh. "This thing we both fight might be older than that," Taalon said. "Well, I did not expect this to be a particularly comradely union. Very well. You deliver Vestara Khai. Together, in an alliance not seen since this galaxy was new, Sith and Jedi will confront and defeat their mutual foe—one way or the other. And after that . . . well, let us see where we stand then, shall we?"

"Vestara stays here."

The Sith girl froze. There was a long silence.

"I cannot permit that."

"Then we have no alliance." Another long silence.

"She has information we require. She comes with us, or there is no deal," Taalon said.

"Information about how to reach and confront our mutual foe?" Luke said, turning Taalon's own flowery words back on him. "That, I do not object to permitting her to share. That *was* the information you were talking about, wasn't it?"

"She will come to no harm while entrusted in your . . . care," said Taalon. "None. Or we will attack and destroy you down to your marrow and obliterate your very cells."

"Provided you keep your bargain, she's perfectly safe. Jedi aren't in the habit of torturing children."

Vestara frowned at being referred to as a child. Ben started to smile a little, despite the situation, then realized that she was the same age as he was. He shot his dad a disappointed glance.

"Then I believe we have an agreement," Taalon said.

"Not just yet. We need to decide who is going to be in charge of this alliance first."

"I would suggest we command as a pair, you and I," Taalon said. "No Sith will take orders solely from a Jedi. And I am sure you would bridle at being told what to do by a Sith High Lord."

"I would indeed. And *I* would suggest we begin this joint command by sharing information. You first."

"Ah, but Master Skywalker, you have *our* source of information right there with you. Start with her. We will be prepared to depart within a half hour."

"So will we. I'll be in touch. *Jade Shadow* out."

"Dad," Ben said, the second the communication was terminated. "You just agreed to help the *Sith*."

Luke shook his head. "No, son. I agreed to let the Sith help *us*."

Ben regarded him, incredulity mixed with curiosity. "You trust them to keep their word?"

"I trust them to do what is best for them. And as long as what is best for them is best for us, then we'll be fine."

"And when it's not?"

"Like Taalon said . . . we'll see where we stand then. I'm prepared for that. There are two old sayings, Ben: 'The enemy of my enemy is my friend' and 'Keep your friends close, and your enemies closer.'"

Luke pointedly turned to Vestara, who stood straight with her hands clasped behind her back. "Now," he said, "High Lord Taalon assures me you know everything they do."

She lifted a small information chip. "Most of it's here," she said.

"And what's not there?" Luke asked.

Vestara smiled slightly and tapped her temple. "And this is where it will stay until it is necessary. We have a card game on my world. It is called *Mahaa'i Shuur,* which means Ultimate Success in the tongue of the natives. The rules are complicated, but the goal is simple.

The winner is the one who never, ever has to play his last card."

Luke Skywalker watched Vestara Khai the way, long ago, a bartender named Wuher had watched him at the Mos Eisley cantina—coldly, expecting the unexpected, and looking for an excuse to cease being civil. Her back was to him, hands on her hips, her long brown hair hanging loose. She was looking out over the gathering of Sith vessels that were starting to fall into formation in preparation for departure, and he didn't have to sense her in the Force to make a damn good guess as to what she might be thinking. As soon as he had the thought Luke amended it.

She was Sith. So were they. In Luke's mind, that automatically meant they could not be trusted. Even if they were sincere in this desire to unite forces and approach the Maw with a lot more firepower than the *Jade Shadow* would have mustered alone, there had to be a trick, or a trap. They were Sith. Deception was a keystone of their culture.

Vestara Khai was Sith. But she was also a girl who seemed to have at least a few virtues along with her vices, something Luke found unexpected and disconcerting. No doubt she was contemplating treachery. But he was willing to admit that she also might just be missing her people. A soft sigh escaped her, as if confirming his thoughts.

He had assigned Ben the job of being the first to read through the information Vestara had given them, thinking the task would distract his son from the admittedly attractive female his own age who was going to be living in such close quarters with them. He was not worried for Ben's state of mind regarding the Force. Ben had been through more things in his short life than most beings had in century-long ones. He wasn't likely to be tempted by offers of power or greatness, the usual tools those who tried to corrupt Jedi liked to employ.

But it was, Luke realized, entirely possible that Ben might get a little confused now and then. Vestara was strikingly attractive, and had presumably been through things comparable to what Ben had undergone. And she was extremely, in fact exceptionally, strong in the Force. It was a combination that might make any father at least a little anxious for his Jedi son's well-being.

The *Shadow* was quiet, the air heavy with all the "not talking" that was taking place. The only sound was Vestara's single, almost inaudible sigh and the occasional sounds of Ben shifting position in his chair as he read and occasionally cross-referenced data.

The sudden noise alerting them to an incoming message therefore sounded especially loud. No one actually jumped, but a sense of surprise rippled through them all. Luke glanced at the screen and frowned slightly. Three words flashed.

VESTARA KHAI. PERSONAL.

As far as Luke was concerned, they might as well have been EMERGENCY INCOMING ATTACK.

"Who's it from, Dad?"

"I don't know. But it's for our guest. Do you know who might want to contact you, Vestara?"

Vestara actually looked surprised. Luke felt the faintest flicker of worry, like an echo of a whisper, in the Force. "I've no idea," and it sounded genuine. "Is there a place where I can—"

"I can't let you receive a private message, especially from someone who won't identify him- or herself," Luke said matter-of-factly.

Vestara nodded. "Of course not. If I were in your position, I would take similar precautions."

Luke flipped a switch. "This is the *Jade Shadow* to the anonymous sender of the previous message directed at

Vestara Khai. You must understand I cannot permit her to receive a private missive."

There was a long silence. Luke could feel young ears straining. Then another message appeared, addressed to LUKE SKYWALKER.

THE MESSAGE MAY BE PUBLICLY VIEWED.

"Well, a reasonable Sith, what next," Luke muttered, and touched another button on the console.

A small holographic figure took shape. It was a human male, wearing the traditional Sith black robes. A lightsaber of antique-looking design was clipped to his belt. His long dark hair was pulled up in a topknot. His face was chiseled and handsome.

Vestara's startled gasp revealed her emotions, but the Force did so even more prominently. There was a rush of warm, affectionate feelings, quickly clamped down, as if a lid had been put on a pot. Luke's eyes flickered to the girl, then back to the hologram. Both images appeared to be trying hard not to smile, although Vestara often looked as though she were smiling when she wasn't due to the little scar on her mouth.

"Daughter. You are well."

Luke's eyes widened. Daughter?

Vestara bowed. "Father. I am. It is good to see you. I am pleased that you were among those selected for the honor of this mission."

"You, it would seem, have already brought honor to the Tribe," the elder Khai said. "I understand you are the sole survivor of the . . . initial exploratory team."

"Thank you, Father. I have always striven to elevate the standing of our household."

"Master Skywalker," Khai said. "I understand that you are graciously providing hospitality to my daughter."

"That's . . . a word for it," Luke said.

"And that High Lord Taalon has agreed that you may continue to provide hospitality. Despite a father's wishes to the contrary."

"Let's face it," Luke said. "Sith and Jedi don't exactly mesh well. Put us together and we're about as volatile as Tibanna gas. If you were tentatively allied with eleven Jedi vessels, and my son were aboard *your* ship—well, I think you'd like to keep him there for a while."

Khai considered this for a moment, then nodded slowly. "Very well, your point is taken, and it is a shrewd one. You have promised she will come to no harm. I am sure that if Luke Skywalker gives his word, then every hair on Vestara's head will be safe," said Khai. His voice was melodic and rich and beautiful, just like the voice of every member of this lost Tribe they'd encountered so far.

"It seems we have nothing more to discuss then," Luke said. "Say your farewells and—"

"Dad?"

Luke frowned a little, turning to Ben. "Yes?"

Ben jerked his head a little in the hologram's direction, and Luke muted the sound. "I know we can't just turn her over to them," Ben said, glancing over his shoulder at Vestara, who had been silent as the grave during the debate between the two parents. "But what harm can there be in letting them talk for just a few minutes?"

"A lot," Luke said. "You know that." Neither of them had ever bothered to hide their suspicions of Vestara, and Luke did not attempt to do so now.

"But . . . you said it yourself, what if it were me?" Ben's blue eyes were intense. "What if this situation were reversed, and Vestara's dad was keeping a tight grip on me? A hologram is nice and everything, but you know it doesn't beat actually being with someone. And it's clear they really miss each other."

That much was true. "A private conversation would

enable her to relay anything she's learned from us," Luke reminded him.

Ben rolled his eyes in exasperation. "Dad, let's face facts here—she already *has*. Otherwise how would the Sith know about the Jedi going crazy?"

Luke glanced at Vestara. He was not expecting a sheepish grin and a nod—even if their bluff was called, Sith were not likely to simply docilely show their hands—but neither did she make an earnest effort to contradict Ben. She was a smart kid.

He didn't reply to Ben, but turned around to the console and unmuted the channel. "Since I am prepared to admit that even nexu are fond of their cubs, I'll permit you to see Vestara for a brief visit. I will extend my hospitality to both Khais. You will be permitted to come aboard the *Jade Shadow,* alone, and without weapons." He knew, as he knew Khai knew, that any powerful Force-user did not need weapons to pose a deadly threat. But acquiescing would take this arrogant Sith down a notch. "Any hint of treachery from you and this alliance is dissolved."

Khai frowned. He was clearly struggling to contain his offense. "I would never dream of doing anything to harm a union that my superiors have deemed necessary."

"Then if you are truly simply a concerned father anxious to be reunited with his child, I *certainly* wouldn't stand in the way."

The two regarded each other for a long moment. Out of the corner of his eye, Luke saw Ben and Vestara exchange glances, and the young man stepped closer to her. He seemed to want to put a hand on her shoulder, but stopped just short of making the gesture.

Khai was good. He gave away nothing. At last he said, "Your terms are acceptable."

\*　　\*　　\*

A short time later, Khai's small, podlike ship was secured to the docking port of the *Jade Shadow*. The port was located on the underside of the vessel. Vestara, Ben, and Luke stood awaiting him as he emerged from the connecting tube.

Khai was, not unexpectedly, an imposing presence, both physically and in the Force. He was tall, much taller than Luke, and while not bulky, was clearly muscular. Luke guessed he was in his early forties, but there was no trace of gray in the jet-black hair, and the lines on his face seemed to be either furrows of concentration or laugh lines rather than the marks of age.

Khai's belt was empty of weapons, and scans that would detect even the smallest bits of metal on his person had turned up nothing. He paused before stepping fully onto the *Shadow* and spread his hands. They were strong and callused, with long, clever-looking fingers.

"Saber Gavar Khai," the Sith said, bowing. "Permission to come aboard."

"Permission granted. I am Master Luke Skywalker. This is Ben Skywalker, my son and Jedi Knight. And Vestara, of course."

Vestara had locked down her feelings. Save for the brightness of her eyes, she looked composed, almost bored. She bowed, deeply, respectfully.

"Father."

Saber—whatever that meant—Gavar Khai opened his arms and Vestara went into them. For a brief moment, they were simply a reunited father and daughter, and Luke felt a brief flicker of embarrassment. It was swiftly quashed. Father and daughter they might be, and Luke was willing to grant that there might even be familial love between them, but they were still Sith. They probably fought pretty well as a father-child team, just like he and Ben did.

Vestara pulled back, keeping her face averted from Luke and Ben until the mask was back in place.

"Thank you for permitting me to see her," Khai said, his arm still around his daughter's shoulders. "Her mother and I have missed her greatly."

That comment raised a hundred other questions in Luke's mind, but he didn't think any of them would be answered. At least, not honestly.

"I'm a father myself. I know how it is," he said instead. "If you like, you two are welcome to use my quarters for a chat. A very brief chat."

Vestara glanced first at Luke, then at Ben. Ben shrugged slightly.

"Thank you," Gavar Khai said again. "That is most kind of you. Our chitchat about Vestara's mother and servants and the state of the household would likely not interest you anyway."

"I doubt very much that it would," Luke said. Both men smiled. Both knew that if any mention of mother, servants, and the state of the household did indeed occur, it would be only in passing. Between Sith, there were other matters to discuss.

Luke indicated his cabin, and the two Khais entered. The door slid shut, and Luke and Ben made their way back to the cockpit.

"How come you did that?" Ben asked. "I thought you were against a private visit."

"I said they could have a chat. I never said that it would be private."

"I see. But it's not going to do us any good. I mean— Khai's acting all polite, but he's not going to speak Basic just so we can eavesdrop more efficiently."

"No. They'll speak the other language we've heard from Vestara before." Luke flicked a switch. Gavar Khai's voice was heard, speaking in a lilting tongue. Then Vestara's, light and musical.

"It's pretty," Ben said, and Luke wasn't sure if he meant the language or Vestara's voice. "But what's the point? We've got no reference in the databanks. There's no way we can translate this."

Luke gave him a grin. "We can't. But I know someone who can."

"They will be recording everything we say," Vestara said.

"Of course they will. It is what I would do. But they have never heard Keshiri before. I doubt they will be able to translate it swiftly enough for our conversation to be useful to them."

Vestara nodded. "This is not a diplomat's vessel," she agreed.

"You have been given free rein of it?" Khai said, reaching into his robes and producing a piece of flimsi and a writing instrument. When Vestara nodded, he said, "Good. Draw it for me while we speak."

At once Vestara obeyed, laying the flimsi down on a flat piece of furniture and beginning to sketch. She heard a slight rustling and turned, curious. Her father was reaching inside his robes, searching for something, and a moment later his hand emerged.

He held out a shikkar.

Vestara smiled. Of course. The sensors would detect no weapon, as the shikkar was made entirely of glass. She recognized this one as one from her father's personal collection. It was a piece crafted by one of the most famous shikkar glassmakers, Tura Sanga. Sanga's work was distinctive, and this was no exception. The shikkar was narrow and elegant, stark black-and-white, the hilt slender and long, the blade barely the width of a finger. Its fragility was deceptive. The only weak spot was where the blade joined the hilt—a quick snap would separate the two. Vestara wondered who she would use it on. Ben? The great Luke Skywalker himself? Perhaps, if she was lucky. After all, she had already cut him once. She could do so again, should the opportunity arise. She accepted the noble weapon with a humble nod of thanks, and stashed it carefully in her own robes.

"How is Mother?" she asked.

"She is well. Missing you, but proud of what you are doing."

Vestara smiled a little. "I am glad. I strive to make you proud." *And to become a Saber like you . . . or even soar higher than you.* She did not attempt to shield her emotions from her father; he encouraged her ambition and would not take offense.

"You did fine work on Dathomir," Gavar continued. "And even though your Master is dead, you are still to be granted the rank of apprentice. We will find a new Master for you when this business with Abeloth and the Skywalkers is complete. I am sure many will be eager to teach you."

Vestara straightened slightly, basking in the phrase. "The so-called Nightsister prisoners we took are being sorted out according to their abilities and Force-strengths," her father continued.

"They go willingly?" Vestara was surprised.

"Some do, most do not." Gavar shrugged his broad shoulders. "It matters not. They will go and do what we tell them, or they will suffer. And a little suffering often changes minds." He smiled. "And so another world has yielded to the Tribe what we need if we are to be strong and spread across this galaxy."

Vestara nodded. "I am glad they are proving useful." She glanced over her shoulder at him. "The apprentices . . . how are they doing?"

He looked confused for a moment. "Apprentices?"

"The ones that Abeloth is turning mad," Vestara said. Khai chuckled. Warm affection spread from him in the Force. "Dearest daughter, there is not a single thing wrong with any of the Tribe Sith apprentices that a good beating will not rectify."

"But—"

"I know what Taalon told Skywalker. It is an utter fabrication. We got the idea from you, my clever girl. We needed a good reason for the Skywalkers to ally with us, and it made sense to claim that our apprentices were suffering the same fate as the Jedi Knights."

"I see," Vestara said. It was an excellent plan, one that played well upon the idealistic natures of both Skywalker men. It was sound enough that she herself, who ought to have known better, had believed it. "So . . . what is the *true* reason we are allying with them?"

Gavar gazed at her shrewdly. "You have held your tongue and guarded your feelings well thus far. But I think perhaps that information should come later."

For an instant, a dark flicker of resentment welled up in Vestara, but she extinguished it almost as soon as it came. She was fairly certain her father hadn't noticed. "Of course. As you see fit."

"I share your grief about Lady Rhea and Ahri Raas," Gavar continued, changing the subject. Vestara's brow furrowed slightly as she worked on the sketch, smudging out an inaccurate line with her fingers. She would have to remember to clean them before she left Luke's cabin.

She had respected and had a healthy fear of Lady Olaris Rhea. She had been devoted to her, as befit a proper Sith apprentice to her master. But there had been no affection between them. Vestara did grieve for Ahri, although at one point, she had been willing to kill him herself if need be. Lady Rhea's words came back to her: *Want everything you wish—hunger, burn for it, if that fuels you. But never love anyone or anything so much that you cannot bear to lose it.*

"They died well, at the hands of the Skywalkers," was all she said to her father. "You have met them. You know that there is no dishonor in falling against them."

"True," said Gavar Khai, stepping beside her and squeezing her shoulder affectionately as he peered at the sketch. "But I would just as soon neither of *us* fell against them."

Vestara grinned. "I agree."

"My decision to come here was sound. I learned a great deal about them just from the little exposure I had a few moments ago. The journey before us will give us ample opportunity to learn more."

Vestara examined the sketch critically. She added a few more notes. "I will continue to share with you everything I learn."

"You might be able to learn even more . . . or perhaps insinuate yourself better with them."

Finished, Vestara handed the sketch to her father and cleaned her hands at the sink. "I will do what I can, but I am a Sith, and their prisoner. What they have let me learn is only what they want me to know or the occasional accidental slip."

Khai turned her around to face him, his hands on her shoulders. "I am willing to wager that the slips have not come from Master Luke Skywalker."

There was something in the tone of his voice that made Vestara instantly alert. "No," she said. "It is Ben who has told me the most."

"You are attracted to the Skywalker boy."

It was a statement, not a question, and Vestara's stomach clenched. She wanted to deny it, but this was her father, who knew her better than anyone. Even without the use of the Force he would know if she lied to him about this.

"Yes, I am," she said softly, not meeting his eyes. "He is appealing to me. I am sorry. I will do my best to—"

Khai tilted her chin up with a finger. "No, you will not."

"I—" Vestara floundered. She had not felt this off guard since the first time she had killed, when she had been surprised at how hard it had been, how much blood there was, and how the sensation of the victim's life slipping away at such close range had unnerved her.

"This is something we can use," Gavar Khai continued. "I certainly do not want you to fall in love with Ben Skywalker. But if you do feel genuine affection or desire for him, do not be afraid to let him sense that. Especially if he can sense it in the Force, he'll know it's real, and that will take him off guard. He will begin to lower his own walls, tell you more, trust you more. You can use that." His eyes brightened as a thought came to him. "You might even be able to turn him."

"To the dark side?" A strange little jolt swept through Vestara at the thought. She recognized it as . . . hope. If Ben were to become Sith, then she wouldn't have to worry about the growing feelings she was having for the Skywalker boy. It wouldn't matter. They would be on the same side—fighting, killing together, advancing the Tribe agenda to rule the galaxy. Ben would, she was certain, become as powerful as his father one day. He might even become a Lord—or a High Lord. They—

Her father's indulgent chuckle snapped her out of her reverie. "That would be my hope as well. Ben Skywalker as a Sith would be a glorious achievement for our family, and you could enjoy him to the fullest. But if you fail to turn him, you must be prepared to be content with toying with him. At least until the time comes when he is no longer useful."

Vestara nodded. "I understand, Father. You do not need to worry about me."

He regarded her for a long moment. "I never had to lay a hand on you for punishment, child. You have always excelled. You are driven by the dark side to achieve, to rise." He placed his hands on her shoulders, squeezing them slightly in approval. "Vestara, you are a true Khai. I know you will not fail me in this."

She stood a little taller at the high praise, craving it, craving the power that lay, unspoken, behind his words. She had once dreamed of becoming a Lord, but now her ambition knew no bounds. Fate, or the dark side, had placed the Skywalkers in her path. In, perhaps, her hands—literally and figuratively. She would make certain she took full advantage of the opportunity.

For her family, for the Tribe—and for herself.

# Chapter Two

ABOARD THE *JADE SHADOW*

"I'M NOT LOOKING FORWARD TO GOING INTO THE MAW again," Ben said bluntly. "It was tricky enough the first time."

"Well," Luke said mildly, "you've done it once, you know what to be aware of."

Ben grimaced. "Doesn't mean it's going to be any easier."

Vestara nodded. "Agreed. We had difficulty as well."

Luke scratched his chin thoughtfully. Tadar'Ro, of the Aing-Tii, had told them the safe path to follow through the Maw to go where Jacen Solo had gone so many years before. Not surprisingly, though, considering how mysterious the Aing-Tii liked to keep themselves, he had couched it in the form of a riddle. "The Path of True Enlightenment runs through the Chasm of Perfect Darkness. The way is narrow and treacherous, but if you can follow it, you will find what you seek." Ben and Luke had indeed been able to follow the "Path of True Enlightenment," although the way had been treacherous indeed. It had led them between two black holes into an area known as Stable Zone One, in which "stability" was a bit of a misnomer. Ben had been the one to do the navigating of the yacht, and while he'd managed it by a combination of good piloting and trusting his feelings in the Force, it had still been an unnerving journey. Luke wasn't looking forward to repeating it either, especially not having to worry about a dozen other vessels all making the journey successfully.

"I'm wondering if we might get a little help," he said at last. "I've got an old friend who lives near the Maw who might be able to lend us a ship."

Instantly, like a nexu scenting danger, Vestara was on the alert. "More ships? You are calling in reinforcements?"

"I said *a* ship. A specialized asteroid tug that could help us offset the gravitational pull of the black holes. It's large and it's designed with more tractor beam emitters than ought to be legal. I have a friend who is very fond of tinkering and upgrading."

"Oh, Lando?" Ben looked pleased and amused. "We're going to go to Kessel?"

Vestara was listening attentively, filing away everything. Luke didn't care. He was not attempting to keep this information from anyone.

"Hopefully not to Kessel," he replied to his son. "I'm hoping Lando can come join us. Meet us at the Maw so we can just head on in as soon as possible. I don't want to delay any longer than we have to." His voice became not hard, but determined. "The longer that being sits in her lair, the stronger she'll become and the more harm she can do. We need to stop her as soon as possible, but we've got to make sure we've got every advantage."

"Well," Ben said, glancing at Vestara, "Why *wouldn't* more reinforcements be a good idea? Lando doesn't have an injunction against warning him not to associate with you. He's not a Jedi. Why can't he help?"

"I think once we reach Abeloth, all of us combined can take her," Luke said. "All we really need is the *Rockhound* to get us there safely."

Vestara's brown eyes narrowed. "It seems foolish to

me that you do not take advantage of your friend's connections, Master Skywalker. If he will give us more ships for our endeavor, why not?"

"There might be a thousand food items on a table, but you do not need to eat them all in order to satisfy your hunger," Luke replied. "Others might need to eat as well."

"Or," Vestara said, "you might decide to come back for seconds later. When you are hungry again."

Ben grimaced and leapt up, striding purposefully toward the galley. "All this talk of food is making *me* hungry right now. Anyone want anything?"

"I'll come help you," Vestara said quickly, rising. The two moved out of the cockpit and down toward the galley.

"Oh? You like to cook?" Ben asked, grinning at her as they walked.

"No, I like to hunt," Vestara replied. "I am very good with the parang. We also had trained hunting reptiles. Cooking meals is left to the servants."

"I wouldn't like to see what See-Threepio would do with preparing a meal. Appetizers are about all we trust him with."

"Who is See-Threepio?"

Their voices grew fainter until at last Luke could not hear them. He sent a short message to Tendrando Arms, and a moment later he was smiling—despite the direness of the situation—at the miniature holographic form of Lando Calrissian. Even at only a third of a meter tall, Lando managed to look impressive. He was missing the hip-length cape and his silky red shirt looked a touch more casual than usual, but his boots gleamed and the black trousers had sharp creases that were even visible in miniature. Lando looked genuinely pleased to see him, and spread out his arms in a welcoming gesture.

"Hey, buddy, long time no see!" Lando said expansively. "I didn't expect to hear anything from you till you proved that cranky biddy in charge of the GA wrong."

Luke smothered a grin at hearing Admiral and Chief of State Natasi Daala referred to in such a manner. "I respect Chief of State Daala's leadership qualities."

"You gotta say that in case there are any eavesdropping devices, right?" Lando grinned, his eyes dancing.

"Maybe," Luke deadpanned.

"Hear you've gone off on some kind of odyssey with your boy."

"Something like that," Luke said. "It's good to see you, Lando, but this isn't a social call. I've got a favor to ask."

"For Luke Skywalker? Name it."

"I'm in need of the *Rockhound*."

Lando's jet-black eyebrows shot up. "The *Rockhound*?" he echoed. "What makes you think I've still got that beat-up antique hanging around?"

"Because you have a nostalgic streak a thousand kilometers wide. Because the thing is one of only three ships made by the BramDorc Corporation known to exist. And because you never get rid of *anything*."

Lando shrugged self-deprecatingly and chuckled. "I am what I am. You got me. Yeah, I've still got her. I take it you've got some asteroids you need moved?"

The *Rockhound* was a Colossus I Beta Series asteroid tug constructed by the now-defunct BramDorc Corporation. Little was known about the corporation, other than the fact that it had been based somewhere in the Unknown Regions and it specialized in massive vessels. It had vanished from the Galactic record with no trace some five years before the Battle of Yavin. Luke was right—there were only two other remaining ships manufactured by BramDorc: a waterhunter called the *Icebreaker* and the amusingly named liquefied–Tibanna tanker *Gasbag*, that had been turned into the orbital fortress of a two-bit Hutt crimelord.

By all rights, Luke knew, the old ship belonged either in a museum like the *Icebreaker*, now forever planet-bound in the New Brampis Starship Museum, or a scrapyard. No one knew exactly how old the *Rock-hound* was, though the Arkanian Orbital Logs mentioned it as far back as 524 years before the Battle of Yavin. Lando had flown it solo for many years back in his younger days as a prospector. Han had revealed quite a few things he found amusing about the *Rock-hound* to Luke one night when the kids were dead to the world and both their wives had gone to bed. . . .

*Mara, I still miss you, and I swear I feel you here with me now.*

. . . and Luke had never forgotten them. One was the interesting fact that, as seemed to be the case with several ships in Lando's possession, he had won the *Rock-hound* from a Brubb prospector in an epic, six-hour, arm-wrestling match. Which, Han hinted, may or may not have been rigged. The other intriguing tidbit was the fact that the crew were all droids with a rather unique programming. Han had refused to elaborate further, returning Luke's queries with smug, self-satisfied grins. Luke supposed he would now get the chance to find out what Han had been talking about.

"Not exactly," said Luke. "I'm actually heading into the Maw."

Lando's jovial good humor, which Luke suspected was largely for his benefit, abated somewhat. "The Maw? Why? It's hardly a vacation paradise in there."

"Certainly not," Luke agreed. "But it's part of what I'm doing with Ben right now. We're retracing Jacen's five-year journey."

Lando sobered, his eyes kind. "Yeah, I heard a little something about that."

Luke thought, not for the first time, that while Lando did an effective job of hiding his innate decentness behind his swashbuckling façade, he wasn't always the bluffer he liked to think of himself as. Lando Calrissian cared deeply for those he called friends.

"Our path so far has led us here. And we've come to find out if there's something . . . or more precisely, someone . . . in there who needs taking care of," Luke continued.

Lando nodded. "Yeah . . . I was wondering if something was going on there. You heard about what happened here on Kessel, right?"

Luke had. Leia had told him about the strange quakes that had threatened to destroy Kessel, and incidentally Tendrando Arms in its entirety, right along with them. Too, his sister had mentioned that Allana had heard something through the Force. The girl had insisted that "something was waiting" for her "up in space." It had wanted to know who she was, and was "sad but scary." True, the girl was just barely eight, but she was the daughter of Tenel Ka and Jacen Solo, the granddaughter of Leia Organa Solo, and the great-granddaughter of Anakin Skywalker. If anyone could claim Force sensitivity was in her genes, it was Allana.

Both Leia and Han had been convinced that their granddaughter had been telling the truth, at least as she was able to comprehend it. It was a disturbing thought. Luke was more certain now than ever that Abeloth had contacted Allana.

He nodded. "Yes, I heard. Sounds like everything is stable for now, though."

"For now," Lando allowed. He looked thoughtful for a moment, then as if suddenly becoming aware of the potential for solemnity, flashed a trademark rakish grin. "And hey—I guess that's all anyone's ever got, right?"

"I guess so. I had no idea you were quite so profound, Lando."

Lando waved a dismissive hand. "Don't let it get around. Bad for my reputation. So, you going in with just you and Ben? Even with the *Rockhound*, it could be tricky. I hate that place."

"Actually, Ben and I managed it with the *Jade Shadow,* but it was close," Luke replied. "But with a group, the *Rockhound* will be particularly useful. Come on—that thing's so big it almost creates its own gravimetric field."

Lando glanced at him curiously. "A group?"

"I have a few . . . associates accompanying me."

Even via holographic communication, Lando knew how to read people. His bright eyes narrowed as he regarded Luke.

"Associates, eh? What kind of associates? Not swindlers and scoundrels keeping the noble Luke Skywalker company, surely."

Luke debated demurring, but decided not to. He had known Lando for a long time, and certainly the former space pirate could not sit in judgment on Luke, considering the company he once kept—and, probably, still did keep.

"Er . . . They're um . . . well, they're Sith, actually."

Lando's expression of shock was almost comical. His mouth dropped open and his eyebrows shot up, and the carefully cultivated "I've seen it all" image went right out the airlock.

"S-Sith?" He could barely get the word out.

"Sith," Luke confirmed. "Quite a few of them. It's . . . a long story."

"No kidding. I'll want that story in addition to my fee, Skywalker."

There would be no fee, of course, and Luke didn't bat an eyelash. "As soon as I can share it, I will," he replied, grinning. "So, I take it you'll surrender the *Rockhound* for a bit?"

"Bring her back home safe and sound, and yourselves, too, if possible, and she's yours," Lando said. "But I have to warn you. You'll have to cultivate that Jedi patience. She's been out of service for a while, and it's going to take some time to bring her up to speed. I've made a few . . . adjustments."

Luke couldn't help but smile. Lando, just like Han, was always tinkering with his ships. It was as if the two simply couldn't stand the notion of flying a ship the way it came out of the factory. While it amused him, Luke was certainly not one to dismiss the pair's inclination to improve—the *Jade Shadow* was testimony to what a customized vessel could do.

"I'm sure it will do everything but make me a cup of caf and deliver it to me in bed," Luke said.

"You know . . . that's a great idea, Luke. I'll get right on it," Lando said with a straight face, stroking his chin thoughtfully.

"How long do you think it will take?"

Lando considered. "Hm . . . the old boat's been sitting in dock for a while. A week? Maybe two?"

Disappointment knifed through Luke. "That long?" He did not regret his decision to ally with the Sith. He'd thought it over carefully and knew that it was the right one. He also knew that the longer one spent hanging around with garbage, the greater the chance a dianoga would show up. He wanted to confront Abeloth as soon as possible and be rid of the promises he had made before the Sith decided to turn on him, which was as inevitable as Ben getting hungry every few hours.

Lando spread his hands in a don't-look-at-me gesture. "Hey, you're the one who wants a specialized vessel to go chasing Big Bads in the Maw, not me. I'll do my best to make it a week. But seriously, Luke, I do have to warn you, this thing is *old*. And so is her droid crew. You gotta be gentle with her, understand?"

"She's not going to break down on me in the middle of the Maw?"

"Hey, hey, did I say that?" Lando looked wounded, but it was just over the top enough for Luke to know his friend wasn't serious. "That's what I need the time for, to make sure that doesn't happen. I'm just letting you know that she will need a little extra love, that's all."

Luke sighed. He needed every advantage he could in going after Abeloth—that much had been made excruciatingly clear. If Lando said one to two weeks, then he would have to wait one to two weeks, and hope the Sith didn't chafe at the delay too much. The tug could make all the difference.

"I'll keep that in mind. Thanks for the loan. It's appreciated, Lando. We'll lay in a course for Kessel and—"

"Oh, no, no, no, you're not bringing Sith into orbit around *my* planet," Lando said at once. "That would be bad for business if word gets out."

Luke thought it would be bad for everyone's business if word got out, but he said nothing.

Lando continued. "We'll rendezvous at Klatooine. It's close to the Maw, part of the Si'Klaata Cluster," Lando continued.

"Why do I know that name?" Luke asked. He wondered if it was only because it was so similar to "Tatooine" that it stuck in his mind so.

Lando grinned, showing perfect white teeth. "Because it's the last stop on the famous Kessel Run. You can't possibly have forgotten that."

"Of course," Luke said. "The Kessel Run. Han has to regale us at least once a year with that story."

Lando chuckled. "Believe me, the Run was even more interesting when the place was crawling with Hutts," he said. "Or slithering, since Hutts don't have legs. It's still

Hutt space, officially, but they got badly hurt during the Yuuzhan Vong wars. It's pretty quiet there now. You and your, uh, *associates* shouldn't have too much trouble. A few days in orbit, maybe even a planet landing to stretch your legs, should be just fine."

Luke touched the console and a map popped up on the transparisteel screen. There was the Maw, and near it was Kessel. Hutt space was clearly defined, and sure enough, there was the Si'Klaata Cluster, consisting of Klatooine, Nimia, Ques, Lant, Iotra, Yoruibuunt, and Sriluur. Klatooine was firmly within Hutt space, but Luke was not worried. Lando might be adventurous, but he would never deliberately put Luke in harm's way for something as inconsequential as a rendezvous point.

"Thanks, Lando. I appreciate it."

"Anytime, Luke. Just treat my old vessel with care and respect. And . . . watch your back, huh kid?"

Lando grinned, winked, and his image vanished.

"Threepio's a protocol droid," Ben was saying as he rummaged about in the galley. They had restocked somewhat on Dathomir after Ben had depleted their supplies by helping the Mind Drinkers in the Maw, but there was still not a lot to choose from. He selected some fruits and vegetables and began to cut them up into a sort of salad, tossing in a few chunks of cooked something-or-other. He hadn't paid much attention to the flora and fauna of Dathomir, except to make sure it wasn't going to try to sting, poison, choke, or eat him.

"He knows all about etiquette and stuff. Languages, histories, customs—"

"But not recipes," Vestara said, smiling, as she reached for the salad he had made her.

"Definitely not recipes," Ben confirmed, smiling back. So often, she seemed to hold herself rigidly in check, projecting a cool composure. When Vestara Khai did smile, she looked her age. Her face lit up and her brown eyes warmed and . . . well, he liked it when she smiled.

Ben realized she was looking at him expectantly and he blushed a little at where his thoughts were going. He returned his attention to making his own salad. "It's not as if my aunt Leia hasn't tried to improve on his programming. She does this spiceloaf that—"

He caught himself. This was not an ordinary girl, with whom he could chat casually about family recipes, good or bad. And he'd just named his aunt.

Vestara continued to smile and look at him curiously. "What about the spiceloaf? What kind of spices were used in it?"

"Uh, I don't know, but let's put it this way," Ben said, glancing down as if the preparation of a salad was as important a task as navigating through the Kathol rift. "It would be nice if Threepio could learn how to cook."

Vestara slid into a seat, folding her tall body in with feline grace, laughing a little. "You speak of this droid as if he were a family member."

Ben poured them each a glass of blue milk—his dad hated the stuff, but Ben found he kind of liked it—and shrugged. He slid the glass over to Vestara, and as she grasped it, their fingers brushed.

"Well," he said, "he kind of is. I mean, he's got a personality." He grinned suddenly. "He *definitely* has a personality. And he's been with the family a long time."

"How long?" Vestara took a sip of the milk and peered at Ben, apparently highly interested.

*I bet you are,* Ben thought. *You're just waiting for me to get too chatty and let something slip.*

"Very long," he said. It was time to turn the tables. He forked up a chunk of vegetable. "You said you liked hunting. What sort of animals did you hunt?" *And are you hunting me, stalking me, waiting patiently?*

It was the briefest of pauses, as Vestara chewed and

swallowed, but pause she did. She patted her lips delicately with a napkin and graced him with another one of her radiant smiles. But somehow to Ben, this one seemed just a little forced.

"Dead, once we were done with them."

She was closed down, guarded. Just like he was. Ben had to make an effort not to sigh.

They finished their meal in an uncomfortable silence.

# Chapter Three

OFFICES OF THE IMPERIAL HEAD OF STATE
GALACTIC EMPIRE EMBASSY COMPLEX,
CORUSCANT

THE HOUR WASN'T ALL THAT LATE, NOT AS JAGGED FEL
was starting to reckon hours, but it was late enough that
his brain was tired and having difficulty focusing. He
rubbed his eyes, strained from staring at datapads all
day, and put the one he was reading atop a pile. On a
whim, he assembled them all into a little tower. There
were quite a lot of them.

He turned his expensive—and incredibly comfortable,
which was more a necessity than a luxury, considering
how much time he spent in it—nerfhide chair toward
the vidscreen and touched a button.

A too-familiar face filled the screen: the visage of a
man with tawny, perfectly coiffed hair, a stylish suit, and
a faux-sincere expression. The so-called journalist, Javis
Tyrr. Behind him, framed artistically off center in the
cam, was Raynar Thul, looking as if he were listening to
something no one else could hear.

Thul had been a Jedi who had gone missing years earlier. He had reappeared, alarmingly and unexpectedly,
as UnuThul—a Joiner who was leading the Killik ex-
pansion into the Chiss territories. He was mad, and dis-
figured, and had been under the care of the Jedi healer

Cilghal for a long time. His burn scars had healed but still left the face framed by the cam looking stiff and artificial. Free now to come and go as he pleased, Thul had not yet chosen to leave the Jedi Temple.

"I'm sitting here, on the steps of the Jedi Temple, speaking with Raynar Thul, who—"

Jag glowered and changed the channel.

"—former Jedi Tahiri Veila," a human woman with long black hair swept up into a bun was saying. "The charges are—"

Jag's glower deepened. He wanted to hear about Tahiri's situation even less than he wanted to stare at Javis Tyrr's smirk. He changed the channel again.

Another reporter's face filled the screen. By human standards, Javis Tyrr's perfect features were more appealing than the one Jag regarded now, but Fel would take the homely, oversized face of Perre Needmo and his levelheaded reporting over Tyrr's pretty looks and sensationalism any day. Needmo was a Chevin, and his face was long and solemn with a wrinkled, expressive snout. He had the calm mien of an elder statesperson, and evoked trust and confidence. His show, too, tended to include positive things as well as negative, so one didn't feel the need to take a sanisteam right after watching. It made a nice change from *Javis Tyrr Presents*.

"—from reporter Madhi Vaandt," Needmo was saying, and the scene cut to a young female Devaronian standing in what looked to be the heart of the Coruscant Underlevel. Not for the first time, Jag was struck by how extremely different the genders were in Devaronians. The females didn't even look like they belonged to the same species, and their behavior and natures couldn't be more different from the males. That they needed one another to continue the species had always seemed to Jag like some great cosmic joke.

Whereas the males had bare, reddish skin, two prominent horns of which they were extremely proud, and sharp incisors, the females were covered in short soft white, brown, or reddish fur except for their hands, feet, and faces, which were pale pink, and had merely darker pigmented ovals where horns would be on their male counterparts.

The males had a reputation for irresponsibility and wanderlust, and tended to roam the galaxy. They were not the finest representatives of their species, so most of the denizens of various worlds did not have the highest opinion of Devaronians. The females, however, were precisely the opposite. They were the ones who ran the businesses and the government, with level heads, calmness, and insight.

The female before him seemed a fine representative of her gender. And an appealing one, too. Javis Tyrr would have killed for the charm and sincerity she radiated. Whereas Tyrr's hair stylist and makeup artist probably got paid overtime, Madhi Vaandt's hair was cut short and was rather wild, as if all she had done was run her fingers through it. She wore makeup to offset the brightness of the harsh cam lighting, but even through that he could see the dark ovals on her forehead peeping through wispy locks of white hair and smaller dots on her forehead that were freckles. Her clothing, too, was unremarkable and practical—tan-colored pants, a linen blouse with the sleeves rolled up under a vest with lots of pockets. She looked right into the cam, slanted green eyes intense and captivating, long pink ears swept back.

"Thank you, Perre," Vaandt said. Her voice was captivating, musical and lilting with her native accent. "I'm coming to you live from one of the dark, dirty secrets of Coruscant—a place known variously as Lower Coruscant, the Coruscant Underworld, Undercity, or the Coruscant Underlevel. Oh, its origins are no secret."

Vaandt began walking as she spoke. Behind her, Jag

could see yorik coral covering railings and stairwells, and slashvines and other plant life growing wherever it had a chance to set hungry roots. Now and then, a figure darted past; it was almost impossible to tell what species it was. It didn't matter. Jag knew that, in this place, all suffered. He found himself wincing in sympathy.

"This is an ancient place, filled with ruins and stories. And recently, it was given a new name—Yuuzhan'tar. While the rest of Coruscant has been reclaimed since the end of the war, this part of the planet never fully recovered."

She paused, tilted her pink face upward. "Above me are towering buildings. Civilization. Order. Order the Galactic Alliance has established over the years. But in the midst of all the rebuilding, all the recovery, all the positive steps the GA has taken . . ."

She turned and gestured with a slender, white-furred, graceful arm. The cam panned over to a cluster of young human males dressed in pieces of plastoid armor and wearing white tabards. When the cam's light hit them, they scattered like creatures one finds when a rock is overturned.

". . . this place has been forgotten. There's no order, no civilization here. There's no health care for beings trying to eke out an existence. There's no stopping the sale of illegal drugs, or halting illicit activities, or investigations of murders here. No interference with zap gangs, or protection from Cthons. Violent deaths are an everyday occurrence, and the bodies are looted before they become food for Ferals. This is a dark place, a frightening place, and it's just easier to forget about it since we are not forced to see it every day."

She raised disturbing points. Why, indeed, hadn't more been done about this place? Jag found himself wondering.

Madhi Vaandt beckoned off cam, her pink, freckled face soft, a gentle smile on her lips, and a young human male came into view. He was thin, with the pinched face of the malnourished, dirty, and looked as skittish as a young animal. Madhi slipped an arm around him.

"We'll be following young Tarynd here for the next few weeks. We'll see what he has to endure on a daily basis, simply to survive, in the heart of this planet, the very seat of the Galactic Alliance. We'll discover—"

"I've got a favor to ask," Jaina Solo stated.

Jag hadn't heard her come in, so focused had he been on Madhi Vaandt's reporting, but he didn't miss a beat.

"So do I," he replied, gazing up at his fiancée as she stood in front of his desk, hands on her hips. "Announce yourself first when you come into my office."

She pushed the stack of datapads to the side and perched on his desk. "Imperial Head of State Jagged Fel, Sword of the Jedi Jaina Solo wants to see you. Proprieties observed. *Now* can I ask my favor?"

"I could have been right in the middle of delicate negotiations or working on something highly classified, you know."

"You weren't. Ashik would have told me." Ashik was the "core name" of Kthira'shi'ktarloo, the Chiss male who was Jag's assistant, attendant, and head of his personal security. Jag trusted the Chiss completely, and it had surprised no one when a member of that species had been appointed to such a position. Ashik—tall, soft-spoken, with a sharp nose, full lips, and piercing eyes—was genial enough, and certainly understood the relationship Jaina and Jag had, but he had no compunctions about denying her, or anyone, entrance if he did not feel it appropriate. Jaina had bridled initially, but it was clear she also respected Ashik's determination.

Jag sighed. He had a feeling he knew what the favor was about to be, and he didn't want to get involved. It seemed that more and more, events—and people, even people they loved—were conspiring to drive them apart. Even though he had vowed to her that nothing as petty as politics would come between them, a vow he fully intended to keep, he had to admit that it was certainly causing things to become frayed around the edges.

"I suppose he would have, yes," he said. "So what's the favor?"

Jaina smiled, slipped her legs neatly over the edge of the desk, and slid off it to sit in his lap. Despite his worry about the nature of the favor, Jag found himself smiling as he pulled her into his arms. They kissed, passionately but sweetly, and he felt the tension inside him ease. He loved Jaina Solo, was looking forward to marrying her, and nothing in the galaxy was going to change that.

She sat back and grinned at him. "Okay," Jag said, "That's a favor I can get behind."

She punched his shoulder in mock annoyance. "That's not the favor, that's the bribe. I figure if I'm going to become a politician's wife, I have to start thinking of things like that."

"So you should," he agreed in his most serious voice, nodding and settling her into his lap. "And I approve of the nature of the bribe. So, Jedi Solo. You have my full attention. Ask your favor."

The playful smile faded from her lovely face, and her eyes turned serious. "It's about Tahiri Veila."

Jag felt his own good humor bleed out. "That's what I thought."

"Jag, she's already lost two advocates. She's going to get someone the court appoints, and the court has it in for her," Jaina said.

"I know that both you and I have had our issues with the Chief of State, but I really don't think she'd go so far as to pack the jury or deliberately appoint someone to lose Tahiri's case for her."

"I do," Jaina said.

He eyed her. "Really?"

"Of course! Daala's smarting from Niathal's suicide. Tahiri Veila is a perfect target for her frustration. You think she's going to let that go? She'd be like Anji with her stuffed eopie."

It was an apt analogy. Jag and Jaina had been over to dinner at the Solos' residence before Han, Leia, and Allana had been forced to find new quarters. Jag had met the latest member of the family, Anji, a young nexu cub. Leia had been forced to kill its mother when the Jedi Knight Natua Wan had snapped and let loose the dangerous animals at the Coruscant Livestock Show and Exhibition. Allana, according to Jaina, had argued that they therefore had a responsibility to care for the orphaned animals—one of them, at least. And that fortunate cub had been Anji.

Anji had dulled quills, clipped claws, and a restraint that prevented her from biting hard enough to draw blood. She adored Allana and seemed gentle enough, for what she was, but kept attacking a stuffed eopie. She would let no one come near it, growling and gnawing upon it despite the bite restraint until Jag was certain that bits of the eopie's fabric innards would be strewn over the carpeting and furniture. It was testimony to how well made the toy was that that didn't happen. Jag thought perhaps he should invest in the toy company; their products seemed to hold together better than some armor he had worn.

"You do have a point," he allowed, shifting her slight weight on his lap. "I'm sorry that Judge Lorteli wouldn't permit Nawara Ven to represent her, and that Mardek Mool didn't work out, but what do you expect me to do about the situation?"

"You know people. You have a lot of connections. You could find someone."

He blinked at her. "Jaina, I can't use my connections to influence the outcome of a trial."

"I'm not asking that. I'm just asking that you see if you know anyone who'd be willing to tackle the job. You *know* she's not going to get a fair trial otherwise."

Jag sighed and leaned his head back against the soft leather of the chair for a moment. Jaina knew better than to press her attack, and just nestled against him quietly. Probably because she knew, like he knew, that he usually did his best to do the right thing within the constraints of his duty. And the right thing in this situation was to get someone who was accused of murder a lawyer who actually cared about representing her fairly and was capable of standing up to what was sure to be an ugly trial.

"It will have to be completely unofficial," he said at last. "It won't be through the offices of the Empire."

"Of course not."

He opened his eyes and looked down at her and his breath caught for a moment. She was smiling gently at him, her face soft, her eyes warm. It wasn't an expression most of the world ever saw. She reserved it for family, and for him, and it was as rare and as lovely as a Krayt dragon pearl. At this moment, she wasn't the "Sword of the Jedi," or the daughter of a perhaps-too-famous couple, or the woman who at the cost of ripping up her own heart had slain a Sith Lord who also happened to be her twin. She was just Jaina now, open and vulnerable. He felt his own heart soften to look at her, and lifted a hand to tenderly brush away a stray lock of dark hair from her forehead.

"All right. I promise you that I will find her the best, most decent, most honest, hardest working lawyer I can," he said.

"Oh," Jaina said. "I was trying to get her someone who'd win."

Cell 2357
Galactic Justice Center
Coruscant

Tahiri Veila, seated in her very clean and very bright GA cell deep in the bowels of the Galactic Justice Center, her head in her hands, found that she was surprised at what she missed.

She'd expected to miss her freedom, of course. The ability to putter as she wished in her own small, private space. The choice of whether to stay home or go out, perhaps even to visit the Temple. The comfortable, familiar weight of her lightsaber at her hip.

And she did miss those things, but above all else was an odd pang at something else she probably ought to have anticipated—how terribly much she missed the feel of soft grass beneath her bare feet. She had carpeted her apartment with grass, and now, deprived of it, it was the thing she missed most.

She could take her shoes off here, of course. After all, this was a Galactic Alliance prison cell, not a primitive cage. But there was only the cool tile of the too-antiseptic, too-well-lit cell to walk on. And the tile was cold, and hard, and unpleasant, and made her miss everything else just a little bit more.

So Tahiri kept her shoes on, stared at the incredibly white-and-black décor, and thought about how things sometimes just weren't white-and-black. She sighed and rubbed her face for a while, ran her hands through her blond hair, then rose and paced the cold tile floor. *Like a caged animal,* she thought. *Which, just maybe, I am.* With the additional irony of knowing that the Jedi Temple was close at hand. The Justice Center was just across Fellowship Plaza from it.

She could have escaped all of this. All she'd have had to do was do what she had done once before—turn her back on people who cared about her and do something reprehensible. Then, it had been to fall under the sway of Jacen Solo, of her own achingly lonely yearning for a boy long dead, of her own wants. She'd killed a decent old man. Not in combat. Not in self-defense, or defending innocents. She'd killed him in cold blood, deliberately. Broken into a room by using the Force to overcome the lock, ordering him to control the Moffs and to violate a surrender. To attack civilians. And when he'd done the right thing, which was to say no, she'd fired at him point-blank.

That had been the deal that Mardek Mool had proposed. He hadn't said in so many words that it had been Daala's idea, but he hadn't had to. It was ironic that Chief of State Natasi Daala, who had been so incensed at that type of action when ordered by Jacen Solo, had been so comfortable with asking Tahiri to betray those who trusted her a second time. It seemed that Daala thought that two wrongs made a right. Because Tahiri had killed Gilad Pellaeon, and lied and deceived in order to do so, it was somehow "right" for her to lie and deceive again. The only difference was, this time it was Daala's enemies, not her friends, that Tahiri was supposed to betray.

But it wasn't right. Tahiri was not about to walk the same misguided path again. She realized that her chances of being found not guilty were, to put it mildly, poor. Make that slim to none. Not even Han Solo would gamble on it.

She didn't believe the courts were completely corrupted. Just mostly.

The Jedi had tried to get Nawara Ven to represent

her—something she hadn't expected, something that moved her. She wasn't surprised that Judge Lorteli had forbidden Ven to do so. Mool, the next advocate, had been sincere in wanting to help, but hadn't been up to the task.

Real help had come from an unexpected, but welcome source. Jaina Solo had come to visit her two days ago, smiling as she told Tahiri that "someone was able to find a good representative for you." The someone, of course, had to be Jagged Fel, and the knowledge, like the willingness of the Jedi to support her, had surprised and touched Tahiri.

This new attorney would be arriving at any minute. She knew that he had once been highly respected, but had retired some years ago. That he was a Bothan named Eramuth Bwua'tu. She wondered if he was any relation to Admiral Nek Bwua'tu. There was a lengthy list of cases he had won, but she had no way here to research them, and they had all transpired before she'd even been born. She wasn't sure what to expect.

The door swung open and she stood, her heart beating slightly faster. *Tahiri, don't, just don't, don't hope too much—*

She blinked. He was, without a doubt, the most elegant being she had ever seen.

Taller than most Bothans, and very thin, he looked like he had stepped out of another era. His fur was dark brown and sleek, though it was thinning slightly with age. Around his muzzle and cheeks, it was snowy white, in stark contrast with the brown, and perfectly groomed. He extended a hand to her, and she took it, noting that he wore gloves.

The rest of his attire was equally as formal. A small, oddly jaunty hat sat between his two ears. His vest, long coat, and trousers looked perfectly tailored, the coat fitting his narrow shoulders, the trouser creases knife-sharp. His boots gleamed, and he sported a cane, black and simple, but with a stylized handle sporting the finely carved head of some animal Tahiri did not recognize. In the same hand he had a small black bag that looked to be made of nerfhide.

"Eramuth Bwua'tu, Esquire," the dapper being said. His handshake was firm, but not too much, and he looked her right in the eye in an interested manner. His voice was deep and mellifluous and resonant. Tahiri could just imagine it carrying in a court of law, with Eramuth crying out something like "I object!" or, more floridly, "Beings of the jury, search your hearts for justice!"

"Tahiri Veila," she managed. A small smile played at the corners of her mouth. Why?

"I've been asked to represent you," Eramuth continued. "Please, miss, do sit down."

"I'd rather stand."

He smiled. It was utterly charming. With a rueful shake of the cane, he said, "Ah, but I'm afraid that *I* would rather sit, and good breeding forbids me doing so unless you do." He winked.

Tahiri sat. Again, she fought the urge to smile.

"Thank you, my dear," Eramuth said, putting a hand to his heart and bowing ever so slightly before pulling out a chair for himself. With anyone else, Tahiri would have thought it a calculated, over-the-top gesture. But with him, it seemed completely natural. There was a grace to him, not just of mannerisms or clothing, but somehow simply emanating from who he was.

Hope started gnawing on her like a mynock on a power cable. She pushed it down, ruthlessly.

"Are you related to Admiral Nek Bwua'tu?"

He gave her another quick smile, focusing the full force of his attention on her. "Indeed I am. He's my nephew. He's done the family proud. Unlike his notoriously eccentric uncle."

He was still smiling, but Tahiri's slightly giddy feeling of hope suddenly turned cold. "Eccentric uncle?" It would be just her luck, she thought, to have landed a madman for an attorney.

"Only in Bothan circles," Eramuth said. "Are you familiar with our culture, my dear?"

Normally, the endearment would have annoyed her, but she sensed only kindness. "Well, I don't want to stereotype, but your people are known for political . . . um . . . maneuvering."

He chuckled. It was a warm, rich, happy sound, and Tahiri instantly wanted to hear it again. "You've the makings of a diplomat."

"Oh, trust me, not really."

"Let me put it this way. Sometimes certain clans want certain outcomes in trials. Sometimes that means a verdict of not guilty for my client . . . which, of course, I desire as well, providing I believe that said client is, in truth, not guilty. I've never taken on a case where I don't believe, with my whole heart, that that being is truly innocent. And I can assure you I never shall."

His voice rose with the passion of his beliefs, and his face went from pleasant to intense and righteous. Tahiri stared at him. She felt a strange catch in her throat and the hairs at the back of her neck rose.

"I am, however, enough of a son of Bothawui to want to be on the winning side." He gave her a somewhat abashed smile. "I do not take on cases I believe I cannot win. And most certainly, I would not come out of retirement and leave my comfortable professorial position for one."

"That's . . . very comforting to know."

He beamed at her for a moment, reached across the table and patted her hand, then turned to business. He pulled off his gloves with quick, precise movements, opened the case and pulled out—

"Flimsi?"

"Of course." He reached into the bag and pulled out a datapad. "I do have datapads, my dear. Never fear, I'm not *entirely* out of date. I simply prefer to have the feel of something a little more permanent in my hands. Data can be erased. Ink . . . is a little harder."

He handed her one of the datapads. "All the information on your case is there. I have the same documents here," and he indicated the flimsi, "all written down in that ink I so love. We can go through it together." Eramuth shuffled through the papers, carefully setting aside a blank piece and a writing instrument.

"Now, my dear," he said, looking at her kindly. "Tell me everything."

# Chapter Four

"TAHIRI VEILA HAS ACCEPTED AN ATTORNEY FOR HER defense," Wynn Dorvan was saying. He sat across the desk from Chief of State Natasi Daala at their daily morning briefing and politely refused a cup of caf she offered him. His pet chitlik, Pocket, was curled up in the part of his jacket for which she was named. The room was tidy and gleamed in black-and-white, evocative of the old Empire of which Daala had once been a part and for which she obviously still harbored nostalgic fondness.

"Good," Daala said. "She'll need one since she forced our hand."

Dorvan suppressed a sigh of irritation. He had not approved of Daala's initial plan to deal with Tahiri. The GA had brought charges of treason and murder against the former Jedi, an accusation which, if she were convicted, could mean the death sentence. Daala had sent in a negotiator to speak with Tahiri's attorney and offered her a quiet under-the-table deal. If Tahiri were to spy on her fellow Jedi and report back to Daala, the charges would be commuted.

It was not the sort of thing the GA should be doing, in Dorvan's opinion. Spies were one thing. Dorvan completely accepted the necessity of espionage, but this was something else entirely. This was betrayal and backstabbing on the part of someone who had been attempting to move her life away from that sort of direction. He had found himself quietly admiring Tahiri for refusing both the deal and the advocate who had brought it. It was not good for the GA, but he could respect it.

A fair trial would, on the other hand, be quite good for the GA. And that was a point Dorvan planned to press today. Again.

"Who did she get?" Daala continued.

"One Eramuth Bwua'tu, uncle to Admiral Nek Bwua'tu. He has quite a reputation as a lively and fierce defender of his clients, but he has been retired for some time. He currently is a professor."

Daala paused in mid-sip. "You're teasing me."

Dorvan looked up and blinked at her. "Ma'am, I'm offended. I would not joke about something of this nature." Dorvan seldom joked about anything, but when he did it was dry, acerbic humor usually about something of no real importance. Pocket sensed his annoyance and shifted position, a warm, soft weight against his hip.

"Quite true. That makes this even more amusing. Admiral Bwua'tu and I are pretty close."

"Eramuth Bwua'tu has a reputation for being incorruptible," Dorvan continued. "Admittedly, that is an unusual characteristic for a Bothan, but it is in the rather exhaustive notes that Desha has compiled for me."

Desha Lor was the overly ebullient young Twi'lek that Daala herself had assigned to him. She was impossibly naïve and quite idealistic, and Daala was not at all surprised that she had seen fit to include such a comment in her notes.

"Not really a cold, hard fact about the man, is it?" Daala was no longer amused.

"No, ma'am. But perhaps you might have thought

about Desha Lor's predilections prior to hiring her as my assistant. Now we both must learn to live with the consequences of such a decision."

The smile returned for a moment. Few could be as blunt with the Chief of State as Dorvan. She had a vast tolerance for his honesty, choosing to value it rather than let it rattle her. He never abused the privilege, but it was a tool in his arsenal in order to get done what he believed was best for the GA.

"Point taken. Still, moral attorney or no, Veila's got about as much chance of being found not guilty as an eopie has of surviving being dropped into a rancor pit."

Daala seemed absolutely sure of the fact, and Dorvan was inclined to agree. While one might feel a certain amount of sympathy for the girl, one didn't pardon someone simply because one felt sorry for her. Tahiri had coasted for the last year because Daala hadn't wanted to pursue the matter. She had spent the time stabilizing the Galactic Alliance after what Jacen Solo had done to it. Dorvan had approved of her decision to focus on healing. The GA had benefited greatly. But now Daala was going after those she perceived as enemies both of herself and of the GA. First Luke Skywalker, and now Tahiri Veila.

Daala had appointed Sul Dekkon, a famous—some would say infamous—Chagrian lawyer who had a reputation for going after a case the way a Kowakian monkey-lizard went after a bad joke. Known for being a stickler for doing things by the book and adhering to the letter of the law, Dekkon was a good choice as far as Dorvan was concerned. Tahiri would need someone equally powerful in order for the trial to do what a trial should do—look at the evidence impartially, and make a decision not based on anyone's need for a particular outcome.

Not even Natasi Daala's.

And fortuitously enough, it was Daala herself who had given Dorvan the perfect opening.

"The case against her is quite strong, and Dekkon will do a fine job," Dorvan said. "That being so, ma'am, I wonder if you see the real opportunity here."

Her red brows came together in a frown. "Explain."

Dorvan leaned back in his chair, folding his hands across the datapad, and looked the Chief of State right in the eye. "You've just stated that Tahiri is certain to lose this case. Barring unforeseen developments—and frankly, ma'am, with you the chance of anything being unforeseen would be extremely rare indeed—I agree. This certainty gives you the chance to spin this to the GA's advantage."

"Go on." Daala's green eyes were fixed on his even as she reached for her cup and took a sip of caf.

"My recommendation to you would be to abolish the special Jedi court. Let Tahiri be tried and, as everyone, including Veila and her attorney *must* know, most likely be convicted in the same court as anyone else. It would demonstrate that while the Jedi get no special privileges, neither do they have special handicaps."

The piercing eyes narrowed. "Not you, too."

Dorvan blinked, which for him was demonstrating a great deal of surprise. "I beg your pardon?"

"Head of State Fel has been after me to do that exact thing." Daala sighed and stared irritably at her caf for a moment. When she did not immediately continue, indicating she was willing to listen, Dorvan went on.

"Unfortunately, the incident with former Judge Lorteli *did* harm us in one court—that of public opinion."

Daala almost, but not quite, winced. It was a sore spot with her. Judge Arabel Lorteli had been appointed as the chief judge of Daala's special Jedi court. Dorvan disliked using the word corrupt, but Lorteli was certainly eager to do all she could to appease the woman who had given her the job. Such eagerness usually did not go hand in hand with a strong sense of will, and the Jedi had taken advantage of it. No one knew for sure if they had used the infamous Jedi mind trick on Lorteli or if they had just managed to sweet-talk her, but the end result was the same.

It had been Daala appointee Judge Arabel Lorteli who had signed the writ permitting Corran and Mirax Horn to visit their children at the Palem Graser Office Tower. What had transpired had not quite been a public relations disaster, but had certainly complicated Wynn Dorvan's day. Brandishing the writ, and with a pack of voracious newshounds, including the ubiquitous and despised Javis Tyrr, capturing every moment, Jaina Solo and several other Jedi had entered the building demanding to see Valin and Jysella Horn.

The two Horn siblings had indeed been found—hanging like wall art in the executive offices of one Colonel Wruq Retk, a Yaka who was in command of the facility that amounted to a not-so-secret secret prison. An outraged Mirax had punched the Yaka, Daala had been forced to do some instant backpedaling, and subsequently and publicly had dismissed Lorteli. Since that time, her position had remained vacant, and the special Jedi court had been inactive.

"The timing is excellent," said Dorvan. "It's been technically inoperative since the incident anyway. Having this trial take place within the regular court system would place you above any hint of scandal, even make you look sympathetic. To my mind, ma'am, there is no downside. Either Tahiri will be found guilty, and thus be subject to what the law decrees as proper punishment, or in the unlikely case that she is found *not* guilty, both you and the GA will come out looking like you have done the right thing, accepting this particular defeat with grace and aplomb."

"Tahiri Veila killed Gilad in cold blood," Daala stated coldly. "She deserves to be punished for what she's done. Others certainly have."

Dorvan knew that Daala was still upset about Admiral Cha Niathal's suicide. He knew why she wanted Tahiri Veila to suffer. She had not wanted to bring charges against the Mon Calamari, but had done so, ironically, in an effort to appear evenhanded. For Dorvan to ask her again for an appearance of evenhandedness specifically directed at Tahiri Veila was pushing it, and he knew it.

Niathal had taken an ancient and honorable way out for those facing political ruin—she had taken her own life in a time and place of her own choosing. It was distressing, certainly, but he suspected that Daala was perhaps taking the suicide—taking *everything* surrounding the case—much too personally.

"Ma'am, if I may . . . I understand that Gilad Pellaeon was a personal friend of yours. And I cannot help but observe that Admiral Niathal's suicide has caused you some distress. But you should not let this become, or at the very least not let it be perceived as, a personal vendetta."

Her patience with him seemed to have reached its limit, for Daala snapped, "Niathal paid the price for aiding Jacen Solo and she didn't even pull the trigger. Veila should, too. Murdered is murdered. It doesn't matter if Pellaeon was an old friend, an old enemy, or someone I'd never met."

Unruffled, Dorvan nodded his brown head. She had him on the last point. Daala folded her arms, thinking.

"If I did this," she said, "the Jedi would think of it as a concession."

"Perhaps," Dorvan said. "One for which they might be very grateful."

"Or one that might make them smug and think they'd scored a point."

"Pardon me, ma'am, I had thought we were trying to do what was best for the Galactic Alliance and its people, not participating in a game of sabacc."

To his surprise, Daala smiled slightly. "Politics is always a game, Dorvan. You'll need to learn that one of these days."

"I hope not, ma'am. I've a dreadful sabacc face." He said this with his usual deadpan voice, and that actually got a chuckle out of the Chief of State.

"Let's say you're right," she continued. "Let's say they're grateful. Perhaps they might be willing to give me something in exchange. Say . . . Sothais Saar."

Sothais Saar was the latest "Jedi crazy," as the press sometimes liked to call them. He was a Chev, tall, powerful, and, like all the "Jedi crazies," extremely dangerous. And he was currently in the Jedi Temple, and nothing that Daala had been able to say or do had persuaded Master Kenth Hamner to release him.

"It's possible," Dorvan said. "It would certainly put you in a stronger negotiating position. And ma'am?"

She glanced at him. "Yes?"

"Quite frankly, it's the right thing to do, and you truly lose nothing."

She sighed. "I will think about it. Anything else?" The clipped, cool tone of her voice told him she hoped there wouldn't be.

He would have to disappoint her. "Well, this is probably nothing of import but . . ."

"Then you wouldn't mention it," Daala said. "I know you too well."

"Well, ma'am, that much is true. It seems that there

have been some uprisings and protests on various worlds."

"Uprisings and protests? Against the GA?" Daala sat up straighter, her brilliant emerald eyes narrowed to slits, her body as still and taut as a predator on the alert.

"No, ma'am. All localized incidents. Suppression of religion, unfair representation, a history of slavery that the suppressed populace has decided is outdated. That sort of thing."

She extended a well-manicured hand for the datapad and he gave it to her. "Mostly backwater worlds," she said after perusing it quickly.

"Hence my initial hesitation in bringing this to your attention. However . . ."

"Such things can be like wildfires," Daala agreed. "If one revolution is successful, another world might take heart and try their own."

"Precisely. And as the Galactic Alliance denounces slavery, I felt it was the right thing to do to mention the situation."

She looked over the list again. "Vinsoth? Really? That's unusual. As far as slavery goes, they're positively civilized about it. The Chevs are treated better by the Chevins than many so-called 'free people' on other worlds."

"Perhaps it does not quite seem so to the Chevs," Dorvan said mildly.

"Perhaps the Chevs might do a little research," Daala said, irritation creeping into her husky voice. She handed the pad back to Dorvan, sighed, and rubbed her temples. "You know, one day I'd like to make it to noon with no bad news."

"I'll have Desha deliver the morning briefing in the future, then."

Daala smiled a little, but it did not reach her eyes. "Anything else?"

There was. Dorvan ran down the list. Rumors of discontent among the Moffs—nothing new. The Senate was locked in debate over extending certain treaties. Species pride parades were blocking off certain sections of the city, and extra guards were being required to make sure order was maintained.

"And finally, I will be continuing my lunch breaks on the steps of the Temple."

He had started these a few days ago, taking his packed lunch—Dorvan always ate at his desk, he never had time to actually leave it to visit the cafeteria—and sitting next to Raynar Thul, who kept a strange sort of vigil every afternoon.

Thul would come out and simply sit at noontime, an eerie personage who was Jedi, but not convincingly so human, but not fully so. His mind went in interesting and fascinating directions, and while Dorvan ostensibly went to see if he had anything that could possibly be of use to the GA, he enjoyed the conversations on a personal level.

For a while, Thul had been thronged by reporters, but they seemed to have dwindled after the first few days. His conversations with anyone were always public, including those he had with Dorvan.

"How's that going?" Daala inquired.

Dorvan shrugged. "Thul is a fascinating person. I haven't enjoyed lunch quite so much in some time. But as for assisting us, I don't think he really thinks in those terms."

"Well, you've not taken a vacation in the entire time you've worked for me, Dorvan, so if you feel like spending your lunch breaks listening to a madman spin tales, then I certainly won't stop you."

"Thank you, ma'am." He rose to leave.

"Wynn?"

"Yes ma'am?"

"That game of politics—I think it's time you started to learn to play. You may tell Raynar Thul that starting today, he'll be having lunch with Wynn Dorvan—my Chief of Staff."

He paused and looked at her. She smiled and nodded; she was quite serious. "Well, then," Dorvan said, "I'll accept his congratulations, or perhaps condolences."

Daala chuckled.

Klatooine was an arid planet. Ben, Vestara, and Luke peered down on a sandy yellow ball of a world, marked only by a few areas of vegetation or the blue of oceans.

"Lovely," Vestara said, wrinkling her nose.

"Do you not like desert worlds? Is your homeworld lush and green, Vestara?" Luke said casually, locking them into orbit.

Vestara's full lips thinned and she remained silent, but otherwise she showed no sign of the irritation Ben knew she must be feeling. Ben didn't know about his dad or her, but he was getting awfully tired of all this dancing around everything.

He wished he could just talk to her, like a regular girl. He wished he could trust her.

He wished she weren't Sith.

"So what's worth writing home about this place?" he asked his father, more to break the uncomfortable silence than because he was actually curious.

"Not a lot," Luke replied. "Here are the beings we'll be interacting with. We have a couple of days while we wait for Lando, and it's a good opportunity to resupply before heading into the Maw."

He touched a button and a hologram appeared, slowly turning. It was of a bipedal being, with a bald pate, deep-set eyes, and heavy jowls around a mouthful of sharp teeth. The hands and feet looked humanoid, but there was something about how the face was arranged that made Ben think of a—

"Dog," he said. "The Klatooinians evolved from canines, didn't they?"

"Sharp eyes," Luke said. "And you're right."

Vestara's lip had curled in repugnance. "What ugly creatures," she said.

Luke smiled at her thinly. "I wouldn't dismiss them quite so quickly. They may not be attractive to your eyes, Vestara, but their culture predates even the Old Republic. You're looking at one of the oldest species in the galaxy."

"Hmph," Vestara said, but Ben noticed that she looked slightly impressed. He, too, had a new respect for the Klatooinians.

"They've been in service to the Hutts for over twenty-five thousand years," Luke continued.

Ben grimaced and sighed. "You know, Dad, when you told me on Sinkhole Station that you thought I hadn't spent enough time with Hutts and were hoping to correct that . . . I thought you were joking."

"Strange are the ways of the Force," Luke said with mock seriousness. Ben could almost see Vestara's ears prick up at the word *Hutts,* but she did not ask what they were. Ben hoped she would not get to find out first-hand.

"The Klatooinians saw the Hutts as near-gods, and the Hutts took advantage of this," Luke continued, returning to his explanation. "They tricked the Klatooinians into signing a treaty that ensured their service for an undefined period of time."

Vestara raised a brown eyebrow. "That is quite the feat," she said. "These Hutts sound like very clever beings."

"Clever? Some of them are, yes," Luke agreed. "But most of them are not anyone I'd care to get to know well. Because of this treaty, the Klatooinians are forced to part with most of their younglings after they reach a certain age. Well-behaved younglings are given good assignments on other worlds, or even permitted to stay with their families on their homeworld. Disruptive youths receive harsher assignments. Basically, the not-nice word for it is slavery."

"Assignments based on merit," Vestara said slowly. "I see."

"No, not based on merit," Luke corrected a touch sharply. "Based on obeisance. That's not the same thing at all."

"The Hutts were weakened after the Yuuzhan Vong war," Ben said. "They can't possibly enforce this everywhere. Why do the Klatooinians continue to put up with it?"

"They are an honorable people, and the treaty is respected," Luke said. "Where they serve the Hutts, they are loyal and dependable. There are a few pockets of discontent here and there, but as a whole, they will not rise up against this servitude until and unless the Hutts do something to violate it. Certainly, their government would never do such a thing."

"But from what you have said, the Hutts are not a stupid species, and they have the advantage here," Vestara said. "So it would be foolish of them to do anything to damage it. They possibly stand to lose much and gain little."

"What was their end of the treaty? Just being gods?" Ben asked.

Luke held up his hand. "Hold on to that thought." He flicked open a channel. "This is the *Jade Shadow* out of Coruscant, requesting permission to land," he said, speaking clearly.

"*Jade Shadow,* this is Docking Control Agent Barada K'lar, operating out of the capital city of Treema. What is the purpose of your visit here?" The voice was gruff and deep, though the speaker's Basic was completely intelligible.

"We wish to restock our vessel with supplies, and to respectfully visit your beautiful Fountain."

Ben frowned. He caught his father's eye and mouthed, *Fountain?*

"Ah," and the voice became much friendlier. And suddenly Ben grinned, clearly now understanding why his father had mentioned it. "The Fountain of the Hutt Ancients. All are more than welcome to behold it. Are you familiar with the rules?"

"It's my understanding that we are not to approach within one kilometer wearing, bearing, or being transported by any contemporary technology," Luke said.

"The Fountain of the Hutt Ancients is out of time," Barada agreed. "We therefore do not sully it by bringing in reminders of the era in which we dwell. Dress simply, leave all technology behind, approach on foot, and you will see one of the marvels of the galaxy. There is a curfew enforced, one standard hour after nightfall. You must be either in your vessel in an established port or within legal boundaries of any city or town you are visiting. The Fountain is in the Derelkoos Desert, many kilometers away from our capital city of Treema. Please plan your visit accordingly so that you have sufficient time to return to your vessel or your lodging. *Jade Shadow* cleared for docking. You may negotiate your hangar with the Dockmaster upon arrival."

"Thank you. *Jade Shadow* out." Luke closed the channel.

"Nice way to get on his good side, Dad," Ben said. "But . . . Fountain of the *Hutt* Ancients? This isn't a Hutt native world, it's a Hutt-conquered world."

"Apparently, the name is a new thing," Luke said. "In the database it's just called the Fountain of the Ancients.

It's a natural formation located, as Barada said, in the Derelkoos Desert. It's supposed to be quite beautiful—tourists come from all over the galaxy to see it."

"Will we have the chance to see it?" Vestara asked.

"I think you'll be too busy getting us supplies to play tourist," Luke said.

"You're not coming with us?" Ben asked.

Luke was annoyed at how pleased Ben sounded at getting to wander around unchaperoned with Vestara. The two young people exchanged glances that were clearly not meant to be interpreted as happy and equally clearly were precisely that. And he was irritated with himself that he was annoyed.

"I'll be sending Dyon Stad along, too. But I think I have a few things to discuss with my new allies. Besides," and Luke permitted himself a small smile, "I grew up on Tatooine. I think I've emptied enough sand out of my boots to last a lifetime."

# Chapter Five

LUKE HAD NOT INTENDED TO SLEEP LONG, BUT HE WAS weary from the time on Dathomir and a short rest would refresh him more than simple meditation. Having sent Dyon off with the two teenagers to gather supplies, he felt, for the moment, that it was safe for him to grab a nap.

He had not told Ben, but he had opted not to remove Mara's things from this cabin that they had shared. It was Mara Jade's ship; it somehow seemed right that her personal effects stay for the duration of this unsought but vital journey that her husband and her son were embarking upon.

So it was that her clothes still hung in the closet, and from time to time Luke would go in there to dress, hesitate, then reach and touch a jacket or tunic or dress she had once worn, remembering when he had last seen it adorning her lithe, graceful body.

He murmured her name in his sleep, and turned over.

In his dream, he opened his eyes and looked out at the stars streaking past. And he felt the press of a warm, living, female body against his back. He did not dare to breathe, did not dare to move, to turn over and take his wife in his arms and kiss her fiercely, whispering *what a terrible nightmare that was, love. I dreamed I lost you.*

And she would laugh softly and whisper back, *You've got too lively an imagination, farm boy. Come here and I'll show you how real I am.*

He knew it was a dream, and yet it seemed so real. He could hear a soft sigh, the rustling of the sheets as she nestled closer to him. But something was not quite right. It wasn't Mara. It couldn't be. She was dead, killed by Jacen Solo.

*I'll show you how real I am.*

"I am real," the faint whisper came from behind him.

And Luke Skywalker, desperate to believe it, flung himself on his other side, reaching out to take her into his arms—

Nothing.

He blinked, knowing he was awake, even though everything seemed as if he had been awake a few moments earlier, though of course he couldn't have been.

He realized he was shaking and that tears stood in his eyes. This surprised him. He had not wept for Mara in a very long time, not even when he had been able to see her . . . ghost? . . . in the Lake of Apparitions inside the Maw. Why, then, did he feel so raw, as if the wound had been made only a few days ago instead of two years? He was at peace with her passing, he knew it. And yet . . .

He reached out a hand and smoothed the pillow, cool to his touch, not warm as it would have been had a living woman lain upon it seconds earlier. With a sigh Luke rolled over on his back, staring up at the ceiling.

It was the ship, he decided. And the recent vision he had been granted of his beloved, late wife. He suspected Ben felt it, too. The *Jade Shadow* was a part of Mara, a part that held them, kept them safe, and took them on their journey to, he hoped, find answers that would help heal the mentally wounded Jedi Knights.

And determine what exactly had happened to Mara's killer, Jacen Solo.

Too, another female presence was aboard the ship—
Vestara Khai, Sith apprentice. And Luke was not so old
that he couldn't see the first hints of a budding romance
when it was happening right under his nose. Ben would
deny it, of course, but Luke had seen how his son's gaze
followed the young woman, how he found excuses to be
in her presence. It concerned him, and he knew it would
concern Mara.

It was no wonder he felt her strongly.

But still.

Even the brief, dream-heavy sleep had refreshed him.
He had wanted that, wanted to feel more rested and
alert, before he talked to High Lord Sarasu Taalon
again.

ABOARD THE BLACK WAVE

"Ah, Master Skywalker," Sarasu Taalon said. He leaned
back in his command chair and smiled. It was an elegant, if predatory smile, for Taalon's pale purple face
was ideally proportioned. His features were sharp but
strong, epitomizing masculine beauty. The tone of his
skin was considered particularly attractive among the
Keshiri and humans as well, even, with no unsightly ir-
regular pigmentation. His strong hands, fingers steepled
in front of him at the moment, showed calluses from
years of using weapons, but had no disfiguring marks
such as scars or misshapen fingers, which indicated that
from a young age he usually won what sparring he engaged in. He kept his dark purple hair short, a departure
from current fashion, but one he found convenient.
Taalon's eyes were large, expressive, and missed nothing
as he gazed at the small holographic image of Grand
Master Luke Skywalker, the hated enemy with whom he
was currently allied.

"Any further word from your friend?"

Luke Skywalker smiled back with what was easily discernible as forced courtesy. "Yes, as a matter of fact. He reports that he is on schedule to join us within ten to twelve days."

"Pity he cannot work faster to update this . . . *tug*?" Taalon did not sneer, not quite.

"You'll have no reason to regret the delay, I assure you. Lando's work is excellent. And since you've not navigated the Maw, you don't appreciate quite yet how useful it will be to us."

Taalon gritted his teeth, both at the delay and the utterly unsubtle jibe. He already had reason to regret having to spend more than five minutes in orbit of the planet turning slowly beneath the vessel. Taalon, like most of the Sith Tribe, burned with ambition and chafed at anything that stood in his way. He had no interest in wasting time orbiting a backwater world. Or back *sand* world, as a cursory glance at the information on Klatooine had revealed. Brown and yellow and ugly.

"Well, then. Let us hope the vessel proves as useful as you say it will," he said, pouring sincerity into the Force to mask his irritation. "I am anxious to take the fight to Abeloth."

"It is my hope that it will not be a fight," said Luke. "Like I said earlier, the goal is not to destroy her, it's to try to understand her and reason with her. Make her understand what she is doing, if possible. She's an alarming being, that much is certain, but I'll need more time to assess the situation before I'm willing to fight her."

Taalon deftly covered his annoyance and forced himself to smile in an indulgent manner, stretching his lips thinly across even white teeth. "Of course, but remember, she is damaging our younglings. She must release them."

"Of course," Luke said, "but killing a sentient being

should always be a last resort. Also, her death might mean our young Jedi and your apprentices would never be released. We have far too little information on her nature to know exactly what is going on."

"You raise a good point," Taalon agreed. "Is there anything further?" Taalon intensely disliked Luke Skywalker. He itched to blast the Jedi with Force lightning, to choke him, to cleave him in two with his lightsaber. With a little luck, and the blessings of the dark side, he would have the opportunity to indulge his desire once Abeloth had been forced to cooperate with the Sith. He allowed himself to fantasize briefly about the moment.

"No, nothing more. Will you be visiting the surface?"

"Doubtful," said Taalon. He did not elaborate.

"Me neither. I'm not very fond of sand. *Jade Shadow* out."

"Captain?" It was Leeha Faal, his second in command, a slender female and fellow Keshiri who stood rigidly at attention. Following her commander's example, she, too, had cut her hair short. Soft bangs, however, fell over her high forehead.

"Yes, what is it?"

"We have been researching Klatooine, and—"

"There cannot possibly be anything remotely interesting in that ball of dirt," Taalon snapped.

"Well, sir . . . there is one thing you might want to see. With your permission?" She indicated the computer. He regarded her for a moment. This had better be good, otherwise her impertinence would not be overlooked.

"Go ahead, impress me," he said.

She didn't flinch, but her resolution in the Force wavered, just for an instant. Then she leaned over him and tapped in something.

What appeared on the screen was a vision of beauty. It looked like a geyser at the moment of eruption, captured forever in time, each finger of water, each splash, each droplet, frozen so that one could admire its power and grace. Swirling, turning, it was vibrant, creative motion somehow paused, and Taalon's heart leapt. Like all the Sith Tribe, he put a great value on beauty, whether it be in the lines of a being's face, the drape of a handmade garment, or the curve of a shikkar handle.

This moved him to his core.

He had to have it.

"It is . . . exquisite," breathed Taalon. "Is it a statue?"

Pleased at his response, Leeha smiled. "No, sir. It is a natural formation. It's a type of glass."

He turned his head sharply to look at her, but she was serious. Glass . . . glass more lovely, more dramatic, than any piece he had ever owned. Ever seen constructed for any building in Tahv.

"How is this possible? What is it?"

"It is called the Fountain of the Hutt Ancients. The planet produces deep in its core a substance called wintrium. Back before recorded time—and that's a long time here, sir, tens of thousands of years—there was some kind of fissure in the planet's crust. The wintrium erupted. There was a chemical change when it came into contact with the air. Rather like water freezing instantly, except it was transformed into glass rather than ice."

If it had been a statue, Taalon mused, he would have abducted the artist on the spot and forced him or her to create a piece of equal or superior beauty for Taalon's private collection. But as it was a natural formation . . .

"I imagine this Fountain is highly regarded among the Klatooinians?"

"Oh, definitely. It's a sacred object to them. Time is very important to their mind-set and culture," Leeha continued, warming to the subject. Clearly, she'd done a lot of research before bringing the Fountain to her captain's attention. "The wintrium continues to harden through the centuries, becoming stronger instead of more fragile."

*Interesting,* thought Taalon. *A material that grows stronger over time. Weapons . . . that grow stronger over time . . .*

He pulled thoughtfully on his neatly trimmed goatee, his eyes never leaving the image of the Fountain as Leeha spoke.

"The Klatooinians, too, believe they grow stronger over time. One of the reasons they agreed to become servants of the Hutts twenty-five thousand years ago was because the Hutts promised to always keep the Fountain safe."

He shot her a quick glance. "Hutts? As in the name of the Fountain Hutts?"

"Well, yes, although it was originally just called the Fountain of the Ancients."

"What are Hutts?"

Leeha didn't miss a beat. She leaned over, not bothering to ask his permission a second time—he liked that, it showed initiative and confidence—and called up another image. This was of a large wormlike creature, with a large head, grinning mouth, and two small armlike appendages. It was most certainly *not* beautiful.

"Hutts can live to be a thousand years old, which was why when they descended upon Klatooine they were revered as being connected to the mythological ancients. The Hutts are intelligent, self-serving, and manipulative, and they took advantage of the Klatooinian belief that they were akin to gods. They tricked the Klatooinians into signing over their younglings to be sent to work for the Hutts wherever they saw fit. In dangerous mines, as tradespeople, as soldiers in an army—for whatever the Hutts needed, they used the Klatooinians."

Ugly they might be, but Taalon felt a new respect for the giant worm things.

"For how long?"

Leeha smiled openly. "Forever."

"My, my. I think we can learn a thing or two from these Hutts."

"The Tribe is always learning, always improving itself, in preparation for our eventual control of the galaxy," Leeha said, very correctly. Smart girl, Leeha. She'd advance far.

He changed the picture back to the Fountain and regarded it for a long moment.

"Are nonnatives permitted to approach it?"

"Oh yes, sir. It's apparently something of a tourist attraction. There are a few rules, though. Because the Klatooinians look at it as sacred, and frozen in time, they don't want anyone bringing anything technological within a one-kilometer radius. They would find that terribly offensive."

"I see. Frankly, I had not intended that any of us land on the planet's surface while waiting for Master Skywalker's little friend," Taalon said. "However, I find I am feeling a need to visit this exquisite, unique natural phenomenon. I think it will do my soul good to gaze upon its beauty with my own eyes."

Leeha's smile widened, making her lovely Keshiri features even more attractive.

"Oh yes, sir, I think that would be an excellent idea."

Taalon grinned.

ABOARD THE JADE SHADOW

There it was again, the strange, but not altogether unpleasant feeling as if he were being watched. Luke turned away from the control panel and glanced around, then closed his eyes and looked with other senses.

No, he was not alone. In a way, he would never be alone, as long as he could touch the Force. All living things created it, and even those who were no longer among the living contributed. Mara would always be there, at least in part. And he would be able to see her always whenever he looked at Ben.

Luke kept his eyes closed and felt the faintest, almost imaginary brush of a feminine touch over his cheek, and sighed audibly.

*I miss you,* he thought.

*I miss you, too. But we will be together.*

*One day,* he agreed. A soft chime from the communications array caused him to open his eyes, and he grinned when he saw who was calling. He tapped the controls and a miniature version of a golden droid appeared. He looked extremely pleased, if droids could look pleased, and See-Threepio definitely managed it.

"Master Luke!" The protocol droid was all but bouncing in his delight. "What an unexpected pleasure. I am so very flattered you were interested in consulting me. I do not get very many messages myself, you know. Usually I am relegated to the task of conveying the identity of the caller when Master Han and Mistress Leia are contacted. This is quite a treat."

Luke found himself smiling. "Hi, Threepio. I've missed you."

"Oh, goodness, we have missed you, too, Master Luke. How may I be of assistance?"

"I need some help, and you're the droid to provide it," Luke replied, tapping the controls. "I'm transmitting a conversation. I need you to translate it."

"Oh! As you know, I am fluent in over six million forms of communication."

"Yes, I know. But not this one."

"Oh? Are you certain?"

"Very certain. It's from a completely unknown world.

I don't know the planet, don't know the name of the language, or the people who created it. I need you to cross-reference it as best you can and translate it for me as soon as possible."

Technically, he supposed the argument could be made that he was in violation of the terms of the agreement he had made with Daala. Some would say that in contacting Leia's droid, he was initiating a request for information from Jedi sources. But Threepio also belonged to Han, and he was no Jedi. He'd ducked the issue entirely by contacting the droid directly. It made good legal sense, and also, it made Threepio feel good.

"Oooh. A challenge! I shall get to it immediately, Master Luke. How delightful to feel truly useful again. It does become rather tiresome to be relegated to cooking, cleaning, and answering comms. One yearns to do what one was designed for."

"I know you'll do your best. Let me know when you've got something."

"The very nanosecond," Threepio assured him. Luke had no doubt that Threepio meant it literally.

"Talk to you then," he said.

"Take good care of yourself, Master Luke. And of Master Ben as well."

Luke clicked off and leaned back in the chair, and wondered what sort of mischief his teenage son and the teenage Sith girl had gotten themselves into.

# Chapter Six

DYON STAD, WHO HAD SERVED AS A GUIDE FOR HAN, Leia, and Allana during their time on Dathomir, was a pleasant, cheerful fellow who seemed to harbor no resentment at all toward Luke, Ben, or even Vestara for their superior ability to use the Force. Ben had taken an instant liking to him. His time on Dathomir had caused him to be a lot more relaxed about things than Luke was, and he was closer to Ben's age than anyone in his immediate family.

So Ben was rather pleased that if he had to have an "escort" because his dad didn't trust him to shepherd Vestara properly on his own, it was Dyon rather than Luke. Ben had traveled enough and seen enough that Treema, the capital of this arid world, was not all that impressive to him. No doubt it showcased the finest Klatooine had to offer, but truth be told, that wasn't much. At least, not from what he had been able to glean as the *Jade Shadow* had come in for docking.

Luke had told Ben that the Klatooinian species was an ancient one, and Treema was the oldest city that had not fallen into ruins, most likely because of its proximity to the Fountain of Hutt Ancients. The city seemed to like to build on top of itself, and the end result was something that looked to Ben's eye like an extremely tall stack of hotcakes. Ships were permitted to dock in the center of each level. The most expensive docking bays were on the top level, with the price falling the closer one was willing to be to the ground. The reasoning was simple: the upper levels offered better protection from sandstorms, greater security, and simply were newer. Luke and Ben had opted for something in the mid range, on Level 34.

As Ben, Vestara, and Dyon emerged from the *Shadow* and walked toward the turbolifts, Ben said, "So . . . what are your orders?"

Dyon grinned cheerily down at the two adolescents. "To keep you two *in* my sight and *out* of trouble."

Vestara looked at him intently. "Did Master Luke really instruct you to say that?"

"No," Dyon said, his grin widening. "He just said to keep an eye on you two."

"So, no stipulations on where we can go or what we can do?" Ben pressed.

Dyon shrugged, glancing down at the datapad in his hand. "I think as long as we get everything on this list and return with all our limbs intact, we're pretty free to do whatever we like."

Ben gave Vestara a quick grin, and her own curved in an answering, if slightly sardonic, return smile.

Next to each of the turbolifts were two large maps. One identified the main purpose of each level, the other was a map of Level 34. Ben suspected they'd find something identical on each level. Vestara paused and began analyzing the main map.

Ben rolled his eyes. "Let's just jump into the turbolift, pick a floor, and be surprised."

She frowned. "That is not very efficient." She glanced at Dyon for support. "Surely you agree. Your profession is tracking things down."

Dyon nodded. "It is," he agreed. "But we've got

plenty of time to explore. And it's by exploring that you learn the lay of the land."

During the height of the Hutt control in the galaxy, this place must have been impressive. While Klatooine had not fallen to the Yuuzhan Vong, the war had crippled their masters the Hutts, and as such the world clearly did not receive the attention or the traffic it once had. The docking bays on Level 34 were adequate, but not much more, and a good two decades out of date. The turbolifts that connected the levels varied from efficient to erratic to let's-not-get-on-this-one.

Their exploration took them to random places all over the city. Some levels were living areas, again with the most expensive and attractive dwellings near the top levels, and what essentially amounted to hovels down at ground level, and in some cases lower than that. Others were devoted to trade: repair shops, stores, markets, and so on. Still others seemed to exclusively feature restaurants and taverns, and more were dedicated to recreation. These areas appeared to be the hardest hit, with some levels actually closed off, their extravagant luxuries having no takers.

The turbolift opened on one level that was dimly lit, loud with voices and music, and thick with smoke. For a second Ben thought something was on fire, but then he realized it was simply the haze floating out from one of the establishments.

Vestara coughed, but moved forward. Dyon gently took her arm. "I don't think Luke would be happy if I let you two poke around this level too much," he said.

Ben extended his senses in the Force, was able to figure out the nature of some of the "entertainment" being offered in the various places, and glanced at Vestara. She hadn't said much about her homeworld, but one thing was sure. Even though she was a Sith, and had by her own admission killed in cold blood, there was an innocence about her that denoted a sheltered life in many respects. He somehow thought she wouldn't quite be prepared for some of the things she would see if she went into these seedy places.

Then again, she no doubt sensed, as he did, that the emotions of the beings within ran to the darker side of the Force. The proprietors of these taverns, gambling houses, and worse fed on greed, fear, despair, and loneliness. That had to execute a powerful pull for a Sith apprentice. His heart sank a little at the expression on her beautiful face, eager and curious. She was disappointed at Dyon's words, but nodded and stepped back into the turbolift.

"Let's see what's on the ground level," Dyon said. If he had noticed Vestara's response to the pull of the dark side present on this floor, he gave no indication.

When the turbolift doors hissed open, Ben almost gaped. "Did we just step into a circus?" he asked, looking around at the noise, bustle, and colors, and inhaling a staggering variety of smells, not all of which were pleasant.

"I think it's an open-air market," Dyon said as they stepped forward into a crowd of beings. Ben's feet encountered not duracrete, but hardpacked soil. It actually made sense—produce and other market wares would come by air and by land. Judging from the smell, many of the natives of this world still relied upon living transport.

Like most originally arid worlds that still sported a fairly generous populace, Klatooine had learned to wrest sufficient moisture from the soil by means of technology in order to grow a decent amount of crops. It was cheaper, in the long run, to invest in droids, irrigation technology, and up-to-date vaporators and mechanics to take care of them than it was to import food. Especially, Ben mused, if you had been under the thumb of the Hutts for almost forever. He took a second to recall Hutt anatomy and then let it go, content with Yes, Hutts did have thumbs.

So it was that in the shaded marketplace, with artificially moist, cool air blowing about them and a few musicians standing about playing strangely complicated-looking instruments with cases looking sadly empty of credcoins, he, Vestara, and Dyon found themselves looking at a pretty impressive amount of fruits, vegetables, nuts, grains, and meats.

He liked to watch Vestara when she encountered new things, and this was much more to his liking than her curiosity about the goings-on occurring on Level 7. *You like to watch Vestara whatever she's doing,* a little voice inside his head spoke up, but he pushed it down. For him, this was another market like dozens he had seen before. But while Vestara refused to say how many new worlds she had seen or species she had encountered, Ben could tell by her reactions that she was nowhere near as well versed with such a variety of beings and cultures as he was.

She was apparently insatiably curious, wanting to look at, sniff, touch, and if possible, taste everything. She asked question after question, listening intently to the answer, learning, always learning. Dyon's interest seemed piqued by the marketplace, and he was engrossed in glancing at the list Luke had given them and stocking up on a variety of intriguing-looking foodstuffs. As a result, Ben and Vestara found themselves several stalls away from the Force-using tracker. Ben didn't mind at all. He glanced over to where Dyon was animatedly chatting with a red-cheeked, elderly human female about the contents of an aquarium, nodded to himself, and returned his attention to Vestara.

"They cannot be grown anywhere else, you say?" Vestara was asking, her musical voice intense, her brown eyes fastened intently upon a young male Klatooinian. Despite her initial repugnance of the species, Vestara had no problem looking the other being in the eye, or being courteous.

"No, nowhere else in the galaxy," the young male was replying. Vestara nodded, then bent her head over the lumpy purple fruit currently under discussion. She lifted it to her nose and sniffed delicately, running a thumb over its surface. The young Klatooinian eyed her appreciatively as she did so. Ben suspected that if she had noticed the youth ogling her so openly, she might have wiped the smirk off with her bare hands. Luke had forbidden the Sith apprentice to take her lightsaber on the visit with her.

Ben, for an instant, wanted to use his own lightsaber for just such a purpose, but he sighed and let the impulse go.

He contented himself with stepping close to Vestara, reaching out a finger to run along the skin of the fruit she held as she had, though in actuality the thing held no interest for him at all. A meter or two away, the owner of the booth, possibly the youth's father, gave them a quick smile before returning to weighing and marking prices on bags of produce.

"Why is that?" Vestara said so firmly that the question almost sounded like a demand.

"No one knows for sure," the youth said. "No lab has been able to replicate quite the same conditions that are found here. Could be traces of wintrium in the soil, but we're not certain. If you're hungry, take it. Free sample."

Vestara's always-almost smile widened into a real one. "Thank you," she said. "And . . . how do I eat it?"

The boy chuckled slightly, took the fruit from her, and peeled it quickly with a knife. "There you go."

The fruit was amber in the center and dripping juice.

Vestara took a healthy bite of the succulent flesh and wiped as the liquid dribbled down her chin.

"My son Kelkad is correct," the grocer said, moving forward to join the discussion. "The general conclusion is that the wintrium in the soil enables the pak'pah to grow and reach that unique sweetness. Wintrium is found nowhere else in the galaxy but on our humble world."

"Can it be artificially replicated?" Vestara again.

"No," the grocer replied. "And we have refused to let it be analyzed. Any scientific analysis would require more than could be obtained with a soil sample, as wintrium is such a complex element. And the only way to get that would be to violate the Fountain."

Fountain. Ben knew a cue when one was presented to him. He stepped in quickly. "When my father requested permission to dock, he was told a little bit about the Fountain. It's called the Fountain of the Hutt Ancients, right?"

Kelkad had been turned away from his father, placing the priced and bagged items on the table. Both Ben and Vestara saw him wince at the word "Hutt."

"Yes. All are free to behold it. You can even walk right up to it. We would not dream of attempting to come between the Fountain and those who approach to respectfully admire it."

"There are rules, I understand," Vestara said. "Visitors to the Fountain are forbidden to approach with anything technological on them. Or to ride on ships or any motorized vehicles."

"You are quite correct," and the grocer smiled at them. Still turned away from his father, Kelkad continued to quietly fume. Ben frowned a little. Why was the youth so upset?

"The Fountain is not like any other fountain. You see, it does not spout water. It spouted wintrium—so long ago that its origins are lost to time. It is because of that sacred timelessness that we do not approach with anything technological."

"And wintrium is unique to your world," Vestara continued. "And there is no other place on Klatooine where one could get such a pure sample other than at the Fountain."

"And no one would violate the Fountain, so no one else gets to grow pak'pahs."

"Why would no one violate the Fountain?"

Vestara's blunt question clearly offended the elder Klatooinian. "Because not only is it wrong, and most of our visitors are enlightened enough to know that," he said, rather pointedly, "but because it would violate the Treaty of Vontor."

"What's that?"

The grocer drew breath to speak, but his son interrupted him. "Over twenty-five thousand years ago, Barada M'Beg, the Klatooinian for whom most males on my world are named, including my father, signed a treaty with the Hutts. In return for the Hutt's promise to protect the Fountain, Barada M'Beg promised the Hutts the servitude of my people forever."

Kelkad's voice was polite and cool, almost disinterested. But Barada shot him a worried look and glanced around. The market was crowded and noisy and nobody seemed to be paying any attention to the conversation.

"That is correct," Barada said. "And the Hutts have always kept their bargain. No one has violated the Fountain in all that time. Is there anything you two would care to purchase?"

His point was clear. "Uh," Ben said. "Yeah. You liked the pak'pah, right Vestara?"

Vestara caught on at once, as he knew she would. "Yes. We'll take—oh, about a dozen."

"Sure," said Kelkad. "Let me help you select the best ones."

There was nothing further for Barada to do other than walk away, casting a worried glance at his son and a not-very-friendly one at Vestara and Ben. The three bent their heads together, selecting out the most succulent pak'pah fruit while softly continuing their conversation.

Vestara cut right to the point with lightsaber keenness. "You don't approve of the treaty, do you, Kelkad?" Her whisper was soft and husky.

"No," Kelkad said. "And there are many who think like me scattered throughout the galaxy. Some have escaped their bonds of servitude and live free, on free worlds."

"What's meant by 'servitude' anyway?" Ben queried. "Is that polite code for 'slavery'?"

"It can be," said Kelkad. "It can be whatever the Hutts want it to mean."

Ben frowned a little, confused. "It's got to be dangerous to voice dissent here. So how come you're talking so freely to us?"

"Because I heard that you're Jedi."

Vestara continued to look sincere and earnest. Ben supposed that it didn't matter if she heard Kelkad's impassioned opinion. Vestara didn't work for the Hutts, and he couldn't imagine the Sith Tribe caring one way or another about a species on a remote world and its twenty-five-thousand-year bond of "servitude."

"Well, some of us are Jedi," Ben said. "I'm a Jedi Knight."

For the first time, Kelkad gave him a genuine smile. "Jedi despise slavery."

"We do, but the treaty's kind of . . . legal, isn't it? I mean, you weren't snatched up and carted away someplace against your will."

Ben did not look at Vestara as he said these words, but

he felt her shiver in the Force, ever so slightly. She had done exactly that to the Nightsisters. He was starting to grow highly attuned to her nuances in the Force, as well as learning how to read her usually impassive face and body language.

"No, but I did not sign the treaty," Kelkad continued bitterly. More loudly he said, "This one looks good," and made a show of dropping another fruit into Vestara's bag. "And I do not get to decide my own fate. That is wrong. Jedi know that it's wrong, don't they?"

He looked Ben full in the face, his large dark eyes pleading. Ben felt a stab of guilt. Not for the first time, Ben found himself confronted with what was right versus what was legal. It was an issue that seemed to be cropping up an awful lot these days. He wanted to say something calming and wise like his father so often did when confronted with things like this, but found no words would come.

Fortunately, Kelkad did not appear to want to wait for Ben's comment, and he had no such problem speaking. He continued, the words tumbling out of him.

"I am almost of the age where they will come for me. They might let me stay here and continue to help my father. Or they might drag me away to some dangerous world and I will be told to fight and kill enemies of the Hutts. And the same will be true of every youth my age on this world. All because Barada M'Beg got the Hutts to agree to protect the Fountain of the Ancients. I refuse to sully it with the word 'Hutt.' They are not our ancients. A few guards with blasters, and their commitment is met. But our commitment—"

He broke off. Ben glanced over at Barada, who was starting to again take note of the conversation.

"Your dad's watching," he said quietly. "I think he's worried for you."

"Of course he is," hissed Kelkad, his jowls shaking

with barely suppressed outrage. "He knows he could lose me forever if the Hutts get wind that I am saying this. But I cannot keep it inside me any longer!" His fists clenched, and the pak'pah he held in one of them split under the pressure, juice dripping freely to the hard-packed dirt floor.

Impulsively, Ben said, "I wish I could help. But we're just a couple of Jedi. I'm sorry."

"I know. But . . . when you go home . . . you will return to the Temple? You will speak with the Masters there? We hear of them."

Vestara was watching them both closely. Ben only nodded.

"Tell them that we are a patient people. But we are also a people with a deep regard for time. For what it does, how it shapes everything. Everyone knows that in the face of time, all things fade away." He smiled, drawing his jowls back from sharp teeth. "Even treaties."

Ben nodded slowly, then handed over some credcoins. Vestara took the bag, smiling. Without a word exchanged between them, they turned back to the street, out from under the canopied market stalls.

Where they could talk freely.

Ben selected a pak'pah, fiddling with it absently. He wasn't really hungry but he had to do something with his hands.

"So the Jedi help slaves?"

"Well, of course we do, where we can," Ben said. For no real reason he could fathom immediately, he was annoyed with Vestara. "To take a being and force it to do something against its will when it's completely innocent of any wrongdoing—" He sighed, peeling the fruit.

"Servants and slaves are useful things," Vestara said quietly, simply stating what was, for her, a fact. "Your father was not quite right, I believe. From everything I have heard, even from Kelkad, the Hutts place the Klatooinian youths where they are best suited." She took another bite of the pak'pah, wiping the juice from her chin.

"Where the *Hutts* think they are best suited, not their own people," Ben said. "That's a huge distinction."

"We place the—" Vestara suddenly fell silent, one hand creeping up to her throat. The half-eaten pak'pah fruit tumbled from her other hand as she clutched Ben's arm. She appeared unable to breathe.

The argument utterly fled from Ben's mind, replaced by quick, cold, slithering fear as Vestara choked. Almost immediately he reached out, both physically to slip an arm around her, and in the Force, and focused his attention on the object lodging in her throat. He needn't have worried, of course. Vestara, even while choking, was levelheaded and a powerful Force user. She had already thought of the same thing he had, and the small piece of fruit moved from blocking her airway to her mouth, where she spat it out.

"You okay?"

She nodded. For a second there he wondered if she had been faking it, but he had sensed the blockage was serious. She gave him a grin.

"Well, *that* was attractive," she said, her cheeks coloring a little. "Sorry about that."

"Hey, it's fine," Ben said. His arm was still around her. He found he didn't want to remove it. Nor did he want to revisit the conversation they'd been having. It was an argument, a clash, and he was growing increasingly weary of struggling against her. For the time being, they were all supposed to be working together. She was beautiful and smart, and they were simply walking through an outdoor market. Did they have to be fighting while doing so? Couldn't it all be—he didn't know—set aside for an hour?

Vestara was still embarrassed, and the thought

pleased him a little. She cared about how he thought of her. He squeezed her shoulder reassuringly, and she didn't protest. She even leaned into him a little, smiling at him. The scar, that tiny little scar that she disliked so much, stretched with the gesture and made her smile even wider.

He wanted to tell her, *I don't want to fight with you. There's enough strife and anger and bad feelings running around as it is. I know there are things we can't agree on, and things that make my gut hurt to think that you really believe. I know that I want to show you my world, my thoughts, what I believe is right. And I think that maybe you might listen, one day. But for now, I just want to walk around with you and just . . . be us. Can't we just be us?*

Instead he said, keeping his voice light, "So, how'd you get that scar?"

Her smile widened, became mischievous. His heart did something strange in his chest. "Oh, that was when I was beginning my apprenticeship training," she said, her voice deadly serious but her eyes bright. "In order to prove that I was worthy to be trained, I had to fight four rukaros, all fed enough to keep them strong and deadly, but kept so that they were not at the height of their aggression. I had a sporting chance."

They had started walking now, ambling, heading no place in particular. She continued melodramatically.

"They all came at me at once, four sets of claws as long as my hand, a mouthful of teeth, tails that were barbed with poison. I killed all but one before they could get me, but before that one died, right as my lightsaber sliced him neatly into six pieces, he struck out with a claw and tore my mouth. And that's what caused the scar."

Ben grinned at her. The argument they had had earlier was forgotten, gone like a cloud blown away by a cleansing wind. "Well, I have to say, I'm not impressed. I—"

A sudden scream sounded from inside the market, followed by a loud crash. For half a heartbeat Ben and Vestara stared at each other. Then Ben grasped his lightsaber and raced back toward the marketplace as fast as he could go. Vestara was right beside him.

# Chapter Seven

MOS EISLEY, TATOOINE

SHE WAS ELEVEN, DIRTY, TOO SKINNY, AND TOO CLEVER for her own good. Or so her master told her. Her name was Kitaya Shuul, and she was a slave.

Inserted just below her shoulder blade was a subcutaneous chip that transmitted a signal. Her master, Truugo the Hutt, could tell where she was at any time of the day or the night. And she knew she was monitored nearly constantly. If Truugo didn't like where she was, he would order that the chip be detonated. And Kitaya would no longer be dirty, too skinny, and too clever for her own good; she would be a messy, gooey collection of small pieces of flesh and bone.

That didn't stop her.

Fortunately, one of the duties Truugo liked to utilize her for was the occasional—more than occasional—round of espionage. He had done his best to teach her several languages, making his other slaves teach her everything they knew. Kit could speak four different languages and comprehend eight more; her human ear could understand certain languages when spoken, but her human tongue could not replicate them.

It was ironic, that while conducting her service to her master, she was also plotting his downfall.

Slavery was an institution as old as there were sentient

beings. In the days of the Republic, Tatooine was too far afield to warrant the enforcement of the antislavery laws. And now, in the era of the Galactic Alliance, because it had not joined said Alliance, there were no antislavery laws to enforce at all. Tatooine, as it had for most of its history, was left to take care of itself.

And Kit wanted to be among those who would "take care" of the institution of slavery.

It had begun with books, smuggled to her on chips or encoded among repair manuals on datapads. Poetry, history, fiction, or truth, Kit drank it all in as thirstily as she drank water on this arid world. Stories of revolutions and of peaceful negotiations, accounts of brutalities and unspeakable kindnesses, tales of the individual and tales of a society. All inspired her.

Then, she began keeping in contact with certain individuals who had "business" here. And they often conducted their "business" in locales where Truugo sent Kit to spy. For a while, Kit had held her breath, certain that at some point she would be discovered. Would find out when it was too late that the being she was sent to eavesdrop on was one of her contacts.

They called themselves the Freedom Flight. Their burning passion was to eliminate slavery throughout the galaxy, not just on those worlds whose leaders had enough integrity to do so themselves. Sometimes they were able to help fund planetary representatives who would work to bring about change. Other times, the organization, if such a term could be applied to something so mysterious and elusive, functioned on more of a personal level, helping individuals to escape and finding them new lives and identities elsewhere. Those involved in such activities were called "pilots," and the routes they took were called "flight paths." The "flight paths" had several stops, and most pilots knew only their small portion of the route to freedom for the slaves they transported. It was safer that way if anyone was ever caught.

Kit couldn't escape. Technology, it would seem, kept up with the slave trade, and every time it looked like someone had figured out how to deactivate the transmitter, a new, improved one would be invented. She'd resigned herself to that. Besides, her life was not as bad as that of others she had heard tell of. She at least was beaten only if she disappointed her master, and she had enough food most of the time. Kit knew she could help best if she stayed here, on Tatooine, owned by a giant slug.

Kit swept up a lock of dirty, unkempt black hair behind her ear, and hurried on bare, callused feet to the appointment site.

She had no fear of being recognized. She was not a well-known slave, as she had few interactions with the public. The most basic of disguises—hair coloring or a wig, cleaned up or scruffy, posture, simple prosthetics—made her look different each time. She moved swiftly, not quite running so as not to attract attention, through the streets of the spaceport. There were people out even at this hour, for Mos Eisley knew no curfew. Curfews were bad for business—of all kinds.

Kit slowed as she approached the cantina. Formally known as Chalmun's Cantina, although nobody bothered to call it that anymore, it had a decades-old reputation for being a place where shady goings-on took place. It also, according to Truugo, served the best Sarlacc Kicker in town. As usual, business was brisk, and she had to dodge quickly as a stumbling Gamorrean lurched out of the doorway. It glared at her with its tiny, piggy eyes, and grunted. She knew the language, but had been called more insulting things in her day, so she simply stepped out of the way and let him trundle drunkenly off into the night.

She waited for a pause in the flow of customers, then settled herself down near the entrance. Not so close that she would be inadvertently stepped on, but close enough so that she could see those who entered and left, and could hear very well thanks to the auditory enhancer.

She sat on an old blanket and put out a ceramic bowl, letting her body droop in mock weariness and pain. Her left arm was bent so that her hand rested on her shoulder and tightly bound, the sleeve flopping free. In the dim light, even if a being looked closely, she would seem like a poor amputee begging for food or credits from the kinder-hearted. The auditory enhancer in her ear screened out extraneous noises, and she had learned from an early age how to focus on one voice above all others.

Feet, hooves, talons, and wheels all moved swiftly past her, stirring up the dust from the street as they went. Kit stretched out her good hand imploringly, her pinched face with its too-large blue eyes peering up at the passersby.

"A few credits? A bite to eat? Please, whatever you can spare—"

Kit did not expect to be noticed, for few people here had time for the destitute and unfortunate, and for the most part she was ignored. Now and then, though, a bite of food or a credit or two would fall into the little bowl she had set before her. Her eyes darted about, seemingly on the lookout for a kind face, but in actuality searching for one being in particular.

And there he was. A Bothan, swathed in dark, travel-stained robes with a cowl that hid most of his face. She could determine his species only when he glanced up and she caught the briefest glimpse of his feline features. They were a species that was widely traveled and not above less-than-reputable dealings, so they were not uncommon on Tatooine. Nonetheless, he was the right species, in the right place, at the right time, and that was good enough for Kit to focus on him.

She'd been listening to the chatter inside the cantina for a while now. The musicians, clatter of chairs, and clink of glasses had been tuned out, and she'd already gotten a good sense of who was present. There were a few Twi'lek females soliciting customers for acts best performed in private; the Toydarian gambler Yol Saan, who cheated brilliantly and who lost just often enough that he didn't end up facedown in the alley behind the cantina; a couple of Jawas who were utterly drunk by this point and performing their species' version of hysterical giggling; and several strangers of all species discussing the purchase of, or obtaining passage on, vessels. In other words, she had heard nothing out of the ordinary.

The Bothan stepped through the doorway, ignoring Kit completely. Kit continued to enact the charade of a poor, orphaned cripple, but her full attention was focused on what was transpiring inside.

The Bothan's voice was soft and pleasant. He spoke in his native language, one that Kit understood completely, all soft, husky purring punctuated with the occasional growl. He approached Ackmena, the night bartender, and asked for a Starshine Surprise. She greeted him pleasantly enough, mixed up the drink, and turned her attention to other customers. The Bothan moved away, making idle chitchat as he settled on a table. One of the Twi'lek girls approached him, but before she could get well into the oft-rehearsed invitation, the Bothan cut her off.

"Not interested, sorry my dear. Not that you're not lovely."

Compliments, it seemed, did not equal credits in the Twi'lek's opinion, for she responded to it with a vulgar phrase. Kit smothered a grin.

There was not a lot to be heard from the Bothan for some time. Kit began to grow worried. Maybe the information Truugo had on this being was inaccurate. If she came back without any information for him, he'd be very displeased. She shifted uneasily on her blanket.

"You're late."

Kit frowned. The voice was human, female and gravelly, and Kit knew it well. It belonged to Ackmena, the bartender. Ackmena was something of a celebrity on Tatooine. She'd started out as the night bartender, and gone on to fame with her singing. She'd come back awhile ago and had her own place now, but apparently she was still drawn to Chalmun's, for it wasn't unusual to see her tending bar, presumably just for the fun of socializing. While there was certainly a lot of traffic in the cantina, there were many regulars as well, and they adored the gruff but cheerful woman. While she never revealed her age, everyone knew she was well into her eighties by this point, but she still had the energy of a woman much younger. It surprised and saddened Kit to realize that Ackmena was involved in the sort of shady affairs that would interest her master.

"Unavoidable, I'm afraid. I appear to have attracted a bit of attention."

The sound of fingers drumming gently on a table. "Attention on your company isn't a bad thing. Attention on the pilots is."

Kit gasped and then bit her tongue. She glanced around; fortunately, no one seemed to have noticed. Both the Bothan she had been sent to spy on and the beloved, famous bartender were members of the Freedom Flight!

"Indeed," said the Bothan, his voice still soft, barely a murmur. "The pilot whose route I am presently flying has retired."

It all made sense now. Kit swallowed a lump in her

throat as she realized her contact, a Ryn named Tohrm, must have been killed by one of the organizations who stood to profit from the slave trade. It had been several weeks since he had come to Tatooine; she had simply thought it had gotten too risky for him and he was lying low for a while. She had been right, but apparently the risk had been more dangerous than she had realized.

The question was, what should she do now? She had been assigned to watch the Bothan. She'd have to report back on something, and obviously she was not about to tell Truugo the truth. She wished she knew exactly why the Hutt wanted the Bothan watched, then she could at least make up something creative. Kit's mind gnawed on the problem even while she continued to listen intently.

"I'm sorry to hear that," Ackmena said, and Kit could tell she meant it. "I'd hoped he had found another company to do business with." Then, more loudly, "I hope you'll be as careful with the shipments of Tedonian wine as Tohrm was."

"I've not lost a shipment yet," the Bothan said, also more loudly, and chuckled.

That was it . . . Kit could make up something about smuggling. She wouldn't need to implicate Ackmena, she could—

Kit noticed a figure across the narrow, crowded street. It seemed to have a great deal of interest in watching the door. Kit was instantly alert. She kept an eye on the figure while still pretending to be a crippled beggar and listening to the conversation.

For the next several minutes, there was idle chitchat. The figure across the alley didn't move, but did such an excellent job of blending in that once or twice Kit thought it had.

"Well, I have customers to attend to, and my little Chadra-Fan waitress tends to get her hands full after about twenty minutes left on her own," Ackmena said.

"Come back day after tomorrow and I'll have that shipment ready for you."

Kit felt a little pang. The "shipment," of course, consisted of escaped slaves. But not Tatooine slaves, not with the transmitter. Other slaves from other worlds were sequestered away somewhere on the planet, awaiting their freedom. Hers would not come for a long time, but she was resigned to that.

The Bothan stepped out the door, ignoring her with a swirl of his long cape. Of course, a pilot wouldn't want to be seen showing charity or compassion. They had to maintain a tough demeanor. She watched him go, then turned her eyes back to the figure.

It was gone.

"Stang!" she whispered. Her heart started racing in her chest. She could stay here for a little while longer, then go back to Truugo with her falsified stories, and no one could blame her.

No one except herself.

Kit made her choice and rose. She threw her belongings into a small sack and hurried off in the direction in which the Bothan pilot had gone. As she walked swiftly, threading her way through the crowds with the ease of long experience, she deftly undid her tied-back arm, wincing a little as life came back to the limb with sharp stinging sensations.

The Bothan was up ahead. The crowds were beginning to thin out now, and Kit fell back, looking for the mysterious watcher. There he was, a few paces behind the Bothan, just as Kit was a few paces behind him. He was definitely shadowing the pilot.

A bit farther on, and the streets became practically deserted at this time of night. Kit's mouth was dry and she felt her legs quivering as she moved. But she had to keep on. The Bothan didn't know he was being followed. Or did he? She couldn't take that chance.

Her sharp ears, trained since she was four, heard the slight snicking sound of a knife being pulled from its sheath.

She acted without thinking, springing on the being's back, strong little hands clawing at its face. At the same moment the Bothan whirled and fired some sort of weapon point-blank into the stalker's chest. It was almost silent, making the merest little puff of sound, but the being dropped like a stone. Kit sprang off lightly, panting and staring at the dead human.

"Who are you?" Kit turned to see the strange weapon pointed directly at her and felt the blood drain from her face.

"I-I'm Kit," she said. "I knew Tohrm. I'm a slave."

His eyes narrowed. "Prove it."

She turned around and slipped her shirt low enough to show the little pucker of skin where the transmitter had been inserted.

"Ah," the Bothan said. "I'm sorry. You shouldn't have done that. You could have been injured, or even killed. I knew he was following me."

Kit turned back around and tugged her sleeve back into place. "Could have fooled me," she sniffed.

"I fooled *him*, didn't I?" the Bothan replied. Their eyes met and they exchanged a grin. He knelt beside the corpse and searched it. Kit noticed he had gloves on.

"Who was he?"

"No way to tell for sure. Probably a member of some criminal organization that deals in flesh. They've started to get wind of some of the Flight's activities."

Kit's grin faded as he spoke, and she recalled the nature of her errand tonight. "I uh . . . was sent to spy on you. Don't worry, I'll tell my master some kind of story. You're the last person I would want to get in trouble. Well," she amended, "you and Ackmena."

He nodded, his fur rippling. "Thanks, kid. I hate to

ask anything more of you, but . . . can you talk to Ackmena? Let her know we're going to have to delay the shipment until I can send a replacement?"

She nodded energetically. "Sure, I can do that."

"Thank you. I wish I could do something for you."

Kit looked up at him, her pinched face serious. "You *are* doing something for me," she said quietly, then added the motto of the Flight, "We will be free."

The Bothan stepped forward and squeezed her shoulder gently. "Yes," he said. "You will."

He gathered his dark cloak about his slender feline form, looked about one last time, then turned and slipped into the shadows.

Kit realized she never learned his name.

# Chapter Eight

*NO, NO, NO, NO, NO.*

All gone. All taken. Dyon didn't know how he knew, but he did. Fake fake fake. No one was real, no one was who he pretended to be, they all wore masks, didn't they, imposters all, and he was the only one who was who he said he was.

Why had they come here, to Klatooine? Why were they bothering to impersonate *fruit vendors*? And what did they want with him? He wasn't even a Jedi, just a dabbler who had ended up taking people around Dathomir for credits . . .

"Sixty credits," the Nikto merchant said. He peered expectantly at Dyon with small, beady, black eyes.

They could read minds. They knew he was thinking about credits. Sweat popped out on his brow, beneath his arms. He wanted to run, to scream, to upend tables and flee, a cornered beast about to be captured—or killed. Or copied.

He fought to steady himself. Something that had just danced across his mind would help. What was it—a beast, he was an animal they wanted to capture.

No, he wasn't. He was a man, they were the monsters, the animals, and he knew how to track them, how to hunt them. The Nikto—

*—no, he wasn't a Nikto, he was some alien species that Dyon didn't even know about yet, wasn't he, some*

*imposter who'd stolen away everyone on this whole kriffing world; the scope was enormous, just enormous, the mind couldn't even grasp it, not really—*

—started to frown at him. Since their normal expression was somewhat dour, this made him look furious. "You good for the money or no, human?"

He was pointing it out. Rubbing it in. That he, Dyon Stad, was the only human left. That meant—

Dyon turned to look for Ben and Vestara. They were gone. Of course. Blast! They were in on this. They were part of it. They weren't who they were pretending to be. Or maybe Vestara was; she was a Sith after all, and everyone knew you couldn't trust a Sith. He would have to let Luke know at once so he could—

And then the realization struck him like a blow to the gut. Luke had to be in on this, too, or, rather, the thing that had killed or captured the real Grand Master Luke Skywalker and wore his face and body like a costume.

He licked dry lips and forced himself to be calm. Calm, that was it. He had to stay calm. Not-Ben and Not-Vestara were out there somewhere, hiding where he couldn't see them, no doubt ready to spring on him the moment he showed signs of awakening to what had been done around him. He couldn't let that happen. Dyon smiled weakly at the Nikto.

The Nikto sighed. "All right. You drive a hard bargain. Fifty credits. But no lower, and it's a steal. I grow the best skappis on the whole planet."

Amazing, keeping up the façade so smoothly. Dyon almost found himself admiring these Others. How to get out of it? Just buy the fruit and walk away? No, he didn't want his hands encumbered if he had to fight.

"I've changed my mind," he said, and fought to keep his voice from quivering.

The Nikto glowered, and pointed with a sharp-nailed orange finger at the fruit Dyon had in his hand. Dyon had completely forgotten he was holding it. He had squeezed it so tightly he had split the skin, and juice and soft pulp were oozing in rivulets down his arm.

"You gotta pay for that one at least," the Nikto growled. "And then move on and quit blocking the aisle. Make room for people who are actually going to purchase something."

Dyon's shirt was clinging to his torso, soaked in sweat that did not come from the desert heat. He fished in one of the pockets of his vest and grasped a credcoin, then thrust it at the vendor.

The vendor chuckled, his good humor restored. "Now, while these *are* the finest skappis on Klatooine, they *don't* cost that much per piece. Hang on a moment, lemme get your change."

Dyon turned and moved at a fast walk toward the glaring whiteness of the sand outside the tent. He didn't know where to go, he just knew that he had to get away. Had to—

"Hey! Your change!"

Dyon walked faster. Suddenly looming in front of him was a Klatooinian in plastoid armor. At his hip was a WESTAR-34 blaster pistol, which, though dented and dinged, certainly looked functional. The Klatooinian was smiling at him. Smiling the lie.

"Slow down, looks like you forgot your change," he said cheerfully.

The Other was blocking his way. Was not going to let him escape. Dyon panicked. He had to do something.

Without knowing exactly what prompted him, Dyon reached out, placed a hand on the being's neck, pinched, and said, "Sleep." Wordlessly, the guard crumpled to the hard-packed ground, his eyes closed, already snoring.

Someone screamed. Dyon shot out his hand. At once dozens of small objects whirled about: hand-crafted knives, hard-shelled fruits, haunches of meat, small paddy frogs. He hurled them into the thickest part of the crowd of Fakes, and then jerked up his other hand, palm flat. A table laden with yellow spherical fruits lifted, and then came crashing down on the crowd. More screams, this time of pain as well as fear.

Dyon bent over, grabbed the blaster from the sleeping Klatooinian's belt, and raced as fast as he could for the freedom of the sand.

There was a cluster of vehicles and beasts of burden outside the ground level of the city, and beyond that was a hardpacked dirt ring that was clearly more for symbolism than function. The vehicles were lined up in neat, precise rows, except for a conspicuously empty spot near the gate where a bleeding Klatooinian lay on the sand, struggling to rise, one hand clapped to a shoulder that still smoked. He was wounded, but would survive. Already people were rushing to help him.

A trail led off toward the desert. "He stole a vehicle," Vestara said unnecessarily.

"Yeah," Ben said. They both had known it was Dyon. Ben had reached out immediately and felt for Dyon in the Force. The man was terrified, recoiling from Ben's touch as Ben had once recoiled from the "tentacle friend" in the Maw. Vestara had known it at once, too.

Ben glanced around quickly. Most of the vehicles were old and had seen better days, but there was a speeder bike that looked as if it might not fall apart when touched. If it wasn't touched too hard. "So it's time for us to steal one and go after him."

"Jedi? Steal?" Vestara stared at him, astonished.

"Well, borrow, really," Ben said. "It's a fine old Jedi tradition, actually. Come on. Let's take that one."

Vestara shrugged, reached out a hand, made a fist, and tugged. The speeder lifted up, careened over the rows of speeders, farming equipment, and one or two animals that bleated and hooted in alarm, landed, and bounce slightly in the soft sand a meter away from them. Now it was Ben's turn to stare. She'd maneuvered the speeder as if it were no more cumbersome than a pak'pah fruit. Vestara noticed his expression and shot him a grin. Ben recovered quickly.

"Yeah, well, then I'll drive," he said, jumping onto the speeder and starting it. Vestara slid behind him as the speeder roared to life, slipping her arms around his waist. Safely facing away from her, Ben permitted himself a small private smile at the touch, then yanked the handles around and followed the trail that the insane Dyon had so conveniently left them.

"Where does he think he's going to go?" Ben asked rhetorically, yelling to be heard over the sound of the speeder bike.

"According to the map," Vestara yelled back, "Treema is the only major city within several hundred kilometers. If he wanted to escape, he should have stolen a ship."

"Thinking clearly does not seem to be a trait when these Jedi snap," Ben retorted.

But where *did* Dyon think he was going? On a land vessel, he'd run out of water before he made it anywhere. And yet the trail led due west, toward the sinking, bloated magenta sun.

"The Fountain!" Vestara exclaimed.

"The Fountain of the Hutt Ancients?" Why would he go there? Then again, why did the Force users who went mad do anything? To a crazy mind, he supposed it made . . . some kind of sense.

"It's the only thing other than sand that is due west of Treema," Vestara continued. Keeping one arm firmly around his waist, she pointed with the other. "Look. Right there. That slight glint right on the horizon. That's it."

Oh, this was just wonderful. A crazed Force-user on a speeder bike heading straight for an ancient, sacred place that insisted that no modern technology approach within one full kilometer. Ben started to reach for his comlink, but he was going too fast and the speeder swerved. Ben swore under his breath.

"Contact my dad. Let him know what's happened."

"Master Skywalker?"

Vestara. Her voice was drowned out by what sounded like wind snatching away her words. Luke frowned slightly. "Vestara? Everything all right? Where's Ben?"

"No sir, everything is not all right, and Ben is right here with me," she said. "We are in pursuit of Dyon Stad. He appeared to go insane inside on the ground level market and began attacking civilians."

Luke closed his eyes briefly. No, not here, not now . . . At least Vestara's strict Sith training had taught her to report calmly, briefly, and accurately. First things first.

"Any casualties?"

"Negative, unless you count a few bushels of exotic fruit and several wooden crates."

Ben was rubbing off on her. So much for reporting calmly, briefly, and accurately.

She added, "Several people were injured, but neither Ben nor I sensed any deaths."

"Well, that's something, at least. Do you know where he's heading?"

"Due west of Treema," she said. "He's on a speeder bike and so are we. Anticipate broaching the kilometer barrier around the Fountain in approximately five minutes."

"I assume the authorities are also en route."

A pause. "Yes, sir. Behind us and closing in are four land vehicles and above us are six air vehicles."

"What kind?"

Another pause. "Sir, I don't know your vessel classifications."

Ah, the Sith. They could always be trusted upon to lie. Luke suspected that Vestara knew exactly what type of "vessel classifications" she was regarding, maybe even better than Ben. But he chose not to challenge her on it.

"It doesn't matter. Are they—"

He was about to say "attacking" but was saved the trouble as the unmistakable sound of blaster fire was heard.

"Vestara!"

"We're all right," she said, her voice calm and cool. "They appear to be poor shots, and I'm deflecting most of the bolts. And most of their attention is focused on Dyon rather than us."

"Where's Ben?"

"Driving."

They were getting closer. Ben wasn't a big fan of art and culture per se, but even he had to admit the Fountain of the Hutt Ancients was a true wonder.

It rose up out of the sand like a giant tidal wave, a thing frozen in time and dreadfully, beautifully, out of place. The glasslike wintrium caught the light and glinted brightly, causing Ben's eyes to water slightly. He narrowed them further against the glare of the sun on the sand. He hadn't anticipated needing goggles and there had been no time to find any. He was beginning to understand why his father hated desert worlds so darned much.

Still, the fountain was gorgeous, and Tatooine, as far as Ben had been told, had nothing of beauty to recommend it other than the dual sunset. Certainly nothing like the Fountain. He could tell even at this distance that it was much larger than he had expected it to be. No wonder the Klatooinians revered it so much, and attached such significance to it. He wished he could spare it more than a glance out of the corner of his eye, as his attention was demanded elsewhere.

Blaster fire kicked up little sprays of molten glass from where the bolts struck the sand. Behind him, he felt Vestara's body, pressed against his back, move in various pleasant and somewhat distracting ways as she gestured to deflect the fire that was directed at them. He was closing in on Dyon, the tracker having selected an older vehicle. Ben grimly pressed his lips together and began to steer erratically, trying to avoid the attack and still stop the mad Jedi from violating a treaty that was twenty-five thousand years old. He felt a sudden stinging pain emanating from where Vestara's arm encircled his waist and inhaled quickly in surprise and annoyance.

"Stop that," Vestara shouted. "It's harder for me to deflect them!"

"Avoiding is better than deflecting," Ben shot back. "And don't use your dark side poodoo on me."

"I'm better at deflecting than you are at avoiding," Vestara retorted. "And I'll do whatever it takes to stop this crazy Force-user, even dark side poodoo."

She was utterly serious, and he realized she didn't know the slang term. He couldn't help it, and he laughed. Hard. Until she sent another bolt through him.

"I'm bringing the *Jade Shadow* down to assist, but I'm not sure I'll get there in time," Luke said through the comlink. "Dyon has to be stopped, but we don't want him killed if we can avoid it."

"Of course not," Vestara said, sounding indignant. Ben felt her lift her arm, then heard a sizzle as she batted back a bolt. "He's ill. We need to help him."

"Sorry, Vestara, but that sounds a little too compassionate coming from a Sith."

"Not all of us take delight in hurting or killing unnecessarily," Vestara said. "And remember, our apprentices"—

pause, sizzle—"are being harmed by Abeloth as well as your Jedi. We might need them all alive if we want to find out what's going on."

She made a good point, but to Ben it almost felt as if she were making excuses for her original comment. As if she were embarrassed at showing compassion. He wondered if that was real or just wishful thinking. Then he forgot completely about the conversation.

Up ahead was a wall similar to the one that enclosed Treema. It was, apparently, the only barricade that protected the Fountain from its admirers. There were gates at various intervals and these were closed, but . . . seriously, it was only a ring of dirt and wooden gates. Apparently, even the barricade around the place had to be low-tech.

The guards patrolling it, however, had no such hindrance. They wore plastoid armor and sported DL-44 heavy blasters that looked like they meant business. And the extremely businesslike-looking blasters were trained on the figure of Dyon Stad as he barreled in, seemingly intent upon crashing through the gates.

"Off! Off!" shouted Ben.

Vestara understood immediately, and as one, they vaulted upward, soaring and then landing easily on their feet even in the soft sand. Ben's lightsaber was in his hand and activated by the time he straightened. Even as he brought it up, he was batting back blaster fire. The driverless speeder bike kept going, heading straight for the wall and two guards standing there. The guards were not there a second later, having intelligently dived out of the way. The speeder bike rammed at top speed into the barrier. It did not break through it, but there was a good-sized hole around the now-crumpled speeder.

A sharp scream caused Ben's head to whip around, although he kept good focus on the fight. Vestara stood with her long legs set wide apart and her hands, fingers splayed hard, stretched out in front of her. Her beautiful face was set in a harsh, unforgiving expression. Blue Force lightning crackled from her hands in a jagged, dancing line to two other guards. They convulsed, shrieking in torment. The Sith apprentice lifted her hands and tossed the two guards aside. Her head turned, her brown eyes narrowed, then she reached out in the direction of Dyon Stad.

"Vestara!" Ben shouted.

She was going to do it.

She was going to do just what his father had warned him that Sith did, that Sith *always* did. She was going to betray him and murder Dyon Stad, because Sith killed Jedi. The promise meant nothing to her, Ben meant nothing to her, she was lost to the dark side, and—

Less than a second before Dyon Stad's speeder bike impacted with the barrier, Dyon himself suddenly shot upward as if grasped by an invisible hand. He yelled in protest, his legs and arms flailing, and then was thrown several meters away to land on the soft sand.

His speeder slammed hard into the wall and was rendered into so much scrap metal instantly. Had Dyon still been on it, he would now have been little more than a collection of bloody tissue.

Ben blinked. The attacks ceased as everyone started to converge on the stunned man, who only now was moving and trying unsuccessfully to sit up. Vestara beat them all, leaping with the grace and power of a narglatch to land beside Dyon, straddling him, drawing her fist back, and slamming it into his jaw. Dyon's head jerked to the side, and he stopped moving. Vestara hissed slightly, shook her stinging hand, then yanked up Dyon's arms and trussed him up with cord from her belt.

Ben lowered his weapon. Vestara rose, dusting the

sand from her knees, and stepped aside as the locals seized Dyon by each arm and hauled him upward. Ben fumbled for his comlink and clicked it.

"She stopped him. Vestara," Ben said. He was panting a little from the chase. "The local authorities have him right now. Do you want me to step in?"

"No, not at this point," Luke said. He did not acknowledge Ben's first comment. "He came close to violating their most sacred area, and he's stolen property. The GA doesn't have any kind of jurisdiction here, and neither do we. I'll come down and talk to someone once they've processed him. When everyone's a little calmer, they might agree to release him to my custody."

"Dad," Ben said, "did you hear what I said? Vestara got him. She could have killed him, but she didn't."

"I'm glad she didn't violate the terms of our alliance," was all Luke said, and then clicked off.

Ben glowered at the comlink. His father wasn't going to give Vestara anything, no matter how trustworthy she continued to prove herself. It was starting to irritate Ben.

"You look annoyed," Vestara said suddenly by his ear. He started; he hadn't noticed her approach. "Why? We stopped him in time. Everyone should be pleased."

"I'm not exactly happy that we had another Mawdweller go nuts right in front of us," Ben said, dodging the real issue. "But at least you see what we're up against."

Vestara nodded. "It's one thing to hear about it, another to actually witness it. I'm just happy it wasn't someone you were close to. That's hard to see."

She looked genuinely concerned as she said it. She was about a foot away from him, her face dewed with sweat and smudged with sand. Her chest rose and fell slightly with exertion, and her hair, which she had not braided today, was a tangled, sandy mess. Her eyes were kind, and met his evenly, and when he sensed her in the Force, he found nothing to contradict his impression.

"Thanks," Ben said. "Sounds like you might have to face the same problem."

"I don't know any of the apprentices who have gone mad," she replied. Again, honesty. "I'm sure it would be very difficult if I did, though."

"You're Sith," Ben said suddenly, feeling a bit petty. "You're not supposed to care about other people, even your so-called friends."

Vestara shrugged. "Of course I care. I'm human, Ben, not a droid. I love my family and my pet Tikk and—and I loved my friend Ahri. Whom *you* killed."

Ben winced inwardly, but pressed on. "Did you love your Master? Lady Rhea?"

She shook her head. "No, but I respected and feared her."

"Isn't fear better than love?"

Her nostrils flared and her eyes narrowed, and he immediately sensed she was growing irritated with his combative questioning.

"Sometimes. Sometimes not." She turned away from him to regard Dyon Stad, who had been unceremoniously tossed into a vehicle. "So what are we going to do with him? Are you letting the Klatooinians just take him?"

"For now, that's what Dad wants. He's going to come down later and talk to the authorities, try to get them to turn him over to us. In the meantime, I think I am in dire need of a sanisteam."

And just like that, the tension went away as Vestara gave him a quick, playful grin. "Yeah, I was going to say something."

Ben mock-glared at her, then looked back. "Oh," he

said. "It's a bit of a hike back to Treema." Suddenly, his danger sense prickled, and both he and Vestara turned at the same time to see one of the guards aiming a blaster right at them.

"I think perhaps *I* can give you a lift," said the guard.

# Chapter Nine

"OUR DADS'LL BE HERE SOON," BEN SAID.

Vestara frowned at him. "We wouldn't have to wait on them to get us out of here if you'd just let me convince the guards to let me go."

"Here" was an old, dilapidated holding cell located deep inside the Treema Courthouse and Detention Area. The security systems were utterly inadequate to the task of confining two powerful Force-users. They could have left any time they wished. Vestara was well aware of this and irritated with the fact.

"Problem is," Ben said, "my dad would want us to cooperate with the officials. And if you try to use mind tricks on the wrong person, they notice and they get pretty ticked off with you. It's just easier to go along with them."

She snorted slightly and folded her arms, shifting a bit farther away on the cold durasteel bench. She clearly would have liked to put more distance between them, but there was only one bench in the cell. The only lighting came from glow rods older than they were, and the tiny room smelled musty and unused.

"My father wouldn't have handled it that way," Vestara said.

"*Your* father—" Ben began heatedly, then choked the words back. "Never mind."

She eyed him, but with more curiosity than irritation. "My father what? Go on."

It was Ben's turn to fold his arms. "I said, never mind. They're just . . . very different."

"Well, of course, one is a Jedi and the other is a proud and well-respected Saber," Vestara said.

He turned to her, angry, then saw that she was smiling at him. Not just her it's-almost-but-not-really-a-smile, but a genuine one. She was teasing him. Or was she trying to lure him out? He could never tell.

Ben decided to play along. Maybe he'd learn something. At the very least, it was an entertaining way to kill time.

"You seem close to your father, but it's very . . . distant," he said, firing the first volley.

"And you seem overly familiar. Almost rude to him. He should beat you more often."

"My dad *never* beat me and never would!" Ben said indignantly, then immediately modified the statement. "Well, when I was younger, I *did* usually end up a little battered after sparring with him, but that's completely different."

"Ah, so that's what's wrong with you!" The smile had reached her eyes. "Not beaten enough. A good Sith upbringing and you'd be just fine. No more of your smart-mouthed comments to your father, to whom you should show respect."

"I somehow think my dad would like Sith more if he heard that last bit," Ben said. He unfolded his arms, clasped his hands behind his back, and stretched out his legs. "I think he'd approve of no more smart-mouthed comments. 'Yes, dear Papa.' 'No, dear Papa.' 'You are amazing, dear Papa.'"

Vestara grinned. "Somehow, I just can't see that coming from you," she said.

"Good."

"And I'm not that bad with my father!"

He relented a little. "No, you're really not. But you *are* awfully formal."

"And you aren't."

Ben shook his head. "No. Dad likes to say I got my mouth from Mom." He was comfortable telling her this. If the Tribe, as they referred to themselves, had access to vessels as comparatively sophisticated as the ChaseMaster frigates, they had access to decent databanks.

"Well, whatever else Luke Skywalker might be, he is obviously an extremely patient man. My father would take no back talk from my mother. She isn't even a Force-sensitive."

"And that matters? To how you treat someone?"

A slight frown furrowed her pale brow. "Of course it does."

"Yeah, I suppose it would. To a Sith."

She leaned forward, her palms on the bench beside her. She seemed to want him to understand. "It is how we are, Ben. The more skills you have, the further you can advance. Advancement means wealth, power, and safety."

"Yeah?" Ben turned to her. "Then if it was so important, how come Gavar Khai didn't marry a fellow Force-sensitive?"

Vestara's eyes widened, and he realized she had never thought to ask herself that question. "I—I suppose because he loved her."

"Careful, that's Jedi thinking!" Ben's smile softened the words. She blushed a little and looked away.

"They do love each other, and he loves me," Vestara said, almost as if she were trying to justify something. "It's just . . . this is how we are. *Who* we are."

"You know," Ben said, working his way through the thought even as he spoke it, "There was a time when I wasn't particularly close to Dad. It's really been since Mom's death that—" He caught himself, and thought, *ah, the heck with it,* and continued. She'd know sooner or later . . . and maybe this would help open her eyes a little bit. "—that we've gotten close."

"I'm sorry," Vestara said, and she sounded like she meant it. Her emotions in the Force did show sincere regret. "It must be hard to lose a parent. I would be very upset if anything happened to either of mine."

*Then I hope I'm not the one who has to lop off your father's head with my lightsaber,* Ben thought, with a slight bitterness. She sensed his change of mood in the Force and drew back, confused and suddenly slightly wary.

"It was hard on both of us," Ben said, sending her a gentle brush of reassurance. "She was . . . an amazing woman. And a *great* mom."

Vestara hesitated, then said, "You and your father seem to have . . . fun."

"Do we?" Ben thought about the time he had shared with Luke on their journey thus far. He'd hardly call it "fun." But then again . . . there had been a lot of good conversations, and they constantly exchanged playful zingers with no barbs to them. And he'd laughed. A lot. "Yeah, I guess we do."

Vestara did not reply. Ben knew that she loved her family, but she certainly didn't have "fun" with Gavar Khai. The impression Ben got of the man was that living with him must be like constantly walking on the edge of a blade. He didn't think that Khai would tolerate mistakes of the sort Ben had made throughout his short life. He wondered if Sith, like certain animals Ben had heard of, killed their offspring if they found imperfections in them.

He didn't like that line of thought. And he didn't like to see Vestara looking melancholy. So he said, "Speaking of fun . . . know any jokes?"

As Luke brought the *Jade Shadow* in for a landing, he reflected that the building that served as a courthouse and a prison had seen better days. It was a large duracrete dome whose paint had been weathered and chipped. There were a few windows, small ovals low to the ground, and several unprepossessing doors. This was not a species with much time or money with which to indulge any love of beauty that might exist among its populace. Nearly everything here, save for the breathtaking Fountain of the Hutt Ancients, was practical, weathered, and stolid.

Luke sighed, recognizing the type of design. Domes weathered sandstorms better; there was less roof surface for sand to pile atop of, and less wall surface for the winds to pound against. He had not been back to Tatooine for many, many years, and had hoped to avoid venturing out into this arid world, but fate seemed to have other plans.

He settled the vessel down into the soft sand, then went down the ramp, squinting against the brightness of midday sun striking pale yellow sand. As he stepped off the ramp, he saw a figure coming toward him and sighed.

It was Gavar Khai. He must have been baking to death inside his heavy black-and-silver robes, but he gave no sign of it. His broad shoulders were straight, his dark head high, and he actually managed to somehow *stride* in the yielding sand. He had to be using the Force, Luke thought. The idea bothered him. To use the Force for something so trivial seemed a violation to him. But then again, Sith were hardly known for their respect toward the power of the Force. They used the dark side to further their own selfish ends and indulge their whims.

Whims like striding through sand.

He must have been alerted by Vestara as to the situation. Luke supposed Ben couldn't have stopped her at this point. Luke moved toward the Sith, nodding a greeting. He opened his mouth to speak but was interrupted.

"My daughter is being detained because of your son," Khai said bluntly. "This does not please me, Jedi."

Luke's blond eyebrows rose, but he kept his voice mild. "It was my understanding that an unfortunate young man snapped and was heading to defile the Fountain. Your daughter and my son took it upon themselves to prevent him from doing so."

"I am certain that Ben forced her to go along with him. Let us not mince words, Skywalker. My daughter is currently what amounts to your prisoner. Even though we outnumber you, we are choosing to work together to end this threat that is mutually damaging. I am most certain that Ben had instructions to never leave Vestara unattended."

Luke found himself grinning. "It's clear that you've forgotten the spontaneity of youth, Khai." He did not use the honorific "Saber." "From what I have learned of Vestara, she is not one to sit idly by while others have all the fun."

Khai's nostrils flared as he took a deep, calming breath. "No. My daughter is bold. Still, my point stands."

"Why don't we go in and find out exactly what happened rather than standing out here arguing?" Luke suggested. "I'm sure those heavy dark robes aren't the most comfortable thing to wear in a desert climate."

Khai shrugged. "I had not noticed. Sith must become used to all climates, and with the Force, we can bend even heat and cold to our will. I am puzzled that you choose to not do so. I would think you had sufficient skill."

"It's sometimes easier just to dress appropriately," Luke said, and headed for the courthouse door. Khai snorted and fell into step beside him.

Two Klatooinians stood guard by the door and demanded their names. Khai and Luke gave them, and were permitted admittance.

Inside the dome it was darker, if not much cooler. There was a *clank-clank* sound coming from somewhere that grated on the ear, probably some out-of-date cooling system in dire need of repair. A rather agitated-looking Klatooinian was seated at a battered desk. In front of her were several datapads in a haphazard pile. A small plaque read ABARA MUN, SECURITY AND DETENTION OFFICER.

"Master Luke Skywalker and Saber Gavar Khai," the guard stated.

The female, presumably Abara Mun, glanced up swiftly, her jowls quivering with the movement. "Ah," she said. "Excellent. Your children have been detained for questioning. As they are under the legal age according to our laws, we've held them until you arrived."

Khai started to say something, but Luke stepped in smoothly, "We understand. I hope there are no charges brought against them?"

Mun rose. "Oh, not at all. Their quick action actually aided in defeating the would-be defiler. I imagine you're proud of them. Their litter should be astonishing."

She tossed out the comment offhandedly as she rose. It took both Sith and Jedi a second to realize what she was saying. Understanding broke over them simultaneously and both of them spoke at once.

"Oh, they're not involved," Luke said.

"There will be no children," stated Khai. They turned

to glare at each other for a moment, then Luke smiled at the confused Mun.

"Our children are not involved in any way. They're . . . just friends."

Mun raised an eyebrow, then shrugged. "Didn't strike me that way, but suit yourself. We personally value strong litters and wise breeding, but I know not everyone shares our sentiments."

The words were tolerant, but her voice revealed her contempt for their attitude. She beckoned them to follow her as she led them through dimly lit, narrow corridors winding their way between thick duracrete walls. It reminded Luke of a bunker.

He wondered what she might have seen or sensed to come to that conclusion. Had Ben and Vestara's behavior led her to think that, or was it just her species' social conditioning? He'd have to talk to Ben when they had a few moments alone. There was no such thing as "harmless" flirtation when it came to a Sith. Vestara would take his son's innate goodness and optimism and seek to turn him to the dark side. Luke knew she would fail, and when she realized that too . . .

They turned a corner into a wider room with a mere four holding cells and a door that presumably opened onto yet another corridor. Luke thought that a surprisingly small number for such a major city, then realized that there probably was very little crime. For all intents and purposes, the Hutts owned Klatooine, thanks to the sweeping terms of the Treaty of Vontor. Luke was certain that any threat of misbehavior would result in being sent someplace extremely unpleasant. It was a deterrent to crime, but one that Luke would not wish on anyone.

He was mildly amused to see that the old doors were completely inadequate to housing anyone with even a modicum of Force ability. Ben and Vestara, both possessed of a great deal more than a modicum of ability, would not have been kept there for longer than about half a minute if they had not agreed to be. Mun stopped in front of the first cell and keyed in a code.

Ben's voice floated out to them. "—and then the rancor says, 'Then what did I just eat?'"

A peal of girlish laughter was heard, abruptly cut off as the door jerkily retracted into the wall. They were standing stiffly by the time the door was open completely, looking vaguely guilty.

"Oh, hey Dad," Ben said. "That was uh . . . fast."

Vestara's hands were clasped behind her back and she executed a slight bow. "Greetings, Father. Thank you for coming."

"Not a moment too soon, it would seem," Gavar Khai said. "Come, Vestara. Let us leave the Skywalkers to their business." Before Luke could protest, he gave the Jedi a sharp look. "Do not fear, I shall not abscond with her. We will be waiting for you outside." Vestara gave Ben a quick, sidelong glance from underneath her lashes, then moved quickly to obey her father.

Luke didn't much care for it, but he supposed there was nothing he could do. He was just sorry he had no way to record a conversation while they were outside melting in the sun.

"This shouldn't take long," Luke said. "We'll see you shortly, then."

# Chapter Ten

GAVAR AND VESTARA BOWED, PERFECTLY IN TANDEM, AS if they had rehearsed it, then turned and went back the way Luke and Gavar had come. When the sound of their feet had faded, Luke turned to Mun. "Where is Dyon Stad being held? I presume these cells are inadequate to the task."

Mun growled softly. "You presume correctly. We do not have a great deal of violent crime here, and our population renders very few Force-users. We have had to take special precautions. Follow me."

She moved to the door at the far end and keyed it open. Ahead was, as Luke suspected, yet another corridor. Reaching out in the Force, Luke gently probed the area above, to all sides, and below them. There was Dyon Stad . . . several meters below. His Force energy was dull, but steady. Ahead were two other presences, standing in tandem, presumably guards.

Ben was apparently doing the same because he said, "You've got a cellar down here."

"Not precisely," Mun said. The lighting from the glow rods that ran the length of the corridor wasn't particularly powerful, and several of them were inactive. Luke could now see the two Klatooinians standing on either side of a large door in the floor. They did not appear to be too happy about their assignment, their lugubrious, canine features looking even more jowly with resignation.

Luke understood why. The door was rigged with a WW-47 Cryoban grenade. It appeared to have been modified so that it could be activated from a distance. Once detonated, all the heat in the area would be absorbed, creating an area of freezing cold. It wouldn't kill Dyon, but it would immobilize him and likely cause nerve damage.

"I guess he could be perceived as that dangerous," Ben said.

"Here he certainly could be," Luke agreed, thinking of the conspicuous lack of Force-sensitives or weapons among the general populace—and even among what passed for the military.

"He is heavily sedated and as restrained as we could manage," Mun said. She knelt and quickly began to disarm the grenade. "And there is a third guard down there with him."

"We brought along restraints that might be more efficient for a Force-user," Ben said.

Mun shot him an irritated look, but Luke could tell that the irritation wasn't really directed at his son. "You can say it. A flimsi box sealed with vartik tree sap would be more efficient to hold a Force-user than what we've got. We simply don't have the resources here to deal with this sort of thing, so I'm more than happy to turn him over to you two."

She opened the hatch. A scent that one wouldn't expect on a desert world wafted out—the dank, murky odor of fetid water and mildew.

"It's not a cellar, it's an old well," Ben said, peering down. It went down a long way. There was a dim light at the bottom, just enough so that Luke knew that the unlucky guard likely pointing a decades-old blaster at the unconscious Force-user had a glow rod to help him see better. It would be of little comfort to the hapless fellow to be able to see it clearly if Dyon awoke, snatched the blaster out of his hand and snapped his neck with the Force.

Mun nodded. "On our world, most buildings are built over wells. It's an old, old tradition to guard against water shortage."

Water vaporators of some variety had been around for a long, long time. This well must indeed have been ancient.

Ben was thinking along the same lines for he said, "Surely, this is dangerous to just leave around. How come you didn't fill it in some . . . you know, ten thousand years ago?"

Mun looked at him evenly. "Because technology sometimes fails. Or fails to arrive when needed, young Skywalker."

"But—you're the last stop on the Kessel Run. The Hutts—" Ben stopped in midsentence. Mun's smile widened, but it was a bitter one. Ben had just answered his own question. The Hutts gave—and failed to give— as they saw fit.

Luke thought about what he had learned of the treaty and about what he knew of the Klatooinians themselves. They honored the treaty, and had for twenty-five-thousand years. And yet, they believed, like the Fountain they so honored, that they grew stronger with time.

Luke suspected that, valid as the reason Mun gave was, there were perhaps other reasons.

But now the pressing need was to get Dyon out. Luke caught Ben's eye, nodded, and father and son Force-leapt down into the deep well. Luke slowed his fall and landed, bending his knees, beside the prone and cuffed figure of Dyon Stad. The guard had obviously been notified at some point because he did not attempt to shoot either Jedi, and merely seemed a little alarmed at their manner of arrival. Ben was already bending over Dyon with stun cuffs from the *Jade Shadow*. Squatting beside the older man, Ben glanced up at his dad and nodded.

"He's fine. His injuries have been attended to. He's out cold, though, and should be for some time. These guys did their jobs well on all counts."

Luke smiled at the still-flustered guard. "We'll take it from here. Thank you."

Ben rose and together the two settled themselves and reached out for the Force's aid. Luke half-hid a smile of fond remembrance. Long ago, when he was only a few years older than his son, he had stood on soggy soil, as he did now, surrounded by the stench of rotting wetness, and tried to levitate a sunken X-wing. He had gasped and panted and shuddered with the effort, only to watch the greedy waters of the Dagobah swamp claim it again.

And then tiny little Yoda had lifted the thing up as if it weighed nothing at all.

His smile grew as he reached out to his son in the Force and they met there, moving as one to surround and support the limp, bruised, and scraped body of Dyon Stad. Ben used both his hands, holding them out as if miming lifting Dyon's form, and Luke barely moved a finger or two as the figure rose swiftly but steadily upward. When Dyon neared the top, they maneuvered him gently onto the floor.

Ben leapt up first, followed by Luke. Ben looked back down into the old well, then over at Mun and the two guards. "What about him?"

"We have a rope ladder," one of the guards said.

"We could bring him up." Luke smothered a grin. Ben had a sabacc face Han would envy at the moment. "Wouldn't be a problem."

"I think Rommul will be happy to emerge the old-fashioned way," Mun said. "Now if you two and your . . .

charge . . . will follow me, we'll finish up the paperwork and you can take him out of my detention area."

Vestara stepped out into the bright sunlight, blinking quickly. She and Ben had been in the holding cell for about a half hour. It was illuminated, but dimly, and moving from the dark, dome-shaped building to full sunlight made her eyes water.

Her father didn't waste a second. "What do you think you are doing?" he demanded, speaking in Keshiri. He kept his voice modulated and made no attempt to lay a hand on her, but she could feel his anger, narrowly channeled, almost buffeting her in the Force.

She stared at him, utterly confused. "I did what I was supposed to do," she said. "What you asked me to do. I did not let Ben Skywalker out of my sight."

"You *helped* him!" Gavar replied, the anger cold and unyielding. Vestara was taken aback. Her father had never, ever been this angry with her. Irritated, frustrated, of course, like any parent with any child. But most of the emotions she had experienced from him were approval, love, and pride. This wounded her to her core, but even though it was completely new and unexpected behavior, she had been well schooled. She did not let her hurt show. She used the Force to even out her skin tone so that the rush of heat to her face would not betray her, and spoke in a calm, measured voice.

"It was my understanding that we wish the Skywalkers to believe that we share a common goal. We have claimed that our apprentices are going mad, as their Knights are. When one of them began to act erratically, there was no question in my mind that the right course of action would be to subdue him, to preserve the façade of cooperation."

His anger wavered slightly. "It would have been better

if you had been able to contrive to kill, or better yet, capture him."

"Had I been in a position to do so, I would have," Vestara said. It was a lie. She watched her father carefully, but he gave no indication that he sensed it. Vestara regretted the necessity, but his apparently irrational reaction warranted the deception.

"I had no weapon, and Ben and I were far from the only ones in pursuit of Dyon Stad. Ben now counts me as a true ally, as I have proven my apparent trustworthiness twice now. Was that not what you asked of me? To win his confidence?"

It was a classic tactic—to turn the argument back on the adversary. Vestara had put her father in the defensive role and had taken the offensive.

"True." The anger was all but gone now, and Khai looked thoughtful. "You did not hesitate to offer your aid?"

Vestara shook her head. "Not for an instant. We worked together as a team. That is how he will continue to think of us. And Ben will desire his father to think of us that way as well."

"You have bedded him?"

Another pang, quickly shuttered. Vestara was Sith. She had been trained to utilize every weapon in her arsenal, and was well familiar that being able to manipulate another's physical desire was a powerful tool. Still, to have her own father speak so casually of it—

"No," she said. "Not yet."

"Keep him wanting you," Khai said. "Do not let him have you unless you judge that it will get you something truly important. I expect you to have Ben Skywalker eating out of your hand like Tikk by the time you are done with him."

Vestara smiled a little at the thought of her pet. She did not ask what had happened to Tikk. He had been left behind at the Sith Temple when she had departed Kesh to explore the galaxy. She had no idea if he was still there, or if he had been returned to her family. She did not want to risk her father's irritation by inquiring.

"I will endeavor to do so. Master Skywalker is endeavoring to keep us apart. I think he senses what you and I intend."

Another hit—reaffirming her bond with her father as a conspirator. All traces of anger were gone now.

"Of course he does. You are a lovely young human woman, my dear, and Ben is a healthy young male. Of course he is attracted to you. No doubt he aspires, for the moment, to 'save' you and bring you to the light side of the Force."

Vestara nodded. She and her father had both read what information Ship had on the Skywalkers. Doubtless her father was right.

"I wonder then why Master Skywalker does not encourage him," Vestara mused.

Her father slipped a forefinger under her chin and tilted it up. He smiled at her kindly now, the alien anger replaced by the more familiar pride and affection. "Because, Master Skywalker is not the besotted fool that Ben is. Ben is young and idealistic and full of hope. Luke Skywalker is much wiser. He sees how strong with the dark side you are, and knows, as I do, that you cannot be turned."

"Yet his own wife was the Emperor's Hand," Vestara offered. "And he himself turned one of the most powerful Sith Lords in history. If there is anyone who has seen that people can be swayed from the dark side, it is Luke Skywalker."

"I did not say Skywalker thought it impossible to sway someone. I said that he very wisely thinks it impossible to sway *you*."

"That is unfortunate," Vestara said. Things would be

much easier if Luke thought, as Ben probably did, that she could be persuaded to leave the path of the dark side. "Should I attempt to behave as if I am considering betraying you?"

Khai considered for a moment. "No," he said, finally. "I am sure you would be convincing, but Skywalker would be on to you immediately. Continue as you have."

He glanced up and Vestara followed his gaze. Luke stepped out from the entrance to the dome, squinting against the sunlight, one hand raised. Behind him floated the limp shape of Dyon Stad, and Ben brought up the rear.

"So, Skywalker was able to negotiate for Stad's release. Interesting. Dyon escapes his prison, but it is clearly time for you to return to yours," said Khai, almost but not quite growling. He turned to her. "It is only because you are serving the Sith that I permit it."

"I know, Father."

He bent and kissed her forehead. "Make me proud, daughter," he said. She bowed to him and went to rejoin the two Jedi. Ben saw her coming, a step or two behind his father, and gave her a quick smile, his attention still on levitating Dyon. She did not dare return the smile, as Luke was regarding her with that same intent gaze he always did.

"I am glad that the boy was released to your care, Master Skywalker," Khai called. "I would hope that if it were one of our apprentices, you would be as pleased for us."

"Honestly? Doubtful," Luke said.

"Your honesty is . . . refreshing," Khai said.

"I imagine it would be unusual to a Sith," Luke agreed. "Glad you're appreciating it. Vestara? Let's go."

"And that's the news. Until tomorrow, this is Perre Needmo. Good night."

The cam droids closed in on Needmo's long face and wise, calm eyes encircled by wrinkles.

"And cut," said the director, Jorm Alvic. A human in his early middle years, Jorm had thick black hair turning to gray at the temples in a rather dashing and dramatic manner. It was the only thing dramatic and dashing about him physically. He was slightly shorter than average, with a belly that lapped over his belt and a face that, while pleasant, wasn't really remarkable in any way save for an easy smile. He had been friends with Needmo for many years and had directed nearly every episode of *The Perre Needmo Newshour* since its inception. "Great job as usual, Perre."

"Thanks, Jorm. But I'd say that goes for everyone. Well done tonight. The interviews in particular went very smoothly," Needmo said. He placed the datapads neatly on his desk, then descended from his anchor's chair. He peered up to the control booth. "I wonder if perhaps we'd all be willing to stay a little later tonight? I have an idea I'd like to propose."

"What's that, Perre?" asked Sima Shadar, the producer, also in the control booth. The tech crew paused in their nightly shutdown routine, exchanging glances and shrugs. A mouse droid peeped in irritation as its normal path was blocked by human feet, then zipped off to clean another area of the set.

"I've been thinking about this for a while. I'd like to start including a new recurring segment."

"Well, our staff meeting is day after tomorrow; we can put that on the top of the agenda," began Sima, but Needmo was shaking his huge head.

"No, I really would like to begin this as soon as possible."

Jorm and Sima looked at each other and shrugged. "You got it, Perre," Sima said. The Chevin nodded, satisfied. He hadn't really expected any protest. Sima pressed a button, and her voice carried throughout the studio and back rooms.

"Attention staff. Perre has requested our presence for a brief meeting before you all head on home. Please come to the main set."

There was a silence, then "Sure," "Of course, boss." The writers, directors, and editors all filed onto the stage. Most had cafs or snacks in hand; it was a fairly relaxed show. Everyone was ready to go home, of course, but everyone also liked their jobs, and they all knew Needmo didn't usually pull this sort of thing unless he felt it was really important. Some grabbed seats, some just plopped down on the floor.

"We've had a few guests commenting on the situation on Tatooine, Karfeddion, and Thalassia, along with some very lively debates on the issue and on the Freedom Flight," Needmo began. He trundled to the center of the set and looked about at his team. "But all my instincts are telling me that this is going to be a big story. I'd like to make sure we address it. Keep tabs on it, keep people aware of it. It's an important issue, and one that doesn't really have any gray areas." While *The Perre Needmo Newshour* worked diligently to report the news without bias, one of the reasons Perre had left Vinsoth to start his own show was to broadcast good news. Or, if that wasn't possible on a particular evening, to at least get something out there people could support.

"Good idea," Sima said, tapping on a datapad. "We can get Darric Tevul to report regularly on—"

Needmo waved his hands. "No, no, not just commentary. I think we should put someone on the scene. Visit some of these worlds, conduct interviews with the governments and the insurgents both."

Eyes widened. Some beings whistled. Jorm scratched his head, but nodded.

"It's a good idea," he said. "Very good idea. Boost our

ratings, no doubt about it. But it's not exactly the sort of thing we're known for."

"We all work very hard to disassociate ourselves from the likes of Javis Tyrr and his type of sleemo journalism," Needmo said, "and to do that we've chosen a more staid format. I'm not suggesting we change that, just augment it. I have a feeling this is not just a few isolated incidents."

No one on *The Perre Needmo Newshour* was Force-sensitive, but they all had finely tuned instincts, the clichéd "nose for news." The joke was that *no* one had a better nose for news than Perre Needmo. And, far from being insulted by the comment, Needmo sometimes said it himself.

"We'll get on it right away," Jorm said. "Any of our regulars have any field experience?"

"Madhi Vaandt," said the lighting director immediately. A chorus of positive murmuring went around the room. Madhi had been on a short while ago, with a segment on the atrocious living conditions in the Underlevels of Coruscant. She stubbornly remained a freelancer, but the same station that ran *The Perre Needmo Newshour* had hired her for various spots.

"Oh, perfect," said Jorm. "That last segment she did with us got a lot of attention. Someone even started fund-raisers to help provide medicines and fosterage for some of the younglings in the Underlevels. She's got no whiff of scandal and the holocam loves her."

Needmo's snout wrinkled in hearty approval. "Hear that, beings?" he said, pleasure and pride warming his voice. "You bring injustice to the attention of the viewers, and they do something about it. I liked what I saw of Vaandt. Get in touch with her agent right away. We'll want her on two, perhaps three different worlds. And one of them," he paused and centered himself, "one of those worlds must be Vinsoth."

The team exchanged glances. Vinsoth was Needmo's own homeworld. For thousands of years, his people, the Chevin, had enslaved a humanoid race known as the Chev. Granted, their domination had not been a particularly violent or brutal one. Indeed, some might even call it civilized. The Chev culture, far from being quashed, was encouraged to flourish, and full support was given them if they chose to pursue the arts. Physical violence against them was discouraged and blatant violation of that law resulted in stiff fines and occasionally prison time for the offender.

Needmo looked from face to face, his eyes crinkling in a benevolent smile.

"Come now," he said, his voice gentle. "How can we do otherwise? We cannot in good conscience report on slavery on other worlds without addressing the fact that the being for whom the show is named comes from such a world himself. We'd be hypocrites and lose the trust and faith the viewers have placed in us. And furthermore, it just wouldn't be right."

"Perre," Jorm said, "you've made your reputation on who you are and what you've done, not where you come from."

"As all beings should have the right to do," Needmo said. "No being should be judged on his or her—or, frankly, its—species, or what world they were born on. It is who you are that matters. Trust me on this. I have striven to be neutral in reporting the news. But to omit Vinsoth would *not* be neutral. I will not be reporting, or personally commenting on the situation—although informally my views are well known. Madhi would be. She's got no personal agenda. And I won't have her censored," he added, looking sharply at Sima. "The viewers will make their own conclusions, and it will be good for the show and good for our viewers. Isn't that what we've always wanted to do?"

Needmo knew his team realized there was little point in arguing with him. His instincts had proven to be sound for several years. He'd bucked the trend of slick, fast-paced "journalism" in favor of calm reporting of actual facts, not possibly faked action scenes better depicted in a holodrama. Even bringing in Madhi was shaking up the format.

But Needmo knew he was absolutely right on this. Madhi Vaandt was already making her reputation by calling things as she saw them. Fit, impulsive, she went to the heart of the story to bring things out of the darkness into the light. She'd had no compunctions at all about traveling to the Underlevels with just a cam crew for "security." And if she covered the situation on Vinsoth in that same way, on a show hosted by a Chev, there would be no question of biased reporting.

Everyone present knew that Needmo heartily disapproved of the current situation on his homeworld. He had chosen not to be politically active, but it was one reason he had left his homeworld for Coruscant. Some things in this galaxy were just *wrong*.

Finally, the producer shrugged. "It's the Perre Needmo hour, boss. If you want to do this, we'll do it. And I bet it will boost ratings better than 'The Jedi Among Us with Javis Tyrr.'"

The laughter broke the nervous tension. "Well, then," Needmo said, his trunk undulating with amusement, "that alone should be a reason to do it, don't you think?" More laughter. They were on board with him, and he was proud of every one of them. He'd assembled a great team over the years, and went to bed every night knowing that they'd all worked hard to inform and enlighten their viewers. And maybe, just maybe, help make the galaxy a better place.

# Chapter Eleven

ERAMUTH BWUA'TU HAD ONE GLOVED HAND GENTLY pressing on the small of Tahiri Veila's back to guide her through the throng of journalists restrained only by a red cordon and a few scowling guards. Eramuth's other hand grasped the ornately decorated cane, with which he tapped quite deliberately on the marble floor as they strode forward.

The holojournalists, their tabards a colorful array of logos, all were vying for her attention. Each of them wanted "the" shot to lead on the evening news.

"Miss Veila! Over here!"

"Tahiri! How are you feeling on this first day of your trial?"

"Former Jedi Veila, at what point do you consider that your betrayal began?" This last from, of course, the biggest sleemo of them all, Javis Tyrr. Tahiri kept her head held high and her gaze focused straight ahead.

"Good girl, you're doing beautifully," Eramuth said, his voice soft. "Hateful beings, the press, but utterly necessary to a free society. Are you ready for this, my dear?"

"Yes," Tahiri replied, her voice just as soft, knowing his sharp Bothan ears would pick up the faint sound. She was ready. She'd known from the moment the arrest warrant had been served that it would come to this, and she harbored no illusions as to how difficult the journey to "not guilty" would be, if it was even successful.

But Eramuth, dapper and debonair and antiquated, had given her hope. He had listened and taken copious notes as she told the story of how she had come to be influenced by Jacen. She hadn't sugarcoated or omitted anything. She fully owned her part in what she did, but did not take on those burdens that were not hers to bear.

For his part, Eramuth managed to grill her gently, which she would have thought an oxymoron. By the time he was done with her, Tahiri mused to herself that he knew more about her than her closest friends. Of course, she didn't *have* close friends, not anymore.

Not since Caedus.

The main entrance was a set of double doors that slid open as they approached. Tahiri got her first look at the place where she would be spending most of her time for the next . . . however long it took. The courtroom of the Ninth Hall of Justice at the Galactic Justice Center looked exactly how she would have imagined it to look, and she realized that her elegant, eccentric attorney would appear right at home here. Certainly she knew Eramuth would *feel* right at home—he had told her that he had argued, and won, more than twenty-seven cases in this very room.

The walls were dark wood paneling. The floor was a continuation of the marble tile of the hallway, the path through the "general public" seats in the back covered with a soft, thick, red carpet. On her right were the seats for the jury beings. There were many different shapes and sizes, and Tahiri realized that a variety of beings would determine her fate, not just humanoid. She wondered if that was a good or a bad thing, but trusted her lawyer to have vetted any obvious GA plants. Regardless of the shape, the seats were padded and comfortable-looking. Jurors had an important responsibility, and they would be well tended to for the duration of the trial.

On the right were places for members of the press. A staggering variety of technical equipment was on display there, and each box was carefully marked to indicate which station was which. Thankfully, a small, single seat was reserved for *The Perre Needmo Newshour*. At least it wouldn't *all* be luridly over the top.

Just mostly.

Straight ahead were two exquisite, caf-colored antique marble desks from Ithor. The defense's station, Tahiri had been told, was the table on the left-hand side. There were two equally ancient wooden chairs beside it. They were polished so they seemed to glow in the morning light coming in from the row of windows placed near the top of the high walls. Apparently, defendants did not get the same attention to physical comfort as the jurors did. The prosecution's desk was on the right. And at the far end of the room was the judge's elevated bench, also of antique Ithorian marble, and the witness's chair.

The judge's chair, in contrast with the practical but comfortable chairs for the public and the jurors and the elegant and uncomfortable seats for the defendant and prosecution, was almost thronelike. It also appeared to be an antique. It was an elegant, high-backed chair with thick upholstery and a variety of buttons on its long arms that looked at odds with the nostalgia the rest of the piece evoked. The desk it faced had been polished till it gleamed, and it, too, had had modern technology imposed upon it.

At the front of the desk was the insignia of the Galactic Alliance. A large protocol droid stood stock-still at attention, gleaming brightly. It would translate, no doubt, if there were any witnesses who did not speak Basic, and Tahiri guessed it would probably record the events as well. Standing by one of the two doors that led to the judge's chambers in the back of the room was a large, burly, human male. Tahiri knew the proper, respectful term was "bailiff," but looking at the man's oft-broken nose and low brows, she thought "bouncer." Even though he was dressed impeccably in the proper uniform for the task, he still cut an imposing, fear-inducing figure.

Behind Eramuth and Tahiri, the journalists were permitted to enter. They hastened to their stations, speaking in low voices and adjusting equipment. Eramuth directed Tahiri to her chair, courteously pulling it out for her before sitting down himself. He seemed relaxed and confident, looking around the room with what seemed to Tahiri a bit of nostalgia.

"Never lost a case in this room, Tahiri my dear," he said, "and I don't intend yours to be the first."

She nodded, suddenly becoming overwhelmed. This, more than the arrest, more than having to wear specialized shock shackles and stun cuffs—the irony did not escape her that they were twins to the ones she had forced Ben Skywalker to wear—more than anything else she had encountered, this room, with its smell of furniture polish and leather, with dust motes dancing in the slanting light, the murmurs and *blips* and *clicks* of recording devices running through their paces, this brought home to her the true reality of her situation.

She was glad that Eramuth seemed so calm and confident. Because despite the dangers she had faced since her earliest years, Tahiri was nervous. Combat, she understood. But there was a stiffness, a formality, an order that permeated this room to its very core that was more intimidating than any enemy she'd yet faced.

Eramuth's hand on hers squeezed. "Here comes Sul

Dekkon, the prosecuting attorney," he said quietly. Tahiri craned her neck as unobtrusively as possible. A tall, blue-skinned Chagrian wrapped in meticulous black- and rust-colored robes entered the room along with the press of spectators and newsbeings.

A few paces behind the Chagrian were two familiar faces—those of Han Solo and Leia Organa Solo. Their eyes fell on her and they smiled reassuringly. They had been present for her arraignment, and now it seemed they intended to be here for the trial. At least, Tahiri amended, as much of the trial as they could. It was a heartening gesture.

She nodded slightly at them, then returned her gaze to the prosecuting attorney. Both sets of his horns were long and glorious. The sharp ends of his lethorns, which extended from two trailing pieces of flesh on either side of his head that reminded Tahiri of a Twi'lek's lekku, were capped with two polished spheres of some kind of metal that gleamed in the yellowish light of the courtroom. His eyes were deeply set but clearly sharp. Now those eyes fastened on Tahiri.

"He and I have tangled before. One of my last cases." Eramuth hadn't looked up himself, but poured her a glass of water from a pitcher that had been set at the table. He handed it to her, giving her a good excuse to look away without appearing as if she had broken Dekkon's gaze.

"Did you win?" Tahiri murmured, taking a sip of water.

"Naturally."

"Great," she said, putting the glass down. "Now he's got a score to settle."

"Let him try," Eramuth said airily. He rose and extended a hand politely to the Chagrian who had, with a swirl of his dark, elegant robes, now stepped up beside him.

Sul Dekkon was much taller than the Bothan, towering over him as they shook hands. Eramuth didn't bat an eye.

"Sul," he said, his voice sincere, warm and rich and rolling. "You look well."

"And you, Eramuth," came the response. The voice was harsher than Eramuth's, the words clipped and cool. "I see academia is treating you well."

Eramuth smiled. His right ear flicked. "It is always an honor to pass to the next generation what one has learned."

"Next? I'd say more than that," Dekkon said, smiling. It did not reach his eyes. "These could be your grandchildren you're instructing, Eramuth."

"Many things improve with age," Eramuth said. "The Bothan mind is one of them."

"Perhaps," the Chagrian agreed. "However, you're a bit out of practice, aren't you?"

Eramuth chuckled. "Practice means nothing when you've won as many cases as I have. I believe you're up to half that number now, aren't you?"

Both were lawyers. Neither was a Force-user, but they hid their emotions well. Still, for someone as sensitive as Tahiri was in the Force, they might as well have been screaming at each other for the hostility that was flowing between them. Or rather, Dekkon might have been screaming. Eramuth was enjoying himself, baiting the other attorney with a deftness that a dancer would have envied. Still, there was something off—something the Chagrian had said had gotten to him.

Dekkon's eyes flashed and he opened his mouth to retort, but movement from the back of the room interrupted the conversation. The bouncer-bailiff had opened the door, and the twelve jurors filed quietly into their seats. Dekkon gave Eramuth a brief nod and turned to his seat, pulling datapads out and arranging them on the table. Eramuth bowed, then slid back into his chair beside Tahiri.

"I think we've got ourselves a good jury," Eramuth said, his muzzle to Tahiri's ear. "Most of them are open-minded. Some of them were even somewhat sympathetic to you."

She watched the jurors out of the corner of her eye. Humans, Bith, Chadra-Fans, Wookiees—it was almost as if every species whose planet was a member of the Galactic Alliance was represented here. She wondered if any of them were Force-users. It was, after all, supposed to be a jury of her peers. She dismissed the hope at once. It would be all too easy to argue that the Force was being misused by the potential jury member. A Mon Calamari looked at her with one eye, clearly thinking his expression was neutral, clearly kidding himself. He did not like her.

"And some weren't," Tahiri said, watching as the Mon Cal took his seat.

"And some weren't, quite right, but that's to be expected," Eramuth said without missing a beat. "I give a little, he gives a little. The only thing Dekkon has going for him, really, is the facts."

Tahiri couldn't help it. She stared at him. "Wait a minute—what did you just say?"

He smiled and poured a glass of water for himself. His hand shook a little, but he seemed completely calm and she had noticed the slight trembling before. Eramuth was, after all, definitely an elder.

"I said, all Dekkon has is the facts. We have something more. We can decide how the jury interprets and internalizes those facts. Moreover, my dear, we have you." He took a long drink. "We have who you were, and are, and wish to become. And believe me, I'd rather have those things on my side than something as simplistic as cold, hard facts."

"But . . . why?" Tahiri's heart felt like it had been squeezed by a prosthetic hand. Was the Bothan crazy?

"Because, my dear, beings don't really want things that are cold and hard. They are sitting there, most of them, bless them, really, truly, trying to do the right thing. If they find you guilty, it must be beyond a reasonable doubt. And that, Miss Tahiri Veila, is what you and I are going to give them. Many, many reasons to doubt."

Before Tahiri could splutter out more questions, the bailiff strode forward and bellowed in a voice that almost shook the walls, "All rise for Her Honor, Judge Mavari Zudan."

Tahiri recognized the name, though she had never seen the Falleen woman who now entered the room from the back door. For a moment, Tahiri wondered if she'd simply traded one bad situation for another. While the farce that was the Court of Jedi Affairs had been abolished, and the clearly biased Judge Lorteli had been quietly removed from the bench, Zudan was the woman who had sentenced Luke Skywalker.

She wore dark judicial robes that made her look to Tahiri more like an executioner than a judge. The woman's stern, pinched expression didn't help the impression. She ascended to her chair, reached for an old-fashioned gavel, and banged it.

"This court is now in session."

"You have visitors," the guard said. "Step away from the door and sit on the chair."

It had been a long first day of the trial, and Tahiri was exhausted, but not too tired to be surprised and curious at the words. The only being who had been able to visit her since her arraignment had been her lawyer. She obeyed, and sat patiently while two guards entered. One had a blaster pointed at her, the other painstakingly bound her wrists and ankles with stun cuffs. The idea was, of course, that she was adequately contained as long as the door was closed and locked. When it was open, she needed additional restraints. She suffered the indignity quietly, more focused on who could possibly be coming to see her than on the inconvenience and discomfort of the manacles.

The guards stepped back. Two dark-haired humans stepped into the room, one tall and rangy and male, and one petite and female, and smiled at her.

"It took us awhile, but we were able to get in to see you," Leia said.

Tahiri indicated the manacles. "Forgive me if I don't get up," she said. "But . . . it's good to see you."

"Be better to see you over a cup of caf," Han said. He glared at the guards. "Didn't your mothers ever tell you it's rude to eavesdrop?"

They didn't budge, nor did they reply.

Han and Leia exchanged glances. Leia straightened to her full diminutive height and looked at them each in turn. "I understand you have your duty, and that is to monitor any information that comes to the prisoner through any method other than her lawyer. The only reason we're here is because we have some deeply personal news to deliver. I think you'd both feel very uncomfortable having to overhear it. Would it be possible to have a little privacy?"

Both of them were male and looked uncomfortable already at the thought of hearing "deeply personal news."

"Your reputation precedes you, ma'am," one of them said deferentially. And glancing at Han, he added in a slightly harder voice, "As does yours, Captain Solo. But orders are orders."

"You think we're going to try to bust her out of here or something?" Han said. "Kid, she's a Jedi, and a damn good one. These little toys you've got on her wouldn't do much if she wasn't willing to be here of her own accord. Right?" He shot Tahiri a look for confirmation. Despite the situation Tahiri fought back nervous laughter. She suspected that whatever the Solos had to say, Han was doing more harm than good.

"They're pretty effective," she said. "But I also am indeed here of my own accord. I wouldn't try to escape."

"Wouldn't want you to," Han continued. "We want her to stay so everyone can see how wrong they've been about her."

Leia moved forward. "Gentlemen," she said, "everything I have to tell Tahiri Veila concerns only my own family situation."

Family . . . oh no . . . "Is something wrong? Did something happen to Amelia? Or Jaina?" The words came quickly from Tahiri's lips.

Han dropped a big hand on her shoulder and squeezed. "They're fine, they're all okay," he said, his voice gentle. "Look—I can step out if—"

"I want you here when I tell her," Leia said quickly. She turned to look at her husband and Tahiri could see the glitter of tears in her eyes. She had been shut down in the Force, but now she opened to the Solos. There was pain, but there was also a strange, quiet joy.

The guards exchanged glances. "We'll leave you alone, but your conversation will be monitored," one of them said.

"I appreciate even that much," said Leia, gracing them with the smile that still managed to melt hearts. The guards left and the door slid heavily back in place. True to his word, the small cam focused on Tahiri continued to blink, indicating it was still active.

"Leia, Han—what's this all about?"

They each drew up a chair to sit beside her. Han draped an arm across her shoulders, while Leia placed her small hands on Tahiri's own. Deep concern was in her brown eyes. Tahiri thought it little short of a wonder that, barely two years after the two of them had tangled in a very violent lightsaber battle, when Tahiri had foolishly tried to arrest the Solos on Jacen's orders, there was this level of caring between them. The Solos, as she knew they did, had great hearts. This was just one more example.

Leia gave a quick, casual gesture in the direction of the cam monitoring Tahiri. It sputtered, and Tahiri smiled a little as she realized that Leia, unable to get the guards to agree to privacy, had simply and practically Force-flashed the device.

"I have to be careful about what I tell you," Leia began. "I've gotten certain information—from Ben and Luke."

"They're all right?"

"For now," Han said. "They—"

Leia cleared her throat and shot him a meaningful glance. He closed his mouth with an audible *click*.

"They're fine," Leia said soothingly, squeezing Tahiri's hands. "That's not what I want to talk to you about. They . . . I suppose we can say they had a sort of . . . vision, except much more accurate than that. In their investigations, they made a mental and spiritual journey and came across a place called the Lake of Apparitions. There is a part of the lake called the Mirror of Remembrance. In this place . . . they believe you can speak with the dead."

And suddenly Tahiri knew. She felt the blood drain from her face, knew that her blue eyes were wide and staring, her face and lips ashen. Han's arm across her shoulders tightened. If Luke Skywalker believed this encounter with the dead was real, then Tahiri did, too. And the fact that Leia and Han must have pulled all kinds of strings in order to see her told her exactly whom Ben and Luke had seen.

Tears welled in her eyes, slipped down her face. She tried to lift her hands to wipe them away, but the wrist manacles were connected to the ankle manacles and she couldn't complete the gesture. Instead, Leia's hand, small and soft, gently stroked away the droplets running down the younger woman's cheeks.

"He saw Mara, and Jacen . . . and Anakin." Leia's voice was warm and calm. She had already had her shock of the news and recovered from it, though it still obviously moved her deeply and likely always would. On Tahiri's other side, Han Solo cleared his throat. Tahiri couldn't take her eyes from Leia's, but she suspected that Han, who might very well have been her father-in-law by now had Fate decreed differently, was struggling to control his emotions.

Tahiri opened her mouth, but nothing came out. *Is he at peace? What did he say? Does he remember me?*

"Anakin was the first one who appeared to them," Leia continued. "Luke and Ben told him that his sacrifice saved the Jedi. That there had never been a Jedi Knight like him since."

*And there never will be.*

Leia smiled a little. "Anakin said that the Order couldn't wait for a great Jedi Knight to lead it. That every Jedi Knight has to be his own light, so that the Light that is the Jedi never goes out."

Tahiri bit her lip, but the tears kept coming. She thought back to all the times she had flow-walked with Jacen, trying to find closure, trying to make it all right for him to be dead, to be gone. And it never worked.

"He asked about you. He asked if you were well."

"What—" Tahiri took a breath and blinked hard, forcing composure she did not feel. "What did they tell him?"

Leia's smile widened. "That you would be," she said. "And then he said . . . tell her that I still love her."

Tahiri's composure shattered. She had held her emotions in check for so long, too long. The flow-walking, the dance with the dark side, the trial that was going to force her to revisit some of the ugliest and most painful moments of her past—she had suppressed all the emotions they had stirred up, but now she found herself no longer able to.

He still loved her. He always would, and she would always love him. This, *this* was the closure her lonely, broken, lost self had sought. Even as she wept broken sobs, and as Leia and Han both wrapped arms around her, she could feel things inside her that had been jagged and raw beginning to mend and heal, a terrible cold knot she hadn't even realized was there starting to melt.

He would always love her, and he would always be with her. She could let go, now. Let go of the dream of Anakin, let go of the self-hatred of what she had done and become since then. After a few moments, she lifted her head from Leia's shoulder and looked first at her, then at Han.

"I'm going to be all right," she said. "They're going to find me not guilty. They're going to find me not guilty because I've got too much to do, too much to set right, to fix. Too many bridges to repair. And I'm going to do that."

"For Anakin," Leia said quietly.

Tahiri shook her head, her golden hair moving softly with the gesture. "Not just for him. For me."

"Good call, kid," Han said, his voice a little rough. "That's the way our boy would have wanted it."

And Tahiri knew that it was.

# Chapter Twelve

KENTH HAMNER SIPPED A CUP OF CAF AND GLANCED AT a pile of datapads on his desk. So many things were getting neglected, but that was the nature of command, of leadership—one had to prioritize, practice a sort of political triage. Not everything was going to get accomplished. Hamner's job was to make certain that if something had to slide, it wasn't the important things.

To that end, taking a cue from the woman who was starting to become the chief thorn in his side, he had promoted one of the most promising apprentices, a young woman named Kani Asari, to the role of an assistant. It was, like many decisions he had been forced to make recently, not a very popular one with some of the other Masters. He had heard grumblings, especially from the more outspoken people like Kyp Durran and Han Solo—who wasn't even a Jedi—who hadn't bothered to try to hide their displeasure. Luke, the Grand Master, the creator of the new Order, hadn't had to have an "assistant." Couldn't Hamner get his own caf and read his own datapads? Did he need pillows fluffed for him, too?

None of them quite understood the volume of activity that passed across his desk on any given day—any given *hour*. He did not think even the intrepid Han Solo would be able to juggle everything. And of course, everyone who had any kind of an issue with him or the Jedi felt that his or her problem was the single most dire thing in the known universe.

Hamner ignored the grumblers, and only hoped that the fair-haired, rather petite human girl who was doing a superb job was either ignoring them, too, or, better yet, hadn't overheard them.

He sensed Kani on the other side of the door and called, "Come in," rising and going to a small sideboard.

She poked her golden head in with a bright smile that belied the circles under her eyes. Again, Hamner felt a stirring of resentment on her behalf. It seemed that only he understood how hard she worked.

"Good morning, Master Hamner," she said, taking her usual seat.

"Morning, Kani. Care for some caf?"

"Oh, yes please," she said, thankfully. He warmed up his own cup and poured a fresh one for her, bringing it back to his desk. She took a sip, then put the cup down and retrieved her datapad. She looked up at him expectantly, peering out from a fall of bangs that had escaped their comb.

His eyes narrowed. He took in her robe, her hair, the fading makeup. "You didn't get to sleep last night, did you?" She had promised to leave shortly after he did, right before midnight. Apparently, she had not kept that particular promise.

"Um . . . no Master. But it's fine. I'll try to leave early today if I can."

"I'll see that you do," he said, frowning. "It is important to take time to rest. At the very least, meditate."

"Yes, Master," she said. "I'll go to the fountain room this afternoon for a bit."

"Good. Now, bring me up to speed, since you stayed later than I did." He settled back, sipping the hot caf.

"Well, I have good news, and I have bad news."

He rubbed his eyes. "Well, at least there is some good news. Let's start with that."

"You probably know this already, but Tahiri Veila's trial is going well so far. The news media is reporting positively on it, and I spoke with Nawara Ven last night. He's impressed with how Bwua'tu is handling it. Have you watched any of the proceedings?"

"Some."

"Then you'll know that Eramuth Bwua'tu is quite . . . colorful."

Hamner smiled a little, something he did not do often these days. "Perhaps a little color is just what is needed," he said. "At any rate, that *is* good news. Though it was quite the blow when Daala's 'Jedi Court' did not permit him to represent Tahiri, Ven did say he had every hope of getting a favorable verdict. Although I'm afraid that it's impossible to exonerate her completely." Tahiri's sincere regret at her actions, and her behavior since she had turned away from the dark side, were clearly standing her in good stead. He, and all the other Jedi, had been surprised—pleased, but surprised—that Chief of State Daala had agreed to dissolve the Jedi court prior to the trial. He knew it was because Daala thought the case was open and shut. However, obviously, it was far from that.

"Ven cautions us that the outcome is far from certain, and that the current climate of pro-Jedi sentiment is going to make the Chief of State unhappy."

"Let her be unhappy," Hamner said, his voice almost, but not quite, a growl. "She wants to do things by the book; we are. She's got to live with the consequences. Now . . . what's the bad news?"

"Master Cilghal is very concerned about the recent . . . well, wave, I guess is the word . . . of Jedi . . . um . . ."

"Snapping?" supplied Hamner. Kani nodded. "Well, I am, too." There had been no fewer than five reports of Jedi—all of whom had been at Shelter in their childhood years—going mad. Two incidents have occurred within the last thirty-six hours.

Even Luke Skywalker himself had found his hands full with one. Not a Knight, thankfully, nor even a Jedi proper, but a Force-user who met the profile. One Dyon Stad, Hamner believed his name was. Of course, Luke had not contacted him. Young Ben had contacted Cilghal, and the information had reached Hamner through her. Hamner found himself longing for the days when one did not have to go through something akin to gymnastics in order to get and share information among the Jedi.

He found himself longing for Luke Skywalker's return.

"She's written a report, going into detail about the most recent ones, Jedi Kunor Bann and Turi Altamik." Both Kunor and Turi were humans, male and female. Bann, fortunately, had succumbed right here in the Temple, and been captured and confined without anyone outside knowing a thing about it. They had not been so lucky with Turi, who had led them on a brief chase when she managed to escape the Temple. They had recovered her, but not before good old Javis Tyrr had captured it on holocam. There she had been, bigger than life, large green eyes wide with fear and determination, full lips shouting out accusations, short golden hair damp with the sweat of terror. She had made almost as big an impression on the public consciousness as Jysella Horn.

"Anything unique or unusual?"

"She's afraid that the rate of . . . snapping . . . might be accelerating," Kani said. "They're not having any luck at all with Sothais Saar. They've often been reduced to sedating him at times, and Master Cilghal says they're actually getting low on supplies. She'll be getting another order in shortly, but she's concerned."

"Accelerating? Perhaps we're just now starting to get reports from elsewhere, now that we know what to look for." Even as he said it, he could hear the hope in his voice. It might be true. Or Cilghal's concern might be warranted. Only time would tell. "Have her come in to talk to me personally when she has a moment," he told Kani, who dutifully wrote down the request.

There were a few other items of import—certain worlds were asking for Jedi aid in various skirmishes, or in two cases, in potential uprisings designed to overthrow governments that were deemed harsh and unduly cruel. When Kani mentioned an underground organization that seemed to span several worlds, something called the "Freedom Flight," whose purpose was to eradicate slavery throughout the galaxy, Hamner sighed inwardly. He was reminded harshly of Saar and his report on surviving slavery practices. More than ever, he wished the rather dour Chev was well enough to hear that the cause about which he cared so passionately was gaining support.

He would bring up the request at the next Master's meeting, but he did not think that it was possible at this time to grant any request for resources or public support. He knew some would want to, but felt certain that, given the current situation with Daala, cooler heads would prevail.

Finally, two cups of caf later, Kani had finished her briefing. "I'll notify Master Cilghal that you wish to see her, and continue monitoring the trial," Kani said. "And I've heard back from all of the Masters but two that they'll be present for the meeting later today. Will there be anything else?"

"Yes," Hamner said. "You go right to the Room of a Thousand Fountains when you're done talking to Master Cilghal."

She gave him a tired grin, finished her caf, and left. Hamner eased his chair back, resting his eyes for a moment, collecting his thoughts. A chiming sound from his comlink caused him to open his eyes again, slightly irritated.

"Hamner," he said.

"Master Hamner," came a female voice.

He sat up quickly in his chair. "Chief of State Daala," he said.

"I'm sure you're surprised to hear from me."

"I confess that I am. Usually, it's your chief of staff, Wynn Dorvan, I hear from."

"I decided to go right to the source. I've got a lot on my plate, Kenth, and I know you do, too. We can stop this little tug of war dead in its tracks. No more intermediaries, no more press releases or photo opportunities, no more dancing around the issue. You know what I want. And you know why I want it."

"Yes, Admiral," he said, keeping things formal, "I know *whom* you want, and all the reasons you've given me for wanting him. Sothais Saar is a Chev, and therefore has been property for most of his life. Do him the courtesy of referring to him as a person, not a thing, please. Whether or not he's mentally ill."

"Come off it, Hamner," she said. "Don't play the semantics game. You know what I meant. I want Saar, and I want Altamik."

"You're not going to get them. No one trusts you anymore, Daala. Do you not understand that? Make a show of good faith. Earn our trust again. If this 'little tug of war' is bothering you so much, then you have the ability to end it."

There was a pause. "So do you. Right now. Before things get so bad you'd give a great deal to be having this conversation again."

There was something in her voice that chilled him.

"I do not respond well to threats, Admiral. Nor did the Solos. Nor will the other Jedi. I must ask you to prove your innocence and trustworthiness, otherwise we have nothing to discuss."

"That's terribly unfortunate. You say you represent the Jedi—I hope you represent the families of the Jedi as well when you say that. Good-bye, Master Hamner."

He opened his mouth to speak, but she had gone. Nor would she respond when he had Kani attempt to raise her. Not even Wynn Dorvan would speak with him. The best Hamner could do was talk to a flustered-sounding female who said, "I'm awfully sorry, sir, but the Chief of State has left me explicit orders that neither she nor Wynn Dorvan are to be interrupted."

He stood for a moment, calming himself. Then he looked down at his comlink and called Kani. "Summon the Masters. Immediately. The meeting's been moved up, and I need everyone there."

Jaina got the summons in the middle of Tahiri's trial. She frowned at the blinking light on her comlink, stepped out, heard that she had been requested to attend an emergency meeting of the Masters, and let Kani, known to some of the Masters as "K.P.," Kenth's Pet, know she was on her way immediately.

Most of the Masters had already assembled by the time she had arrived. She went up to Kyp Durran and said, "We have to stop seeing each other like this."

"I know," he said. "It's just so wrong, but I can't help it."

"What *is* wrong," Jaina said, too worried to continue the banter, "is that I keep being asked to attend these meetings. I'm not a Master, I'm the Sword of the Jedi, and the fact that I keep getting invited means that someone thinks the Sword of the Jedi might be needed. Also wrong is that this is an emergency meeting when a regular one was scheduled in just a couple of hours."

Kyp nodded and sighed. "I know. K.P. wasn't much help at all when I asked what was going on."

"You shouldn't keep calling Kani that, she's a good kid," Jaina said, glaring at him.

"Doesn't mean she's not Kenth's Pet," Kyp countered. "And don't look at me like that. Your dad was the one who came up with the nickname, you know."

Jaina's shoulders drooped slightly. "I know," she said.

Hamner was outwardly calm, and was clearly doing his best to suppress his emotions in the Force as well, but some of his agitation leaked out anyway. Jaina stood close to the door, leaning against the wall, arms folded. This was the closest she'd ever come to seeing Kenth Hamner rattled, and her curiosity was eating her alive.

Eventually, everyone who was going to attend had arrived. They took their seats and waited expectantly.

"A little while ago, I was contacted by the Chief of State," he said without preamble. "Based upon our conversation, I suggest we brace ourselves for another attack. Most likely, again from the Mandalorians."

Jaina felt all eyes turn on her, including Hamner's, which she took as permission to speak. "Then we should be fine, judging by how we handled them last time," she said bluntly. "We didn't lose a single Jedi, but they lost quite a few against us. Let's face it, the biggest consequence of that whole incident was forcing us to delay the launch. The StealthX's are still trapped here, but I can't think of anything worse the Mandos could do that they haven't already done."

"There was something new this time," Hamner said, and something in the tone of his voice made the hair on the back of Jaina's neck stand on end. "Right before she ended the conversation—and, I might add, neither she nor Wynn Dorvan has responded to my repeated efforts to contact her—she said that I had a chance to end this little game we were playing with each other. Before things, and I quote, 'get so bad I'd give a great deal to be having this conversation again.'"

"That's a nicely ominous but completely vague threat," Kyle Katarn said. "Did she honestly think such a thing would make you surrender Saar and Altamik?"

"I can't be sure. I told her I spoke for the Masters, and we are deeply mistrustful of her right now. That she would have to prove herself to us before any negotiations would resume. Her response was that she hoped I spoke for the families of the Jedi as well."

If someone had tossed a thermal detonator into the room, it could not have gotten a stronger reaction than those few words. Saba Sebatyne lashed out with her tail so hard she cracked one of the chairs.

"She goes too far! Threatening our families!" cried Saba.

"What kind of threat? Wait, quiet, what kind of threat?" Katarn, calm as usual, trying to get more information and less emotion.

"This is complete and utter bantha poodoo!" Jaina was furious and wanted badly to follow Saba's example and break something. Nearly everyone else was shouting, even some of the quieter Masters such as Octa Ramis and Katarn. Strangely enough, Jaina noticed that Corran Horn stayed silent, though a vein throbbed at his temple. Jaina immediately felt a hot surge of shame. His family had already been taken by Daala, and they were nowhere near getting them back.

Hamner called for silence, finally using the Force to

amplify his voice into a bellow that sliced through the uproar.

*"Quiet!"*

He followed it with an extremely powerful Force suggestion for some which, though everyone assembled could resist, nonetheless had an effect. Calm started to replace the anger in most of those present, though the worry was still there, quivering in the air.

*Our families,* Jaina thought. Her mind went back to the restaurant, and little Allana's terrified shrieks. It was all getting very ugly very fast.

"The threat was deliberately vague," said Hamner. "It could even be empty." It was clear he didn't believe his own words. Nor did Jaina, nor, she suspected, did any Jedi in the room. Daala wasn't known for bluffing. And Jaina's danger sense was tingling, like unfriendly fingers tickling the back of her neck.

"We must launch!" growled Saba. "We should have done so before we were trapped. Now, we must launch before Daala does something to cripple the Order even more."

"She's right," Jaina said. The words escaped her lips without even realizing it.

"Come on, Jaina, *think*," Kyp said, too annoyed to curb his tongue. "We've had this conversation before. The second we launch, we'll be heard and shot down like game birds."

"Not if we've got help," Jaina said. Hamner shot her an angry glance.

"Not again, Jaina. No more Darkmeld, or any other scheme you've come up with. We don't need the bad public response right now. It's a delicate juncture and I will not have you jeopardizing it."

"I wasn't going to—"

*"I don't care!"*

Jaina's mouth slowly closed. For the next few minutes,

she listened to the uproar. Everyone was shouting, no one was listening, and no one was going to do anything.

Except Jaina.

Quietly, unobtrusively, she made her way to the door. She waited for a long moment, then slipped out.

There was someone she thought just might help.

# Chapter Thirteen

"Sir, I tried to stop her—" Ashik said as a small whirlwind burst into Jagged Fel's office.

"As soon stop time as Jaina," Jag muttered under his breath.

"It's important," Jaina said. She turned to Ashik. "Can you leave us alone for a few moments? I need to talk to Jag in private."

Ashik looked at Jag, who nodded. Frowning slightly, the Chiss closed the door.

"So what's so important that you had to practically hit Ashik in the nose?" he asked, leaning back in his chair and regarding her.

"I need your help."

"With what this time?"

Jaina winced a little at his tone of voice. "I know . . . it seems like recently the only time I come to see you is when I need something. I'm sorry, but this time—Jag, this is huge."

He sighed, and relaxed, extending his right hand to her. She took it in her left, moving forward to perch on a corner of his desk, and his eyes lingered for a moment on the bright stone on the fourth finger. The sight took away some of the irritation. Jaina was Jaina, and had always been, and thank stars would always be, Jaina. And he loved her, despite, and because of, that.

"All right. What's going on."

She licked her lips. "Vault time."

". . . okay."

"I can't tell you everything. Not yet. But . . ." She took a deep breath. "Luke's run into something really, really big. Something that's a threat to the entire galaxy. He needs help. The Jedi were going to provide it to him. We have a small fleet of StealthXs ready to go inside the Temple, but since the Mandos attacked, the GA is watching us like a vyrhawk. There's no way we can launch. And today, Daala contacted Kenth Hamner with this very nasty, very obscure threat to our families if she didn't get Saar. Jag—we've got to launch, and soon. We've got to get these ships to Luke or—"

"Whoa, whoa, slow down," Jag said, dropping her hands and lifting both of his up in a defensive gesture. "First of all, Luke isn't supposed to have any aid. Those were the terms of his agreement."

"He doesn't know we're coming. That way he won't get into trouble. And once the threat is ended, everyone, even Daala, will realize that it was absolutely necessary."

"And what is it exactly you would like me to do?"

She straightened, slightly, hearing the ice in his voice. "Distract Daala. Get her to quit watching us. Or else—" Her eyes widened as the idea struck, then she shook her head. "No, I can't ask that of you."

"Spit it out."

She seemed to be having an internal battle. "You've got to believe me—I wouldn't ask this of you unless I felt it was absolutely necessary." The words came slowly, reluctantly, and Jag knew they were true. This wasn't a flippant request.

"Maybe . . . you can give us some of your ships. Some Imperial ships. That way we don't have to launch the StealthXs. We can just—"

"Let me get this straight. You want me to either lie to

Daala to get her off your back, or else provide you with Imperial ships without informing the Galactic Alliance, to go haring off chasing some unnamed threat to the galaxy? Jaina, the repercussions from this—" He was at a loss for words for a moment. "You realize you could be asking me to help start a war? In order to fight some enemy you won't even tell me about?"

She shifted her weight and looked away uneasily. "Okay, so . . . when you put it like *that,*" she said, "it doesn't sound very good. But Jag, this is real. And it's dangerous. It's—it involves the Sith, okay? Please, just trust me!"

Sith. Now he understood a bit better. The Sith were, for Jaina, an almost incomprehensibly personal matter. More than anyone else he could think of, Jaina knew what they could do, and the cost they could exact on one's soul. Daala had stated that she did not think that, in the end, there was that much difference between Sith and Jedi. Now he knew why Jaina wanted to act now, rather than request permission and aid—because it would be denied her.

It was with gentleness and a regret that went bone deep that he spoke. "I understand why you are asking this. But . . . you have to know I can't possibly do it. I can't ask my people to go out and commit crimes that would cause the sort of gigantic diplomatic incident that could possibly start a war. I can't do this for any of a thousand reasons. You see that, don't you?"

She reached out to him imploringly. "Jag, this is me. Jaina. Just trust me. It will all work out, I swear it to you. But we've got to get some kind of fleet to Luke or it's going to be too late!"

"For me, Jaina, I would believe you. I would follow you anywhere just on your word. And you know what that means to me."

She swallowed, nodding. She knew. Trust was something that had once been shattered between them, and the admission that he was willing to trust her again did not come easily.

The door slid open. Ashik rushed in, grabbed a controller, and turned on the viewscreen. Both Jaina and Jag had their mouths open to protest his barging in, but they quickly forgot it as they watched what was unfolding.

The cam focused on the familiar image of the Jedi Temple. Jaina stopped breathing, her eyes going wide. The cam then pulled back to show that the Temple was completely surrounded. By Mandalorians and their vehicles.

Jag quickly took in the sight of at least half a dozen tra'kads, Mandalorian Protector starships. Slow, heavily armed, and built with beskar, the things were essentially flying tanks. They were on the ground now, in various places on the now empty square, but once they were airborne, they could cause a great deal of damage to the Temple's structure. They were augmented by several distinctive orange-hued *Canderous*-class assault tanks. There were other heavy ground vessels, and bombers of various types made slow, ominous passes over the Temple.

"—is under siege," came the too-familiar voice of Javis Tyrr. "A siege, right here in Coruscant. One might think that Chief of State Daala has run out of ideas, or reverted to the days of the past, where one ruled with an iron fist."

"That was fast," Jaina said quietly.

Jag turned his attention from grainy, stock holofootage to stare at her. "You knew about this?"

"I was trying to tell you," Jaina said, her voice unusually quiet. "Daala contacted Master Hamner—"

"—about the families, right, but—"

Jaina looked like she was about to punch a wall. Instead, she took a deep breath.

"Jag. She's laying siege to the Temple. Using Mandalorians. It's too late to get the StealthXs out. She acted too fast. She's not about to listen to us. But you can still help me. Please."

Jag turned from her to the sight of Mandalorians enclosing the Temple. He thought about what Jaina was asking him to do. He thought about Daala, riding this guarlara right off a cliff in an effort to extract two Jedi. He thought about the attack on himself—and on the Solos. The attack they all suspected Daala had orchestrated.

Suspected.

They didn't know for sure.

He closed his eyes for a moment, then opened them and gazed up at his fiancée.

"I will talk to Daala, and try to get her to end the siege," he said, his voice cool and calm and quiet. "More than that—I cannot do."

Jaina froze, like a statue, for a long moment. Finally, she spoke, and her voice was subdued and strangely gentle. "I shouldn't have asked this of you. I shouldn't have asked you to bend so far you'd break, and that's exactly what I did."

"Jaina, I'm sure there's some other—"

"We're not going to be able to make this work, Jag. No matter how much we want to. Our duties are always going to come between us. This is something I have to do . . . just like your refusing to help is something you have to do. I'm sorry."

Then, slowly, she reached with her right hand, pulled off the engagement ring, and placed it with surprising tenderness down on the desk. Tears stood in her eyes, but she rose without trembling and walked out.

He could have called her back. He could have apologized, offered to covertly send her anything she wanted.

She'd have leapt into his arms, holding him tight, and all would be well between them again.

Except it wouldn't. She was right. Jag was who he was, and Jaina was who she was, and once again, for a final time, that had come between them.

Jagged Fel reached out slowly, grasped the engagement ring tightly in his hand, and, expressionless as his heart cracked within him although there was no one to see, watched the news unfold.

Dorvan's comm buzzed. "Dorvan."

Daala's voice. "Turn on the holonews. Now."

Dorvan sighed and obeyed. He had protested the installation of a vidscreen in his office, but recently Daala had been insistent. As she said, it was not as if her chief of staff would be caught watching daytime holodramas.

He suspected what he would see even before the reporter's distinctive, oh-so-irritating voice came on. Mercifully, Dorvan was spared the sight of the fellow. Instead, the cam focused on the Jedi Temple, surrounded by Mandalorians in their distinctive armor.

"—is under siege. A siege, right here in Coruscant. One might think that Chief of State Daala has run out of ideas, or reverted to the days of the past, where one ruled with an iron fist."

As he talked, there was grainy, jumpy stock footage of familiar figures. One was a pleasant-looking older man with thick, wavy silver hair and kindly eyes. He was standing and speaking passionately before the Senate. The other was a shot of a distinctive moving figure in black, with a cloak flowing behind him and a mask that morphed into the face of Jacen Solo.

Dorvan was not a man easily moved by propaganda or calculated images. He had seen enough in his life to know exactly how easily pictures could be manipulated. But he was troubled by watching this footage of Palpatine, Darth Vader, and Jacen Solo because the comparison wasn't altogether ludicrous. Daala *was* behaving in a fashion that called those tyrants to mind. She *did* have her history with the Galactic Empire trailing behind her like Vader's cloak.

"Are you watching this?" Daala's voice trembled with outrage.

"Ma'am, your connections with the Empire have been cast in a negative light before," he said calmly. "It is distressing and inaccurate, but most beings with half a brain can see right through Tyrr."

"It doesn't matter. It's everywhere, and there's no one actually simply reporting on the issue. There's no one just covering it without feeling compelled to hurl images of Vader and Palpatine and Caedus in along with invectives. This can't be permitted to continue."

Something akin to alarm fluttered inside Dorvan's chest. He sat forward in his chair and spoke to her in his blandest, most calming voice—the one he had learned she listened to the most. "Ma'am, it's a free press. Please trust me on this one, it's self-regulating. You don't want to get involved the way the Moffs did."

"Maybe we should. Maybe we should find our own reporter, set him or her up with an inside connection." She was coldly angry now, and looking to go on the offensive.

Dorvan could not let that happen. He'd warned her about being perceived as another Palpatine. He'd not been able to dissuade her from the siege. As far as he was concerned, the Mandalorians were bad news. He'd not wanted her to use them at all, but she had ignored his advice multiple times. It was difficult for him not to say, "Well, ma'am, if you hadn't laid siege to the Temple, then the reporters wouldn't be able to use that against you." That would not help. She had done it, the siege was continuing.

But the minute Daala stooped to the same tactics as her enemies in this situation, or began gagging a free press, there would be even more, and possibly worse and more far-reaching, trouble for the Galactic Alliance. Trouble that could only be temporarily eased by going down the path even farther to try to fix the problems. It was a vicious cycle, and Daala could not be permitted to get caught up in it.

*He* could not permit her to get caught up in it. He sat very still for a moment, thinking.

"You still there, Dorvan?"

"Oh, yes ma'am, quite. I don't think that escalating this into a journalistic war is a good idea. But I think I have a way to muzzle our tawny-haired newshound."

"Really? What?"

"It's best if you don't know the details, ma'am. But I can assure you that it will be legal and not implicate you or the GA in any fashion."

Her voice was warm. "I knew I could count on you, Wynn. You always come through."

"That's my job, ma'am."

He clicked off the comm and leaned back in the chair, eyes on the screen. He'd misled Daala slightly. He hadn't told her the details not because it was best that she didn't know them, although that was most certainly true, but rather because he hadn't figured them out himself yet. Tyrr was still nattering on about "siege of the Temple" and "trapped inside" and so on. Where was his concern for the Jedi when he aired the footage . . .

That was it. That was the key. But how to . . .

He watched the footage very carefully. Tyrr himself was in the shot now. The lighting was excellent, and Tyrr almost—almost—was convincing in his faux concern.

Oh yes. That was it.

He pressed his comm button. "Desha?"

"Yes sir?" Desha Lor's voice was eager and alert, as, Dorvan mused, was the young Twi'lek herself.

"I need you to do a little digging for me." He outlined what she needed to find out, but not why, because she hardly ever needed to know why and thus he hardly ever told her, and she dutifully took notes and assured him, in typical cheery Desha fashion, that he'd get it as soon as possible, if not sooner.

He fished Pocket out of her favorite napping spot and stroked her. She stirred, shifted, opened her tiny mouth in a yawn, and went back to sleep draped over his hand. Tyrr was still continuing melodramatically.

"Enjoy this last story while you can, Javis Tyrr," Dorvan said quietly, and permitted himself the tiniest smile of satisfaction at the thought.

# Chapter Fourteen

IT WAS A DRINKING HOLE WITH THE IGNOMINIOUS NAME of The Drunken Ootak, and from the interior it could have been a drinking hole anywhere in the galaxy. It just happened to be on Vinsoth.

The Drunken Ootak, named for an indigenous primate that was known for searching out fermented fruit and proceeding to gorge until intoxicated, was crowded and noisy and smelly, and a complex variety of beings were laying bets and shouting. Smoke hazed the air, and laughter punctuated it.

The bets and the shouting and the laughter revolved around the activities occurring at a center table. Seated in a far-too-large high-backed chair at one end of the table was a slender, delicately built humanoid female. Her clothing was simple: travel-worn boots, trousers, shirt, and a vest with several pockets. She had long ears, pink skin, a wispy, tousled mop of white hair, and bright eyes. Those eyes were currently blinking very slowly, and her head was nodding. Standing at her side was a human male with graying blond hair, blue eyes, and a rather worried look on his face.

On the other end of the table sat a Chevin male. He was thinner than most, his enormous face seeming harsh and angular. The smoke-hazed light glinted on a gold ring pierced through one nostril. His robes, purple and blue shot through with gold thread in pleasant geometrical designs, proclaimed him as a being of some wealth. Currently, however, the distinctive reek of alcohol wafted from the robes from where more than one glass had been spilled over the course of the evening. There was a little crowd gathered behind him. Some of them appeared to be personal friends or servants, others were simply angling for a good view. Two Chevs, a male and a female, stood slightly behind him.

The Chevin and the pink-skinned female each had eleven small glasses upended in front of them. Between them was a bottle of Twi'lek liquor—a beverage known for its potency.

Brukal, the Chevin owner of The Drunken Ootak, poured them each another shot of the green fluid, then recorked the bottle. It had been unopened not so long ago; now it was nearly empty.

The shot was passed to the female. She started, as if waking herself, and then reached out for the glass with unsteady hands. She brought the glass to her lips, then paused. She took a deep breath. There was muttering and credits changed hands.

"Don't be so hasty," she said, in a voice that slurred only slightly. "I c'n handle this . . ."

She brought the glass to her lips, licked them, and then knocked back the shot with a quick flick of her wrist. There was scattered applause, and credits changed hands again.

"Hey, Guumak," Brukal said, his expression twisting slightly in annoyance. "You gotta pay up. We bet each round. Or you too drunk to remember that?"

The other Chevin looked distressed. His snout wrinkled in agitation. He frowned at the female, clearly unable to understand how it was that one so small could be threatening to drink him under the table. But he waved for another shot.

"Money first," Brukal said, waving his fingers impatiently.

Guumak turned and spoke to the two Chevs who stood behind him. The female, clad in an attractive robe of subdued colors with black hair held back by a jeweled band, held a small sack. Looking as distressed as the Chevin, she said something in her native tongue and indicated the sack, which was obviously empty.

Guumak grunted, reached out a hand and grabbed the wrist of the male Chevin. With a firm tug, the Chevin was yanked forward, stumbling a little.

"Put Shohta up." He gestured. The Chev, presumably Shohta, looked stunned.

"Master?" He glanced uncertainly from the drunken Chevin to the delicate-seeming female with whom his master was competing. This time, Guumak stared at the glass for a long time before lifting it and upending the contents into his open mouth. He gulped the alcohol down.

And that was when his motor skills failed completely. The glass tumbled down to shatter on the duracrete floor, and the Chevin followed it a second later.

Wild cheering went up, although there were also plenty of dirty looks shot the female's way as beings reached for pouches, purses, and sacks. She smiled, satisfied, and rose as the crowd began to disperse, drifting their individual ways. Her unsteadiness had markedly decreased, and the human who had stood beside her, vastly relieved, offered her a glass of pure, clear, nonalcoholic water. She drank it down eagerly. Her companion asked, sotto voce, "How the kriff did you manage that?"

"Devaronians have a second liver," Madhi Vaandt said equally softly, grinning a little.

The human stared, then started to grin in return. "Oh, I get it. So you can't get drunk."

"Oh, we still can, and do. Just takes an awful lot. Find out anything?" The two retreated to a shadowed corner, ducking out of the path of a Wookiee who was lugging out the unconscious body of the Chevin. The female Chev followed closely, looking distressed. She glanced over her shoulder and met the eyes of the male who had been attending Guumak. He gave her what was meant to be a reassuring smile, then turned and approached the human and the Devaronian female. He inclined his head and cleared his throat.

"I am Shohta. It is an honor to serve you," he said, almost mechanically.

A week ago, Madhi Vaandt and her cam operator, Tyl Krain, had just finished a segment on Tatooine. It was there that she had received her first letter, which had revealed the existence of a group called the Freedom Flight. They were a very loosely connected group, the letter told her, who had as their chief concern the extermination of slavery throughout the galaxy. They had been observing her reporting for some time now, and would continue to do so if they believed she could help them.

A second letter had come just hours ago. "We suspected your path would lead you here, to Vinsoth, where slavery has been coated with sweetness and made to appear palatable," the letter had said. "We are watching you and are considering giving you an exclusive insight into our group. However, be warned—any public mention of the Flight prior to such contact would result in termination of any possible leads. Enjoy your stay, and observe how different, and yet how similar, slavery is on different worlds."

Madhi had seen slavery at a distance on Tatooine.

Now she was forced to truly look the institution, as personified by this single being, in the face. She regarded Shohta uncomfortably. He stood quietly, as if he was used to doing so, and simply waited.

"Um," Madhi said, "It's all right. You . . . don't need to serve me."

"Oh, but I do," he insisted. "You won me in the competition. I am considered as good as credits in this establishment. You may confirm this with Brukal." He turned and indicated the proprietor, who was busy pouring drinks. Even over the din of the place, Brukal was apparently accustomed to hearing his name. He glanced up, fixed Madhi with his small dark eyes, and nodded to her.

"He's yours," Brukal grunted, then returned to tending his bar.

Madhi's stomach flip-flopped. "As good as credits in this establishment," she repeated. She shook her head. "Not with me you're not."

"Miss . . . ?" Shohta paused and waited politely.

"Vaandt. Madhi Vaandt," she said.

"Miss Madhi Vaandt, I *belong* to you. If I return to my former master, I will be severely punished and he will be penalized by Brukal for failing to honor his bet. I would ask you please to accept me as your winnings. If I disappoint you in any fashion, I assure you I am a quick learner and will not do so twice. I come from very fine stock."

"Stock?" Madhi and her cam operator exchanged glances.

"Oh, you would wish a pedigree? I'm sure once Master Guumak is . . . er, has recovered from the contest, he would be happy to provide you with proper documentation."

Krain seemed to have recovered, at least somewhat. He glanced at his chronometer. "Well, we were supposed to do the segment in fifteen minutes, but we can wait."

Madhi shook her head. Her mop of white hair became even more tousled with the gesture. "No," she said. "No need to wait."

"But, uh . . . this . . . being here . . ."

"Shohta?"

"Yes, mistress?"

"Your first job as my . . . my slave," and she stumbled over the word, "will be to appear on cam with me. For a holovid newscast."

"I'm afraid I've never performed," he said, shifting his feet and looking nervously. "I'm more of a personal attendant rather than a theatrical performer, although many of my people are known for their thespian skills."

"You'll come on the newscast with me," Madhi repeated, "and you'll just answer whatever questions I ask you. It won't be difficult."

He bowed, deeply, elegantly. "As my mistress commands, I will obey."

"I wish all the subjects I interviewed were as cooperative," Madhi quipped automatically, then sobered. "No. No, I don't."

"Eleven minutes," said the cam operator.

Madhi waved at Shohta. "Come on, follow me."

Seven minutes later, just as dawn was coming, they were several meters away from the watering hole. Krain had positioned the shot strategically, so that it caught some of the establishment without actually including the name. Neither would they mention it. Nothing that had happened inside was illegal, at least not on Vinsoth, and both Tyl and Madhi had been around long enough to know one only riled someone when necessary for the story. And it wasn't necessary this time.

Madhi stood with her microphone, looking as fresh as if she hadn't knocked back nearly a liter of highly alcoholic Twi'lek liquor less than a half hour ago. Shohta stood off to the side, looking poised but uncomfortable. He brushed nervously at his robe.

"And go," Krain said.

"I'm standing here in front of an intoxicant establishment in the capital city of Umalor on Vinsoth," said Madhi. "The dawn is breaking for this city, but there is still not much light being shone on the institution of slavery that has continued without change for thousands of years on this planet, where the Chevs have enslaved the Chevins. Some would argue that it's a very civilized arrangement. That the Chevins are well taken care of, that their culture is respected and allowed to flourish."

Madhi's gaze grew intense. She made no effort to stifle her feelings. "Honest reporting compels me to admit that most Chevins are indeed well treated. Indeed, their lives might be easier than those of many free beings elsewhere. But they are *not* free beings. They are property, they are owned, and they can be bought and sold . . . even submitted as bets in a card game.

"In fact," she continued, "I myself was involved in a game of chance just an hour or so ago. And I'd like you to meet what was offered as currency."

Shohta moved hesitantly into the cam range, glancing uneasily back and forth between the cam operator and Madhi. She smiled up at him briefly, then returned her intense gaze to the audience she always envisioned as gazing back at her on the other side of the lens.

"We know the clichés of what happens when someone doesn't have money in a game of chance. Jewelry gets put on the table. Sometimes deeds to property. Shohta is property, and now, according to all the laws of this planet, he belongs to me just like my jacket does. Shohta," she said, turning to him, "you spoke very eloquently earlier of all that you had to offer me as a slave. Can you share that with the viewing audience?"

"Of course, mistress," he said promptly, looking relieved. This was something he was comfortable with, even proud of. "My name is, as you know, Shohta Laar. I am trained to be a personal attendant. I cook, clean, manage personal affairs such as errands and schedules, and conduct interviews of other slaves you might desire to purchase, among other things."

"I see," Madhi said. "And you said earlier you had a pedigree? Can you tell me more about it?"

"This marks me as a descendant of one of the most sought-after slave families," Shohta said, lifting an arm to show a welded-on bracelet. It was beautiful, as such things went. "I can date my lineage back several dozen generations. The Laar line is a pure-blooded one."

"Good breeding," Madhi said.

"Very," Shohta said.

"And you think I'll be happy with how you serve me?"

"I do hope so, mistress."

"And what could I do to you, if I was unhappy? Legally?" Madhi watched him intently, and Shohta began to squirm, ever so slightly.

"I—well, you own me. You could do anything you wish."

"I could beat you? Starve you? Whip you in public?"

"Not in public. Behind closed doors, yes."

Madhi was relentless. "I could, if I owned your children, beat *them* in order to punish *you*?"

"Yes, you could."

Madhi's eyes bored into his. "I could . . . kill you? Force you to be . . . involved with me?"

The slave was clearly uncomfortable now, but he squared his shoulders and answered the question. "Anything you wished. I am yours to deal with as you see fit."

"Anything I wished," Madhi repeated. "Because I had good luck in a game of chance, I now have a living, breathing, thinking, feeling being that I could do all manner of things to just because I wanted to." She regarded him for a moment more, then turned back to the cam. She could feel the heat of indignation in her face, and hoped it came through despite the makeup.

"This is the ugly reality of slavery. Oh, the Chevins let the Chevs paint, let them perform their traditional plays, so they can make money off the paintings and performances. They are overall decent to their slaves—because you don't damage valuable property. Maybe the Chevs are lucky. But they're only as lucky as the people who own them decide they are. What if Shohta here *isn't* lucky?"

She turned back to him. Shohta's eyes widened, but he stood still. He was, Madhi mused with a pang, a very well-trained slave indeed.

"Well, I am going to do whatever I want with you, Shohta. And do you know what that is?"

He licked lips that had gone slightly dry. "No, mistress. Please tell me, that I may obey."

"I'm going to free you."

His jaw did not quite drop, but his eyes widened even further.

"Do you want to be freed?" This was the moment, and she knew it. If Shohta said no, he was happy being a slave, then this whole thing would have backfired. She'd have to scrap the whole segment and start over, and the most important thing to her—the wants and needs of those who were the actual slaves—would mean nothing.

For a long time, he didn't speak. Then he looked her in the eye.

"A kindly mistress is still a mistress, and a comfortable cage still confines," he said, quietly. "Yes. Yes, I wish to be free."

Madhi blinked rapidly. Her voice, when she turned back to the cam, was quite unprofessionally thick.

"Then consider it done," she said. "And later today, when businesses are open I will make it formal. I'll be hiring you as a member of my staff, if you would like. Otherwise, you are free to go wherever you wish."

"I think . . . I would like to be . . . employed by you," he said, turning over the phrase on his tongue with not a little awe. He bowed, deeply, as he had been doing all his life. But when he straightened, there was a new expression on his face. One of pride, of confidence, of gratitude that had nothing to do with subservience. Madhi couldn't help but smile.

She was sure that on the next world they went to, the Freedom Flight would decide to make actual physical contact. And Shohta Laar would be right beside her when they did.

# Chapter Fifteen

SOLO SAFE HOUSE, CORUSCANT

THREEPIO WAS ACTING WEIRD.

Allana did not think it was a malfunction, but he was definitely behaving in an unusual manner. Over the last couple of days, he had seemed both more pleased and more annoyed than usual. Threepio was always a little annoyed about something, or else he didn't seem to be able to be happy. That puzzled Allana, but she had encountered living beings who were the same way, so she simply filed away this insight into the droid's personality without further worry.

But recently, the golden protocol droid didn't seem to be annoyed with anyone else. He seemed to be annoyed with himself, and *that*, Allana knew, was most definitely unusual behavior.

With Anji padding along on silent paws at her side, she'd begun observing Threepio. Someone else might have called it "snooping," but Allana knew it was simply observing and gathering information. Someone might have tampered with his programming. Or he might need adjusting. But she was able to admit that the main reason she was observing and gathering information was that she was bored. She'd had such an exciting time on Dathomir, even with the dangers she'd faced, that to come home, even with Grandma and Grandpa and Aunt Jaina, seemed terribly dull in comparison. Too, while she understood the need for these temporary rental lodgings, she missed the familiar comforts of the Solos' real apartments.

Grandpa had found her pouting over her lessons just the other day and when she had explained this to him, he'd nodded to her.

"Know just what you mean, kid. But even the best of ships need downtime for repairs."

"I'm not hurt or in need of repairs," Allana had said.

"No, not physically. But sometimes you need time to kick back and take a breath before plunging into things again," he'd said.

"You don't seem to."

He'd grinned, that grin that always seemed to provoke an answering smile and a sort of softness on her grandmother's face.

"Yeah, well, you gotta remember, I got a couple of years on you." He'd tweaked her nose and she giggled. "I firmly believe that by the time you're my age, you'll have seen and done so much you'll find even all the excitement we had on Dathomir to be boring. But for right now, I think a little quiet time is good for little girls."

"Grandpa, I just turned eight!"

A strange look flitted across his face, and she felt a little pang from him in the Force. "That may be, but you'll always be my little girl."

Allana thought she understood. "Just like Jaina will be, right?"

"Yep."

"And . . . like Jysella is to Mirax and Corran. Even though she is a brave and experienced Jedi Knight."

The sorrow increased, and Anji fidgeted, agitated by the emotion. The little nexu's ears flattened slightly and her spines rose.

"Grandpa," Allana said patiently, "we've been over this. You can't feel bad. It upsets Anji."

Han grinned again and pulled Allana into his lap, snuggling her tight. She laughed, and she felt his mood lighten as well, the sadness giving way to profound love. "Okay, how's this then. You don't get mad at me when you're all grown up and able to toss me around with the Force, and I still call you my little girl."

She laughed happily. "You got a deal, Grandpa."

But her grandfather wasn't always there to be a silly distraction for her, and besides, Threepio's strange behavior was ever so much more interesting than this whole "breath-taking" thing Han had told her about.

She would overhear the droid talking to himself, or sometimes to Artoo. He would say things like, "Goodness, I should request an upgrade, this is taking far too long!" or "Such a relief to be doing what I was designed to," or "Oh dear, oh dear, perhaps a newer model would serve the Solos better. I am positively decrepit and tragically outdated."

*That,* he never said to Artoo.

Now she saw him glancing around, his photoreceptors taking in everything. She ducked back behind the wall before he turned in her direction. Anji looked up at her, and Allana put her finger to her mouth. The cub did not make a sound. Twice a week, Allana and Anji worked with a professional nexu trainer. The animals could be trained as hunting companions or guard animals, and with four eyes, responded very well to visual signals. In order to keep her beloved companion with her on her prowling, Allana had quickly trained Anji to respond to the nearly universal signal for silence.

She listened until she heard the clanking, whirring sound of Threepio walking away into the study. Allana felt a little pang of disappointment. It looked like Threepio was about to do nothing more dramatic than relay a message for her grandparents.

Still, that could be interesting, too. She moved through and leaned up against the wall of the study, listening. It was probably going to be boring.

And then she heard her uncle's voice. "Threepio! It's good to see you."

Luke?

"Master Luke, sir! I, too, am very pleased. I am delighted to report that I was able to do as you requested."

Requested? Wasn't that the same as "help"? And wasn't Grandma Leia not supposed to be helping Luke? But they'd gone to Dathomir . . . Allana was so confused.

"That's wonderful."

"I can tell it to you now, if you'd like." Allana's eyes grew wide.

"Actually," Uncle Luke was saying, "could you just transmit it to me? I want to be able to listen to it more than once, and at a time and place of my own choosing."

"Ah! I quite understand, given the clandestine nature of this information."

*Clandestine* was a big word, but Allana knew it. This was just getting better and better. Allana was both excited and worried. She didn't want anyone getting into trouble—not Luke, not Grandma, not anybody. But at the same time she needed to know exactly what was going on.

"I dislike eavesdropping," Luke continued, "but when you have Sith on your ship, well, I dislike not knowing what they're planning even more."

"Indeed, Master Luke. You working with the Sith! Who would ever have thought it! It is a unique situation, and may I say that it is one which I had never anticipated encountering."

Allana's eyes grew as big as the saucers that held their evening hot chocolate. That couldn't be right. Her Uncle Luke Skywalker would never work with the Sith!

"Well, you're not exactly encountering them, Threepio. I hope you're able to stay well out of it."

"I share that hope ardently, Master Luke. I feel like I need a nice hot oil bath after translating such an unpleasant conversation."

So it was true. A wave of fear and confusion rushed over Allana. Anji lifted her head and hissed, her spines raised, agitated by Allana's emotions. Allana winced and grabbed Anji, trying to calm her, but the cub was still young and imperfectly trained, and when Allana's hands closed on her too hard, she yowled and struggled to free herself. Allana released her, and the cub scooted off a distance, fleeing on too-large feet, before sliding to a halt and turning around, mewing pathetically for her master.

"Oh! Who's there! Mistress Allana!" Threepio hastened to the doorway. Allana made no attempt to hide herself. She stared up at Threepio, a mixture of emotions warring within her. She could see past him into the room, where a small hologram of Luke Skywalker stood on the desk.

"Threepio?" the miniature Luke was saying. "What's wrong? Allana?"

"What are you doing here?" Threepio scolded.

"I might ask the same question of you," Alanna retored. "Both of you."

"It goes against the polite conventions of eighty-seven-point-four percent of known cultures to listen to a conversation not intended for one's aural receivers," Threepio continued indignantly.

Allana ignored him, marching up to the hologram of Luke. She was crying, and that upset her because she didn't want to cry; she wanted to be calm and in control like her mother and grandmother would have been. She wanted to ask proper questions.

Instead, what burst out of her was a sobbing, "Uncle Luke, why? Why have you gone over to the Sith?"

Luke's face, barely a centimeter high, softened with compassion. "Oh, honey, it's not what you think. I've not gone over to the dark side. I promise you."

"Then why?" The cry was anguished. "What are you doing even *talking* to them? Why is Threepio sneaking around to talk to you?"

"It's very complicated," Luke said. "Threepio, you still there?"

"Indeed, Master Luke."

"Go get Han and Leia. I think they need to explain everything to Allana."

"Of course." The droid sounded relieved to have an excuse to leave. "I'll go fetch them immediately." Servos whirring, he hastened out of the room.

Allana almost staggered, gripping the back of a sofa for support. "Grandma and Grandpa know about this?"

"Well, some of it," Luke said, and smiled a little. "I hadn't . . . exactly asked permission to use Threepio to help me translate the Keshiri language. That's what the Sith I'm working with speak. It would have put your grandparents in an awkward position. So I just went directly to Threepio."

Allana knuckled at her eyes, trying to make sense of all this. "I know about spies," she said, taking a deep breath. "Is . . . is that what you are doing? What you asked Threepio to help you with?"

"Sort of like that," Luke said.

"So . . . two of them, right?"

"Actually, a whole lot more," Luke said. "It seems that there is a whole planet of Sith out there."

Before Allana could actually fall from shock, a pair of

strong arms went around her and lifted her off the ground and into a bear hug. Allana struggled at first. She was still confused, and angry, but after a second or two when it became clear that Han's stubbornness—and strong arms—weren't going to release her immediately, she relaxed into it. Her arms went around his neck and she placed her soft cheek next to his scratchy one. He held her for a long minute, then set her down. Leia was kneeling, and Allana hugged her tightly as well for a long moment. Leia drew back, touched the girl's cheek reassuringly, then rose, holding Allana's small hand tightly in hers as she turned to face her brother. Artoo had followed them into the room and had come to a halt beside Threepio. He tweedled curiously at his humanoid-shaped counterpart, but Threepio waved a hand in a not-now gesture.

"Threepio said you needed to talk to us, that Allana was upset."

"I'm afraid I was borrowing Threepio's fluency with six million languages to have him translate a Keshiri conversation," Luke explained.

"Oh," both Solos said at once, turning to look at the droid in question. Threepio lifted his hands defensively and took a step backward.

"It's not my fault," he said, "Don't blame me. I am programmed to serve when requested!" Artoo made a booping noise that sounded almost like a rebuke.

"No, it's my fault," Luke said. "If my request was to a droid and not to a Jedi, I was still keeping to the conditions of my exile."

"Easier to ask forgiveness than permission, huh kid?" Han was asking. "You're getting more and more like me all the time. You might even start to look as good as me one of these days."

"No thanks, I don't want to look like a grumpy, thick-headed, craggy-faced old man," Luke replied.

"Who's craggy-faced?" The banter was strained, but helped ease some of the tension. Allana felt it, and it helped her relax slightly as well. She felt something brush up against her leg. It was Anji, who looked up at her, blinking her four eyes solemnly, then butted her head hard against Allana's calf, purring.

"Why didn't you tell me?" Allana was proud of herself. The question was a good one, and she had asked it in a calm, adult manner.

"Apparently, some people aren't telling other people lots of things," Han muttered, but fell quiet when Leia gave him a sharp look.

"Because there's a lot going on right now, honey," Leia said, stroking Allana's short, black-dyed hair. "A lot of things that you don't need to know about. And some that you do. We try to figure out what to tell you when, to keep you as safe and happy as possible."

"I am Chume'da," Allana said quietly. "I'm supposed to know about these things."

Leia didn't back down. "You're also eight years old, and we are your guardians. You can't solve all the galaxy's problems."

"Neither can you, Grandma."

"Kid's got you there," Han said.

"So . . . I know that Uncle Luke was asking Threepio to help translate a language so he could know what some Sith were saying," Allana continued. "But he's also working with them. Do I have everything right, Uncle Luke?"

"Yes," Luke said. "As strange as all that sounds when put together like that, it's all true."

"But you're not going to the dark side." Despite her best efforts, there was a quiver in her voice. Even after two years had passed, when she thought of Darth Caedus—she didn't think of the yellow-eyed man as her daddy—it was as if a hand clamped down hard on her heart and breathing became difficult.

"No," Leia said, in a voice that was both gentle and firm. "No one here is going to the dark side."

Allana nodded, clinging to Leia's hand. "Then . . . why are you being nice to the Sith?"

"Because there's something bad in the Maw," Leia said. "And we think that something is what is making the Knights all get sick."

Allana's eyes flew wide, hope chasing away the fear. "You mean . . . we know what's wrong with Barv and Yaqeel and the others?"

"We're pretty sure we do. And your Uncle Luke can't help them by himself."

"But . . . Sith aren't honorable . . . are they?"

Han and Leia exchanged pained glances. "Well, Sith can usually be counted on to look after themselves," Han said. "And it sounds like they're having the same sort of problems we are in that area. So Luke's teaming up with them to get to the bottom of things."

"What if they double-cross him?" Allana's face flamed as the adults all chuckled. Leia sensed her embarrassment and squeezed her hand again.

"That was the first thing on everyone's mind, honey. Luke's expecting a double-cross."

"That's why I asked Threepio to translate for me," Luke said. "So that I could know if they were planning something, and be prepared for it."

Allana nodded. "I get it," she said. "I think so, anyway."

"It's a pretty complicated and messy situation," Han said.

"So you left me out of it?"

"We would have told you," Leia said. "As soon as we felt you needed to know."

"When would that have been?"

Leia didn't look at Luke. She and Han had indeed planned to let Allana know what was happening when they left as part of the Jedi strike force. But she couldn't let Luke know about it ahead of time. This was indeed a pretty complicated and messy situation, as Han had so aptly put it. They couldn't tell Luke about the strike force because he would tell them to stand down. He wouldn't want to violate the terms of his agreement. And he had contrived to speak to Threepio, and just Threepio, for the same reasons. And no one had told an eight-year-old girl about the harsh realities of recording conversations and making alliances with enemies. It would be nice if she could shield Allana from this sort of thing.

But not shielding her was the only thing she and Han could do. Even more important, it was the right thing. The galaxy needed beings who could look into its darkness and ugliness without flinching, in order to make it a better place. Allana was going to be one such being.

And it was that calm certainty she projected into the Force, and not her worries and regret. It was with the face of a lifetime politician that Leia said to her granddaughter, "When the time was right."

Allana peered skeptically at Leia. "Is that one of those grown-up things like 'we'll see'?" she asked.

Despite the direness of the situation, Leia couldn't help but laugh a little. "Yes," she said, "it is."

Allana sighed.

"Now," Leia said, putting a hand on Allana's shoulder and steering her toward the door, "we all interrupted a conversation that was none of our business. Luke is allowed to talk to a droid he once owned." Leia tugged on Han's sleeve, urging him to exit with Allana and Anji.

Before he left, Han turned back to the hologram,

shrugged, gave a grin that had disarmed many a would-be attacker, and said, "*I* certainly didn't hear anything."

"Let's see if there's anything fun on the holovid," said Leia. Usually, Allana saw right through them when they tried to distract her, but this time the little girl nodded. She was content with the explanation they had given her, and for that small favor Leia was grateful.

Allana reached and clicked and the vidwall sprang to life. Leia had been about to go get them all something to munch on but she did a double take, her brown eyes huge, when she saw the image of the Jedi Temple.

"Oh no," she breathed.

"A siege?" yelped Han. "What the stang is Daala thinking?"

Caught up in the horrible sight of her beloved Temple surrounded by Mandalorians and siege weaponry, Leia didn't even chide him for his language in front of Allana. Anji growled, and Allana tried to comfort her.

"What's happening?" Allana said, her voice climbing higher with worry.

"I don't know, sweetheart," Leia said. "But your grandfather and I are going to find out."

Just then, Threepio entered. "Your pardon, Mistress Leia. I had only just finished with Master Luke when I received a brief, prerecorded message from Master Jagged Fel."

"Jag? What?" said Han, rising. Allana started to slip off the couch, but paused at the rather stern look her grandfather gave her. "Stay here, honey," he said, moderating his look with the term of endearment. "Threepio—watch her for us until we get back, will you?"

"Of course, Master Han."

They rushed into the study and closed the door behind them. Leia's danger sense was tingling like mad. Quickly, she pressed the button and listened. It was typically Jag—cool, precise, informative.

"Leia, Han. If you haven't heard already, the Mandos, under Daala's orders, have begun a siege against the Jedi Temple. Jaina was just in my office. She told me about what's going on in the Temple, and asked for my aid. I couldn't give it to her. She ended the engagement, and my concern is that she has decided to take off on her own. Please know that I intend to talk to Daala as soon as possible, though I doubt that will help matters any." A pause. "Jaina does what she has to. We all know that. I'm sorry it did not turn out that I could be a member of your family."

"She broke up with him?" Han said, disbelieving.

"Sounds like," said Leia, her own heart aching at the news. "Jag was deliberately vague, in case his transmission was being monitored, but it sounds like she told him about the strike force to help Luke and asked for his help in launching it."

Han nodded. "And Jag, being Jag, turned her down, and Jaina, being Jaina, broke the engagement and—" His eyes widened with realization. "And took off on her own. That girl has gone to Klatooine all by herself!"

"Don't glare at me," Leia said. "That's a very Han Solo thing to do."

"We've got to stop her."

Leia shook her head. "No, we've got to stop Daala."

# Chapter Sixteen

ABOARD THE JADE SHADOW

LUKE SAT BACK IN THE PILOT'S SEAT, BLOWING OUT A heavy breath. Little Allana was proving to be a bit too clever for her great-uncle's own good. Leia, as could be expected, had taken charge of the situation and defused it expertly. Threepio, flustered and alternately apologetic and defensive, had hastily transmitted the data and signed off.

It had been a long day, filled with all kinds of things Luke really would rather not have had to deal with. Dyon Stad had snapped, attacked a guard, stolen a speeder bike, and very nearly caused a political crisis that would have shaken a culture to its core.

Luke had overheard his son, the Jedi Knight, telling jokes to a Sith apprentice who was giggling at them as if she were nothing more than an ordinary sixteen-year-old girl. Luke had to admit, he wasn't sure which incident bothered him more—and that simple fact *really* bothered him.

They had returned with Dyon still unconscious, and there was now the question of what to do with him. Luke had realized at once they had to sell the yacht that had once belonged to Vestara and now Dyon. He was fine with that; the credits could go toward supplies. They'd need to keep Dyon very close at hand, and Luke was not about to let one of the Siths have the yacht. Had this still been the vessel of the Emperor's Hand, no doubt there would be a special area used for the stashing of prisoners, and it wouldn't be luxury quarters. But the *Jade Shadow* had been adapted for the use of Mara Jade Skywalker, and while Mara was certainly not one to embark on any kind of journey, short or long, without being prepared for any contingency, there was no prisoner cell per se.

There was, however, a sick bay, which included a bed with pretty decent restraints and a veritable laboratory of medicinal supplies. Dyon was now tranquilized, with a drip pouring a constant, comforting stream of chemicals into his body. He was strapped down at chest, waist, wrists, and thighs, with a set of stun cuffs on his ankles for good measure. He was hooked up to a monitor that would send an alert throughout the ship if his status changed, and Luke had set up a small mouse droid to watch him at all times.

Ben's contribution was to hang his vor'cha stun stick beside the door within easy reach. He had not had cause to use it—not yet—but Tadar'Ro, the Aing-Tii monk who had given it to Ben, seemed to think it was extremely powerful. "It's a gift from rock guys, designed to drop their enemies," Ben had pointed out. "I'm sure it packs a wallop."

All in all, it was a far cry from the setup at the Jedi Temple back on Coruscant, and much less than Luke would have preferred, but it would have to do. He felt fairly confident that they would be able to restrain Dyon for a while. At least Dyon wasn't a trained Jedi Knight, nor was his ability with the Force particularly strong. Luke was grateful for small favors.

After they had secured Dyon, Ben said, with a completely failed effort at casualness, "I'm going to check on Vestara. See how she's doing."

"You do that," Luke had said, "then tell her we're taking a walk and we're locking her in her quarters while we're gone."

Ben's red brows drew together. "What?"

"You heard me, son." Luke's voice was calm, but brooked no argument. "Dyon's restrained, but he could be very dangerous. And dangerous people have often been employed by the Sith."

"I can't believe you just said that," Ben said, his voice rising. His blue eyes snapped with anger and hurt. "She's the one who brought him down, Dad."

"I am aware of that," Luke said, tapping into the Force to keep his own rising irritation at bay. "But you were right there with her. She might well have done something very different had you not been."

"When are you—"

"Ben." Luke put the Force behind the words, so that Ben would know he was very serious indeed. "Go tell Vestara, activate the exterior controls on her door, and then come meet me outside."

Ben's breath was quick and angry, but he had nodded curtly and stomped off with unnecessary noise to do as he was instructed. Luke had lingered for a moment, gazing at the prone figure of Dyon. He shook his head sadly. Cilghal was not going to be happy to hear about this. He'd send her a quick update while Ben was talking with Vestara. The still figure before him represented why he had made the tentative and much-revisited decision to ally with the Sith in the first place—to find out what Abeloth's hold over these unfortunate beings was, and to end that hold.

He had gone to send Cilghal the message, and frowned slightly as he realized someone was trying to contact him at the same time. He pressed a button, and had been relieved when he saw Threepio's gold figure in minature. While the ensuing conversation had some tense moments, it had ended well, and he was now anxious to discover what Threepio had learned.

Luke began to read the translation Threepio had sent. Luke was honestly a bit surprised the protocol droid had pulled it off. Threepio had done a magnificent job, cross-referencing millions of different languages in order to produce something that, while hardly literature, was at least comprehensible and presumably fairly close to what had actually been said. Although, he mused, it did remind him a little bit of how Yoda used to speak.

As he read, Luke couldn't suppress a smug smile at Gavar Khai's comment that the conversation wouldn't be translated swiftly. They obviously did not know Threepio—or the golden droid's ego.

His eyes moved swiftly across the screen. So—Vestara had given Khai a map of the vessel. Not surprising. Luke was not overly troubled. If the Sith had access to all the things he suspected they did, they would be able to get the basic schematics of the SoroSuub *Horizon*-class Star Yacht easily enough. Vestara herself had been traveling in a similar vessel. The modifications to the *Jade Shadow* were more problematic, but nothing dire.

He continued to read, smiling a little from time to time at the technically accurate but inadvertently humorous translation.

FEMALE: How goes maternal parent?
MALE: Without you, but with pride at your doing.
FEMALE: I reach to make you pride.
MALE: Dathomir was fine. Dark women taken ranked by skill and strength in the Force.
FEMALE: Pleased, go they?
MALE: Yes and no. Go they will, obey or pain caused. Pain caused makes second consideration. Learning will make us powerful and widespread.

Luke frowned just for an instant. Dark women—
Nightsisters. He'd known Vestara was responsible for
the abduction of the Nightsisters. They'd obviously been
evaluated according to their skills and ability to use the
Force. Those who didn't obey quickly enough were tortured.

FEMALE: Happy I useful they. Learners status?
MALE: Learners?
FEMALE: Abeloth mind harm.
MALE: Nothing wrong with learners, but that physi-
cal violence will improve.
FEMALE: (untranslatable word for interrupting)
MALE: Aware I of what Taalon told Skywalker. Is un-
truth. You share idea. Skywalker we needed, so we
say what hurts their learners hurts ours also.

Luke smiled bitterly. He'd suspected as much. There
was nothing wrong with the Sith apprentices. The entire
story had been a lie to convince Luke to ally with them.
He gave a mental shrug.

He tensed slightly as Vestara inquired about the real
reason the Sith were allying with him, and frowned in
disappointment as Gavar Khai dodged the question.

The next few sentences yielded nothing of interest to
Luke. And then, what he was expecting came.

FEMALE: Negative. Ben mostly speaks.
MALE: You are drawn to Skywalker boy.
FEMALE: Affirmative, I am. Appealing he is. I regret.
I will attempt—
MALE: Negative. Useful is this. Fall not in love, but
fear not to reveal the attraction. The Force will con-
vey its reality. Defenses will be lowered. Speak more,
trust more. Use this. Possibility of redirecting.
FEMALE: To the Shadow Side?

A chill went through Luke, and a shiver of revulsion as well. Khai was urging his own child, a girl of sixteen, to attempt to seduce Ben—in all ways. Khai continued, excited at the prospect of a Sith Ben Skywalker, but reminding his daughter that if she failed to turn Ben to the dark side, she would be allowed to play with him . . . only as long as he was useful.

Ben needed to see this.

At that moment, he sensed his son's presence and turned around. Ben poked his auburn head in, glowering. "I've been outside for fifteen minutes, Dad."

"Sorry to have kept you waiting," Luke said sincerely. He waved Ben forward. "Close the door."

Ben snorted. He was still agitated. "Dyon's out cold and Vestara's locked in her room. I debated telling her I was sending her to bed without supper."

"There's something you need to see," Luke said, letting his son's anger wash over him. "You remember, of course, when Gavar Khai came on board, and I told you I was recording their conversation."

Ben nodded, blue eyes narrowing. "Yeah . . . you said we couldn't understand Keshiri, but you knew someone who—oh. Threepio?"

Luke nodded. "I think you'll find it very interesting."

Ben went very still. Luke sent the transmission to the copilot monitor, leaned back, and closed his eyes to allow Ben to read in private.

There was the occasional snort of amusement, and then Ben fell silent. When he heard the sound of Ben sinking back in his chair, Luke opened his eyes.

"So she's planning on seducing me," Ben said, his voice carefully devoid of emotion. "Trying to pull me over to the dark side. I guess I kind of figured that was her plan."

"She *is* Sith, Ben," Luke said quietly. "Born and raised. It's in her blood. You couldn't really expect anything else from her. In a way, it's almost not her fault. But you needed to know."

"So that I can pretend to go along with it?" Ben snapped. "So that we can use *her*, get information from *her*, just like she's trying to do with me?"

"No," Luke said, still gently. "So that you don't get hurt."

"I'm *not* going to go over to the dark side, Dad."

Ben was angry, and directing it at Luke. Luke didn't rise to the bait. "I know that. I know better than to think that you're in danger of that happening. If Caedus couldn't get you to join him, with the connection you two had, Vestara doesn't stand a chance. But you can still get hurt. Pretty badly."

"Don't worry about me," Ben said, rising. "I can take care of myself. She's just a girl, Dad. So—what did you want to talk to me about?"

Luke smiled sadly. "That," he said.

"Oh." Ben shifted in his seat uneasily. "Listen, I—I need to get out of here for a bit. That okay?"

"Sure," Luke said. His son had been in rougher places than this relatively calm spaceport, and he had aided the authorities today. He would be fine. As the youth rose, Luke added, "I know that Lando is a few days away from having the *Rockhound* ready, but I'm beginning to think that we need to move sooner rather than later. Start moving the flotilla toward the Maw. Lando can catch up with us."

"Sounds good to me," Ben said, already almost out the door of the cockpit. "The sooner we're done with these Sith, the better I'll like it."

As he watched Ben leave, Luke knew he was not the first parent to feel his own heart ache at his child's pain. But most parents didn't have to worry about their child losing their heart to a Sith, either. Like everything the

Sith were involved with, they made even teenage romance just that much more painful and dark.

Alone in her room, munching on a pak'pah fruit, Vestara sensed that something had happened between Luke and Ben. She couldn't tell what, exactly. Ben had been upset, but not with her, when he had knocked on the door earlier, bringing a few pieces of the fruit as a peace offering.

"Dad and I are heading out for a bit," he said.

"Oh? I thought he disliked this planet," she said, realizing almost immediately how disingenuous it sounded.

"Yeah, me, too, but you know how it goes. Parents." He gave her a grin that did not reach his eyes. "Don't know how long we'll be gone, but I brought you this in case you got hungry."

She let her face fall, slightly. "I see. Thank you."

Ben looked uncomfortable and gave her a shrug. She smiled at him. "It's okay, Ben. My father would have done the same."

"Funny how different but similar they are."

"Agreed." They looked at each other awkwardly for a moment, then Ben flashed her another quick smile and closed the door. She heard the slight hum as it again locked into place.

She was hungry, and was glad of at least something to eat while she focused in on the Skywalkers. She did not know the particulars, but she supposed she did not have to. Luke was uncomfortable with Ben's attraction to her, Ben was upset at being lectured to. Vestara felt certain that if he knew just how guarded Ben was being, he would not worry nearly so much.

He did like her, and as she had confided to her father, she liked Ben as well. It certainly made her job easy, although it added an element of disquietude that was unexpected. Earlier that day, after they had spoken to

Kelkad about the Klatooinian history of slavery, she and Ben had been perilously close to an argument about ideals—something she had tried assiduously to avoid. Ben was good-natured and forgiving, but he was also intelligent. He would not be an easy convert, if indeed he could be persuaded to walk the dark path at all, and if she ever allowed him a moment to think, really think, about just how different they were, she would lose this battle.

She'd acted fast, letting herself choke on the piece of pak'pah fruit, knowing that she could remove the blockage instantly using the Force. The danger had been real—a non–Force-user would have died. It had to be real, for Ben would have sensed an act. The incident had completely distracted him, and greater distraction came shortly thereafter in the form of a mad Force-user heading for the Fountain. She and Ben had worked remarkably well as a team, and as she recalled the event, Vestara smiled slightly. Even sitting in the unpleasant old cell had been entertaining—and informative. In order to get the jokes, Vestara had to ask what many apparently common things were. Perhaps because she had asked out of a genuine desire to know so she could appreciate the humor, Ben had been readily forthcoming with explanations. And so Vestara had learned much.

And now Luke was reining his son in, urging caution. She felt Ben departing the ship, and unease flickered in her chest.

She attempted to distract herself by playing a holographic game, but the sensation continued. An hour or so later, she felt Ben return. Almost at once, there was a knock on her door.

"Yes, Ben?" She made no attempt to hide that she knew it was him. He was very well trained in the Force; he knew she could sense him. The door slid open.

He was still upset, but this time it was cold, not hot.

And his anger was not directed at Luke, but at her. She had been lying on the bed, but now she sat up, peering at him.

"Dad is sending a message out now to the flotilla," he said in clipped tones. "We're going to be leaving soon."

"Oh? Has your friend Lando arrived?"

"Not yet. Dad wants to go anyway. He says that Lando can meet us there whenever he can make it."

"I thought the whole point of getting the *Rockhound* was to help navigate the Maw," Vestara said, frowning a little.

"Yeah, well, I don't know, Dad's getting antsy. And so am I. I'm ready to be done with this. Thought I'd let you know." The door closed.

Vestara's stomach clenched. Something had gone very wrong. Whatever Luke had convinced Ben of, it had taken deep root. She was going to have to work very hard to even recover the ground she had lost. She tried to convince herself that the tension and unhappiness she was feeling was unease at how her father would react, but she knew that was only part of it.

She had enjoyed being friends with Ben, and now that had gone away. It might come—no, she was Sith, she was cunning and strong willed, it *would* come back—but the coldness with which he regarded her troubled her more than she would ever have expected.

"Why weren't you just born Sith, Ben," she said softly, and laid her flushed face against the cool softness of the pillow.

# Chapter Seventeen

IT WAS THE RIGHT DECISION. LUKE KNEW IT THE MO-
ment he opened his eyes. He had had another one of
those elusive, yet sweet and calming dreams in which the
loving female presence had again enveloped him.

*It's time,* she had whispered, her breath soft against
the back of his neck, her right arm draped over his side,
her fingers entwined with his. *You need to go to the
Maw. Too many fates hinge upon it . . . yours and Ben's
not the least.*

The concern, the love—Luke kept his eyes tightly
closed. He breathed in her scent—familiar, cherished. *I
know. The girl is too dangerous for him. I need to find
out what I can about the Sith, and then sever this alliance.*

*Then go. Go to the Maw.*

Luke thought about the time when he had, with the
aid of the Mind Walkers from Sinkhole Station, gone to
that state they called Beyond Shadows. He had seen his
wife there, in the Lake of Apparitions.

*Will I see you again, in the Maw?*

A gentle nuzzle from behind. *Oh yes, my love. You'll
see me again. I am there, and I will be waiting for you. I
promise.*

And with that, he was instantly, completely, restfully
awake. He half wondered, as he always did, if he turned

around and reached out, whether he might find the sheets warm.

He rose, got dressed, and went to check on Dyon. The younger man was still unconscious, his face calm and untroubled. It was hard to imagine Dyon screaming and attacking others, but he had not been the first to fall to this strange malady, although Luke desperately hoped he would be the last. Luke checked the drip, the restraints, and Dyon's stats, then headed out to send a message.

It was early yet, and both Ben and Vestara, with the biological requirements of people their age, were still deep asleep in their respective quarters. Luke breakfasted on something quick and easy, and a scant twenty minutes after he sent the message, he received a reply.

Lando Calrissian looked less immaculate and pulled together than was customary for him. He wore practical and stained work clothing, which told Luke he had probably been working on the *Rockhound* himself, and a frown, which told Luke that he was not at all happy with Luke's message.

"Come on, Skywalker," Lando said without preamble, "You ask for my help with the *Rockhound,* and then you hare off without her?"

"The situation has changed," Luke said. Briefly, he brought Lando up to speed. He did not mention the inner need that was driving him to leave; Lando wasn't a Force-user, and sometimes they looked askance at such things.

"I see your point," Lando said. "I'd not be too happy with a crazy Jedi on my vessel for longer than I had to have him around either."

"He's not a Jedi, just a Force-user."

"Just as bad," Lando said, flashing white teeth in a quick grin. "And I can imagine that sitting around with a bunch of bored Sith doesn't make for restful sleep either."

Luke thought about the dream, and simply smiled.

"We won't get into dangerous territory without waiting for you," Luke promised, "but I'd like to get everyone doing something, at least."

Lando sighed. "I can step up repairs, but it's still going to be another couple of days at the very least. Think you can distract your Sith buddies with shinies long enough so they don't decide that a Skywalker skin might make a nice belt?"

"I think I can manage that," said Luke. "Thanks."

"You got it, Luke. Watch your back."

Luke expected the second conversation to be better received. He was right.

"I completely concur," Taalon said, nodding his purple head, his fingers steepled in front of him. "This vessel does sound useful, as I said earlier, but I chafe at the delay. I am anxious to be about our joint task of protecting our younglings and finding out exactly who and what Abeloth is."

Luke smiled. He kept careful control of his presence in the Force, letting go of all negative emotions connected to the fact that he had conclusive proof that Taalon's words were lies. Any irritation Taalon sensed would be ascribed to Luke's open dislike and mistrust of Sith in general, which he had never made any attempt to mitigate.

"Then we are in agreement. I've already contacted Lando; he will follow as soon as he can. Let's use the next day to double-check everything, and make sure every vessel has proper supplies. Then we depart in twenty-four standard hours."

Taalon held up a long index finger in a chiding motion. "One moment," he said. "It might be wise to leave a small group behind—say, three or four frigates—to wait for your friend. In case any problems arise."

Luke did not like the idea of leaving Sith vessels, even one or two, behind on Klatooine. He liked his enemies in front of him, where he could see them. But communication would be impossible in the Maw. What if there was a problem? What if Cilghal learned anything important? Luke was not about to have her contact the Sith, but she could leave an encrypted message for him with Klatooine security and the Sith ship could deliver it if necessary.

"I hate to admit that a Sith has a good point, but you do," he said at last.

Taalon's very fake smile widened. "Sith always have good points, Master Skywalker. We consider *all* the options."

"One vessel."

"Four."

"Only one is needed to carry messages of delays or difficulties."

"One vessel might have technical problems."

"Two then. I want the rest with us in case *we* run into any problems."

Taalon sighed. "Very well. Two. I shall select which ones and give them their orders. We will be prepared to depart in twenty-four . . . no, twenty-three hours and forty-seven minutes." He gave Luke a smirk.

For the briefest of moments, Luke envied Han's lack of calm, measured response in a situation like this. Captain Solo would cheerfully have punched Taalon in his perfect, purple nose, and Luke had to admit, he wouldn't have tried very hard to stop his old friend.

Taalon leaned back in his chair, a smile spreading across his face. He went over the logistics in his mind, then sent out three communiqués.

He received a response immediately to the first one. His second in command, Leeha Faal, appeared in front of him within seconds of receiving his request to do so.

She saluted and stood at attention. "Yes, sir?"

"You have served me well," he said, "and now, I need you to serve in another capacity. Congratulations, Faal—I'm giving you your first command."

Her eyes widened and he tasted her pleasure in the Force. "Thank you, sir. May I ask which vessel?"

"The *Winged Dagger*," he said. "I've informed Captain Syndor of his new position as your second in command."

A slow, sly smile spread across her pretty lavender face. "I see," she said. "I will collect my belongings and immediately transfer to the *Winged Dagger* to take command. What is your first assignment?"

"One which you yourself brought to my attention," Taalon said, and told her.

Ben and Luke went through the prelaunch systems check. Luke seemed completely at ease, even upbeat at the thought of finally heading out toward the Maw. Ben, however, was still upset by what he had learned.

He'd pretended that he'd expected such betrayal and manipulation from her, and in a way, he had. But that didn't lessen the sting when it had actually happened. Worse, he couldn't even confront Vestara about it. Luke had advised against tipping their hand. "If she doesn't know we can translate her conversations," Luke had said, "then she won't try to hide them. Nor will she inform any of the other Sith that we have a way to understand them. This means that we have a chance to learn more—and Ben, we have to learn as much about them as we can in the time we spend with them. You *know* that."

Ben did know that. It didn't make anything any easier.

He sensed her standing at the entrance to the cockpit. "Vestara, you shouldn't be in here."

"Why not?" she said. "I've already piloted a ship almost exactly like this. I won't learn anything new and highly secret."

Luke glanced over his shoulder at her, then returned his attention to the checklist.

"Okay, true enough. What do you want?"

"I wanted to ask you to tell me about your sick bay."

Ben turned to glare at her. "Why?"

She folded her arms across her chest and gave him an arch look that somehow reminded him of Jaina. "Two reasons. If anything happened to the two of you, I'd be the only chance you have of getting patched up."

"Like you wouldn't light a bonfire and dance a jig if we got injured."

A bright, sharp flicker in the Force—the remark had hurt her. She covered it quickly. "You might still be of use to us. Or maybe we'd just want to keep you alive so we could torture you." Yeah, she was angry all right. Despite himself, Ben felt bad.

"I'm saying this a lot to Sith today, but you do have a point, Vestara," Luke said. "But surely you already know the basics of a sick bay. You yourself said it— you're familiar with SoroSuubs."

"Master Skywalker, you shouldn't play ignorant. It's not becoming. You know as well as I do that the *Jade Shadow* is no ordinary vessel. I'm sure there are quite a few things in that sick bay that aren't standard equipment for this class of ship. Also, in case you've forgotten, you have a crazy man held prisoner in there. I need to know how to best subdue him in case something happens. Which, by the way, would necessitate that you stop locking me in my room when you leave the vessel."

Ben really wished his dad had opted to take someone else hostage back at Sinkhole Station.

"Dad?"

Luke sighed and rose. "Back in a moment. This won't take long."

Ben rubbed his eyes with the heel of his hand, then stretched. He wished Vestara wasn't so . . . well . . . He wished she was uglier, or stupid, or unpleasant. But she wasn't any of those things. He knew she was a Sith, knew that she was trying to manipulate him—but blast it, he also knew that on some level, she cared. She was trying to drag him over to the dark side, but what if he could bring her to the light side? There was good in her. He'd felt it in the Force. She wasn't like Jacen, not yet— she was much more like Tahiri. True, she'd been born Sith and raised with a whole planet full of them. But maybe she was Sith because that's all she knew. Maybe if she was shown another path, she'd take it.

After all, even in her conversation with Gavar Khai, she'd admitted that she liked him. A question formed in his mind. His father returned a few minutes later. Vestara was not with him.

"Dad?"

"Yes?"

"Do you think Gavar Khai would kill his own daughter if she disappointed him?"

Luke considered the question. "I think he cares for her very much. But he is very demanding. Yes, I do think that if she disappointed him and he found out about it, he'd kill her."

Ben had his answer. And it was not the answer to the question he'd just asked his dad.

It was good to be Sith, to be in command of your own vessel, and to be charged with so pleasant a task, mused Leeha Faal. She leaned back in the command chair, enjoying the sensation. *Her* chair, *her* ship. She had been wise to ally with Sarasu Taalon a few years ago. She had observed how his star was rising among the Circle, and had contrived to be assigned to the *Black Wave*. "Contrived" and "assigned," of course, meant that she had arranged for the assassination of her current competition and two other possible threats. Their bodies had never been found. It would seem that although they had been beaten back from the main cities of Kesh, the huge, aggressive rukaros were still eager to feed and continue their species.

Her insight had proven correct. Now she was here, in orbit around this backwater planet, assigned to perform a task that would specifically please the leader of this whole expedition. And once that was out of the way, she would rejoin the fleet and be part of the ultimate Sith victory. With the power Taalon would command and the Skywalkers eliminated, there was no telling how far she could—

"Incoming message, Captain," said Syndor. She smiled prettily at him. He had once been captain of this vessel and was dealing surprisingly well with his demotion to second in command. Which, of course, meant he had some sort of plot up his sleeve. She'd have to be careful. But then again, she was Sith, and there was a joke among the Sith that they were always born faceup to protect their backs. "From Commander Sarasu Taalon."

It was only the commander's voice, but that was enough. "The flotilla is ready to depart for the Maw, Captain Faal," came Taalon's smooth voice. "Join us when you are able."

"Of course, sir," Leeha replied. "That will be soon, I hope."

"As do we all," Taalon said. "I would hate for you and your crew to miss all the fun. Remember your duties, Captain."

"I ever do, sir," said Leeha.

*    *    *

Sarasu Taalon had told Luke Skywalker that he had left two vessels behind to wait for the *Rockhound*. That was not entirely true, although neither could it be said that it was entirely false. The vessels would be well into the Maw by the time Lando Calrissian arrived with his asteroid tug, but Lando would be able to catch up with them quickly enough.

It simply worked better for the Sith if they were not here when the *Rockhound* arrived.

So it was that less than a day later, when Leeha Faal received notification that the *Rockhound* would be there within twelve hours, she sent back a polite and vague response, and issued the orders to the captain of the second ship, the *Starstalker*.

Captain Vyn Holpur had leapt at the opportunity. An older man with pale green eyes and black hair elegantly going to gray, he was a Saber who had once been well on his way to becoming a Lord. No one knew for sure what had happened, but there had been some sort of scandal, and then there was no more talk of promotions. Still, Taalon had regarded him well enough to bring him along. Successful completion of this task would go a long way to restoring Holpur's favor.

The order had come, from Taalon to Faal to Holpur, and he obeyed.

The *Starstalker*'s light freighter, piloted by Holpur himself, soared above the sand, zipping speedily and smoothly toward its destination, due west of Treema. The object of their desire appeared in the distance, the bright sunlight bouncing harshly off it, and everyone had to squint and remember to not look directly at the Fountain of the Hutt Ancients.

Holpur had been sent all documentation of the ancient natural formation. He read disinterestedly about the wintrium that formed the beautiful, glassine "sculpture," how long it had been in existence, how sacred it was to the Klatooinians, what a vital role it had in the making of the Treaty of Vontor. He knew that his ship would not be permitted within a kilometer radius of the Fountain because all modern technology was forbidden.

He did not particularly care about any of it. He did, however, care very much about pleasing Sarasu Taalon and recovering his lost status. And so it was that he was completely calm when the first warnings came.

"Fountain Security to unknown vessel. You are approaching within five kilometers of the Fountain. Please alter your course."

Holpur tucked his robes about him more comfortably as he sat in his chair. He extended his senses in the Force, attentive to his crew's emotions. Some of them were a little uneasy. Not, he suspected, out of any mere qualms, but about possibly being caught and punished. Others were excited, eager, enjoying even this little adventure after waiting and doing nothing for so long. Still others were neutral, not caring one way or the other. Holpur made note of all of it. When this was done, he would reward those who had had faith in him and the mission, and mete out punishment to those who did not.

"Unknown vessel, you are rapidly approaching the forbidden radius of one kilometer. Alter your course immediately or we will open fire!"

Holpur leaned forward and thumbed the intercom. "As we discussed," he said. "We'll have to be fast. Anyul, Marjaak, are you ready?"

"Copy, sir." Anyul, twenty-four, blond and lithe, and Marjaak, a white-haired Keshiri male, were standing ready to leap out of the ship as soon as the hatch opened and execute their task quickly. He'd chosen them carefully. Both were Sabers, given that high honor at comparatively young ages. Both were physically fit, swift, and disciplined. They were prepared.

Now, finally, Holpur's heart sped up. It was a risky maneuver, although Taalon had made it sound like child's play. The very law that they were violating was what would protect them long enough for them to succeed.

The Klatooinians opened fire from several small blaster cannons. Holpur frowned slightly as the ship took a blow and rocked. It could withstand much more than this, but he had hoped that even a minor attack would be avoided. He wanted to bring the ship whole into the Maw, to find Abeloth, glory, and his restored name.

And then suddenly the firing stopped. Holpur actually laughed, a short bark.

They had entered the one-kilometer forbidden zone.

The *Starstalker* opened its hatch. A small, elegant, if older, skiff darted out as the *Starstalker* moved out of range of the land-based blasters.

The Fountain of the Hutt Ancients loomed ahead, bright and beautiful and gleaming. Anything but the most rudimentary technology anywhere in this zone was a blatant violation of both law and tradition, and was not only illegal, it was blasphemy. But the Klatooinians would never willingly violate the sacred law themselves, and so the best they could do would be to come after them with ancient weapons.

The skiff settled down, stirring up sand. Even before it had landed, the hatch had opened and Anyul and Marjaak used the Force to leap out gracefully close to the Fountain. They, like the three Sith behind them cradling blaster rifles, were in full armorweave. They had known they would not need much more.

The pair raced up to the Fountain. Swiftly, calculatedly, Anyul drew her lightsaber and began shaving off samples from a large "wave" of wintrium. Marjaak moved farther down and tried to cut off a thinner, dagger-shaped portion. The wintrium was startlingly strong. Even their lingnan crystal-powered lightsabers were having difficulty cutting through the deceptively delicate-looking material.

The three Sith behind them took up defensive positions, prepared to defend Marjaak and Anyul with their lives if need be.

That need would not come, and when they saw what they were up against, they began to laugh.

"You're joking," said Turg, a red-haired man in his early forties. "*This* is the defense for a twenty-five-thousand-year-old treaty?"

His companions Vran and Kaara, a brother and sister pair with black hair and blue eyes, were laughing so hard they couldn't reply, although they were able to fire quite well.

Outside the packed dirt wall that encircled the Fountain, as they had just witnessed, the guards had blasters and proper armor. But the Klatooinian guards who rushed in, crying, "Blasphemers! You will pay!" wore nothing but simple plate armor and carried spears, arrows, swords, and nets. They looked like actors in a drama, enacting some long-ago battle.

It was ease itself to mow them down, but more came—and from all sides. Turg's laughter died in his throat when, from behind him, a net dropped over him and pulled tight. His companions swore and rushed to cut him free. Kaara, the dark-haired woman, grunted when something hard struck her, only to gasp in surprise when her armorweave began to hiss and smoke as acid started eating away at first the armor, then her skin.

Her brother Vran activated his lightsaber and freed Turg with a single precise, perfect slice of the red blade. In the same motion he whirled, bringing the lightsaber around to slay Kaara's attacker. The Sith woman dropped to the sand, biting her lip to stay silent as the unbearable pain continued. Unable to help her, her brother concentrated on exacting revenge, cursing and letting his fury and hatred augment his deadly speed.

Marjaak glanced over his shoulder at the commotion. "Faster," was all the Keshiri Saber said to his colleague. Anyul nodded, clenching her teeth as her muscles knotted, adding her strength and that of the Force to push the lightsaber through the crystal.

Turg, the redhead, took the offensive, rushing at the approaching Klatooinians. One of them aimed a spear right at him, the other three had swords raised. Casually, the Sith sliced the weapon in two, and did the same to its wielder and the three others who charged, sending three swords—each still with part of an arm attached to them—flying.

Arrows sang as they were released. Turg sensed them and turned casually, deflecting them even more easily than he would bat back blaster fire. They had gotten a lucky blow in with Kaara and the acid, because that had been an unexpected weapon. With the element of surprise gone, Turg and Vran began accumulating bodies. Quietly, as befitted a Sith Saber, Kaara died.

The two Sith assigned to take samples of the wintrium were sweating with effort. "This stuff is almost impossible to cut," muttered Marjaak.

Anyul shot him an angry glance. "Tell me something I don't know, fool," she spat, and continued. The impossibly hard substance was finally starting to yield.

Almost . . . there . . .

# Chapter Eighteen

"Sir," said the communications officer to Holpur, "the Elders are attempting to contact us, telling us to stand down and surrender ourselves for punishment for blasphemy."

Holpur chuckled. "So amusing," he said.

There was what amounted to a palace close to the Fountain, on the far west side. This was where the Elders, the governing body of Klatooine, dwelt. Holpur knew they arose every morning and looked east, to the sun's first rays striking off the Fountain. They were no doubt seeing a quite different view now.

He called up an image of the Elder's palace on the small screen by his chair and regarded it thoughtfully. It had no defenses. Anyone could simply march right up and bang on the entrance. What were these people thinking? He could, with the *Starstalker*'s weapons alone, blast it to rubble. He toyed with the idea, but he was too amused at the thought of these beings, like ants he was about to step on, yapping at him to cease and desist.

"Patch it through," he said.

"Copy, sir."

". . . repeat, stand down! You are in violation of sacred space! We will not tolerate this!"

"Sir," said his communications officer, "they're sending out a distress signal. They're trying to contact the Hutts to come protect them."

"Let them," said Holpur. "I know what the situation is. The Hutts have not cared much for this planet since the war with the beings known as the Yuuzhan Vong. It will be days, or at the very least, hours, before the Hutts deign to send a response unit, and we shall be long gone."

INSIDE THE ELDERS' PALACE

"Repeat, stand down!"

Darima Kedari paced back and forth. The emergency session of the Elder Governors was in chaos. They were shouting at one another, and finally Darima, the Chancellor, abandoned any effort at civility to his fellow Elders.

"Silence!" he bellowed, shaking his staff of office at them. "I cannot hear myself think!"

The moment they had been notified of the blasphemy, they had of course contacted their defenses in Treema. And they were on their way—such as they were. There were approximately five ships of any size that were in sufficiently good flying order that they would be of any use at all. The Governors could hire mercenaries among those visiting Treema, of course, but that took time, and the Fountain was being violated *now*. The Hutts had not left them much with which to defend themselves, assuring the Klatooinians that if the need arose, the Hutts would, per the treaty, come to protect them. Where were they now? An urgent signal had been sent, with the plea that would surely grab the attention of their masters:

*The Fountain is being violated. Come at once.*

All would now be thrown into chaos.

Anger and rage tore at his heart. This precious, exquisite thing, this symbol of beauty and strength and timelessness—blood was being spilt on it, strangers who had no love or understanding of it had come and simply taken what they wanted. How dare they!

"How did we not foresee this?" he cried, clenching his fists as he beheld the sacrilege.

"We never dreamed anyone would harm it," said the frail, elderly female Mashu Tek Barik. Tears stood in her eyes. "It is forbidden to no one—we ask no payment to see it, even to touch it. We could not conceive of . . . this."

She waved a bony hand in the direction of the Fountain.

"Where are the ships?" demanded someone else. "Where are the ships to defend the Fountain?"

"It is too late," said Mashu softly. "It is done. It is done."

And suddenly, the realization broke over Darima with an intensity so strong he broke out in a sweat and had to grasp the back of his chair. She was right. It was done.

"The Hutts will come" came another voice. Blood was thundering in Darima's ears so he could not even tell who was speaking. "They will destroy these blasphemers. They will exact revenge for what they have done. They will pay. They will pay!"

Others murmured hopeful agreement, but Darima glanced over at Mashu. She was rocking back and forth slightly, staring at the light freighter that now opened to let the skiff return. Return with the blasphemers, with the wintrium they had stolen.

And he thought that Mashu was right.


ABOARD THE ROCKHOUND

"What do you mean, the rest have gone?"

Lando Calrissian was seated in a mobile levchair at

the pilot's station of the antique vessel, the *Rockhound*. He was glaring at one of the drop-down display screens that currently showed the head and shoulders of the purple Sith woman who had introduced herself as Captain Leeha Faal.

She smiled. It was not a pleasant smile, but it did not detract from her attractiveness. Sith.

"Your Master Skywalker was most insistent," she said. "He felt that it would be better to have the fleet assembled and ready to proceed closer to the Maw itself. He left the *Winged Dagger* and the *Starstalker* behind in his stead. We are allies, Captain Calrissian."

Allies, right. Sith flying around in frigates. "Of course, Luke told me he was working with you." He was proud of himself. His smooth voice had lost none of its charm, even when he uttered words that unsettled—even disgusted—him. He gave her one of *his* best smiles, lifted his arms, and winked. "Well, here I am. Are you ready, Captain Faal?"

"We shall be momentarily," she said, her voice soothing and easy on the ears. "The *Starstalker* should be here shortly. We will conduct our preflight check, and then we shall hasten to join our comrades outside the Maw."

"That sounds fine," Lando said. "Let me know when you're good to go. Calrissian out."

He clicked an old-fashioned, shiny button. Faal's pretty face was replaced by a blank screen. His smile disappeared as if it were a glow rod he had switched off.

Though he was the only living being on the ship, Lando was not alone. There was a full crew complement; it was simply one composed entirely of droids. He turned in the levchair to regard the one with whom he had the most interaction, the bridge droid Cybot Galactica Model RN8.

"Bust my rear getting you droids and this ship functional, and Luke hightails it out of here without me.

Nice of him to leave such an attractive welcoming committee though."

Ornate straightened and turned her head globe to regard him with her three blue photoreceptors. The transparent globe was alive with the sparkles of her processing unit, and her bronze body casing was decorated with comets and stars. She was extremely old, functioning well, and as lovely as any piece of art. "I am not programmed to evaluate human standards of attractiveness," Ornate said in a deep, purring voice.

"*I* am," Lando said cheerily. Ornate merely turned her globe head back to the navigation console. Lando grinned a little and swung the chair back around just in time to see a white flash indicating someone dropping out of hyperdrive.

Four vessels suddenly appeared, bristling with weapons, their forms bulky and threatening. Lando's gut twisted, his humor gone.

"Oh great," he muttered. "Just what we needed. Hutts." He waited, sweat gathering at his hairline, to see if he would be hailed, but the Hutts were apparently here on other business. After less than a minute, they dived as one for the atmosphere. Lando breathed out a sign of relief that lasted about two seconds.

"Faal to *Rockhound*!" The pretty voice was urgent.

"*Rockhound* here, go ahead, Captain Faal."

"We are under attack! Repeat, under attack! Request aid immediately!"

"What's going on? Ornate, ready the *Stoneskipper*!" The droid inclined her sparkling globe and began the process for readying the *Rockhound*'s small skiff. "Who's attacking you?"

"The Hutts! They are opening fire!"

Oh, this was great. Just great.

"Captain Calrissian, I assure you, it's a huge misunderstanding!" Faal continued. The strain of trying to speak calmly made her pleasant voice less so. "But as our ally, I request that you aid us!"

"I can't take this baby down. Best I can do would be a skiff."

The four Hutt ships, obviously reinforcements to whatever atmospheric vessels were already engaged, were now heading down toward the surface. "Then perhaps you could be of use elsewhere. Do you know beings on this world?"

He did, several, and lots of them would not be particularly happy to see him. Especially if his new "allies" had riled the Hutts. "Uh," he said, "a few."

"They will destroy the *Starstalker* and all aboard if they do not call off their attack," Faal was saying. "If you could—"

Six more Hutt vessels exited hyperspace, splitting up gracefully to encircle the *Winged Dagger*. Fortunately, for the moment, they seemed unaware that Lando had anything to do with the Sith vessel and whatever was going on planetside. Lando was debating the wisdom of simply powering up the *Rockhound* and heading right for the Maw, leaving these two Sith ships to their own devices. After all, he was there to help Luke, not Luke's buddies. But then again, one didn't really want to anger a Sith, did one?

Another ship arrived. "For crying out loud, what is this, a party?" Lando yelped to Ornate. "How many Hutt ships do you need to take down—"

He broke off in midsentence when he saw what kind of vessel it was. Or rather, didn't quite see. It was like a phantom, the slightest distortion against the darkness and starlight. But Lando had a lot of experience seeing things others might miss.

It was a StealthX, and that meant Jedi.

"Hail it," he told Ornate. "Now." The droid complied. Lando knew that the vessels had to maintain silence in order to be undetected, and wasn't sure if the pilot of this particular ship would respond. However, a familiar voice crackled over the antique communications system. It was faint—probably a personal comlink rather than the ship's.

"Hey, Uncle Lando. What are you doing here?"

Lando blinked. "Jaina? I might ask the same question of you."

"I asked first." Lando started to reply that this was a poor time for jokes, but there was a guardedness in her voice that made him pause. She was serious.

"I'm here to help Luke, except he's apparently gone off without me and, uh . . . left a couple of buddies behind." He wondered if Jaina knew about the "buddies." "Jaina, listen, something's happening down there. And Luke's . . . colleagues—"

"I know about them." There was annoyance and anger in her voice.

"Oh, okay then. Well, they're wrapped up in it and asking for my help."

Jaina muttered something under her breath. "Let's go find out what's going on, then. Permission to dock?"

"Of course. But you didn't tell me why you were here."

"Nope. Sure didn't. You coming with me, or not?"

"All right, keep your flight suit on," Lando grumbled. "You don't want to take that baby down there. Bring it into the hangar and we'll go down together in the skiff."

It was, of course, not that simple. While he waited for Jaina, Lando attempted to hail the planet, and for several long, strained minutes, there was no response. Finally, a female Klatooinian appeared on one of the drop-down screens. She looked wary and her voice was brusque.

"This is Abara Mun. Klatooine is currently in an

emergency state and a full lockdown. No one will be granted permission to arrive or depart until further notice." She reached forward to end the transmission.

"Wait!" yelped Lando. "I know Darima Kedari!"

Mun paused in midmotion and eyed him skeptically. The hatchway at the back slid open with a grinding sound. Lando heard Jaina's boots on the old durasteel deck as she came up behind him. "We go way back. Ask him."

A pause. "I suppose that's possible," Mun said finally. "I will contact him and inquire."

"You do that." Her face disappeared, replaced by the insignia of the Klatooinian flag. Lando blew out a breath, then turned and gave Jaina a quick hug. "Hey there, little lady. So come on, you can tell Uncle Lando. You came here to help Luke, didn't you?"

She embraced him, then pulled back and nodded. She looked tired and was more subdued than he had seen her in a long time.

"I was supposed to be one of many," she said. "The Jedi have a whole fleet of StealthXs assembled. Luke and Ben had to handle this completely alone. Sith, for crying out loud, Lando. A whole *tribe* of them. So we were going to come and give him the means to end this forced alliance."

"So why is it just you? Not that you aren't a formidable foe," he added quickly.

"Because Daala has begun a siege on the Temple, and we can't launch without being shot down before we get three meters."

"A what?"

She rubbed her eyes. "It's long, it's ugly, and it's irrelevant right now. We have to get to Luke."

"He's in the Maw right now. He left a very lovely and alarmingly pleasant woman behind to wait for me, but apparently there's been some sort of trouble. I'm not sure if Luke wants me to help out or ditch them."

"Sir," said Ornate in her smooth, silky voice, "Chancellor Darima Kedari wishes to speak to you."

Lando smirked, just a little. "See?" he said to Jaina. Jaina, meanwhile, had done a double take at the droid's voice.

"She's some conversationalist," Jaina said dryly.

"About that . . . I'll tell you later," Lando said, looking a bit nonplussed. "Ornate, put him through."

An elderly male appeared on the screen. He wore stiff robes that were made of some sort of fabric that shone in the light. A collar wound around his neck, and a high, flat hat covered his head and ears. Lando gave one of his famous charming grins. "Darima! How you doing?"

"In desperate straits if I am to converse with you," replied the Chancellor in a querulous voice, "but it seems I must do so."

"Er, right," said Lando. He recovered quickly. "May I introduce Jedi Jaina Solo. Jaina, this is Chancellor Darima Kedari, the leader of the Klatooinian Elder Governors. We go way back."

Jaina smiled and inclined her head. "Sir," she said.

Dark eyes set back in a face surrounded by heavy wrinkles widened slightly. "Jaina Solo. Your reputation precedes you as well. First Master Skywalker, now you. Two of you, no less." He seemed to be considering something. "A question for you both, then, since I believe the Ancestors have sent you to us at this crucial juncture. Are you formally or informally connected with the captains or any crew member of the *Starstalker* or the *Winged Dagger*?"

Lando scratched his head and considered his answer very carefully. "I came here at the request of Luke Skywalker," he said. "I know that Luke was cooperating with them, but I've never met these people before in my life."

"And I came here to see Luke, but he wasn't expecting me." Jaina didn't volunteer anything more.

"We are . . . in a crisis," Darima admitted. His jowls shook slightly. "The crew of the *Starstalker* has allegedly violated the no-technology zone of the Fountain. It appears they even had the audacity to take samples of the wintrium."

Lando's jaw dropped. "What?" No wonder he had seen a bunch of Hutt ships. This was bad. Very bad.

"I know you know what this means, Lando," Darima said grimly. "Now you understand why we are forbidding anyone to come to Klatooine. It is all we can do to contain the riots."

"No kidding. I'm surprised you can even do that."

"Wait, what?" asked Jaina, looking from one to the other. "What happened? Lando, you look . . . serious. That alarms me."

"There's a natural formation called the Fountain of the Hutt Ancients," Lando said, his voice somber. "It's highly sacred to the Klatooinians. No one is allowed to take anything but the most primitive technology within a kilometer radius."

Jaina looked confused. "I don't mean to be rude, but . . . you generally aren't that concerned about something like this." She eyed the Chancellor. "No offense, sir."

"There is more than our racial pride or religious sacrilege here, Jedi Solo. The protection of the Fountain was the key to the drawing of the Treaty of Vontor twenty-five thousand years ago," Darima said. "The Hutts swore to protect it. In return, our people and the Nikto swore eternal servitude. The Hutts did not protect the Fountain. If they do not act appropriately—"

Now it was Jaina's turn to gape. "If they don't act appropriately, the deal's off, and the Hutts lose slaves they've had for twenty-five millennia. Okay. I think I see why everyone's so upset." She looked as stunned as Lando felt.

"The Treaty states that if there is ever a question of violation, at least two, preferably more, offworlders must be present to render judgment, as both the Hutts and the Klatooinians have decided interests in the outcome."

"Oh, come on Darima, surely there's gotta be someone else."

The Chancellor looked at him levelly. "This is Hutt territory, Lando. People who have business with them come here. There are some who come to see the Fountain, but they are few. You two both arrive the very day of the sacrilege. And although I cannot believe I am saying this, I . . . trust you to be fair in hearing both sides. And I can say the same of a Jedi, even one I have not met."

Jaina and Lando exchanged glances. "Give us a moment," he said.

"Of course." Ornate obligingly muted the sound.

"I don't want any part of this," Lando said. "I say we leave them and get to Luke."

"I'd say the same thing except for the fact that the liberty of an entire race of people rests on it," Jaina said. "Your friend is right. This isn't a place known for attracting decent and fair-minded beings. Anyone else they get is going to know what side his bread is buttered on. The Hutts'll win for sure."

"And can you be impartial?" Lando challenged. "Suppose the evidence suggests that the Hutts *did* do everything they could. Could you stand there and tell the Klatooinians they're stuck being slaves?"

He expected her to snap at him. Instead, she looked down, her gaze falling quickly on her left hand. It was then that he noticed it was bereft of her engagement ring. And suddenly he understood why she had been so subdued.

"I've made a lot of hard decisions recently based on what I thought was right, Lando. Decisions that weren't what I wanted," she said quietly. "I'm the Sword of the Jedi. I stand, supposedly, for justice. If the Hutts really did keep their end of the bargain, then my answer is yes. I can look the Elders in the eye and say that."

"I really don't want to do this."

"Then don't. Take the *Rockhound* and join Luke in the Maw. Hopefully, I will be there soon. I'll be one of their offworlders, and they can find someone else. Really, it's okay." And he could tell by looking at her that it was. She was making the decision for herself, and letting him make the right one for him.

"You are far too much like your mother sometimes, you know that?" he muttered. "You damn diplomats." He heaved a sigh and waved at Ornate, who unmuted the hologram.

"All right, Darima. You got yourselves two off-worlders."

# Chapter Nineteen

As they flew over the planet's surface in the small skiff, Lando and Jaina could see that Mun and Chancellor Kedari had not exaggerated. If anything, they had downplayed the violence. Vessels, both on the ground and in the air, surrounded the capital city. Tiny figures of armed guards milled around, and Jaina shuddered involuntarily.

Lando caught the gesture. "You okay?"

"It's exactly like what the Mandos are doing to the Temple right now. And it was by sheer dumb luck that I wasn't trapped there as well. I'd left less than a half hour beforehand."

"Heh. Maybe ol' Darima was right. Maybe we have been sent by the Ancestors."

"I wish the Ancestors would send someone to kick Daala's . . ." Jaina sighed and shifted in the passenger seat.

"You're just antsy because you're not piloting."

"That, too. I can't believe we're going to be listening to Hutts and Sith, and ending up actually siding with one."

"Well, let me put it this way—I *have* known some Hutts who were decent beings. But we've gotta do our best to be impartial."

"We could blast both of them. That'd be nice and evenhanded," Jaina said, giving him a little smile.

"Don't tempt me. We're almost to the Fountain, and the palace is right next to it. You should take a look. It's quite the beautiful object."

Jaina had averted her eyes after seeing Treema, but now did as Lando suggested. And her eyes widened.

"Uh, Lando? *You* should take a look."

A colorful oath escaped him as he did so. Below them was the Fountain of the Ancients, or the Hutt Ancients, depending on who one talked to. And Jaina had to admit, it was beautiful. What was not beautiful was the throng that had clustered around it. They were clamoring to get in, the Klatooinians, to be close to the sacred natural phenomenon that had been so much a part of their culture and history at this time of crisis. Except there were too many, shoving, pushing, an enormous crowd of beings surging forward.

"There must be thousands of them," Jaina said, correcting herself almost immediately. "*Tens* of thousands."

"Hundreds of thousands in a few hours," Lando said. "Klatooine may have a planetwide lockdown, and I bet that includes major communications channels, but beings have a way of finding things out."

They were silent as they were vectored in to a large landing area of the palace. Chancellor Kedari was there, along with several attendants. In person, Jaina found him much less imposing. He was shorter than she had expected, he leaned heavily on a beautifully crafted staff, and his body language was that of someone who was very close to being beaten down. She supposed she couldn't blame him. She couldn't imagine what sacrilege done to something that had been part of her very identity—that of everyone on this world—would have done to her. She was having a difficult enough time handling a broken engagement.

"You are very welcome here, both of you," Darima said. "Ordinarily I would extend more ceremony to this meeting, but I think you have seen by now that time is of the essence. We must restore order as soon as possible, and to that end, we must have a decision. Please—come with me."

They followed him into a utilitarian lift whose simple practicality left Jaina unprepared for the large, lavish room it opened onto. Pillars stretched before her, huge, ornate things that supported a ceiling that had been painted dark blue. Cleverly concealed optics winked and glittered, giving the illusion of a panorama of stars. It was faint now, during daylight hours, but Jaina knew that come nightfall it would be beautiful. Circular windows, running the length of the massive chamber, let in slanting light. Sconces evenly spaced along the stone wall would provide light during the evening. The far wall was completely comprised of transparisteel, and opened onto what would normally be the breathtakingly beautiful sight of the Fountain. Now, of course, the sight was disturbing. Jaina wished they'd find a way to shut out the view, but there were no drapes or shutters.

Chairs clearly designed for the comfort of humanoids ran the length of the room, but the center was left open.

"We have not had a verdict rendered here in centuries," Darima was saying as they stepped into the room. "Now, this is where we host theatrical performances or conduct lectures." His voice was wistful. He waved a gnarled hand and led them to the area of the chamber directly opposite the Fountain. Three chairs were arranged on a marble dais. More chairs set to the side.

"Jedi Solo, you and Captain Calrissian will join me

here. The rest of the Governing Elders will sit near us, so they may watch the proceedings. The two parties will be entering shortly."

Jaina sat down in the chair. While it was obviously designed for a larger frame than hers, it was still as comfortable as she had anticipated. Her legs dangled, but she was used to that. Besides, she hoped she wouldn't be sitting here long.

"So—what do we need to do?" she asked Darima.

"Listen," said Darima simply. "You know what is at stake here. You know what the Fountain means to us. You know what the Treaty of Vontor stipulates. Listen to all who speak. You have certain abilities, as a Jedi, to determine guilt or innocence. You, Lando, are a good judge of beings. You've had to learn how to be given your . . . background."

"Hey," Lando said, bridling a little, "it used to be your background, too, you know."

Darima chuckled slightly. "No longer," he said. "But the two of you must judge fairly, if the Ancestors are to be pleased with the outcome."

"We'll do our best," Jaina said simply.

She could sense other presences approaching now. One group felt similar to Darima. Concerned, angry, heartbroken, but resolute and calm at their centers. This had to be the rest of the Elders. A wide set of doors toward the end of the hall slid open, and they entered, moving slowly but with dignity down the long center of the room toward their seats. She followed Lando's example and rose, regarding them. One of them, a female, seemed to be considerably older than the rest, and met Jaina's gaze with a deep, searching one of her own before settling down into her chair.

She and Lando imitated her. Beside her, Darima leaned forward slightly in his chair, gripping his staff tightly, but otherwise displaying no agitation. Jaina could sense them now, these beings upon whom she was about to pass judgment. Dark side energy was wrapped about them like a shimmersilk cloak. Jaina could almost smell it as something physical, a scent that was almost pleasant, but too cloying to be; a rottenness that gave away the true nature of its power. She swallowed hard, remembering her last fight with Jacen. Knowing that with his death, that awful scent that was not a scent had ceased to permeate his soul. He had been dark, and powerful, but there was a newness to his familiarity with the dark side. The beings—some human, some not—who were just on the other side of the door had been steeped in it. This was an old, old stain.

There were only two of them. One was female, stunningly attractive with almost impossibly perfect features and lovely purple skin. She moved with a sinuous grace, her gaze darting back and forth among the three who awaited her arrival. She wore black robes, but carried no weapon. No weapon, of course, other than her deep bond with the dark side of the Force. Her hair was black and caught the light, moving silkily as she walked. Jaina glanced surreptitiously at Lando. He didn't quite gape or drool, but she gave him a Force nudge nonetheless. A good solid one. He started, ever so slightly, and shot her a look.

The other Sith emanated the same dark miasma. He was an older human, very distinguished looking, with pale green eyes. He, too, wore traditional Sith robes, and walked about half a meter behind the female. Both drew up to the podium and bowed deeply, then stepped to the left and stood at attention, hands clasped behind their backs.

The door opened again. Jaina heard the soft humming sound of a repulsorsled. It bore a particularly corpulent and unattractive representative of the Hutt species, and seemed to be straining to do so. The Hutt's sled moved forward to the dais. He looked around, his eyes almost buried in folds of dark blue, glistening flesh, then waved one of his stubby arms in what was clearly intended to be a gesture of respect and ended up merely looking like flailing. He strained for the controls, then moved the hoversled to the right of the podium, opposite the two Sith. Darima got to his feet, holding firmly to his staff.

"Captain Leeha Faal, of the *Winged Dagger*," he said, addressing the woman, and then, "Captain Vyn Holpur, of the *Starstalker*. Captain Holpur, you have several charges levied against you. You have been accused of violating the no-technology zone of the Fountain of the Hutt Ancients, of killing several guards who attempted to defend it, and most disturbingly of all, of physically damaging the Fountain itself." His voice broke on the last charge. "Captain Faal, it is our understanding that Captain Holpur answers to you, and therefore you are here as well. The same charges apply to you, as Holpur is under your command."

Both Sith nodded. "We understand," said Faal.

Darima turned toward the Hutt. "Tooga Jalliissi Gral, you are in charge of the defense of this world, including that of the sacred Fountain. Considering all that hinges upon protection of the Fountain, one might have thought that it would have been a top priority for you. Yet you have failed to protect it from those who would desecrate it."

Tooga, to his credit, seemed to be taking the proceedings very seriously. *As well he should,* Jaina thought. He rumbled, "These are grave charges, Chancellor, and I hope that I will be able to prove the Hutts innocent of dereliction of our duty."

Darima nodded, and gestured to one of the other Elders. He moved forward. "Six standard hours ago, the guards of the Fountain of the Hutt Ancients reported a vessel approaching . . ."

Jaina listened with horrified fascination as the Elder gave the Klatooinian version of the events. A recording of the warning the guards issued was played, but it offered very little insight. When Lando inquired and asked if there were any recordings of the actual violation, he was told that it was considered blasphemous to even direct such technology upon the Fountain within the one-kilometer zone.

Jaina sighed.

Darima rose when the Elder was finished, and regarded the two Sith captains. "Captain Faal, Captain Holpur, you may speak."

"Thank you," said Faal. She moved forward to stand directly in front of Jaina and Lando. Knowing it was fruitless but having to try anyway, Jaina reached out in the Force to get a sense of the woman. There was nothing; she was, of course, adept at hiding her presence in the Force.

"There are certain facts in this case that I would like our two . . . judges, I suppose? . . . to be aware of," Faal continued. Jaina couldn't help but notice that Holpur stayed where he was. He, too, was blocking his presence in the Force. Jaina thought she could get more information from a potted plant.

"The first is that our vessels have been here for several days. We have violated none of your rules, and indeed, we have been useful in actively preventing an incident of sacrilege. It was one of our apprentices, Vestara Khai, who helped to stop one Dyon Stad from driving his hoverbike directly into the forbidden zone around the Fountain."

Jaina was surprised, but quickly concealed it. She wasn't going to let the Sith know anything more about *her* than they were willing to let her know about *them*. She remembered hearing that Ben had reported another Force-user who had been in Shelter losing control, and that he was currently in custody aboard the *Jade Shadow*. She hadn't known that they'd stopped him from desecrating the Fountain . . . or that a Sith had helped them.

"What you say is true," Darima agreed. "It is duly noted."

"Which is why what you have done is all the more heinous" came a slightly shaky female voice. Jaina turned to see that it was the very old, very frail-looking female who had regarded her so intently when she had entered the room with the others.

Faal turned her pretty face and inclined her head respectfully. "If this had been done under my orders, or indeed, under the orders of anyone in my fleet who was in a position to issue such, then you would be absolutely correct."

"Wait—are you saying that the guards are making all this up? That those recordings were forged?" Jaina asked, knowing her skepticism was plain on her face and not caring.

"No, Jedi Solo," replied Faal, giving Jaina a slight chill as she realized that the Sith knew exactly who she was. "Not at all. I'm saying that Captain Holpur acted completely independently."

Holpur tried and failed to keep the shock from showing. But his feelings of betrayal and surprise spiked hard in the Force before they were quickly subdued. A muscle twitched near his eye. He remained utterly silent.

"I have no idea what he was thinking," and now Faal turned to regard Holpur with anger and contempt. "He knew, as we all did, how sacred that Fountain was. How proud we were of brave young Vestara, preventing such a blasphemy on a world we were merely visiting."

Jaina gave up the struggle to conceal her feelings and let her anger and disgust pour into the Force. She didn't believe one word of this, and she let Faal know it.

Faal didn't bat an eyelash. "Let it be known that Holpur, and the entire crew of the *Starstalker*, acted completely on their own in this matter."

"Is this true, Captain Holpur?" asked Darima.

Lando and Jaina exchanged glances, and Lando was as disbelieving as she was.

"It is true," lied Holpur. His voice was steady; he'd had a few seconds to compose himself. "I thought it might please and surprise our leadership if I were able to obtain samples of the wintrium."

"Whoa, wait," said Jaina. "You took samples? Where are they?"

"Their vessel was searched as soon as it was brought to ground," Darima said. "No samples of wintrium were found anywhere on board."

"So, you can't use that as evidence, then," said Lando.

"Witnesses said they saw two members of the crew attempting to cut pieces off the Fountain." The Elders had been admirably quiet, but now they stirred uneasily.

"But you don't have them?" Jaina pressed. Darima shook his head. That was a pity. Hard evidence like that would have made the case open and shut.

"Even if you did not take samples, you wanted to. You thought to use this sacred Fountain of a people who offered us nothing but hospitality as a way to get ahead," snarled Faal. Jaina had to hand it to her. She was good—better than many holodrama actresses. "Now look what your selfishness has brought on your head. Chancellor—I believe that those who committed this sacrilege should pay. I offer your government the *Starstalker,* and her crew, for you to use as you see fit. Take the ship, imprison the crew—or execute them. Whatever your law decides."

Jaina had never expected to ever, *ever,* feel sorry for a Sith. But as she looked at Holpur, standing there resolutely accepting being used as the ultimate scapegoat, sacrificing perhaps even his life simply so the others would not have to shoulder the blame—even though Jaina knew in her gut that poor Holpur was only doing what he had been told to do—she found herself feeling a deep sense of pity, and even respect.

*But that's the way it is, isn't it, being Sith?* she thought. A Jedi would never let another take the fall like this. Of course, a Jedi would never calculatedly desecrate a sacred site for personal gain.

On second thought, she didn't feel that sorry for him. This was the sort of thing Sith did to one another. Holpur had just miscalculated. Bad luck for him.

"We will take your words into consideration," Darima said. He turned now to address the Hutt. "It seems that while Captain Faal does not feel she needs to be punished, she readily admits that the violation took place. What have you to say to this, Tooga?"

"Did we not arrive within moments of your call for aid?" said Tooga, spreading his short arms. "Did we not attack the offending vessel? Surround the other one?"

"You answer a question with a question," said Darima.

"Very Hutt-like," Lando murmured to Jaina.

"And what is wrong with that? My questions are rhetorical. We did arrive almost at once. We did do everything we were asked to do. We protected the Fountain." He eyed Lando and Jaina, to see if they were buying this.

"Protected?" Jaina burst out. "You were supposed to *prevent* anything happening to the Fountain, according to the Treaty. Seems like you didn't. Seems like it got violated pretty darn good."

"We have suffered, like so many, from the Yuuzhan Vong!" Tooga protested. "Our numbers here are few, we have been forced to flee to other worlds, and yet we maintain a presence here. No one could have stopped this. We responded and ended the threat. We even have the criminals to make an example of!"

Jaina couldn't suppress a snort. She didn't want to decide in "favor" of either party. They were, Hutt and Sith both, self-centered liars, willing to throw anyone to the boarwolves to save their own hides. She was beginning to wish she'd taken Lando's advice and just left. Lando regarded her for a moment, then spoke.

"Chancellor . . . I think Jedi Solo and I have heard enough to reach a verdict. Is there somewhere we could talk privately?"

"Certainly," Darima said. He indicated that they should follow him. They descended the podium. Jaina kept her eyes forward, but she could feel both Faal and Tooga watching her closely. Darima led them to a small room off to the side. While much cozier in scale than the massive hall they had just departed, it was no less lovely or opulent. It was windowless, but glow rods provided more than enough illumination, and the chairs and sofa looked inviting. There was a small table in front of the sofa upon which rested a covered tray.

"We have prepared some food for you, in case you are hungry," said Darima. "There is a comm panel on the right side of the door. When you have reached your decision, ring to let us know, or if you require more food or beverages."

"Don't suppose you've got any Correllian whiskey?" asked Lando. "I prefer Whyren's Reserve, but I'll take whatever you've got."

Darima smiled. "I remember you were fond of that. Unfortunately, I do not have any. However, I will send you a bottle of one of our local favorites."

"Thanks."

Darima nodded and closed the door. Jaina turned to Lando. "You shouldn't joke," she chided.

"Who's joking?"

"You're going to drink? Now?"

"Can't think of a better time. You know your daddy would, too. Especially if he had Whyren's Reserve."

"I suppose he would at that." Jaina sighed and plopped down into a chair. "Lando, what do we do? It's a miscarriage of justice either way. No one's innocent here. The Sith did violate the Fountain—and I don't for a nanosecond believe that Holpur was acting on his own initiative—and the Hutts didn't prevent it."

Lando sat down beside her and lifted the cover on the tray. Inside were unrecognizable tidbits. He picked one up, popped it into his mouth, and nodded appreciatively.

"And you know the Sith were lying how?"

She turned her head slowly and looked at him. "They're *Sith*," she said.

"I suppose I see your point. But that's bias."

"You had to have seen how Holpur reacted when Faal chucked him under the speeder."

"Yeah, I did. But frankly, all we have are the reports, and what the Sith and Tooga tell us. You should try one of these blue things, they're pretty good."

"Not hungry, thanks."

"More for me then." He snagged another one. Jaina felt a flash of irritation, quickly dampened. Lando was who he was. He had his own ways of handling things.

"So this Faal person seems to think you're siding with her, right? Because you had come to help Luke, and Luke had allied with them?"

"Right. But I can't let the fact that they're bringing a frigate and more warm bodies to the fight sway me, and neither can you."

"I know," Jaina said, and flopped back in the chair. "I just need to do the right thing."

The problem was, when all options made you feel like

you needed to take a sanisteam, what *was* the right thing?

They emerged within a half hour, moving quietly toward the dais and standing in front of their chairs. They had entered their comments on a datapad, and Darima cleared his throat and began to read from it.

"We, Lando Calrissian and Jaina Solo, affirm that we have given this matter due thought and care. We act solely from a point of what we perceive as justice, with no influence one way or the other.

"We perceive that there are two issues before us: Whether or not the Fountain was violated, and if so who was at fault, and whether the Hutts acted appropriately in defense of the Fountain. As to the first, it is clear to us from all accounts, even from the accused, that the *Starstalker,* at the very least, did deliberately and knowingly violate the one-kilometer technology-free zone. Captain Leeha Faal has agreed to turn over the entire crew of the *Starstalker* for justice under Klatooinian law."

Slight murmurings and nods of approval from the Elders. From the Sith, two very different reactions. Captain Holpur stiffened, then sagged slightly. The color left his face, then rushed back in. Captain Faal did not smirk, smile, or otherwise express pleasure. Indeed, she had a fine sabacc face. But her eyes flashed, once, with triumph. Jaina knew that violation of the Fountain meant death. Part of her was sorry that it had to come to that, but these Sith knew perfectly well what they were doing, orders or not. It was the law of this world, and she couldn't find them to be anything other than guilty.

"Secondly, as to the actions of Tooga Jalliissi Gral, we find that he did not obey the exact words of the Treaty of Vontor, but he did obey its spirit. The Hutt people have suffered, and their ability to protect the Fountain from such a completely unexpected and overt attack, something that has never occurred in twenty-five thousand years, should not be considered a dereliction of duty. The Fountain was violated, but not due to anything the Hutts in charge of its protection could reasonably be expected to have foreseen."

Tooga closed his eyes in relief, but the Elders looked surprised by the verdict, though almost immediately Jaina sensed that some of them understood exactly why the decision had been made and agreed with it.

"Thus ends this emergency session," said Darima. He pounded the dais with his staff three times, then turned to Lando and Jaina. "Thank you for your help. You may go now."

His presence in the Force was resigned and unhappy. "You don't agree with our decision," Jaina said.

Darima gave her a sad look. "It's not that I disagree, Jedi Solo. Actually, I would say given the circumstances, you rendered a remarkably well-thought-out verdict. The problem is, it doesn't matter. Whatever verdict was reached, it would not have mattered."

"What do you mean?" Lando asked.

"It is too late," Darima said. "There are riots occurring all over Klatooine. Hutts, even decent shop owners who have lived here for years, are being attacked. We are getting reports of uprisings throughout the galaxy. Lando, my people have been loyal to the treaty for *twenty-five-thousand years*. Many chafe underneath it, and this incident . . . I do not honestly think that even if the Hutts had intervened in time, had prevented the *Starstalker* from violating the no-technology zone entirely, that things would be different. Too many are looking for the slightest excuse to call the treaty null and void. And the *Starstalker* gave it to them."

"What's going to happen now?" Jaina asked.

"Only the Ancestors know," Darima replied. "We will

give them the crew of the *Starstalker*. The law is clear upon that. Such a blasphemy calls for execution. But that will not be enough. I fear that Klatooine is at a crucial juncture. We are beholding the end of something—and the birth of something new. And I fear it will be birthed in blood."

"Such things usually are," Jaina said quietly. "I'm sorry we couldn't be of more help."

He smiled, gently. "You cared enough to try to find justice. More, no one could ask. Believe me when I tell you this has little to do with your decision. But at least we can say that all formalities were observed. Go now. While it's still safe for you to fly."

Go. With a smirking, self-satisfied Leeha Faal accompanying them.

Jaina was glad that she hadn't eaten any of the little appetizers that had been prepared. She was convinced that if she had, they'd be coming right back up.

Leeha Faal went over to the doomed Vyn Holpur. "Your family will be rewarded for your action," she said quietly.

"Thank you," he replied formally. "Tell them I died well."

She smiled slightly. "I can't tell them that, because I'm not going to see you die. But we'll assume so, shall we? It shouldn't take too long. The pieces *were* large and sharp, were they not?"

He nodded.

"It is too bad we were not able to take the samples with us, but they can still serve a purpose. And if that does not suffice, then I trust you will bravely face whatever form of execution they deem appropriate. Tell the same to your crew. Their families will remember them. And so will High Lord Sarasu Taalon, when we have achieved our goal in the Maw."

Holpur smiled faintly. "You'll forgive me if I don't bow."

"Of course." She nodded at him, then turned and walked out. She withdrew her comlink and spoke into it. "Syndor? All is well. We are free to depart. But before we do, you must do something for me, and quickly. I need you to . . ."

The conversation became inaudible. He watched her go, hearing the heavy footfalls of booted feet denoting Klatooinian guards coming up behind him, and he placed a hand on his stomach before they bound his hands behind his back.

# Chapter Twenty

HIS NAME WAS BELOK RHAL. HE WAS NOT VERY TALL, with close-cropped blond hair and pale blue eyes. His nose looked like it had been broken several times, a long scar ran the length of his left cheek, and he moved with a fluid grace.

He had been appointed to command the Mandalorian forces laying siege to the Temple, and Daala had largely given him free rein to do as he saw fit. "I want the Chev Jedi Sothais Saar, and the human Turi Altamik," she said. "If the Jedi surrender them, your mission is complete. If they don't—" She had shrugged. "It's time to make them understand what they're really up against."

A slow smile had spread across Rhal's face, and he had nodded. "Understood."

He'd not made any attempts to respond to efforts at contact from Jedi for several hours. The silence would unnerve them. Now, though, it was time to get some movement out of the situation. He was clad in beskar armor, brightly painted in hues of reds and yellows. The armor had seen combat—a great deal of combat. Possibly, it would see more during this mission.

He removed his helmet, so that the watching Jedi could see his face. Enemies, he had learned, found his face more unnerving than an impersonal helmet.

Rhal gestured for the amplifier, and spoke. His voice would carry to the Temple and beyond.

"My name is Belok Rhal. You will remember it. I am here on the orders of the Galactic Alliance to retrieve two Jedi—Sothais Saar and Turi Altamik," he said, his voice deep and rough. "You have been ordered to relinquish them to the care of the Galactic Alliance, and you have refused. All legal methods have been exhausted. Your Chief of State Daala has asked me to ensure that you turn them over. And you will."

He paused to let this sink in. "If you do not comply with this request, which is binding by all laws you claim to adhere to, *there will be consequences*. If you trust nothing else, trust my word on that. I will accept nothing less than seeing Turi Altamik and Sothais Saar coming out of the Temple. You have thirty-six hours to comply."

The voice was cold, almost dead, and Hamner felt his danger sense prickling. All around him, he sensed that the other Masters shared his unease.

Saba Sebatyne grunted. "This one is not Daala's pet," she said. "This Belok Rhal meanz what he says."

"I believe he does," said Hamner. He turned back to the Master. "Master Katarn, report."

"The news isn't good. As we all knew, the vehicles and weaponry he has assembled could deal a terrible amount of damage to the Temple," said Kyle Katarn. "What's worse is, we've sent apprentices to all the exits of the Temple, even the ones we've thought hidden, and there's a Mando presence at every one of them."

"That is impossible," said Saba. "There are many secret passagewayz."

"It's not impossible if someone talked," Kyp said.

"Perhaps Reeqo and Melari," mused Hamner. The two apprentices had quit some time ago, frightened by the thought of being the target of Daala's wrath. It was not outside the realm of possibility that they had been taken in and had told everything they knew. Too, technology properly targeted could reveal hollowed areas beneath the ground and where tunnels so revealed might lead.

"Then we find other exits," Octa Ramis said calmly, arms folded across her chest. "The Temple has been destroyed and rebuilt more than once. It's possible, even likely, that something's been overlooked, or forgotten, or has caved in. Kenth, the apprentices are under a lot of strain right now. They're worried and are looking for something to do to keep busy and to feel like they're helping. I suggest that each of us and every available Knight should take a few of them and start searching for any way out. Seha and I will coordinate this. She's used to finding her way around underground."

"That's a fine idea, Master Ramis," Hamner said.

"We must find some way to get out soon—or at least to get supplies in," said Cilghal. "We are dangerously low on sedatives strong enough to keep the ill Jedi restrained. And of course, we cannot use the Force in any way to aid them." Hamner nodded at her to indicate he understood.

"I think there will be some way to get what we need. Once we are resupplied, we have the advantage—we could sit and wait this, and Daala, out for a very long time indeed."

But Kyle Katarn was shaking his head. "Theoretically, yes, we would have enough supplies to do so. There are other, more pressing reasons not to wait. But I'm concerned about the effect such a large gathering of Mandos will have on the populace. It's one thing when they're targeting us and engaged in active fighting. These are beings of action. If there's any civilian protests, things could get very ugly very quickly. The longer this goes on, the more likely that will happen. Innocent people could get harmed while we sit here quietly playing the waiting game."

"Well, Jaina's out there, and neither she nor her family are the sort to sit around killing time. She'd left to go get some kind of help. Any word from her?" asked Kyp.

Hamner grimaced. He wasn't sure whether to count it a blessing that none of the Solo clan had been present during the onset of the siege. Jaina was resourceful and intelligent, and Katarn raised a good point about civilians, but this was still a balancing act. Daala had the upper hand—again.

"We'll use codes to get word out about what we need," he said, deciding to ignore Kyp and Katarn for the moment and focus on Cilghal's request. "If we can find some way out of the Temple, even one too small for a Jedi or an apprentice to pass through, we can get supplies in and—"

"Sir?" It was Kani, Hamner's assistant. Her pretty face registered dismay. "Security reports the Mandos have just begun utilizing jamming equipment. Communication within the Temple is unaffected, but as for external communications—well, it's carefully designed so it all goes one way. Daala or this Rhal fellow can contact us, but we can't contact them. We're totally dependent upon his choices, and we won't be able to get any signals out for supplies or anything else."

There was a loud, angry oath from Corran Horn. "Hamner, *this will stop*! We're trapped in here with *no* way out, *no* way to speak to anyone on the outside, looking at possible harm to civilians, and a threat to our families hangs over our heads. We've got three Jedi who are convinced we're evil imposters, and we are rapidly running out of the means to take proper care of them. If you would stop trying to appease Daala we—"

"*Appease* her?" Kenth Hamner was a man slow to anger, but Corran's words bit deep. "I'm not trying to appease anyone, I'm trying to find a solution! All I need to do to end this threat, Horn, is to let Saar and Altamik go. She doesn't even know about Bann. Two Jedis, on a gurney, and we can all go home—"

He stopped in midsentence. Corran's eyes were hard and angry. Horn would not get to be with his family, even if he could leave now. He would go home only to his wife, as strained and heartsick and angry as he was. His children were not here, in Jedi safekeeping, tended by beings who cared for them. They were stuck in carbonite, hung on a wall, and treated like decorations.

"I'm sorry, Corran," Hamner said, and he was. "But we've come to this point because we've continued to refuse Daala, and that's hardly appeasement. I'm open to any and all suggestions."

"She sent Belok Rhal to handle the situation. And she's deliberately refusing to talk to us. Maybe we should talk to him instead, while we keep pursuing the other options," suggested Octa Ramis.

"We can't," said Hamner, struggling for patience. "Didn't you hear Kani's report? All outgoing communications are blocked."

Octa smiled a little. "There's a lower tech solution, Kenth. Just send someone to walk out the front steps to discuss terms. We could at least get the deadline extended while we tried to come up with another plan."

"Somehow I don't think that gentleman out there is much of a talker," grumbled Kyp.

"Nor do I," said Kyle Katarn, stroking his beard thoughtfully. "I hate to say this, but at the moment, until we can find a way out of here, Daala really does have the upper hand. She's got many of the Masters right where she wants us. Temple communications are effectively paralyzed; all known exits are watched. Unless we are suddenly sprung by a coordinated effort from offworld—not impossible, but not likely, and it certainly wouldn't be in a timely manner—we might be here awhile. Getting this very brief deadline of thirty-six hours extended is currently the only thing I can think of. We need more time, and the chrono is counting down every minute we delay."

Hamner sighed. "I think you're right. It's worth a try, at any rate. I'll go out and see if I can—"

"No," said several voices at once.

"I'm the acting Grand Master. I'm the one Rhal will want to speak with."

"Right," said Kyp, "and he'll snatch you up so fast it'll make a lightsaber strike look slow."

Kenth's brows drew together. "Daala would not dare."

"We don't know anything anymore about what Daala would and would not stoop to," said Katarn. "She's threatened our families, and sent in this Mando with apparent carte blanche—and we certainly don't know anything about him. I would not tempt either of them with you as the prize."

Slowly, Hamner nodded. "I do not like asking another to take the risk," he said. "But you raise a valid point. Who else would be willing to go?"

Several mouths opened, but someone unexpected spoke first.

"I will," said Kani.

"What?" said many voices at once, and Hamner said firmly, "Absolutely not."

"It makes sense, sir. If any of the Masters or even someone in full Jedi robes goes out, they might suspect a trap or an attack of some sort. I'm obviously not a full Jedi Knight yet. I'm not much of a threat, but I do have your ear, and so I'm a good person to negotiate with."

The Masters regarded one another. "K.P. . . . I mean . . . Kani has a point," said Kyp.

"K.P.?" Kani looked at him curiously. He waved it

aside, looking a little uncomfortable and not meeting her gaze as he continued talking. "We, the Masters, are all well known by sight. Even the Jedi here are mostly Knights. I hate sending an apprentice in, but she might get further with them than any of us."

Hamner glanced at Kani worriedly. "They might arrest you, Kani. You know that."

She shrugged her slender shoulders. "So what? I haven't done anything. I don't *know* anything. Well, not very much. I wouldn't be of much use, and after all, Master Hamner . . . this is the Galactic Alliance we're talking about. Even Tahiri Veila is getting decent treatment and a fair trial."

Hamner considered. She could do what he, or indeed any of the Masters, could not. This Mando would want Hamner—with Kani, he could reach Hamner. But he couldn't do much else with her. She knew nothing about the buildup of StealthXs, nothing about the Sith, and very little about Sothais and Turi. But she'd spent enough time with Hamner to know how he would reply to various terms and conditions. Kani was a bright young woman and could think on her feet. All in all, she was uniquely useful.

"Very well," he said. "Go unarmed, with your hands in plain sight. Don't give them any reason to open fire on you."

She paled a little as the realization that this was actually going to happen sank in, but nodded. "Let's do this, then."

Ten minutes later, wearing only apprentice robes and carrying only a comlink, Kani Asari stood ready to go. The rest of the Masters—and a fairly large crowd of other Jedi trapped in the Temple—were assembled in the formal entrance hall. No one trusted the Mandos not to have snipers, and so everyone was careful to stay well away from the entrance.

Kani looked nervous, her eyes wide, her breathing quick. Hamner placed a steadying hand on her shoulder.

"You don't have to do this, Kani. I'm not making it an order."

She looked up at him. "I know, sir. I want to."

"You know what to tell them."

She grinned. "I do. 'I speak on behalf of Master Kenth Hamner, who is interested in opening negotiations for the peaceful resolution of this situation.' Blah blah blah and lead them in a circle until you all figure out what to do next."

"Don't let them rattle you," Katarn said. "They're Mandos, they enjoy causing fear."

"I won't, Master Katarn." She smoothed her robes, brushed a hand over her blond hair, then looked back at Master Hamner. "Hopefully, you'll hear from Daala soon," she said, patting the comlink tucked in the sleeve of her robe.

"Hopefully, *you'll* be back in time for dinner," Hamner said. He squeezed her shoulder and gave her a gentle push.

Kani stepped forward briskly. As soon as she reached the top of the stairs, she held her hands aloft, then turned around slowly, to show she carried no weapons. There were security monitors in various places in the entrance, and the Masters moved, as one, to regard them.

Hamner realized he had been holding his breath, and now let it out slowly. He had been afraid they'd fire on the girl without seeing that she had come unarmed.

Kani moved down the stairs. A figure detached itself from the ring of Mandalorians and their siege vehicles. It was Belok Rhal, striding briskly up the stairs despite the armor toward Kani.

"That's a good sign," murmured Hamner. "If Rhal himself is going to meet her, then he recognizes her as a formal emissary of the Temple."

Others did not look so certain. Rhal halted halfway and eyed Kani up and down.

"You are not Sothais Saar," he said. He had a mic of some sort attached to his armor, and his voice carried loudly.

"No, sir," said Kani. Her voice was picked up by the same mic. Hamner was proud of her; her voice didn't shake at all.

"Nor are you Turi Altamik, though you resemble her."

"I am Jedi Apprentice Kani Asari, assistant to Master Kenth Hamner. He has instructed me to come negotiate with you concerning this situation."

"Negotiate?"

"That is correct, sir."

The Mando regarded her for a long moment. Then, before anyone realized what he was planning, he had drawn a handheld blaster from his belt, pointed it at Kani from a distance of a third of a meter, and fired.

Kani Asari dropped without a cry, dead before she hit the stairs.

# Chapter Twenty-one

*"No!"* cried Hamner.

He could hear the other Masters and Knights shouting, as stunned and outraged by this grotesque atrocity, this blatant *murder,* as he, but he couldn't make out their words. Blood thundered in his ears. This couldn't be happening! Kani was just a child, coming out, unarmed, to negotiate! She couldn't just have been slaughtered like a—

"I thought I had made myself quite clear, but apparently Jedi need things explained in the simplest terms," said Rhal. "I am here for a single, specific purpose. And that purpose is to take Sothais Saar and Turi Altamik into custody. This," and Rhal nudged Kani's limp form, the hole in her chest still smoking, with his foot, "is not Sothais Saar, nor is it Turi Altamik. I am not here to negotiate, discuss, or even capture and interrogate. No one leaves the Temple until this matter is resolved. Anyone attempting to do so will be dealt with in this same manner. You now have twenty-four hours to turn over the Jedi. At the end of that time, your Temple will be leveled, your people slain, and Altamik and Saar recovered. The girl stays here, as a reminder. Any attempt to recover her body and we will open fire on the Temple."

He turned around and descended the stairs. Kani lay where she had fallen, face up to the sky, eyes wide.

"That . . . ice-blooded . . . heartless— I'm going to get her," said Kyp, suiting action to word.

"No!" Hamner's voice was clear and sharp and cracked like a whip. "No one else is going to get harmed! That is an order, Durran!"

"I'm not leaving her out there!" Kyp's eyes flashed angrily.

"It is foolish for you to join her in death," Saba said. She radiated fury, but it was cold and controlled and focused. "Now is not the time. We will strike at Daala when we are better prepared. And strike we will."

"Daala didn't authorize that," said Katarn with certainty. "This . . . being . . . is acting on his own."

"Daala hired him," hissed Saba. "She is responsible."

"I shouldn't have let her go," murmured Kenth. "I shouldn't have let her go."

"We all thought it was a good idea," said Octa, stepping up behind him. "We thought she'd be safer than anyone else."

"No one is safe," said Corran Horn. "No one can be trusted. Not the GA, not Daala, not anyone. We're on our own. And the sooner we realize that, the better off we'll be."

Kenth Hamner stood alone, staring at Kani's body on the monitor after the rest of the Masters and other Jedi had filed out. They were furious, raging, but they could not fight, not yet, and so were anxious to channel their energies into something positive. Ramis, a subued Seha by her side, had tried to get Hamner to go eat something, but he shook his head without speaking, and eventually she, too, had left to start organizing the apprentices.

He stood here because he realized he didn't know where he wanted to go. Normally, he would go back to his offices, finish up the day's work, spend some time in the Room of a Thousand Fountains, and then on to his quarters here at the Temple. But today was most assuredly not a normal day.

Hamner had no wish to be at odds with his fellow Masters. But Grand Master Luke Skywalker had charged him with a duty, and that duty was to lead the Jedi as best he could. Hamner would do nothing less. It pained, and sometimes frustrated, him that what seemed like obvious, sound, clear choices to him were seldom perceived as such by the Council.

Duties awaited him, even now, even when the Temple was under siege and an innocent girl's corpse lay stiffening on the steps. But he couldn't move, not yet.

His comlink chimed. His eyes still fastened on Kani, he fished out his comm and clicked it.

"Hamner."

There was a slight pause, then a voice that Hamner recognized.

"Master Hamner. Thank you for speaking with me." Pleasant, purring Bothan.

Hamner recovered swiftly, and his voice was steady as he replied. "Admiral Bwua'tu. This is unexpected, to say the least." What was Admiral Nek Bwua'tu doing contacting him on a secure channel out of the blue in the middle of a siege? And how—no, he knew without asking. Buwa'tu was the head of the Galactic Alliance Navy. He'd be able to bypass Galactic Alliance jamming signals if he wanted to.

"I'm certain it is. But this is a matter of some import and timeliness."

"I'm staring at the body of a girl who was murdered by the heartless bastard you picked to lead the siege," he said. "I assure you, sir, I am all attention."

"Not to put too fine a point on it, Master Hamner," the pleasant voice continued, "but your Jedi are in severe peril at the moment."

Hamner actually laughed, though it was an angry one.

"Indeed? *Thank* you for pointing that out, Admiral. I'm sure we would *never* have noticed that we were under siege by order of the Galactic Alliance, or that my assistant was just killed in cold blood."

Bwua'tu appeared unruffled by the sarcasm. "I deeply regret the girl's death. It is in the hope of avoiding more bloodshed that I speak to you now. I do not refer to the siege, Master Hamner, when I speak of peril."

Hamner suspected a trap. Bwua'tu was a decent sort and a fine admiral. His loyalty to the Galactic Alliance was beyond question; Hamner knew that he had even sworn an oath of krevi, a vow so binding it meant that Bwua'tu put the needs of the Galactic Alliance before those of his homeworld or his own people. Hamner respected that. But the being was canny, the oath of krevi meant that he worked for the GA first and foremost, and Hamner suspected that, discreet as the two tried to be, Bwua'tu was involved with the Chief of State as more than a friend and adviser.

"Let us do each other the courtesy of being blunt, Hamner," Bwua'tu said. "It will save us time and possibly lives."

"By all means," Hamner replied, and braced himself.

"It has come to my attention that the Jedi are building up a considerable attack force of StealthXs for some purpose as yet unknown to me."

The knot in Hamner's gut tightened another loop. Oddly, though, his danger sense was not active. He inhaled, exhaled, gathering calm about him.

"When you said 'blunt,' clearly you meant exactly that. But rumors are wild things, Admiral. You of all people should know that."

"True," said Bwua'tu. "But recordings made by Mandalorians as they fought inside the Temple are not rumors. There's quite a buildup going on, Master Hamner. It looks as if you're preparing for something big."

Hamner closed his eyes, opened them. "Who else knows about this?" There was no point in denying it, not if they had footage of the strike force.

"What few Mandalorians survived," Bwua'tu continued. "Myself."

"The Chief of State?"

"No, she does not. And frankly, I'd rather she didn't."

Hamner was confused. "I see."

"No, I don't think you do. Master Hamner, believe this—if I intended you ill, I would not be speaking with you right now. I'd have informed the Chief of State of the content of the recordings. And instead of a siege, you'd be looking at a full-out preemptive attack. Daala could draw no other conclusion than that this buildup of vessels was intended to be used against her and the Galactic Alliance."

"But you can."

"I certainly can, and am entertaining other possibilities."

"Am I speaking to the Head of the Navy, or am I speaking to Natasi Daala's . . . companion?"

Bwua'tu seemed completely unruffled by the comment. "The Head of the Navy. The Chief of State knows nothing about any of this—not the buildup, nor my contacting you."

"Forgive me if I am dubious."

"Then perhaps what I have to say will convince you of my trustworthiness. We are military, you and I. We are beings of honor, beings of duty. It is in this spirit that I ask you this question. Is this buildup of armed vessels intended to be directed against Daala or the Galactic Alliance?"

Hamner didn't even have to weigh the issues. Swiftly, truthfully, he said, "No."

"I believe you, Master Hamner. As I intimated, that was the answer I was expecting. I take it then that the

Jedi have another target. Are you aware of another enemy? A mutual one, perhaps?"

"I believe so, yes," Hamner said. He knew that if anyone on the Council had heard the conversation, they'd be outraged. But all his senses, senses in the Force he had been trained to trust, as well as his rational mind, were telling him to be truthful at this moment.

"But I do not think that the Chief of State is prepared to listen to anything we have to say about this . . . potential mutual enemy."

"She may not be. I am."

Hamner considered for a long moment, then made his decision. "I can't tell you anything more than that," Hamner said finally. He could not divulge the details without feeling like he had betrayed the Jedi, even if doing so might get Bwau'tu firmly on his side. "I'm sorry."

"I understand. Perhaps a bit later, you might feel differently. Here is what I am willing to propose. I would ask you to refrain from launching your flotilla of StealthXs until such time as I tell you that you may do so."

"Absolutely not," Hamner stated, bridling. This was going too far. "I know the nature of the situation, Admiral. You don't. I'm not about to launch or refrain from launching according to your timetable."

A sigh. "Well, then you should be aware that the Chief of State will absolutely and unhesitatingly fire on them the second they *do* launch. I wouldn't be able to stop her from doing so unless there were better relations between her and the Jedi. However, I am in—shall we say—a unique position to lower tensions between the two parties."

Hamner's eyebrows lifted at the admission. So, Bwau'tu was confirming the rumors about him and Daala—a not-inconsiderable gesture of trust on his part.

"I see," was all Hamner said.

"If you agree to stay your hand until such time as I tell you when, I will personally guarantee that, so long as these StealthXs are not involved in any activity that violate GA interests, the Jedi will have complete fleet cooperation with your operation."

Surprise flickered through Kenth. Surprise—and hope. "I'm not sure you're in a position to promise such things."

"I'm Chief of the Navy, Hamner. They're *my* ships. I will deploy them covertly if I must to keep to this bargain."

It sounded too good to be true. "You wouldn't come to me with such an offer if there wasn't something in it for you," he said.

"It would be a poor bargain indeed if I were to walk away empty-handed. The best negotiation, as I know you understand, is one that both parties feel satisfied with."

*Here we go,* Hamner thought. Irritation made his tongue sharp. "What is it—handing over Sothais and Turi? Allowing Jedi to be searched every time they enter a tapcaf? Inserting transmitters so their every movement can be tracked?"

"Nothing so drastic. I want to do what is best for the GA. I have sworn a vow to uphold that. And Master Hamner—frankly, seeing the head of this organization I love so dearly at odds with the beings best suited to protect it is, in my opinion, most definitely *not* what is best for the GA. I *do* agree with some of Admiral Daala's sentiments regarding your order and its place, but not all of them. Both the Chief of State and many of your Jedi are *reacting,* rather than acting, and that is not good for anyone. Soon no one will be able to scratch his nose without someone freezing him in carbonite or lopping off the arm doing the scratching. If you launch that flotilla, Daala will destroy you—not just the StealthXs, but the whole Jedi order, if she can. There will be no going back from it, and everyone walks away—if they can walk—the worse for it. I want exactly the opposite. I want a solution in which everyone benefits. And both you and I know they will."

Hamner was silent for a while, his patrician brow creased in a furrow as he weighed the options.

Daala's heavy hand was causing a great deal of harm. One innocent had already lost her life. For what seemed like the first time in too long a while, Hamner and the Masters he ostensibly led were in agreement—Luke Skywalker needed aid. Everyone, including himself, was chafing at the delay when the ships were prepped and ready to go. They would have been useful before now, when Skywalker was on Dathomir. He had been alone and unaided and forced to strike a dark and dangerous bargain—with *Sith,* for star's sake.

He knew that Bwua'tu was sincere. There was every reason for the Bothan to be telling the truth, and no reason Hamner could fathom that he would lie. The StealthXs were ready to launch, past ready, but there would be no assisting Skywalker if they were blown out of the sky when they tried to lift off. That would be a disaster of epic proportions. Bwua'tu was right. There would be no way either Daala or the Jedi could turn back to peaceful negotiations. Jedi would be killed for no reason, and innocent civilians would be caught in the middle. It was utterly unacceptable.

But if Bwua'tu meant what he was saying, then the strike team would be able to deploy and finally get Skywalker the help he so clearly needed. And they would do so with the GA Navy's support—be it official or unofficial, Hamner didn't care at this point.

There was never a question in his mind of taking this to the Masters for a vote. There was too much negativity there for them to listen and understand exactly how useful and timely a deal this was. They would not want to wait; they burned to act, right now, unable to see the wisdom in patience. He disliked that, but his duty, given to him by Grand Master Luke Skywalker himself, was clear—to protect the interests of the Jedi order and the Jedi themselves.

He took a deep breath and made his decision. "We have a deal. Although Nek—"

"Yes, Kenth?"

"Move as fast as you can. There's not a lot of time. The longer we hold off on launching, the more chance that beings are going to die. And not just Jedi."

"I understand. I believe things are going to come to a head quickly. And then perhaps you'll be willing to tell me what this is all about."

Kenth Hamner, Acting Grand Master of the Jedi Council, said gravely and quietly, "Perhaps the fate of the galaxy."

"Don't you think that's a bit—melodramatic?"

*I don't see how the thought of an entire planet full of Sith and a mysterious, malevolent being in the Maw who can control Jedi all over the galaxy is melodramatic.*

"Not at all," he said. "If anything, it's an understatement."

A pause. Then, "I see. I will make all due haste then, Master Hamner. I will be in touch."

Hamner clicked off the comlink. The mantle of leadership in this case was proving far, far heavier than even he had imagined. He had just made a bargain that he knew probably every single Master would have challenged.

He also knew that he could have done nothing else. He gazed with deep sorrow one last time on Kani's body, then turned away from the Temple entrance, his footsteps, if not light, at least certain.

# Chapter Twenty-two

"The prosecution calls former Jedi Tahiri Veila to the stand," said Sul Dekkon. He turned with a flourish and swirl of dramatic robes and fixed Tahiri with his piercing gaze.

She rose, her face calm. She wasn't looking forward to this, of course, but she was ready for it. She and Eramuth had prepared earlier.

"Just tell the truth, but don't volunteer anything that is not specifically asked," Eramuth had advised her. "And if he seems to score a point, don't worry. I'm allowed to cross-examine, and I'll get things back on track."

"It sounds like a game," Tahiri had said. "A game with my future, maybe my life, at stake."

"Not a game, but an art form, if you will," Eramuth had replied, sipping at his caf. "And I am a master of this art form." He had given her a confident grin and a wink. Now, as she rose to take the stand, he still looked completely confident and relaxed. It was reassuring.

He had told her about the Mando siege of the Temple, so that she wouldn't be taken by surprise while on the stand. "It actually works in our favor," he had said. "Mandalorians in the middle of the city generally do not make people feel calm and relaxed. It's much more likely to generate sympathy for you than the opposite, although you probably will have fewer friendly faces out in the public seats today."

She supposed she could deal with that.

The bouncer-bailiff faced her. "State your name."

"Tahiri Veila."

"Do you solemnly swear to tell the truth, the whole truth, and nothing but the truth?"

"I do."

"Furthermore, do you solemnly swear to not utilize the Force in any way, large or small, trivial or significant, to influence the outcome of the jury's verdict and the judge's ruling?"

Tahiri gritted her teeth. Still, having to take such a vow was more palatable than having to deal with an entire special Jedi court for the trial.

"I would not have done so in any case, but yes, I swear." There was a slight rippling through the courtroom at her tart response. She knew she shouldn't have said it, and Eramuth's ever so slight frown of rebuke confirmed the fact, but she couldn't help herself.

The bailiff trundled off to his usual position, his footfalls so heavy Tahiri thought it a wonder the floor didn't shake. The Chagrian took the bailiff's place in front of her, smiling with artificial pleasantness. Tahiri didn't bother to smile back, just looked at him quietly, expectantly. She wondered if he'd feign solicitude to get her to drop her guard, or go in like an anooba for the kill.

"Before we begin, would you care for some water?" he asked. Solicitude, then. She eyed the pitcher of water and the empty glass to her right.

"No thanks. Even without using the Force I can pour myself a glass of water if I want it."

There was another murmur of disapproval, but she caught a few chuckles as well.

He gave her a thin smile. "Then, since you are obviously not thirsty, would you please tell the court about your . . . *relationship* with Jacen Solo?"

Now he was going in for the kill. He could switch

gears fast. She'd half-expected Eramuth to leap forward with an objection, but he seemed completely at ease.

"Of course," she said, taking her cue from her lawyer and not rising to the bait. "I knew Jacen Solo half my life."

"So there was no personal relationship?"

She'd known this was coming, and replied calmly. "There was."

He tried and failed to hide the gleam of excitement in his eyes. "Please elaborate on the nature of this relationship."

"Objection," said Eramuth. "Surely, the court has no prurient interest in the details of Tahiri Veila's private life."

"Your Honor, I am trying to establish how deeply involved the accused and Jacen Solo were, whether their relationship was personal or professional."

Judge Zudan considered, then said, "Overruled. The prosecution may continue."

Tahiri felt heat rising in her cheeks, but kept her face calm. "So, would it be accurate to say that you and Jacen Solo were lovers?" Dekkon continued.

"We were involved," Tahiri said bluntly. "Love had nothing to do with it."

"So we may assume that you were physically—"

"Objection!" Eramuth said again. His whiskers bristled, and he was the very image of wounded propriety. "Further questioning along this line verges on the salacious. A relationship has been established. No one here needs to know details. This is a trial, not a holodrama."

"Sustained," said the judge. "Prosecution may continue with another line of questioning."

The rest of her history was gone through, all with a subtly negative cast. She felt some agitation, but pushed it down. She'd expected this, and if there was anything

Eramuth felt was damaging, he would revisit it and correct it in the cross-examination.

Finally, the prosecutor arrived at the most recent events. Eramuth looked relaxed, perhaps even a trifle bored, but sufficiently attentive so that the jury did not think he didn't care. The press had been recording everything, but now they started paying more attention. One positive that had come out of the siege was the fact that, while her trial was still obviously news, journalistic attention was now divided. Still, she hated those hungry looks they gave her.

She thought about the Solos, coming to visit her with the news that even after his death, Anakin still loved her. They knew who she was. Ben knew who she was, and Luke, and Jaina. Even Jag, who had found Eramuth for her. Everyone who mattered understood and forgave, and if this trial went badly, Tahiri knew that would be enough.

"So by this point, you were officially working with Darth Caedus."

It was accurate, as far as it went. Tahiri knew now that by the time Jacen had begun seeking her out in order to have her assistance, he had gone over to the dark side. Eramuth's ear twitched slightly, but otherwise he seemed calm.

"Yes."

"There were several orders that you were asked to carry out that most beings of conscience might find unpalatable. What were your thoughts on doing such things?"

"Many beings obeyed orders from Jacen Solo," Tahiri replied, keeping the sharpness out of her voice with an effort.

"Ah yes," Dekkon said, turning away to give the jury a knowing glance. "'I was just following orders.' Famous words, uttered by many who did not wish to take

responsibility for the harm they caused. Yet without beings who obeyed orders, Darth Caedus could not have
wreaked the havoc he did. Many would be alive today
had not beings simply said, 'yes, sir.'"

"Objection," said Eramuth. "My esteemed colleague
knows full well what the consequences would have been
to anyone who challenged a Sith Lord, which was what
Jacen had either fully become or was well on his way to
becoming by the time he got his claws into my client.
Also, this was not a civilian corporation. Tahiri Veila
would not have been a simple whistle-blower. She was in
a military organization and could not have challenged
an order from a superior officer without extremely dire
consequences. Especially when that superior officer was
Colonel Solo. I trust I do not need to remind anyone
here of the power he wielded at that point in time."

"Sustained," the judge said. Clearly, Eramuth didn't
need to remind anyone.

Dekkon nodded, as if he wasn't at all disappointed.
With his grand, almost theatrical robes sweeping the
marble floor, he continued, hands clasped behind his
back.

"May it please the court. I withdraw my implication
that the accused should have disobeyed a direct order issued from her military superior. Ah—"

He came to a dead stop, looking as if the thought had
just occurred to him. "That is, of course, assuming that
the instruction to murder—"

"Objection!"

"—to assassinate," and Dekkon glanced at the judge,
who nodded. "To assassinate Admiral Gilad Pellaeon
was a direct order. *Was* it a direct order, and phrased as
such?"

"Objection!" Eramuth cried again, leaping to his feet.
"When coming from a Sith Lord, surely this court recog-

nizes that even the merest *hint* of that Lord's preference must be construed as an order!"

"Your Honor," Dekkon said, "we are all in agreement that in a military organization, orders must be followed. I am simply trying to establish whether such an order was actually issued or if Tahiri Veila acted on her own initiative."

"Overruled," Zudan said. Her face betrayed no hint of emotion. "Continue with your line of questioning, counsel. Defense Attorney Bwua'tu, please take your seat. The court is worried about your injuring yourself in your ebullience."

"Thank you, your honor," Dekkon said, inclining his head as a titter swept through the courtroom.

Eramuth's ear twitched. Despite his display of energy, Tahiri didn't miss that he reached for the arm of his chair to ease himself down. His face was impassive, but she was sure her own burned sympathetically in response to the rebuke her lawyer had just received. It was an unnecessary and, frankly, petty attack against his age, and she knew he felt the sting. She wanted to use the Force to even out her color, but of course she couldn't. Instead she took deep, calming breaths. She didn't want to give this anooba of a lawyer the satisfaction of knowing that he'd gotten to her.

"Miss Veila," Dekkon continued, smiling at her as if they were just two friends having a pleasant chat over caf, "no one questions that it is a subordinate's job to obey orders from her commanding officer. Even if she disagrees with the orders. So please tell the court, in your own words, precisely the order that Colonel Solo issued."

The words wouldn't come. Tahiri swallowed hard, knowing that Dekkon would see the gesture, that the judge and the jury would see it, that Eramuth would see it.

"The court is waiting, Miss Veila." Again, the congenial smile. The smile of a sand panther about to strike.

She squared her shoulders and looked him fully in the eye. "He did not give a formal order as such."

Dekkon blinked. "He did not?"

"No."

Tahiri waited for the objection. It didn't come. To her surprise, Eramuth didn't even appear interested. He was leaning forward, one hand on his cane, the other thumbing through a datapad. She returned her attention to the Chagrian.

"So you were never issued an order to kill Admiral Pellaeon."

"No. He—"

"So—I just want to be absolutely clear on this—you wouldn't even have violated a formal order had you not lifted a blaster and fired point-blank at an unarmed ninety-two-year-old man."

"Objection." Eramuth didn't even lift his eyes from the datapad.

"With respect, your honor, every one of those words is a fact."

And sickly Tahiri realized they were. Phrased as bluntly as Dekkon had said, they were horrible, vile words, and she saw several members of the jury cringe slightly. One or two of them narrowed their eyes in disapproval.

"Overruled," the judge said. "The witness may answer the question."

"No," and Tahiri was surprised at how calm her voice sounded. "I did not violate a *formal* order. But—"

Dekkon whirled. "I would like my question and the accused's response read back for the jury."

The droid stepped forward dispassionately, lacking the enjoyment C-3PO seemed to get out of performing his programmed tasks. In his precise voice, he said,

"'So—I just want to be absolutely clear on this—you wouldn't even have violated a formal order had you not lifted a blaster and fired point-blank at an unarmed ninety-two-year-old man.' 'No. I did not violate a *formal* order. But—'"

Dekkon turned to the jury and lifted his hands, almost as if in apology. "That is all I needed to hear, Miss Veila. Counsel—your witness."

"Hm? Done already? Oh, thank you, Prosecutor Dekkon." Eramuth took a sip of water and got to his feet. He did not use his cane as he moved forward toward Tahiri, smiling gently at her. She badly wanted to sense him in the Force, to get some idea of what was going on, but she could not without breaking her vow. And jeopardizing the outcome of her trial by doing so was definitely not what she wanted.

"Miss Veila," said Eramuth, his mellifluous voice carrying clearly and seemingly without effort into every corner of the room. "Surely, by this point in Jacen Solo's career, he had truly become Darth Caedus." Eramuth put just enough, but not too much, emphasis on the last two words. "And you were aware of the nature of your superior officer."

Tahiri nodded her blond head. "Yes," she said. "He made no secret of it to me toward the end."

"Now . . . everyone here is familiar with the events of two years past. We've seen the newsvids. But I still don't really think that what it means to those around you to be a Dark Lord of the Sith has really quite sunk in to this court. Perhaps you could, in your own words, tell us a little bit about how you felt about Jacen Solo, and how it was you came to be working with him."

She didn't have to read him in the Force to know that beneath the words were the unspoken ones, *trust me.* She could see it in his eyes. And she did trust him. She had to—there was no other choice.

She glanced over at the droid performing the service as court reporter. "May I please have some water? This might take some time."

It did. She began at the beginning. Tahiri knew it would be hard, but was surprised at how hard it actually was. She spoke of the flow-walking journeys Jacen Solo had taken her on—back in time to undo something she had been regretting for almost twenty years.

"Flow-walking is dangerous, is it not?" Eramuth said.

"Well—" Tahiri hesitated. "Jacen told me that it was. That I was taking a risk that might change the fate of the galaxy if we weren't careful. I've since learned that that isn't true. Things can be changed slightly, yes, but the pattern of the Force flows so that the true path is restored."

"But he forced you to rely upon him, while lying to you, by making you think you were doing something dangerous when he knew for a certainty all would be well?"

"That's correct, yes."

"Objection!"

Eramuth slightly flattened his ears in amusement and turned a calm visage toward the judge. "May it please the court," he said. "With respect, Your Honor, every one of those words is a fact."

There was a slight rippling of amusement throughout the courtroom at the comment. The Falleen's eyes narrowed, but she sighed.

"Overruled. Counsel may continue with questioning."

"Thank you, Your Honor." Eramuth returned his attention to Tahiri. "Help me understand why you went back more than once. It sounds as though you accomplished your goal on your very first trip. To give Anakin Solo the kiss you had withheld before he sacrificed his life."

Tahiri lowered her head slightly, uncomfortable with the personal nature of the questioning. But she had to trust Eramuth.

"I uh . . . Jacen always managed to make it feel as if there were something else. Something left unfinished. And—it was hard not to want to go back."

Eramuth's voice was gentle. "To see the face of someone you loved one more time. I think everyone in this court would understand how compelling such an opportunity would be. Did you ever try to change things? Anything of lasting significance? For instance, it must have been extremely tempting to want to save Anakin Solo—not just for yourself, but for the good he would have done the galaxy."

And despite all that had transpired, despite the years and the horrors that had crowded upon Tahiri since that terrible day so long ago, it was as if it had just happened. She saw again Anakin in her mind's eye. She could feel his cheek beneath her hand, smell him, taste his kiss again on her lips. He was her first and only love, her best friend, and he had been ripped from her far, far too soon. Learning from Han and Leia that even in death, Anakin still thought of her and loved her had gone a long way toward helping her heal in some respects, but in others, it only made the pain worse.

She took a sip of water before she spoke, giving herself a minute to regain her composure. "It was. I had wanted to see Anakin again to give myself closure, but . . . how it happened, how Jacen always managed to drag me away before I was ready to go—it was as if the wound were reopened, rather than healed. And yes, more than once, I wanted to fight alongside him. To save him, somehow."

"But you never did," pressed Eramuth. "As strong as the temptation—as the pain—was."

Tahiri bit her lip. "No," she said, quietly. "I never did.

I couldn't jeopardize the future, and Jacen had me convinced that I would do so."

"The future might have been the better for your intervention. Did you not think of that?" His tone was light, conversational.

Tahiri frowned. "There was no way that I could take that risk. I could never make that kind of a judgment call. It's a violation of everything I believe as a Jedi!"

He smiled, gently, his eyes crinkling. "As a Jedi," he repeated, giving each of the words weight. "And yet there are some in this courtroom who would hold that you are a Sith. Do you consider yourself a Sith, Tahiri Veila?"

Tahiri, her throat closed with emotion, shook her head mutely. She didn't know if she considered herself a Jedi, but she knew—just as Ben Skywalker had known, even when he was suffering at her hands—that she was no Sith.

"But you are convinced that Jacen Solo was by this point?"

She nodded. "I saw—" She cleared her throat. "I saw his eyes turn yellow."

"What sort of things do Sith do to people who cross their paths?" Eramuth now moved away, limping only slightly, his eyes on the jury but his ears swiveled back to catch her words. "Who fail to carry out their orders or even, say, their suggestions or implied desires?"

"I think people know what Sith do."

"Perhaps. But you have firsthand experience. Please tell the court the sort of things that might be in store for anyone who, shall we say, disappointed a Sith."

Tahiri took a moment. Then, calmly, she began to speak.

"They begin with just the threat. Or maybe I should refer to it as the promise, because they're certainly willing to keep it. They'll hint, or imply, or leave a sentence trailing with the single unspoken word that they know you're going to supply for them so they don't have to state it bluntly. It may be something they'll do to you, or to someone you love, or something, some ideal you cherish. And they'll promise to hurt you, or them, or it—hurt it in the exact way that it's going to cause the most pain."

The room had gone silent. Tahiri continued.

"Then there's the physical hurting. One of the most well known is something called a Force choke. That's when they reach out in the Force and just . . . clench their hands. And it's as if that hand is on your throat, except much, much stronger." She clenched her fist, then lowered it slowly. The jury was watching her raptly. "And . . . you choke. They use the Force to crush your windpipe. And of course, they don't stop there. They can hurl you against the bulkhead with a thought.

"Then there's Force lightning. Blue energy comes from their fingers. It burns and stuns and shocks, and it's painful, very painful. Excruciating. Then, finally, there's what they can do to your mind. Jacen Solo interrogated—well, if we're being honest, he tortured—a prisoner by forcing his way into her mind. She couldn't take it. It killed her. Painfully."

She spoke in a dispassionate tone, as if she were discussing the weather. She knew she wasn't trembling, but there was a knot inside her gut that wouldn't go away, hadn't gone away, not since the first time she had flow-walked back in time and given her past self a shove into the arms of Anakin Solo. Since she had started down the path of the dark side. Ben had tried to pull her back, and she thought he had succeeded. She wanted him to have succeeded.

She didn't want to be like Jacen.

She didn't *ever* want to be like Jacen.

Eramuth covered her hands with one of his own,

warm, reassuring, slightly furry. "May it please the court—knowing what lay in store for this young woman if she disobeyed even the vaguest suggestion Sith Lord Darth Caedus made . . . I ask you to consider what you might have done had you found yourselves in this same situation."

The jury was silent. Even the Mon Calamari, who had glowered at her so intently, had his head lowered.

The door at the back of the room opened to admit a latecomer. Tahiri's eyes were drawn by the movement. And then those eyes widened.

He stood there, a ghost come to life. Not the fifteen-year-old boy she remembered and loved, no, but Anakin as he would have been had he survived. Sandy-brown hair, blue eyes, ice blue eyes that were somehow never cold, not when they looked at her—

"Anakin," she whispered. The microphone picked up every syllable.

The crowd murmured and heads turned to where she was staring. The young man looked terribly uncomfortable and tried to duck out. The crowd's agitation increased.

"Order!" cried Judge Zudan. "You there. Please state your name and your reason for being in my courtroom."

And even as he opened his mouth to speak, Tahiri knew exactly who it was. The void left by the adrenaline leaving her system made her shake, and she was glad she had not been standing.

It was, of course, not Anakin Solo, although it looked exactly like him. It was, of course, Dab Hantaq, who had been kidnapped as a child by Senator Viqi Shesh and surgically altered to look exactly like the youngest Solo child. Shesh had plotted to kidnap Ben Skywalker through the deception, but the attempt had failed.

She cursed herself for her reaction. She knew about Dab's existence, had even *met* him before, for star's sake, when he had recently been assigned as a Jedi observer to Jaina Solo. But she hadn't expected to see him here, now, right when she was recollecting how badly she missed Anakin, reflecting on how much his death had shaken her.

"My apologies, Your Honor, I didn't mean to disrupt," Dab said. "I was just hoping to find a seat. If you'd prefer, I could just leave."

"Your Honor," Eramuth said, "a brief recess. The appearance of this . . . being . . . who bears such a resemblance to the late Anakin Solo has obviously rattled my client. I'd like to give her a few moments to compose herself before we continue."

Zudan nodded. "Ten minute recess. You, young man, either find a seat or stand in the back and stay quiet, or else leave."

"Yes, ma'am," Dab said, subdued. He looked apologetically at Tahiri, then away, and busied himself looking for a nonexistent seat. Tahiri's grief and shock turned to anger. She stepped down from the bench unsteadily, ignoring Eramuth's outstretched hand and heading straight for her chair. She lowered herself down and stared at the table, trying to calm her racing thoughts.

What was he *doing* here? Why had he come? Didn't he know how she would react if she saw—

Realization crashed down on her. Eramuth had settled himself into his own seat and had just turned to look at her compassionately.

"You told him to come," she said. Her voice was soft, but outrage simmered beneath it.

He gave her an apologetic smile. "I did, I'm afraid. He picked the perfect moment, too."

"Why?" Her voice started to rise and she forced it down with an effort. "Why would you do that to me? Put me through that?"

"I hope when you're a little calmer you'll forgive me," Eramuth said sincerely. "I told you before, the prosecution has the facts on their side. We have to have something else, and that's the jury's hearts. Your story, my dear child, is a moving one. I've not uttered a single lie, nor have you, and the jury has listened with an open ear, open mind, and an increasingly open heart."

"You want them to feel sorry for me," she hissed.

"More precisely," the Bothan continued, his voice melodious and pleasant even when he spoke barely above a whisper, "I want them to *empathize* with you. You've been through a terrible amount of pain in your short life. I want them to see that, because it is only then that they will understand why you did what you did. And that what you did was inevitable. Your reaction to seeing poor Dab could not possibly have been faked. Every being here *felt* it, even us non–Force-users. I haven't had to work very hard to get them to fall in love with you, metaphorically speaking, and Dab's appearance here and your reaction to him clinched it."

Tahiri buried her face in her hands for a moment. Her fingertips brushed against the scars on her forehead, marks of her time with the Yuuzhan Vong. She took a deep breath, then lifted her head.

"I know you're just doing your best to win this case," Tahiri said, composing herself with an effort. "I understand that. But I'm not sure I want to win it this way."

"Look at it differently, my dear. *When* we win," Eramuth said, "you'll have the rest of your life to despise me and my tactics."

# Chapter Twenty-three

BEN, LUKE, AND VESTARA GAZED THROUGH THE TRANS-paristeel screen at the *Rockhound*. Ben had been told it would be an incredibly useful thing to have, that it was big and powerful and could fly escort over the smaller ships like a protective entity. A huge, hideous, buglike protective entity.

The *Rockhound* was, without a doubt, the ugliest thing he had ever laid eyes on.

The thing was certainly *large,* his dad hadn't misinformed him about that. More than two kilometers long, in fact. But with what looked like at least a hundred telescopic legs with which to cling to asteroids dangling from a flat "belly," a rounded "back," and a circular "head" at the bow where the bridge and the living quarters were, well—

"It looks like an insect," Vestara said succinctly. Her nose wrinkled in disapproval. "How unattractive."

"It's supposed to hang on to asteroids," Ben found himself saying. "It doesn't need to be pretty." Why was he contradicting her? He agreed with her! And yet—briefly he wondered if all girls elicited this response from teenage males, or if it was just Sith girls.

She eyed him. "Simply because something is functional doesn't mean it needs to be ugly. Take the lightsaber, for instance. It is highly functional and very deadly, and yet it is a thing of beauty."

"We can argue about the need for aesthetics in prospecting vessels later," Luke said. There was a trace of exhaustion in his voice. "And I would imagine if the *Rockhound* turns out to save lives, we'll all find it very beautiful indeed. Take us in, Ben."

The *Rockhound* did not grow lovelier the closer it got. It looked barely spaceworthy, dinged, dented, and repaired. But then again, the same could be said for the *Millennium Falcon*. Ben could see now that the legs extended from the rim of the ship's underbelly, and that the flat base of the vessel was covered with huge, circular, tractor-beam projection fields. His respect for the decrepit old ship went up a few notches. If those things still worked as intended, the old tug really could haul something mammoth—or several small somethings.

"You could retool those to extend a field around several smaller ships," Ben said. "Protect them."

"I bet Lando has already thought of that," Luke said. "He's usually a step ahead of everyone when it comes to tinkering."

Ben thought about the first time they had gone through the Maw, imagined going through it again with this behemoth flying above them, and suddenly decided he could like the *Rockhound*.

Luke touched a button. "*Jade Shadow* to *Rockhound*. Glad you could join us, Lando."

Lando's voice sounded surprisingly weary. "Me, too, buddy. Listen, I know everyone wants to head on in, but I want to show you around this old tug before we take her into the Maw."

There was something not quite right about this. Ben saw his father's eyes narrow ever so slightly. Luke was facing away from Vestara, so she probably hadn't caught the gesture. Ben kept tight control over what he projected in the Force as he heard his dad answer casually, "Sure. Be right over. But let's make it fast, okay?"

"About the length of a sabacc game if you were playing against Han," Lando said, with a hint of his old cheer.

"Sounds good. *Jade Shadow* out." Luke rose. "Ben, you're in command until I return."

"Sure," Ben said. "Walk you to the Headhunter." He turned to Vestara. "Be right back. Don't touch anything."

She made a slightly disgusted sound. "Of course I won't."

It was almost, but not quite, a game. Ben knew that the moment they were out of sight, she would be sitting at the controls. She probably wouldn't touch anything; any attempt to contact the Sith vessels would be automatically recorded in the ship's databank. But she'd observe. She knew it, and he knew it.

Ben mentally shrugged. It was what it was, and whatever Lando had to tell his dad was more important. He'd picked up that much from Lando's tone of voice.

They walked together toward the single person Z-95 Headhunter. Quietly, Luke said, "I'm sure you figured out that Lando has something he needs to tell me."

Ben nodded his head. "Yeah, and it didn't sound good."

"Keep an eye on her, Ben. She's likable, and I know that."

"But you don't like her."

"I don't trust her."

"I don't trust her either. Not after what I heard." In the silence, the unspoken sentence, *But I still like her,* hung between them.

They reached the aft docking bay. The doors slid open. Luke put a hand on his son's shoulder. "I'll be back as soon as possible."

"Good," Ben said. Much as he disliked the idea of navigating the Maw again, he wanted to be done with all this. He wanted to get to this Abeloth, get some answers, and maybe go home. Say good-bye to Vestara, get her out of his system, and . . .

And do what? What *would* they do, once the alliance was dissolved? What could they do? She was Sith, from a whole planetload of Sith, and he and his dad were Jedi. His shoulders slumped beneath his father's hand, and he made no attempt to hide his weariness and despair in the Force.

"I know," Luke said. "We'll deal with all that when this is over."

"Mind reading a new Force power you picked up and forgot to tell me about?"

"No. I'm your father. That's my job."

If it had looked old and a little nerve-racking on the outside, the inside made Luke even less certain about bringing the Headhunter into the cavernous hangar of the *Rockhound*. He was worried that upon setting it down, the Headhunter might fall right through the tarnished deck.

But what drew Luke's attention immediately, at the expense of marveling how something this ancient was still spaceworthy, was the sight of a StealthX, its sleek lines and cutting-edge, black, star-dappled form as sharply at odds with the old hangar as possible. And then he felt a familiar presence in the Force. It was warm, loving, but its sharp brightness had dimmed somewhat, veiled by some sort of sorrow or regret. As he settled the Headhunter down—cautiously—and climbed out, the hangar door opened with an audible groan. Two figures entered, one small and female in a flight suit, one tall and male in stylish trousers and a hip cape. Both of them had furrowed brows.

"Lando," he said, nodding briefly to his old friend before turning his attention to his niece. "Jaina," he said, both pleased and irritated to see her, "what are you doing here?"

"It's a long story," she said.

"So is mine," Lando said. "And it's a little bit more immediate."

"I'm listening."

His blue eyes went wide, but he made no move to interrupt Lando as his old friend talked about Sith desecration of a religious site, blatant lies, siding with Hutts, and an imminent revolution.

"I shouldn't have gone," Luke said quietly. "Taalon played me. He insisted on leaving someone behind to wait for the *Rockhound,* and blast it . . . it made sense."

"It *did* make sense, Uncle Luke," Jaina said. "You couldn't have known what they were planning. How would anybody know they'd do something so drastic for some strange glasslike material?"

Luke rubbed his eyes. He was angry with himself. "That's just the point, Jaina. We don't know these Sith. We don't know what motivates them, or what their game is, or why they've really chosen to ally with me. I know what they've said, but that shouldn't be regarded as anything even in the vicinity of truth."

Jaina and Lando exchanged glances. "Look at it this way," Lando said. "The Fountain didn't seem all that damaged. You have at least one frigate's worth of Sith out of your way. And this might be the impetus for the Klatooinians to finally free themselves from a lousy bargain that should never have been made."

"I didn't come to start a revolution," Luke said, and then winced inwardly as he realized how that sounded.

"Not this time maybe," Jaina said. "But it's happening. And I think in the end, it's a good thing. We just wanted you to know what was going on."

"Thanks," Luke said. "Now, Jaina, we come back to my question—why are you here?"

Jaina planted her hands on her hips and looked up at her uncle. "Daala is up to her old tricks again."

Luke sighed. "What's she done this time?"

"We've had a few more Jedi snap," Jaina said. "Two, in fact."

"Sothais Saar and who else?"

"Two in *addition* to Saar." Luke whistled softly, then nodded for her to continue. "Turi Altamik and Kunor Bann. Daala doesn't know about Bann, which is a good thing for us, but she's putting the pressure on for us to surrender Saar and Turi."

"What kind of pressure?" Luke kept his face calm, but inwardly he had a bad feeling about this.

"First, she sent a nicely vague threat to Hamner, hinting that the families of the Jedi might be the ones to pay the price for our failure to ask 'how high' when she says 'jump.' That's when I left, so I wasn't caught when the Mandos started a siege."

Luke stared at her, disbelieving. "A siege. Daala is laying siege to the Jedi Temple. To get the release of two beings?"

Jaina nodded. "It's ludicrous and insulting and scary. I know it's Jedi who are going nuts, but I have to tell you, Daala is making decisions that sure don't sound very sane or smart to me." She hesitated. "Uncle Luke, don't you think it's time that you accepted some help? I know you made a deal with Daala, but she certainly isn't behaving rationally now, and you're being forced to ally with Sith against this . . . this unknown thing in the Maw. Wouldn't reinforcements be a good idea? Isn't this whole situation more important than your agreement with Daala?"

Luke sighed. "It's not for me to ask for reinforcements, or help of any kind. Jaina, you're one person and you're not acting on any orders by being here. You're my niece, and you want to help. That I can accept. But I'm trying to do more than just fulfill the terms of my arrangement with Daala. I believe I'm close to finding out what went wrong with Jacen, and to finding a cure for those who were in Shelter during the war. Daala's entire point is that the Jedi can't be trusted. If the Jedi Grand Master can't be trusted to keep his word, who can?"

Jaina glanced away at that. She was distressed, but he couldn't figure out why. And then his gaze fell on her hand, and he understood that sense of sorrow that muted her vibrancy.

She frowned a little as she followed his gaze, moving her left hand somewhat self-consciously behind her back. "Yes, okay, I ended the engagement. I'm the Sword of the Jedi. You named me so, Uncle Luke. And I've got to always remember that. No matter what my personal wants or needs are. I have a duty."

Luke didn't know the details of the situation. He didn't know if this decision was the right one or the wrong one. But right now, it didn't matter. She and Jag would either work it out or they wouldn't. But for now . . . "Well, I can certainly use another Jedi. I'll send you everything I have on Abeloth. But for now—let's get moving."

Ben glanced up as Luke returned. "So, is the *Rockhound* nicer on the inside?" Ben asked, then turned around to look at his dad. Luke's emotions were tightly controlled, but Luke was Ben's father, and there was a hardness to his normally open features and a set to his posture that made Ben instantly alert.

"No," Luke said bluntly, confirming Ben's initial impression. "Open a channel to the *Black Wave*. I want to talk to Taalon. It's urgent."

Vestara had entered just as Luke spoke. She gave Ben

a curious look and he shrugged and did as he was requested. "Master Skywalker," said Taalon, almost purring. "I see your friend and his . . . vessel . . . have arrived safely."

"They have, and we're almost ready to depart. I assume you noticed that only one of the ships you left back on Klatooine made it."

"Indeed. I understand your friend Lando and your . . . niece, is it? Jaina Solo? . . . were instrumental in resolving the situation."

"Situation?" said Vestara.

"Jaina?" said Ben, at the same moment.

Luke waved them to silence. "They rendered what they felt was a fair verdict. I hope you appreciate the scale of what you've just instigated, and the lives it might cost. Too bad you didn't get any samples."

Ben shot Vestara a look. It was her turn to shrug and shake her head in confusion. She seemed as baffled as he was by the conversation.

Taalon sounded offended when he replied. "*Samples*? Master Skywalker, I think it is obvious by now that the *Starstalker* acted on its own. I admit, the Tribe does have a certain fascination with glass, and with things of beauty in general. But cause that kind of an incident for a few samples? Please. It would create more problems than we need at this moment. No, it was foolish of Holpur, and he paid the price."

"Oh yes, he and his entire crew paid. Because your Captain Leeha Faal left him to twist in the wind," Luke said, his voice cold. "But I suppose that is standard behavior for Sith. I just wanted you to know I know, and I hope you won't leave *me* to twist in the wind like you did your own people. Regardless, we're a full vessel short right as we're going in to confront Abeloth. I hope that doesn't tip the balance."

"You sound like you're expecting a fight, Master Sky-walker," replied Taalon.

"I am always prepared to fight when I must—and who I must. Is your fleet ready?"

"They began preflight checks once your *Rockhound* and the *Winged Dagger* joined us," Taalon said.

"Good. I want to discuss our plan of action before we enter the Maw. Vestara, Ben, and I have all been to Sink-hole Station. I shared my report on what we found there with you."

Luke had agonized over that, Ben knew. He didn't want to share *anything* with the Sith, but if they were going to work together effectively as allies, they had to know what Luke and Ben knew about certain things. Sinkhole Station was on that list.

"Sinkhole Station was not in the best shape when we left it. Before we approach Abeloth's world, I want to go to the station again. I believe we will find information there that will help us."

"What kind of information?" Taalon was instantly alert.

"I'll have a better idea when we're there," Luke said, deflecting the question. In truth, Ben knew, Luke didn't think they'd find information. He wanted to see if there was any way he could effect repairs to the station, bring it back to its proper position. Because the more time passed, the more both Luke and Ben felt certain that Sinkhole Station played a vital role in keeping Abeloth where she currently was.

"Very cryptic of you, Master Skywalker. You'd have made a fine Sith."

Luke took a deep breath, and Ben felt him harnessing the Force to chase away the tendrils of anger and worry, replacing those negative emotions with focus and calm. He would not rise to Taalon's bait.

"We enter in the fan formation we agreed on," Luke

said. "The *Jade Shadow* and the *Black Wave* in the lead, the *Rockhound* in the center and above us all. Communication is going to be erratic at best and will vanish entirely the closer we get to Abeloth's planet. Every ship has the flight path laid in. Negotiating the path through the twin black holes as we go toward Sinkhole Station will be tricky but doable, and much safer with the *Rockhound* standing by. If we get separated, every ship also has the rendezvous coordinates laid in. Once we begin our approach to the planet, we should all be on high alert. Abeloth may come at us with everything she's got, or we might get lucky and take her unawares."

Ben and Vestara exchanged glances. Vestara, who had actually met Abeloth, shook her head slowly. Neither of them thought that would happen, and they knew Luke didn't either, but it was, technically, a possibility.

"We'll regroup there and assess the situation, make the rest of our plans from that point on."

"Agreed. The situation is constantly changing and unknowable, but we will adapt. We are Sith."

"And we are Jedi. We know how to adapt as well. *Jade Shadow* out."

The second the channel was closed Ben blurted out, "Dad—what happened on Klatooine? Where's Jaina?"

Luke turned around to look at Vestara as he replied. "Your Sith friends decided to violate the technology-free zone of the Fountain. Moreover, they apparently used their lightsabers to hack off pieces of wintrium, though no one can find them. It seems that the *Starstalker* acted on its own, and the rest of the Sith very much regret the diplomatic incident. Which could, by the way, lead to the overthrowing of the Treaty of Vontor and the liberation of the Klatooinian people."

Ben's jaw dropped, and Vestara's brown eyes widened. Ben thought about their conversation with Kelkad in the market, and the implication that some

Klatooinians, at least, were not happy serving as their ancestors had. He wondered what was going on on Klatooine right now, and while he was glad at the thought of what was technically slavery coming to an end, he wasn't naïve enough to think that it would be a peaceful termination. He hoped Kelkad would be okay, but supposed he would never know.

"I don't believe that for a minute," Luke was saying, "and I don't think anyone here does either. As for Jaina, she came to report on the current situation back on Coruscant and to bring her vessel to the fight if it comes to that."

Ben looked at the Maw, yawning ahead of them. He thought about tentacles, and cold, slithery need. His reaction was better than before, but he still could think of about a million other things—make that about four million—he'd rather be doing than voluntarily going back into this place to face this mysterious Abeloth.

He was only vaguely comforted when he glanced over his shoulder and saw that Vestara, too, looked like she'd rather be anywhere else but here.

"Here we go," Luke said quietly, and the strange fleet of Jedi, Sith, and a former roguish prospector-turned-gambler-turned-businessman moved forward into the gaping mouth of the Maw.

# Chapter Twenty-four

DAALA WATCHED, HER FACE IMMOBILE, AS THE GIRL went down.

She had authorized the use of lethal force if necessary when she spoke with Belok Rhal and put him in complete charge of the mission. "Do whatever's necessary, but I want those two Jedi."

She'd been surprised at the deadline he'd issued. But when he blasted the child—

No. Kani Asari, as the holojournalist was animatedly telling her the name was, was not a child. She was an adult woman, if young, and a Jedi apprentice. She was not an innocent. And if her death—starkly brutal as it was—had the effect of paralyzing the Jedi and making them think twice about the situation, then perhaps young Kani Asari had actually *saved* lives with her sacrifice.

Still. When the holocam panned back and focused tightly in on the limp form, Daala reached for the control and changed the channel.

This new channel showed something just as disturbing— the herky-jerky chaos and cacophony of a riot. The world was a bright one, a desert planet with blue sky and brown sand. And blaster fire. Lots and lots of blaster fire. The cam panned crazily about as the journalist ran for safety. He was saying something in one of the few languages Daala did not understand, but as he moved the cam about she recognized the species of the fallen.

Hutts. Klatooinians. Niktos.

The hair on the back of her neck prickled. It couldn't be. She clicked on the translator and suddenly Basic poured forth.

". . . attack on the Fountain four standard hours ago. Utter, absolute madness, shouting and singing and spontaneous dancing paired with blaster fire and death. No Hutt is safe here, on this world where they once were unquestioned masters. I repeat, the Treaty of Vontor, which has stood for more than twenty-five millennia, has been declared null and void, and the celebrating is—"

She couldn't believe it. She half-expected to see that Devaronian girl, Madhi Vaandt, reporting. This was her sort of environment, the end of the slavery she kept reporting on ad nauseum, and Daala bet she was kicking herself for missing it. Fortunately, Daala was spared that sight. She was relieved. Given her mood, she might have been tempted to hurl her cup of caf at the screen if Madhi's perky face had filled it.

*The Perre Needmo Hour* had a loyal following, and the series of reports on slavery in various distant and sometimes uncomfortably not-so-distant locales was very popular. It had inspired several peaceful protests and a few violent ones on the worlds from which they were broadcast, as well as motivating local clusters of Tatooinians, Chevs and, probably, Klatooinians to form their own parades and protests here on Coruscant.

Her comm buzzed. She knew who it was without even having to click on it. "Yes, Dorvan, I saw it."

"It doesn't look very good, ma'am. Gunning down an unarmed young woman."

"Jedi are never unarmed."

"Well, that's true, but—"

"I know what you meant. But at the same time, it

demonstrates how serious the situation is. Kenth Hamner has been given every opportunity to turn over the Jedi. Now, he gets to see the consequences of his actions. I regret this very much, but I did give Belok Rhal carte blanche to proceed as he saw fit."

"If there is another incident like this—"

"Wynn. They're *Jedi*. They're not stupid. Do you think, having seen this, that anyone would attempt that again?"

A pause. "No, ma'am."

"This siege, ideally, will result in no further bloodshed, the surrender of the Jedi crazies to me, and hopefully the education and submission of the Jedi as a group."

"I hope you're right, ma'am. There's something else I wanted to bring to your attention."

"The incident on Klatooine?"

"As is so often the case, you're a step ahead of me. It makes my job more difficult. But yes, this combined with the other incidents could spark more activity elsewhere. In fact, Desha has just placed reports on my desk of another freedom march that has all the earmarks of becoming a full-fledged revolt. This incident on Klatooine will no doubt inflame that situation."

Another one? What was going on? "Where?" She had muted the sound, but the silent celebratory rioting on Klatooine continued to unfold as she listened to Dorvan.

"Blaudu Sextus."

"Never heard of it."

"You're not alone, ma'am. And fortunately, given what else they have to cover at the moment, the holonews hasn't picked it up yet."

For an instant, Daala wondered if that was a subtle reprimand. She decided it wasn't. Dorvan either didn't comment, or said what he felt in his usual blunt, dry manner.

"The planet is little more than an out of the way mining colony," her chief of staff continued. "Their police force can handle a minor protest, but if this becomes a true revolt, they're incapable of putting it down. Unless we intervene, the government may fall."

As Daala watched, the cam closed in tight on the sight of a Hutt writhing in agony. Someone had put a blaster bolt right into his tail. She wasn't overly fond of Hutts, but they were sentient beings, capable of hate and greed and love and compassion just like anyone else. Granted, the latter qualities were not often seen in abundance in the species, but they were capable of it.

The protests held on Coruscant had, thus far, been peaceful. But violence was contagious. And the Treaty of Vontor had been the most famous example of slavery in the galaxy. With that gone—

"We can't let that happen," Daala said decisively. "We can't let Blaudu Sextus fall."

"It *is* very much out of the way, ma'am. Given the current situation, it might be advantageous for the GA to avoid intervening in internal politics at this juncture and let the problem solve itself one way or another."

Daala clicked back to the other channel. Javis Tyrr— wasn't Dorvan supposed to be doing something about the man?—was mercifully still muted, but the cam took a slow, loving pan over the armed Mandos standing almost as still as statues in a thick ring of beskar armor and weapons around the Jedi Temple.

"Has the Freedom Flight taken credit for the protest on Blaudu Sextus in any way?"

"No ma'am, this appears to be all localized. Hence my comment."

But Daala knew the Flight would, soon enough. And

then that little reporter would start covering Blaudu Sextus. And then . . .

"No," Daala said. "If the government topples, the rebels would think they can start picking away at the edges of Alliance territory. The Freedom Flight will step up activity there, start egging on would-be revolutionaries, and we'll have uprisings springing up like weeds all along the Outer Rim. This incident on Klatooine couldn't have come at a worse time. We need to stop this now, before it spreads."

"Well, ma'am, the Octusi slaves—"

"We don't *have* slaves in the Galactic Alliance, Wynn." She practically bit off each word.

"Of course we don't. The, ah, Octusi *servants* are pacifists, and if images of GA troops facing off against them in full riot gear start showing up on the holonews, it's not going to reflect well on us."

Daala nodded slowly, still watching the coverage of the siege. Her green eyes narrowed as the cam paused on Belok Rhal's scarred visage. It was the only solution. Things were getting out of hand, everywhere. She couldn't allow this spark to ignite other tinder-dry areas throughout the Alliance. It had to be contained. Stopped. And she knew who could get the job done.

"Well, then," she said, "we won't have GA troops in riot gear on Blaudu Sextus."

"I'm not following you, ma'am."

"Contact Belok Rhal. Tell him I need a rapid response Mando brigade to put this thing down. Now."

"Mandalorians? After what just happened?" Seldom did Wynn Dorvan's voice hold much expression other than dry humor. Now, he sounded incredulous. "That won't look any better than GA troops. In fact, it might look worse."

"If the revolt never has a chance to erupt, it won't

*look* like anything," Daala replied, with every word more convinced that this was the right thing to do.

"If it does? Needmo's Devaronian journalist seems to be everywhere these days."

"If it does, and Vaandt or anyone else picks up on it, the holonews picks up on it, who's to say *we* hired the Mandalorians?"

"Ma'am?"

"You've told me that Blaudu Sextus is a mining colony, correct?"

"Yes, but what—"

"So find a mining company to work with. We'll wash payment through them. If the holonews goes after the story, it will just look like a legitimate corporation is try-ing to protect its interests."

"Ah, I understand. I'll get Desha Lor right on it."

"I'd rather you do it, Wynn."

"Desha has proven herself quite capable of—"

"Mandalorians. Desha."

"I see your point. I'll get right on it, then."

Wynn Dorvan sighed. The small pet chitlik perched on his ear nibbled at his hair. He let her. He stared, but did not see the off-white walls of his office, or the safe art on those walls. He saw a Mandalorian gunning down an unarmed apprentice who had come out under the idea of truce. And now Daala wanted to use them again?

A tentative knock on the door. He knew who it was. "Come in, Desha."

The Twi'lek girl poked her head in. Her eyes were swollen; she'd been crying. He wasn't surprised, and was pleased that she had clearly gone to some effort to restrain the emotions that went with such a soft heart.

"Sir, it's the Solos again."

"Of course it is," he sighed. Orders had been issued to bring them in as soon as the siege began, but of course, they had dropped out of sight. They had been trying to contact him through untraceable means ever since the siege had begun, but Daala would have none of it. She had left very clear instructions that "I intend to speak to no one from that family until the current situation is under control or they're safely in custody."

He couldn't imagine what choice words they would have for him and Daala now that an apprentice had been brutally murdered right on the steps of the Temple.

On the steps of the Temple. He frowned. Something about the phrase . . . He shook it off. It would come to him later.

He knew what Han and Leia would say, and found himself agreeing with most of it, but concurring with them would do no good at this point.

"Tell them I'm not able to talk to them right now. And patch me through to Belok Rhal."

"Yes, sir," Desha said, closing the door behind her as she left. Pocket was now nibbling on his ear. He picked her up gently and put her back in her small nest on the corner of his desk. She rolled over, exposing her belly, and he rubbed the soft fur there with an index finger while he mentally shook his head at the fact that he was about to tell a Mandalorian to assemble a team to put down a pacifists' "revolt." He lifted the chitlik and placed her in the right-hand pocket of his jacket, still petting her.

His stomach rumbled, reminding him he had not eaten breakfast and lunchtime was fast approaching. It would seem, whatever the mind had to deal with, the body still stubbornly had its own needs and made them known.

A few moments later, the cold, almost emotionless voice on the comm said, "Rhal. What?"

"Commander Rhal, this is Wynn Dorvan, Daala's

chief of staff. I am speaking to you with the full authority of the Chief of State. I need you to—"

His eye fell on the chrono, and then it all clicked into place.

The steps of the Jedi Temple. Lunch.

In less than fifteen minutes, on an ordinary day, Raynar Thul would be coming out, as he had every single day since he had first embraced his freedom, to have lunch on the Temple steps. Dorvan had joined him for many of those lunches.

And he knew in his gut that something as trivial as being surrounded by a bunch of Mandalorians willing to gun him down was not going to stop Raynar Thul from having his lunch where he had always had it.

"Dorvan. Continue."

Dorvan felt sweat break out on his forehead. Nonetheless, he spoke in his usual calm, almost bland tones. "I need you to withhold fire on the Temple. I have it on good authority that Raynar Thul is about to come out."

"I've just promised the Jedi that we'd gun down anyone who wasn't Saar or Altamik," Rhal said, irritation creeping into his cool voice.

Wynn thought at hyperdrive speed. "I know, but I've been working on Thul for months. We've had lunch on the steps every day about this time. I might be able to use him to convince the Jedi to surrender."

A pause. Dorvan began to think that the Mando wasn't buying it. They would slaughter Thul, just as they had slaughtered Kani, and public opinion would simply not stand for it. There would be furious protests, perhaps even the riots that Daala was seemingly ready to practically sell her soul to prevent. Public sentiment would turn against the GA, and then—

"This is an order from the Chief of State." Wynn usually didn't lie, but this time, he felt the situation warranted it. "I will be there myself in a few moments. Stand down."

"I will not go back on my orders to my soldiers or my promise to the Jedi. It will weaken my standing with them, and Daala assured me I was free to use my best judgment. I answer to her, not you."

"You wouldn't dare fire on me!"

"Of course not." Rhal's tone suggested that he thought Dorvan considered him an idiot. "But you are not a Jedi."

"There will be no firing if I am on those steps!"

"No, sir. But five of your fifteen minutes have just gone by. If this Thul person is due to come out, I suggest you hurry."

Dorvan sprang from his chair and sprinted for the door.

# Chapter Twenty-five

DORVAN KNEW THAT IT WAS UNBECOMING OF SOMEONE in his position within the Galactic Alliance hierarchy to be running flat-out across the square to the Temple. He knew that Daala wouldn't like it. He knew that it would provide fodder for the reporters. He knew that if any of the Mandos whom he was racing toward had an itchy finger, he'd be dead.

None of that mattered. A man's life was at stake.

His eyes were on the steps of the Temple. Thul had not yet emerged, but Kani's body was still there. He slowed down slightly, holding out his ID, as a small group of Mandos broke formation and began trotting toward him.

"Wynn Dorvan, chief of staff to Admiral Daala," he said, panting slightly from the exertion. "Let me through. Commander Rhal knows to expect me."

They took seemingly forever looking at the ID, at him, and back at the ID again. A terrible thought struck him: what if Rhal had told them to delay him so that Thul could be executed? He wouldn't put it past the man, after what he'd seen today.

The precious seconds ticked by. Finally they waved him through the thick lines of machines and humans, two of them dropping into formation behind him, ostensibly acting as an escort. *Fine, then,* Dorvan thought, *let them escort me.* He began to push his way through, moving as fast as he could. One of his "escorts" laughed.

"Where is it exactly you're trying to go?"

"The entrance," Dorvan said. "On the steps to the entrance."

The Mando, her face hidden by her helmet, turned to regard him. "Not the best place in this world to be."

"Doesn't matter. Get me there."

"All right. Your funeral." He realized that she might very well be right—literally.

Still, having agreed to do so, she shoved her way effectively through the circle of beskar armor. Dorvan did not see Rhal, though he was most certainly here. Probably taking aim at the Temple entrance right now.

And then he was there. The steps loomed before him, looking impossibly high, taunting him that he'd never make it up there before Raynar Thul stepped out into firing range. He took them two at a time and had just cleared the top when he saw a movement beyond the pillars.

He'd been right.

Raynar Thul stepped forward, hand outstretched, and Dorvan moved to take it, clasping it hard in relief.

"Wynn," Thul said. "You shouldn't have come. It's dangerous." He tilted his head in the direction of the Mandos.

"I know," Wynn said, gasping a little. He wasn't unfit, but his job did render him sedentary, and he was trembling with the release of adrenaline.

"But you knew I would be here, even after what happened to Kani," Thul said. His face was shiny, almost artificial looking, and stretched in an odd way as he smiled.

"I did," Dorvan said.

Thul and Dorvan stepped out into what passed for sunlight on Coruscant. There was a strange sound, and Dorvan realized it was the noise of hundreds of weapons being trained on them. He swallowed hard, but Thul appeared unperturbed. He went to the first step and sat down. Several more steps down, almost to the bottom, lay Kani's body. Thul regarded it for a moment, then he reached for the small satchel he carried. Dorvan moved to stand in front of him, lest any of the Mandos decide that the satchel held something more dangerous than the sandwich Thul now produced.

Dorvan let out a sigh and dropped to the step beside Thul.

"You didn't bring anything for lunch?" Thul asked.

"I was . . . in a bit of a hurry."

Again, Thul smiled. "Here," he said, and handed half of the sandwich to Dorvan. He took it, not hungry at all, and gazed at Kani's body.

Thul ate methodically, as he always did. Dorvan knew the man intended no disrespect to Kani, and in fact, suspected that one of the reasons he was here right now was to honor her sacrifice.

Oh, no, despite what Rhal had done, the Jedi weren't cowed. Kani hadn't been, and Thul wasn't, and as Dorvan broke off a piece of crust to feed to Pocket, who had stuck her head out at the smell of bread, he wondered just exactly how the Jedi were going to get out of this one.

Because for all the show of force Daala had made, for all the Mandos who still kept careful aim on them both, if Dorvan were a betting man, he'd be betting on the man beside him rather than the soldiers in front of him.

"Han? You might want to take a look at this."

Leia's voice floated to Han, who was in the office of their safe-house apartments cleaning his blasters. They were in perfect condition, but it gave him something to do that at least marginally cheered him up.

"I don't want to take a look at anything, unless it's Daala's head on a pike." Hopefully, he added, "*Is* it Daala's head on a pike?"

"No, not quite, but it *is* her chief of staff running up the steps of the Temple at top speed."

Han rose and went to look at the holovid. "Huh . . . ?" he said, baffled at the sight of the normally calm, almost emotionless Wynn Dorvan running full tilt.

"And we have confirmation that it is indeed Chief of State Daala's right-hand man, Chief of Staff Wynn Dorvan, who is racing headlong up the steps of the besieged Jedi Temple," Javis Tyrr was saying. "He did have a Mandalorian escort as he fought his way through the crowd, and I don't see anyone taking aim at him, so one must assume that he is here on official Galactic Alliance business. Looks like the Jedi must have agreed to—"

Han's mouth fell open. "Thul?"

Leia didn't quite gape, but her brown eyes were wide.

"Why, it's Raynar Thul," said Javis Tyrr. The cam focused in on Thul and Dorvan shaking hands. "As our viewers of Episode 14 of *The Jedi Among Us: Where Are They Now?* know, Raynar Thul has been rehabilitated and has kept a kind of vigil every day at this time, having lunch on the steps of the Temple. I've conducted a few interviews with him. It looks like nothing, not even a Mandalorian siege, is going to keep Thul from enjoying his regular lunch break."

"What the hell is Dorvan doing there?" Han demanded. "You think he's trying to strike a deal with Thul?"

Leia shook her slightly-gray-streaked head slowly. "No, neither of them works that way," she said. "I think he may have been trying to save Thul's life."

"Well, that's noble of him, but he could have saved K.P.'s—aw, blast it, Kani's—life and maybe a whole bunch of others if he and Daala would just back off."

As if on cue, the cam left the two lunching men to linger on Kani's body and the pool of drying blood in which it lay.

"I don't know how either of them can eat, sitting there

looking at her," Han continued, his voice growing angry again.

"Well, nothing Thul does would surprise me at this point, and Dorvan's feeding his half of the sandwich to his chitlik." Indeed, the cam, with the nanosecond memory that the holojournalists appeared to have had these days, had gone from the grisly sight of a corpse to a close-up of a small, adorable animal sitting in Dorvan's lap, holding a piece of bread crust in its forepaws as it ate.

Han snorted in disgust, but Leia suddenly froze. Han eyed her. "What is it? What did you just figure out?"

She turned to him, smiling slowly. "How we can help the Jedi."

Seha Dorvald was exhausted, filthy, and hungry. She and her Master, Octa Ramis, each with six apprentices, had been exploring as many sealed-off, built-over, or otherwise inaccessible egresses from the Temple as they could for the last seven hours. Some of the apprentices were small enough to wriggle down shafts that were impassable for adults. Thus far, however, there had been nothing large enough for even the smallest ones to scramble through.

The good news, if there was good news, was that none of these secret . . . airholes, Seha supposed was the most accurate way to describe them, had attracted the notice of the Mandalorians. That was something. And initial signs indicated that some of them could possibly be enlarged.

She was crawling through a narrow passageway to report back to Master Ramis. A glow rod was tied around her neck, offering at least some light. The tunnel was covered on all four sides with ancient tile slicked with mold. Some of the tiles were broken, and the smell of moist soil and rotting things assaulted her nostrils. Seha moved forward slowly, her gaze two meters ahead. She was tired, and damp and chilled, and as she was returning rather than venturing forth, she wasn't paying close attention. Her hand came down on something soft that squelched beneath it. A fetid stench assaulted her and she had to struggle not to vomit. It was some sort of vermin, she didn't really want to know what. She shoved the decaying corpse aside, wiped her hand on the tiles, and continued on.

Her comlink chirped. She made a slight face of irritation and halted, turning awkwardly on her side to bring it out.

"Seha here."

"Seha . . . have you noticed anything . . . unusual?" It was her Master.

"Um, no, Master, not really. I gave you all the information I gathered on the way out. I don't know how old this tunnel is, but it hits a dead end." She was confused by the question.

"Well . . . make haste, child. There's something here you need to see."

Exhausted as she was, Seha felt curiosity stir, and she picked up the crawling pace. Within fifteen minutes, the ancient tile lining the sides of the tunnel gave way to some kind of metal, and then she saw a glimmer of light ahead. A few minutes later, she dropped down from the shaft into a supply room, where Octa was waiting.

"Okay, so what's so . . ."

Her voice trailed off. Octa Ramis stood beside a set of shelves that were loaded with small boxes of various sizes. Seha didn't know what they contained, and right now she didn't care. Because at Octa Ramis's feet were no fewer than three rodents. They were in no way cute or appealing; these were vermin, plain and simple. But they sat on their haunches as if they were trained, and there was something tied to each of their backs.

"What . . . ?"

"There are more. Lots more. They've come in through every aperture wide enough to permit them passage," Octa said. She was grinning. "We didn't understand what was going on at first, and some of them were frightened away or killed. We thought we'd disturbed some kind of huge, secret nest. But then Master Horn noticed this."

She reached and picked up one of the filthy things and held it out to Seha. The animal remained quiet and calm.

Bound to its back was a small vial of liquid.

"The medication Cilghal was running out of," Seha said quietly. "The sedatives to keep the sick Jedi from harming themselves." Suddenly, the little animals didn't look like disgusting, filthy vermin at all. Suddenly, they looked like the most beautiful, most wonderful creatures in the universe.

"Exactly," Octa replied, her grin widening. "I don't know the identity of our mysterious benefactors, but I can make a guess."

"Valin used the Force to command the creatures that lived here to help him escape," Seha recalled. "No wonder Master Horn was the first to notice something different about these rats."

"But this time, they're coming to help the sick Jedi. We are still short, but there are enough vials to get us through the next twelve hours, at least. And who knows, more may come."

"And if we can get medicines *in*," Seha said slowly, "We might be able to get messages *out*."

"It's already in progress," said Octa. "Now come on. Let's get the vials off these little fellows and in the hands of Cilghal. And," she added, "let's get you a sanisteam."

For the first time since the siege began, Seha laughed.

# Chapter Twenty-six

THE THREE OF THEM CURLED UP TOGETHER ON THE sofa, mugs of hot chocolate warm in their hands. Allana slurped hers rather noisily, and Leia smiled gently.

"You need a shave, young lady," Leia said playfully, reaching over to wipe off the whipped cream mustache with a napkin. Allana giggled, then returned her attention to the show. She took another sip and gave herself another mustache, and Leia simply shook her head this time. Han sprawled on the sofa, loosely cradling his granddaughter. Anji was draped over both their laps, snoring softly.

It was odd, that this was a tradition. And yet not so odd. Leia was the adopted daughter of a prince and a politician, and had been a Senator of her world at nineteen. Politics, galactic events, this had been as much a part of her childhood as small pets or toys or her beloved, and foul-smelling, thranta. Allana came from a similar background. As long as the news was not too graphically violent or disturbing, and *The Perre Needmo Newshour* usually wasn't, Leia was more than content for the breather in their day.

The theme music played and then the visage of Perre Needmo, sitting behind his desk, filled the screen. To humanoid eyes, Chevins were not particularly attractive, but there was something about Needmo that Leia always found appealing. The wisdom and calmness in his wrinkled face, the white in the small tufts of hair. Maybe it was the fact that even if the ugliest being in the known galaxy was hosting the news, and it was as neutral or even upbeat as the show currently was, she'd be happy to watch it.

The Jedi Temple siege, of course, was the lead story. As was usual with the show, coverage downplayed the graphic violence. They even scorned to show what could have been a ratings-grabbing image. Leia had learned that after Dorvan had finished his "lunch" with Raynar Thul—during which he had inadvertently given her the idea of how to smuggle medicine and messages in to the besieged Jedi—he had picked up Kani's body and borne it away. A statement had been issued shortly thereafter from the office of the Chief of State: "It is regrettable that any lives needed to be lost in the Galactic Alliance's pursuit of justice. Our sympathies are with Kani Asari and her family. It can be hoped, however, that her sacrifice was not in vain."

The Perre Needmo Newshour did not focus on that admittedly powerful image; instead, it homed in on the political impasse. Beings on the streets were interviewed, and most of them looked unfavorably on the siege.

"Someone's already been killed," one Ithorian said, blinking her large eyes. "The Chief of State is, I think, right to want to restrain any Jedi that might be harmful to the populace. But at the same time, this is the wrong way to go about it. I'd rather see negotiations than sieges or attacks, since I think that both Daala and the Jedi want to do what is right."

Others espoused the same opinion. The holocams panned over a not-inconsiderably-sized gathering that waved cards that said TRAP THE JEDI, TRAP OUR FREE-

DOM and other sentiments. One had a poster of Daala swathed in Palpatine's robes that read NEVER AGAIN.

"Huh," said Han. "Is it me, or does Daala look good in those robes? Like she was made for them?"

"Chief of State Daala looks best in her admiral's uniform," Leia said diplomatically, "when she is remembering where her real duty lies."

"I think she's beyond remembering. She tried to kill us."

It was hard to argue with that, and Leia wisely didn't.

They had all recovered, as much as one could recover, from Kani's murder. They had found renewed hope in action. Leia had remembered that Cilghal's supply of sedatives was running low, and the last thing the Jedi needed right now was to worry about the three distraught beings attempting escape or violence, to themselves or others. It had been a long shot, but it had worked—the rodents had come when summoned, and had sought out any entrance small enough for them to slip through. And when one of them emerged with a message, Leia felt a terrible knot in her gut ease, if only slightly.

*To our benefactors,* Kenth Hamner had written in the encoded note—he had not signed his name, of course, but Leia knew his flowing, precise script—*we are all well. It would take more than a display of Mando brutality to crush the Jedi spirit. If this reaches you, return correspondence.*

Leia had done so, using the same code and in her own hand so that her handwriting would be recognized by the Jedi as Kenth's had been by her. The chance of interception was small, but not nonexistent, so she kept it brief and cryptic until she received a reply that would indicate the messages were getting through. It had come shortly—a report that all avenues of escape were being pursued and that the Jedi were standing firm. The strike team was still ready to launch, once such a thing was physically possible; they had not abandoned her brother. The letter closed with a request for more medicines, and a list of specifics. Han and Leia had spent the better part of the evening rounding up as many vials as they could, strapping them to the backs of Force-calmed critters, and sending them forth from the safety of several hundred meters away from the encircling ring of Mandos and their machines of death and siege.

More they could not do at this hour, and had come home just in time for some quiet time with their granddaughter. Leia focused on the love she felt for these two people, letting go of her worries about the Jedi for the moment and permitting love for Han and Allana—yes, and Anji, too, who lifted her head and tilted it inquiringly at Leia at that instant—to fill her heart. There was no segment from Madhi Vaandt tonight, and Leia was sorry about that. She liked the spunky young Devaronian, and her coverage always left Leia feeling reenergized.

"Finally tonight, a news item and an editorial in one." Needmo looked grave. "We at *The Perre Needmo Newshour* have long believed in a journalistic tradition of unbiased, honestly obtained, accurate information. We report. We do not spy, we do not invent, and we do not resort to illegal methods of obtaining information. We occasionally have guest journalists on the show who are passionate about what they cover, and seek justice as much as they seek accuracy. We take care to always identify such things as editorials, such as Madhi Vaandt's continuing coverage of the institution of slavery throughout the galaxy, and also this current editorial." He smiled, his small dark eyes crinkling and his snout twitching.

"For the last few years, our honorable profession has come under attack. Not necessarily from governments interested in suppressing a free press—although that has happened on occasion as well—but from within our own ranks. A cancer has formed, a cancer of greed, ego, and ruthlessness that has led to a mind-set of ratings and personal fame at any cost. While those of us who work on this show despise such action, we have never publicly reproached a fellow journalist who has chosen to follow that path. We have stayed out of the fray—out of the pit as it were—trusting in the good sense of the viewers to support whomever they feel is correct."

Leia glanced over at Han, and read the hope in his brown eyes. She didn't dare to voice it. After all this time, all they had been forced to put up with, she didn't want to jinx it. Even so, she found herself crossing her fingers.

"However, once a journalist has violated the law, and there is evidence of such activity, then such a being has gone too far. Taking money for slanting the news in a certain direction violates any decent journalistic code of ethics, and the utilization of advanced technology to illegally obtain information without the knowledge and consent of the individual whose words or actions are being recorded constitutes breaking the law of the Galactic Alliance."

And there it was. Leia felt a grin stretch her face. Han actually whooped out loud and came close to spilling his hot chocolate. "Well, it's about time!"

Never had Leia been so glad to see Javis Tyrr's smirking face fill the screen. Except this time the smirk was notably absent, the finely coiffed hair was messy, and there was a look of panic in the reporter's eyes. Needmo's words continued as the footage rolled.

"They stopped the lying journalist?" asked Allana.

Leia was hard-pressed not to laugh out loud. Out of the mouths of babes. "Looks like, honey."

"At fourteen hundred hours this afternoon, based on

an anonymous tip, journalist Javis Tyrr was arrested at his residence on charges of illegal espionage. While hidden cams are, sadly, nothing new in the arsenal of those determined to get a story at any cost, there are laws in place that prohibit the use of illegal devices. Unfortunately, the device that Tyrr used to record certain events seems to have disappeared, but there is other evidence. A recording has come to light that shows Tyrr inserting said illegal device and revealing its source."

Han and Leia exchanged glances. "Are you thinking what I'm thinking?" Leia said.

"Jaina wouldn't have given them the chip."

Leia frowned, confused. "Then how . . ."

"Who knows," Han said. "Does it matter? Sleemo's got what's coming to him. Someone was on the ball and found him out." He lifted his half-drunk mug of hot chocolate. "Here's to whoever it was. If I find out, I owe you a drink."

Anji was purring madly at the delight so obviously present in the room. Leia petted the creature, then stroked Allana's short, black-dyed hair.

And then she knew.

"Han?"

"Hm?"

"Who do we know who's smart, methodical, patient, appreciates fairness, and works well behind the scenes?"

"A lot of people," Han said.

"I'll narrow it down for you. Who's all that, who also supports Daala?"

"Dorvan?" Han said at once.

"Daala came out looking pretty bad whenever Javis Tyrr got her in his sights," Leia said.

"Yeah, that's true. Plus he's got the resources to do some snooping if he had to. Well, at least he did us a favor, as well as Daala. Hell, he's done the entire journalistic field a favor."

"I just don't know what to think about that man," Leia said. "One minute I think he's on our side, the next he's on Daala's."

"He's walking a very fine line, that's for sure. I hope he ends up on the right side when things finally come to a head."

Leia looked at him. She agreed, but had not wanted to say so. She, too, anticipated a crisis in the near future. Dorvan was a good man, but there were plenty of times where good men were on the wrong side of things when the point of no return came.

Allana was quiet, watching them carefully, and Anji's purring had stopped. Leia smiled at her family, willing away the unease and again summoning calmness and love to close out the evening. Tomorrow's troubles could come tomorrow, not tonight.

"Who wants more hot chocolate?" she asked.

# Chapter Twenty-seven

THE NEWS OF THE DISSOLUTION OF THE TREATY OF Vontor had been stunning. Madhi had been torn between elation for the Niktos and Klatooinians and journalistic irritation that she hadn't been there to cover it while it was all unfolding. She had immediately ordered a change of plans, to go to Klatooine to cover what she could of it. Tyl Krain and the pilot of the *Shooting Star*, a Twi'lek named Remmik Kulavinar, hadn't been too enthusiastic, but she found that Shohta was. Watching him over the last few days had been alternately fascinating, heartwarming, and distressing. The former slave had a great deal to work through emotionally. Sometimes he seemed almost childlike, other times angry. But most of all, he struck her as vibrant, perhaps truly alive for the first time in his life.

On the flight to Klatooine, she recorded a brief essay to transmit to Coruscant. It would be played on the next *Perre Needmo Newshour*.

"To watch this . . . rebirth, almost, into who he now is—it is a privilege," she said, looking right into the cam. "It is humbling and frightening and exciting. And to think that his story, from slave to freed being, could be reenacted literally billions of times over—well, in this reporter's opinion, the galaxy is unprepared for the outpouring of emotions and contributions liberty and freedom could bring it. Governments stand to gain more than they lose. A freed being contributes so much more to a society than a slave. I'm excited to be living at such a monumental time in our history. This is Madhi Vaandt, reporting aboard the *Shooting Star*."

Tyl usually gave her a smile and some kind of word of approval, or else requested to do another take if he wasn't satisfied with the quality of her work, sound recording, or lighting. But this time, he said nothing, and Madhi was instantly alert.

"What is it, Tyl?"

"Remmik says you've got an incoming message," he said. "I didn't want to interrupt the filming, but he says he hasn't been able to identify or trace it."

"What did it say?" Madhi had few secrets from her crew, and they were all free to listen to any incoming messages. They were part of a team, with the same goal.

"It's scrambled," Tyl said. "Requires you to give a voice sample in order to play."

Madhi frowned. "That's very—" Her eyes flew open wide. "I wonder . . . Come on!"

She raced from the room that served as the set while traveling toward the cockpit, her small crew following her and crowding into the cramped space. Remmik glanced up as she entered.

"Tyl told me," Madhi said. Remmik nodded and rose, giving her the controls. She sat down and thumbed a button. "This is Madhi Vaandt, activating voice recognition. Please decode the message."

She was trembling as she waited, and then a voice began to speak.

"Greetings, Madhi Vaandt. I know that you are in receipt of our last letter. Thank you for staying silent on the nature of the Freedom Flight. While we are proud of what we do, and while rumors certainly abound, we would have you reveal more about us at a time of our own choosing."

Everyone was grinning nervously. Madhi couldn't have wiped the smile off her face if she had tried.

"Detour to the coordinates you are about to receive. I will meet you there. Come alone, and I will tell you more about our mission, and give you some information that you will find to be to your benefit."

"Alone? Mist-Madhi," Shohta said, stopping himself from using the phrase that, to him, denoted that Madhi owned him, "I don't like the sound of that. This could be a trap. I am sure you have amassed many enemies doing these reports."

"I'm sure, too," she said, "but the message referenced the letter."

"Which could also have been written by someone trying to entrap you," the Chev said. "Think about it. You were cautioned *not* to speak. Not to talk about the Flight until such time as this mysterious unknown being chose to speak with you."

Madhi, seated at the helm, glanced up at him. His history made him mistrusting. She imagined he had seen a lot of lies and betrayal in the service of Guumak. And the honest truth was, his argument made sense. She didn't discount that her pieces might be responsible for instigating protests on some worlds or that more than a few beings might be delighted to see her dead.

"There's something called a journalist's instinct," she said. "Some people call it a nose for news. My instincts are saying that this contact doesn't mean me any harm. I've been in worse situations than this, Shohta. Really, I have. Thank you for your concern, though." She turned to Remmik.

"Let's make that rendezvous," she said.

*      *      *

The place they were sent wasn't even named. A moon over a planet called Vartos, it was essentially a rock. An out-of-the-way rock, with a thin but breathable atmosphere. There did not appear to be any native plants or animals, nor was there any water. The specific area to which they had been directed was almost entirely flat, with only a few rock formations dotting the landscape here and there.

The ship landed gently, raising a furious cloud of dust. A second moon and Vartos shone like a pair of eyes in the dark nighttime sky. Madhi was running on adrenaline; she hadn't slept for two days straight. But she was used to that. Her career had frequently taken her to dangerous places where hot food, a warm bed, and personal safety were not always in abundant supply. And like any journalist, for Madhi, the thought of a good story made everything worth it.

"You sure you won't let me put a tracking device or a recorder on you?" Tyl asked. Madhi shook her head vigorously.

"Come on, Tyl, who do you think I am, Javis Tyrr?" The laughter broke the tension. "I know the contact said come alone, and I want to show I can be trusted. I'll take my comlink and bring a recorder, and ask his or her permission before turning it on. That's how I work."

Tyl sighed. "I worry about you, Madhi. You take a lot of risks."

She shrugged into her many-pocketed vest and went to the open hatch. Before jumping down she turned around and gave him a playful smile. "That's how you get the good stories, Tyl. You should know that by now."

And then, armed with only a glow rod, she stepped forward into the night.

The glow of the moon and planet cast a significant amount of light in a place utterly bereft of light pollution, and she was able to stride briskly and with confidence. The coordinates were quite specific, and Madhi quickly figured out that her destination was one of the few rock formations they had spotted from the air. She paused after walking for about fifteen minutes and looked back. She could still see the small lights of the ship, and nodded.

Madhi continued forward, until she stood in the shadow of the looming rocks that looked like jagged, broken teeth. She saw nothing, heard or smelled nothing, but just the same, she sensed someone was there.

"I've come alone, as you asked," she said.

"Thank you," said a voice right by her ear.

Despite herself, she started and turned quickly. A Bothan stood less than a third of a meter away from her. He was dressed in dark clothes, and most of his face was hidden by a cowl. He moved it back, revealing his features, and smiled, teeth flashing white in the moonlight.

"You must do this a lot," Madhi said, recovering.

"Indeed I do." He gave her a slight bow. "You handle it better than most."

"I take it you're the being who gave me the letter on Vinsoth?" she asked, recovering her professional composure. Her hand slipped down into her pocket. "Mind if I record the conversation?"

"I assumed you were already doing so."

Madhi shook her head. "I do interviews, not surveillance," she said.

"I approve," her contact replied. "You may record it, but only for your personal use. My voice and features must not be broadcast. Beings could die—including me."

She nodded. "Of course." Madhi clicked it on. "So . . . can you give me your name?"

"Not my real name," the Bothan said, "But you may call me Blink."

"As in, don't blink or you'll be gone?"

"Precisely."

"Okay, Blink. You are a member of the Freedom Flight. How long has the organization been in existence?"

"Formally? Only about six years. Informally, individuals and small groups have been assisting slaves to escape ever since the institution of slavery began. Always, where there is a hand to hold down and crush, there is another to release and nurture."

*Beautiful words,* Madhi thought. *Wish I'd thought of them. This guy's a natural.*

"Tell me how you operate."

"It is a loosely knit organization," Blink said. "Each chain knows of only a few links. That way, if one of us is caught, there is a finite amount of others we can betray if tortured."

"You expect to be tortured?"

His eyes glittered in the light. "Some cultures would not hesitate to use torture. Think about what we are doing, Madhi. We could topple governments, destroy cultures, ruin worlds, according to what some beings believe."

"Do you believe that?"

"Yes," he said firmly, surprising her. "It will have to be the result of finally and completely stamping out the institution. The change will be drastic, more so in some places than in others. Understand, though, that it is not the chaos we are after. It is the order after *that* which we seek—the just order that must come once all beings are able to breathe free. If that order can come calmly and peacefully, then all the better. But it must come. You know that yourself, or else you would not be moved to cover these stories as passionately as you do."

He was right, she realized. She was proud of that, but at the same time knew she needed to maintain proper journalistic impartiality. She steered the conversation back toward its organization.

"So for instance, if you were captured, how many could you betray?"

"Only four," he said. He smiled, again showing white teeth. "But I would not talk."

"I believe that," Madhi said, and she did. "So you use aviation terms: flight path, pilot, cargo, and so on."

"We do. It is safer if we are accidentally overheard. Nine hundred and ninety-nine times, if you are in a spaceport and hear those terms, they are not Freedom Flight members uttering them."

"But that thousandth time they might be."

He nodded.

"What do you think of the situation on Klatooine? Was that instigated by the Flight?"

Blink started to answer, gave her a slightly crafty tilt of the head, and said, "Off the record."

Madhi immediately clicked off the recording device. "For my ears only," she said.

"And charming ones they are," the Bothan replied. Madhi chuckled. "For your ears only, then—no. We do have pilots and other Flight crew stationed there, of course. But the violation of the Fountain—such a thing is reprehensible to us. We respect the enslaved cultures we are struggling so hard to liberate, and endeavor not to do anything that would offend them. Later, perhaps, we will reveal this about the Flight, but for the moment, let beings wonder. Let the Flight scare those who stand to lose much through the abolishment of slavery."

"But the results?"

"The violence is regrettable, but under the unfortunate circumstances it is understandable. The Hutts, the Klatooinians, and the Niktos will have to reach some kind of accord—or not—on their own. Our Flight crews are already departing Klatooine to put their efforts elsewhere where they are needed."

"And where might that be?"

Blink chuckled. "Here's a question for you," he said, "and then I must depart. Where are you heading next?"

"I'm not sure I should be telling you," she replied cagily.

"I would assume Klatooine. But that's not where the story is. If I were you, I would be heading for Blaudu Sextus."

Madhi looked at him, confused. "I've never heard of it."

"Look it up." He stepped back, merging with the shadows of the jutting rock formation. "I think you'll be very glad you did."

# Chapter Twenty-eight

"I'VE . . . GOT A STRANGE FEELING," BEN SAID AS THEY moved slowly through the Maw. He frowned slightly.

"What is it?" Luke asked.

"As if . . . *as if I've been here before!*"

"If I weren't such a tolerant parent I'd box your ears," Luke said. Ben grinned.

"I'll do it," Vestara offered.

"You would," Ben said. Vestara smiled with mocking sweetness that melted into a genuine smile.

The banter was weak, but Luke did not discourage it. Communication had been spotty since they entered the Maw, and everyone, including himself, was on edge. To call this alliance "uneasy" was an understatement, and he did not like being incommunicado with nearly a dozen Sith frigates and the *Rockhound*.

Information had been exchanged. Everyone had the same star charts of the area; everyone had the course plotted and explained. The *Rockhound* hovered over all of them like some extraordinarily ugly mother hen with its chicks, ready to latch on to the *Jade Shadow* or the frigates if any of them showed signs of drifting. Or, Luke had told Lando privately, signs of veering off with possible hostile intent.

Up ahead loomed the twin black holes, looking, as

Ben had described, uncomfortably like eyes. Ben was in the pilot's seat, and Luke made no move to take his place. He'd done a fine job taking them through this once before; Luke had confidence Ben could do so a second time.

"All the caranaks in a row?" Luke asked.

"All present and accounted for. We're a little ahead of the flock, and judging by the *Rockhound*'s pace she's going to drop a bit behind in case there are stragglers."

Luke nodded. "Take her in, son."

Ben closed his eyes for a moment, breathing steadily. His instruments were practically useless for this maneuver, and the Force would be a much more reliable guide. Vestara leaned forward in her seat expectantly.

Ben swore softly. "Stang. It's not there. Never thought I'd be happy to say I didn't feel that tentacle, but it's not there."

"What do you mean?" Luke asked.

Ben's blue eyes flickered to Vestara. Luke felt him weighing the merits of explaining or staying silent. Ben chose to speak. Luke approved; at this juncture, the more information they shared, the better. At least about this.

"I used the Force to bring the *Jade Shadow* between the black holes through Stable Zone One. To Sinkhole Station. I felt a weird dark tentacle thing reaching out to me. I recognized it from when I'd lived in the Maw before, as a kid. It was needy. It wanted to find me—keep me safe, with it. And instead of shutting down, I kind of used it as a rope to guide the *Shadow* in."

"And it's not there now," Luke said, nodding. "She doesn't want us to sense her. I'm not surprised that she's able to hide herself in the Force so well, as powerful as she is."

"Well, it doesn't make my job any easier," said Ben. "I can try, but I have to tell you, Dad, I don't feel at all certain about navigating the *Shadow,* let alone guiding the way for the whole fleet."

"That's understandable," Luke said. "Let me take the helm."

"I can get us there," Vestara said abruptly, surprising them both. "I know the way."

Luke and Ben exchanged glances. "You got to Dathomir on a rickety vessel," Luke said, "but I don't think you can handle this."

"Perhaps I'm not as skilled as Ben or you, but good enough. I learn fast."

"Learn fast?" Ben said, instantly alert. Luke was, too—did she mean she hadn't had much training? But she had shut down and had now turned to the console.

"You are very strong in the Force, Master Luke."

"Thank you."

"It is not a compliment to accurately assess one's en—allies," Vestara said. "You stand the best chance of getting us there in one piece. I ask to be allowed to plot the course and copilot."

"Fair enough," Luke said, slipping into the pilot's seat. Vestara threw him a quick glance, as if reading his thoughts, then sat beside Luke. Her fingers, long and elegant, flew over the console deftly, as if she were playing an instrument, and her smooth brow furrowed in concentration.

"Here," she said. "This is . . ." Her voice trailed off.

Luke had to fight to keep his shock from registering strongly in the Force. The star map she called up was exactly what he had seen at Sinkhole Station, when he had entered the room with the white cabinets and seen several holographic representations of other places, the station itself, and what seemed to be a complete map of the entire Maw cluster.

There had been a crescent-shaped gap on the map. When Luke had touched it, an outline had appeared of a long crack in the shell of black holes. And it was into this void, this crescent, that Vestara was taking them. He and Ben had come this way, but not so far as to see this. In the center of the crescent was a pinpoint of brightness—a blue star.

Except it had changed since the last time Luke had seen it displayed at Sinkhole Station. And apparently, judging from her reaction, it had changed since Vestara had seen it. The crescent had been a sliver, like a few-days-old moon. Now it was a semicircle, like a half-moon.

"It's grown," Vestara said. "This area here," and she pointed to the half-moon of darkness, "used to just be a crescent. It's gotten larger."

"I saw a map of this area at Sinkhole Station, and you're right," Luke said.

"That star is the sun of Abeloth's world," Vestara continued, recovering from her shock. "The light is blue. It's quite lovely. The world is very hostile, completely unnatural. The animals thrive by photosynthesis, and the plants prey upon them." She gave Ben and Luke a half-smile. "Keeps you on your toes."

"And Abeloth controls everything," Luke surmised.

"She does."

"Great," said Ben.

Luke did not reply. More than ever, he was convinced that Sinkhole Station's job was to keep this being in line—keep the black holes surrounding her world, so that she couldn't escape. When he and Ben had been there, the station had clearly been falling into disrepair and it looked like the situation had worsened just in the short time they had been away. Now the area to which Abeloth had been confined had shifted ominously, and this bright blue star burned like a defiant flag run up a pole, daring them to come and get her.

Which, Luke mused, they would.

"We will likely encounter Ship," Vestara said, as if she were just making conversation.

"Yeah," Ben said. "Probably."

She glanced over her shoulder at him. "You know about Ship?"

"I know more than *about* him, I piloted him for a while."

"I'm impressed," Vestara said. She attempted to relay the information about the crescent to the other ships in this most peculiar of fleets. "Ship is strong. It takes a powerful will to command him."

"I take it you have?"

She did not look back at Ben, but replied, "Ship contacted me first when he arrived on our world."

Luke hid a smile. Vestara was intelligent, cunning, and surprisingly strong in the Force. But she clearly was attracted to Ben, as unfortunately his son was to her, and she wanted to impress him. And in so doing, in bragging about her connection with Ship, she had revealed that it had been the strange vessel that had come to them, not the other way around. He didn't know what that signified, not yet, but it was an important piece of the puzzle that was the Lost Tribe's history.

"Once we got close," Vestara continued, "we felt a presence other than Ship's. It was . . . cold. It . . . squirmed its way into you. It was very needy." She glanced over her shoulder. "Like, oh, I don't know. A dark tentacle, perhaps?"

"You, too?"

"It is definitely Abeloth," Luke said. "Interesting that it feels the same to both Sith and Jedi."

"I guess a tentacle's a tentacle, no matter who it's poking or prodding," Ben said.

"It makes our task of finding her that much more challenging," Luke said. "But challenges are what make one grow."

"You sound like my father," Vestara said.

"Sith or Jedi, I suppose fathers read the same handbook," Luke said. "Any response?"

"No. It's doubtful it got through. They'll have to just follow us closely."

"But I'm sure you told them about Abeloth's world and how to find it."

Vestara regarded him levelly, her brown eyes cool. "Of course I did. Would you not do the same for your Jedi?"

"I would. Then let's hope we don't lose any stragglers."

And he moved in.

Luke had always loved his son. In recent years, Ben had grown into a young man whom Luke respected as well as loved. As Luke maneuvered the *Jade Shadow* through the "Chasm of Perfect Darkness," the way was indeed "narrow and treacherous," as the Aing-Tii had told them, and he appreciated what a good job Ben had done the first time. Even with Abeloth's Force presence to hold on to, it had to have been challenging. Luke found himself taxed as he cleared his mind and focused on the Force. Again, as it had the first time, the primary display offered only bright static. Turbulence caused the yacht to shudder, although the protective hovering of the *Rockhound* offered stability that Ben hadn't had access to. He hoped that the other vessels were negotiating the difficult crossing as well as or better than the *Jade Shadow*.

The hull temperature climbed as they entered Stable Zone One. Smoothly, with skill borne of long practice, Luke slowed the vessel. All was going as well as could be expected, but there was something wrong. Something was not as it had been the first time. Abeloth's presence was of course hidden from them, but Luke knew that. Something else . . .

And then he knew.

The last time they had come this way, both of them had sensed what they first assumed to be a hive-mind. Later, of course, they realized it was the Mind Drinkers, or Mind Walkers as they called themselves, on Sinkhole Station. Their connectedness had initially made them seem to be more akin to Killiks than individual beings. But now, Luke could sense nothing. Was Abeloth so powerful she could cloak their presences in the Force as well? They were in thrall to her. It was not impossible.

The only other explanation was one Luke did not want to consider.

"Dad," Ben said. "The Mind Walkers—I'm not sensing them."

"I know," Luke said quietly. The silence filled the cabin. Luke continued to extend his senses in the Force, trying to find any hints of life from the station that was now not far.

He found none. But his danger sense began to tickle at the back of his neck. Instantly he dove, throwing himself, Ben, and Vestara back against their crash webbing. With only centimeters to spare, the *Jade Shadow* slipped under a huge chunk of something that had not been there the last time they were here.

"I've got a bad feeling about this," Ben murmured.

Luke brought the navigation sensors back up, turning on the floodlights, and instantly realized why they had not been able to sense any life emanating from Sinkhole Station.

Sinkhole Station had been destroyed.

# Chapter Twenty-nine

THE LARGE, SPINNING CYLINDER RINGED BY A DOZEN AT-
tached tubes that had been Sinkhole Station was
nowhere to be seen. All that was left of the enormous
station, and those beings who had lived on it—if you
could call Mind Walking living—was chunks of debris.
Huge pieces of what were once the gray-white domes,
looking like broken eggshells, hung in the icy cold of
space, with flotsam and jetsam that were once vessels of
all varieties. They were not close enough yet to see bodies, but bodies there would be as well.

In addition to managing his own shock, Luke attempted to send calm to the rest of the fleet even as he
continued to maneuver the *Shadow*. He sensed the as-
tonishment and almost—affront?—of the Sith, as if they
were offended that anything would dare get in the way
of their plans.

"It's—just gone," Ben said quietly. It was stating the
obvious, but the shocked silence had to be broken.

"Detecting no life signs, no infrared," Luke said.
"Whatever happened to it did a fine job of destroying it
completely."

Vestara was silent. Ben glanced at her over his shoulder.

"This wasn't anything you did, was it?"

She had been staring, wide-eyed, as they had been, but now she snorted derisively. "Oh, of course, I planted a bomb that was able to blow apart the entire station, but was unable to escape from two Jedi. Right."

Ben flushed. "Sorry. Just—really shocked, you know?"

She seemed slightly mollified. "Yeah, I know. I am, too. This does seem the sort of thing Jedi would do rather than Sith—destroy technology rather than let bad people have it."

"Oh, trust me, we wouldn't want to destroy this," Ben said. Luke shot him a quick look.

"Oh? Why not?" Vestara asked.

A bright flash of light caught Luke's eye. "Blast it," he said. "Who among your Sith is foolish enough to keep going into this mess?"

Sure enough, a pair of the Chasemaster frigates had decided to ignore what seemed to Luke as common sense and instead had moved forward at far too great a speed to negotiate such a debris field. Doubtless the hapless captain was hoping to score points with Taalon by gathering some information or perhaps looting a body. Daring, but foolish. Luke, Ben, and Vestara watched as, too late, the frigate realized its mistake and tried to avoid a collision.

That was when something very large moved into place, as fast as it could but with agonizing slowness. Luke caught a strong hit of determination as the *Rockhound* activated its extremely powerful tractor beam and tried to catch both frigates with it.

One of them slowed, stopped. The other one slowed, but not enough to keep it from its fate. Ben, Vestara, and Luke all watched, not averting their eyes at the sudden bright flash of light. Luke felt the dozens of lives aboard the frigate wink out, some immediately, some more slowly.

"What a waste," Luke said. "A useless sacrifice. All they've done is create more debris."

He felt a surge of anger, quickly shuttered, from Vestara. "One might expect more compassion from a Jedi," she said.

"Compassion is for those who deserve it," Luke said.

"Looks like Lando was able to get one anyway," Ben said before Vestara could retort. "You're right, Dad. I'm sure to the crew of that frigate the *Rockhound* is the most gorgeous thing in the universe." The *Rockhound* was now towing the surviving vessel away to a safe distance. It moved ponderously back toward the debris that had been fatal to the Chasemaster, extended telescoping stabilizer legs, and sunk them deep into the chunk of what had once been a station, or perhaps a ship. It was hard to tell.

"Abeloth," said Vestara, breaking the silence.

"You think she could do this?" Luke asked.

Vestara shrugged. "She has great power. She is very strong in the Force. But the Maw strikes me as an enormous place, so it's possible something else did this."

It was, Ben had to admit. No one knew exactly what was contained in this vast cluster. It was large enough to contain Shelter, and Daala's Maw colony, where she had hidden for many years rebuilding her fleet. Neither organization had had a breath of knowledge about the other.

Ben was not a big believer in coincidence.

"A pity," Vestara continued, "that we lost the option to explore the station more."

"I feel pity not for us, but for those beings who were destroyed," Luke said quietly. "It's impossible to calculate how many lives were lost in this . . . incident."

Lando's *Rockhound* continued to clear a path through the debris. It was slow but steady, and after just a few moments Luke felt it was safe to begin moving forward.

"I wonder how long it will take to clear the debris field," Vestara said. "My people are impatient."

Luke glanced over at her and wordlessly pointed at the wreckage of the Chasemaster frigate.

Vestara fell silent.

Luke was now more certain than ever that Sinkhole Station had been designed to contain Abeloth, and that she was, as his beloved Mara had said, something very old, and very dangerous. It had probably been suicidal to think that he and Ben could have approached her alone. Even though he had asserted to the Sith that he wanted to try to reason with her, understand her, he suspected that such overtures would not be welcomed. He suspected, in fact, given what he was looking at now, that they might be flattened like insects.

Vestara had reported the bare bones about Abeloth, but now, as they crept through the litter of what Luke suspected was that being's latest struggle for freedom, he said quietly, "Looks like we have a lot of time to kill. Tell us about Abeloth."

She looked at him warily. "You have everything I have told my own people."

"So tell us something you haven't told them. Tell us about how you felt around her. What she was like."

She narrowed her brown eyes. "Come on, Ves," Ben said, and Luke wondered if his son was even aware that he was calling the girl by a nickname, "the only reason you haven't told the Sith is because you've not had a chance. We're in this together—and it was your High Lord who proposed the alliance."

Whether it was the logic or Ben, Vestara nodded. "Abeloth . . . she strikes one emotionally. I know you Jedi don't like that."

"On the contrary," Luke said, "we are taught to trust our feelings."

"Really? Interesting. Abeloth . . ." She paused for a moment, then spoke with more sincerity than Luke had ever sensed from her before. "Her world is, as I have told you, unnatural. And terribly dangerous. We—we lost many. And when we found her . . . it was just such a relief to not have to be constantly aware of everything around you that you were grateful to be with her. And she was lovely—at first. She—captivating, I think is the word."

"Physically beautiful?" Luke inquired.

"More than that. You couldn't stop looking at her, whatever she chose to look like. It was all you wanted to do—look at her, be around her. Like an intoxicant."

Luke and Ben exchanged glances. "Her looks varied, then?"

"From day to day, or depending on whomever she was around," Vestara said. "Always more or less human, though. Sometimes fair hair, sometimes brown, sometimes long, sometimes short. The features shifted, the eye color changed a little. Until . . ." Vestara paused. "Until the moment I really *saw* her."

Ben leaned forward. "What happened?"

"I told you, everything obeys Abeloth. That's why we wanted to be with her—because she kept us safe. But at one point, the plants attacked Lady Rhea. While Abeloth was still there. She let them. That's when I understood that we had been betrayed, and the next time I saw her—"

Vestara had a great deal of self-control. She was a Sith, from an entire Tribe of them. She had to have self-control. But Luke saw her pale slightly, and her gaze dropped for an instant. And when she spoke, her voice was slightly unsteady.

"Her hair was long and yellow and fell all the way to the ground. Her eyes were tiny, sunk deep into black eye sockets—like two small stars. Her mouth was—it reached literally from ear to ear, and her arms were short, stunted—with writhing tentacles instead of fingers. She was hideous."

Luke nodded. "She was. She is," he said. "I've seen her."

"What? And you did not see fit to tell us? When did you encounter her?"

"It wasn't a literal encounter," Luke said, "but a sort of spiritual one. The people on Sinkhole Station taught me a technique called Mind Walking. One can leave the physical body and travel elsewhere. I'm beginning to think the places I visited were real. Certainly Abeloth was. And—other things."

"Leaving the body," Vestara said. "All those living corpses . . . that's what they were doing, isn't it?"

Luke nodded. "It's very appealing. Most of them don't want to go back."

"And you saw her? Through Mind Walking?"

"You described her perfectly."

"Well," said Vestara with false cheer, "at least we three will recognize her when we see her."

They had entered orbit around Abeloth's planet having expected to be attacked every light-year along the way. That nothing had happened worried Ben much more than an open attack.

"I still don't sense her at all," said Luke. "She's deliberately concealing herself."

"A spider in her web, waiting for the flies to come to her," muttered Ben. "She—"

And then he felt, not Abeloth's presence, but another one. A familiar one.

Ship.

Vestara's eyes widened at the same time, and a soft, almost tender smile touched her lips. Ben shuddered at the thought that she felt such affection for the Sith training vessel.

"Ship," he told his father. "It's here. And . . ." He frowned, trying to put a name to what he was sensing from the Sith meditation sphere.

He had expected Ship to be gleeful. It served Abeloth, who was clearly tremendously powerful and utilized dark side energy. Ship was designed to seek out strong wills, and to obey them. It was created to serve the Sith, and presumably, it would be just as "happy" with Abeloth. But instead he sensed . . .

"It's despairing," he murmured. "It's . . . lost."

Vestara's eyes darted to him. He couldn't read her expression.

"Elaborate," Luke said.

"It's hard to say but . . . I don't think it likes having to serve Abeloth very much."

"She tried to use it against us," Vestara said. "Abeloth set Ship against the Sith—the beings who created it, whom it was made to serve. It could not perform one duty without betraying another, and this troubles it."

Ben made an amused sound. "A dark side meditation sphere and training vessel with a conscience," he said. "Who'd have thought it?"

Ship reminded Ben that he was a very complex vessel, and Ben was forced to agree.

"Then we should be prepared for it to happily attack us, Ben," Luke said. "We're the one target Abeloth can send it after that won't cause it any discomfort to kill."

Ben nodded. "And Jaina and Lando."

"If we can free him from her will somehow, Ship would be a powerful ally," Vestara said. "He likes me. He doesn't want to be used to harm me, or the Tribe. But he can't resist on his own."

"That may be," Luke said, "but let's take this one step

at a time. I'm happy enough it's not firing on us at the moment. Time to go planetside and see what's there."

He and Ben were in the pilot and copilot's seat. There was still no way to communicate with the Sith aboard the frigates, so Ben waited until they were all assembled in orbit. Each frigate opened up to emit two well-armed atmospheric vessels, no doubt crammed to the gills with Sith.

"Stang," said Ben. "We'll have to land the *Shadow,* won't we?"

"Yes . . . Why? Is that a problem?"

"Dyon," said Vestara, as if reading Ben's thoughts.

"Yep. Abeloth might try to free him somehow."

Luke glanced over at the monitor. "He's conscious, though still under the influence of the drug."

"Let me go check him out while you two take the *Shadow* down," Vestara said.

"Give him another dose," Luke called after her.

The drug was coursing through his system. Dyon Stad could feel it, could sense it, even though he knew on one level he shouldn't be able to. He knew that it was clouding his mind, slowing down his body, holding him hostage to the physical needs of his form as surely as the stun cuffs held his body hostage here in this sick bay.

It was not sufficient, however, to shut *her* out.

Tears leaked beneath his closed lids as he struggled, futilely, inevitably, against the restraints, and his heart ached as if it were squeezed by an invisible hand.

*Come to me. Come home.*

A sob escaped him, hastily bitten back. The Others couldn't be permitted to think they had broken him. If he could, he would happily tell them, as he spat in their faces, their perfect replica faces, that it wasn't they who had broken him. In fact, he was not broken at all. He was actually awakening to what had been going on for who knew how long. To the truth. And he was here, here where the greatest strength of understanding and resistance could be found.

He knew her, and he did not know her. All he knew was that she was kind, and good, and understanding, and somehow she held the answers he sought.

*You are true and real, Dyon. There are others. You are not alone. Come to me, find me—*

He was not alone.

His eyes snapped open, red from crying, but sharp and hard. He stared at the Sith girl—or rather, the Other who was masquerading as the Sith girl—and remained silent, waiting for her to speak.

"She's calling to you, isn't she? Abeloth?"

He said nothing.

She stepped closer. Her face, sweet, innocent-looking, no doubt as perfect a replica of the original Vestara as the Not-Luke was of the original Jedi Grand Master, furrowed slightly in speculation.

"I know that you think we're all imposters," she said quietly. "I know that Luke and Ben keep telling you that you're wrong, that you're insane. I know you're sure you're not."

Dyon Stad said nothing. This was likely a trick.

She smiled, a little sadly. "The real Vestara would be trying to play you. She was a Sith, after all."

His eyes narrowed. "And you're standing there telling me that you're not Vestara." It was a statement, not a question. She nodded slowly, dark brown eyes watching him.

"You know the imposters who have taken the place of Luke and Ben—you know them to be hostile. I play along with them, but there are some of us that are secretly opposed to them. Think about it. Do you think that Jedi and Sith would ever really agree on anything?"

"But you're not really a Sith."

"No. But I am one who opposes those who have taken the places of those who were Jedi. And I'm trying to fight them. All of us who have opted to replace the Sith are."

He blinked, the drug coursing through him, making him feel like thick honey was flowing through his veins instead of blood. It didn't make sense. The imposters were taking over everybody. Why would "good" imposters choose to be Sith and "bad" imposters choose to be Jedi? They were all the same.

"You're all fakes," he said. "You're all the enemy. I've got no reason to believe you and every reason to think that you're trying to fool me."

She smiled. "You're smart, Dyon Stad. Even drugged, you're smart. But what would I have to gain? You're already locked up. What would I get out of tricking you?"

He frowned. He couldn't think of anything. But he was sure there was something.

She moved closer. In one hand was a syringe filled with a pale blue liquid. Her other hand closed tightly around something he couldn't see.

"Those of us who are Sith—we're really on Abeloth's side," she said. "And Abeloth knows exactly what's going on, and how to stop it."

Dyon stopped breathing for a moment. How did she—

"Think about it, Dyon. I know it's hard with the drug in your system, but *think*. Who did the Sith ally with? Who does Ship serve?"

"Abeloth," Dyon whispered. It was all wrong, terribly wrong. The fake Jedi evil, the fake Sith good? It went against everything he had been taught to believe, everything he *had* believed. But then again, nothing was the same, not since the coming of the Others.

"Think about Ship."

"Ship?"

"Ship is a Sith training vessel. And it's here . . . protecting Abeloth. It's not fake, it's not been replaced—it's just a vessel. And it's serving Abeloth."

A tendril of thought, cold, piercingly clear, stabbed into his brain. If Ship was a Sith training vessel, then it served the dark side. And if it served the dark side, and now served Abeloth, then Abeloth must—

White-hot pain blossomed in his temples. He cried out and sagged against the restraints.

What had he just been thinking of? He'd just had some thought, some idea, but it had slipped away. The drug hadn't permitted him to hang on to it. It was something important, something key to understanding what was going on—

A shadow fell over him. It was Not-Vestara, the good fake Sith. He looked up at her, mute, shaking with the agony that still shivered through him. She knelt down beside him, put her face to within centimeters of his.

"Abeloth calls to you. And we—the beings who have replaced the Sith—we are on your side. Can you lead us to her?"

He nodded, the gesture causing pain to shoot through him. "I can," he rasped.

"Will you?"

Again, a shadowy tendril of clear thinking tried to force its way into his brain, to be batted aside and ruthlessly crushed.

"I will."

She smiled, a sweet smile, her brown eyes warm. "I have a medication that will clear the drug from your system," she said. "But first . . . time to fool the fake Jedi."

She went over to the monitor and waved a hand over it. Dyon watched as the indicators that represented his pulse and brain activity both slowed down. Not-Vestara gave him a smile.

"Now Luke will think I gave you another dose of the drug to keep you docile, and not the antidote."

She returned to the bed and pressed the needle into his skin. He heard the pop, felt the hot little jolt of pain. For an instant, he wondered if he was wrong to trust her, if this was a fatal moment of weakness, if this needle was the delivery method of death. Instead, a heartbeat later, the confusion cleared from his mind like mist evaporating under a hot sun. He blinked, startled.

She'd kept her word.

"I'll be back shortly. When I return, I'm going to unlock the stun cuffs."

"No," he pleaded, "unlock me now. I must go to her!"

"You will," Not-Vestara promised. "But not right now. What I need from you is for you to pretend to be unconscious if Luke or Ben comes in. Then, when the time is right, I'll free you. But if you betray me, if you reveal I helped you, then everything is lost. Do you understand?"

He nodded, slowly. "You promise you will be back?"

"I do." She smiled at him one more time, then turned and left. Alone in the sick bay, Dyon Stad closed his eyes.

She had helped him. She would help him more.

After all . . . he seemed to remember that the Sith always kept their promises.

# Chapter Thirty

"IT WAS REAL," SAID BEN AS THEY CAME IN FOR A LAND-ing. "What we saw with the Mind Walking. Look at this place."

Luke nodded. Everything was tinged azure, bathed in the light of the cold-seeming blue star that served as the sun for this world. Below them, they could see the crater of a volcano, and below that, somewhat obscured by the dark tendrils of smoke coming from the volcano, a crimson river twining like a scarlet snake.

Vestara had guided them to where the Sith had first landed. En route they had passed a battle cruiser locked in a decaying orbit.

"That is the *Eternal Crusader,*" Vestara said. "The vessel that brought us here."

Ben whistled softly, impressed. "Why did you leave it and go to Sinkhole Station in Ship?"

Vestara didn't answer, and Ben sighed and shook his head. "Fine. Keep your secrets. Just find us somewhere safe to land."

"That's a relative term here," Vestara said. She peered over Ben's shoulder, then said, "I know this place. This is where we first met Abeloth. Set down on the beach. I will at least know the lay of the land."

As they drew closer, heading for the stretch of blue

sand Vestara indicated, she said, "See that cave there? About a kilometer up from the base of the volcano? That is where we found her."

"Oh great, so we're ringing the doorbell within minutes of landing," Ben said.

"Not necessarily," Luke said. "I never saw her here when I Mind Walked. She could be anywhere. But it's as good a place as any to start." He frowned, as if something had occurred to him.

"What is it?" Ben asked.

"There might be a better place . . . but let's land here for now, and regroup with Taalon."

Luke brought the *Jade Shadow* to a very gentle landing on the wide stretch of blue-colored sand. A few Sith vessels were able to land close to him; others had to find space elsewhere as best they could.

The steamy heat hit Ben almost physically as he, Vestara, and Luke stepped out onto the sand. Vestara's lightsaber had been returned to her, and she activated it at once and looked around. The red glow of the blade looked purple in the blue light, and it seemed to burn more brightly than Luke's and Ben's lightsabers.

Her eyes were on the tall ferns that clustered against the bank, and as Luke watched, she sprang forward, severing those that protruded over the sand. They writhed, as if in pain, and pulled back, fluid dripping like blood from the severed pieces. Even those Vestara reduced quickly to pulp, then stepped back.

"Stang," said Ben. "The plants really *are* carnivorous."

"Vestara said so, did she not?" came a melodious, arrogant voice. It was, of course, Gavar Khai, his own red blade lit, striding over to them. With him were High Lord Sarasu Taalon and a female Keshiri, slender and lovely, her short hair framing her perfect features. "Did you think she could be mistaken about something like that?"

"Not at all," Luke said. "I thought she lied."

Gavar Khai did not look insulted on his daughter's behalf. "She also said that Abeloth was first encountered right over there," Luke continued. He pointed to the mouth of the cave, a tiny, fingernail-sized dark oval against the base of the volcano. "But I feel certain she is not there." He nodded to Taalon. "It is good to finally meet you, High Lord Taalon."

"And you, Grand Master Skywalker. This is Captain Leeha Faal."

Luke inclined his head cursorily to Faal. Ben remembered the name—this was the woman who had cheerfully abandoned her companions when they got caught in the act of desecrating the Fountain. Great.

"Now that the courtesies have been observed, I think I know how best to proceed," Luke said.

Ben took petty pleasure in watching a High Lord bridle, and then be forced to calm himself. "I am open to suggestions. However, it seems to me that if Vestara knows that this cave is one place Abeloth visits, then we should investigate it."

"I agree, but first, let's do a search."

"That is a waste of time and resources," Taalon said sharply, his patience wearing thin.

"I disagree. We wouldn't even have to leave our ships."

"You know as well as I do that sensors are useless here!"

"I wasn't talking about sensors. I was talking about Mind Walking."

Ben looked sharply at his dad. Vestara's brown eyes widened. The other Sith looked blankly at Luke.

"It's a technique that the Jedi on Sinkhole Station taught me," Luke continued. "They are able to leave their bodies and—"

"I saw what Mind Walking did to them on the station," Vestara snapped. "You may join them if you wish, but High Lord, I recommend that *no* Sith attempt this."

Luke turned to her. "They became as they were after many exposures. Also, they were, I believe, being manipulated by Abeloth. Mind Walking is appealing, but I think everyone here has a strong enough will not to become seduced by it."

"It killed them. We saw what was left of them," Vestara protested. "Empty shells that—"

"Vestara." Gavar Khai's voice was sharp.

Vestara bowed toward her father. "Your pardon, Father, but I believe what Master Skywalker is proposing is dangerous."

"Of course it is," Luke said. "But so is wandering around hoping to somehow stumble across Abeloth. I'd much rather target her than the other way around."

Taalon considered this for a moment. "I will need to know more of this Mind Walking before I agree."

Luke obliged, explaining the procedure and emphasizing the need for monitoring on the part of those who stayed behind. Ben listened with half an ear, extending all his senses and keeping a sharp eye on the carnivorous plant life.

"When Ben and I Mind Walked the first time, we went to several sites. I wasn't sure if they were real, physical places or not, but I am now. We found Abeloth at a certain point—she was trying to get me to come closer. I'm glad I didn't . . . at that point, in that . . . space, she might well have been stronger. But now, understanding how to Mind Walk, it might be a way for us to find out where she is without having to risk physical injury hiking off in some random direction. The dangers posed by Beyond Shadows are real. And it will be a very pleasant experience. It will be tempting to linger, but that would mean death."

Taalon growled. "Anyone who does deserves what he or she gets," he said. "I will abandon anyone not strong enough to resist the appeal of this place Beyond Shadows."

Luke said nothing. He wasn't sure if fewer Sith was a good or a bad thing. Abeloth was powerful, and she was dangerous. They might need everyone they could get.

"Do not worry, Commander," said Khai. "You have selected only the strongest and most powerful Sith for this mission. No one will fail you."

"And I select only the strongest and most powerful Sith to accompany me now," said Taalon. "Khai. You and Faal will accompany me."

Luke didn't miss the flicker of worry that crossed Vestara's face . . . or the smile of vindication that curved Khai's lips into a triumphant smile. He turned to his son, who looked resigned.

"You know what I'm going to ask," Luke said gently.

"You want me to stay here, to keep an eye on you in case something happens."

"That," Luke agreed, and then inclined his head in Vestara's direction. "And to keep an eye on *her*." He didn't add, *which shouldn't be too hard for you*. Vestara heard and rolled her eyes.

"When will you two be convinced that I am not about to violate the agreement the Tribe has made?"

"Not right now," was all Luke said. Ben seemed suddenly very interested in busily picking at a hangnail. Luke regarded the others. "Take an hour to prepare. I'll transmit instructions on how to reach the state of Beyond Shadows, and where we will all meet."

The Sith tried and failed not to look uncomfortable. Luke permitted himself a small smile at their discomfiture.

\*          \*          \*

Dyon could feel her. They were on her world, now, and
she was out there. He wanted so badly to go to her, but
he couldn't, not until Not-Vestara came back and—

He heard a sound and opened his eyes. As if he had
summoned her by simply thinking of her, Not-Vestara
had appeared. She looked as if she was in a hurry.

"Ben and Luke are going to be here any minute now.
I'm ready to loosen your cuffs, but I need you to promise
me something first."

His eyes narrowed. Here it was. "What?"

"Luke is going to Mind Walk, to try to find Abeloth.
Ben will be—"

"No!" Dyon cried, and started struggling. She placed
a hand on him, and he felt her using the Force to send
him calm. "He mustn't reach her!"

"Be quiet and let me finish!" she hissed. "Luke won't
be Mind Walking alone. Three Sith will be joining him,
including my commander. They're going to keep him
from finding her in that realm of reality."

He ceased his struggle. "I'm listening."

Not-Vestara graced him with a lovely smile. "Meanwhile, while Ben is stuck monitoring Luke, you escape
and find Abeloth first. Tell her of our plan. Tell her that
those who have replaced the Sith are on her side. It's
Skywalker she needs to be wary of, not us. If I loosen
these cuffs, do you give me your word that you will wait
to escape until I tell you the time is right?"

He could lie, of course. He could say yes, then bolt
whenever he felt the time was right. He didn't have to
trust her.

"Yes," he said.

She searched his eyes for a long moment, then nodded.
"Okay," she said. "We trust each other, and we both
benefit. And so does Abeloth."

Now Not-Vestara moved quickly to unlock the stun
cuffs. The right one opened, and she moved to undo the

left. This was the moment when he could take her by surprise, attack the imposter, render her helpless, even kill her if he chose. But he didn't. She had proven worthy of his trust. He was not like the real Sith or the fake Jedi. He would not betray one who had helped him.

"When you're on your way to Abeloth, watch out for the plants. They're carnivorous."

"Thank you," Dyon said quietly. He lay as if he were still imprisoned.

Not-Vestara tensed, paying attention to something Dyon couldn't sense. "They're coming. I've got to go, but I'll be back with them soon. And as soon as possible, I will tell you when you may escape. Here's what you have to do. . . ."

"You know the drill," Luke said to his son as they entered sick bay, with Vestara behind them.

Ben nodded, giving Dyon a cursory glance as they entered the small cabin. He lay on the gurney, still strapped down, still asleep.

"Yep. Hook you up to an IV, monitor the signs, and hope I don't have to go Beyond Shadows to rescue you this time."

Luke smiled. "I don't think you will. We have a very specific task. This time, I know where I want to go and whom I'm looking for. And trust me, I don't want to take more time than I have to on this."

"She knows we're here," Vestara said. The words were uttered without undue emphasis, but with such complete certainty that Ben felt a chill.

"Well, I haven't felt any tentacles yet," Ben said, trying to shrug off his unease.

"If you do, you know how to handle it," said Luke, dropping a hand on Ben's shoulder and giving it a good squeeze. He lay down on the bed next to the unconscious Dyon, and Ben inserted the IV quickly and almost casually.

Luke knew now, as he had not known the first time he had Mind Walked, that this place had a counterpart in physical reality. All of the places he had visited did. He was on Abeloth's world, and this, the Lake of Apparitions, could be visited awake, on foot, with a lightsaber in his hand, if he knew where to find it.

On Sinkhole Station, his guides were being bent to Abeloth's will, to take him to her, to keep him trapped in this place until his physical body perished. Only Ben's decision to come after him, putting himself at great risk, had saved Luke. On this second spirit-voyage, he was again hardly among friends. But no one with whom he journeyed now wished Abeloth well.

He had, as promised, instructed the Sith who had insisted on accompanying him on the techniques. As he expected, they grasped the concept quickly. He had warned them to expect a sense of elation, of euphoria, and to not trust it. He had advised them to have someone watching over them, to monitor their vital signs, and to be prepared to go in after them if things began to look dangerous. They had sniffed at his warnings as if he were a child telling them fire was hot, and said they were certain they could handle it. Still, they had all agreed to be hooked up to IVs and have someone monitoring them at all times.

He had instructed them all to follow the crackling violet light that appeared as they "awoke," for want of a better term, in Beyond Shadows, and had given them a very detailed description of the site at which they needed to appear.

He was the first to arrive, no doubt because of his familiarity with the technique, and looked around at the Lake of Apparitions. He stood again on the shore in front of the narrow lake, bathed in blue sunlight. The surface was as still and dark as it had been the last time he had come here. On one shore was the granite face, on the other, the boulder-strewn meadow, with knee-high hummocks of moss and small streams winding their way between them.

And ahead, at the far end of the Lake of Apparitions, was swirling silver mist. The Mists of Forgetfulness. This time, though, Luke saw no hovering female figure beckoning him onward.

They appeared one by one. First was Taalon, lurching into existence as if stumbling, but then recovering quickly. A second later, Khai and Leeha Faal appeared. They looked around curiously.

"What is this place?" Faal demanded.

"My guide called it the Lake of Apparitions," Luke said. "This end is known as the Mirror of Remembrance. If you want to get from one end to the other, you have to follow a tricky path or else you'll fall into the Depths of Eternity."

Gavar Khai snorted. "Such pompous names," he said.

"I actually have to agree with you on that," Luke said, "but that's what I know them as."

"Apparitions," said Khai slowly, looking into the water. "I see nothing."

Luke shrugged. "I don't know how a lot of this works," he said honestly. "I saw several people I recognized. Perhaps it is different for each individual."

Khai shot him a searching look. "Really? I'd be very interested to know the sort of people Master Skywalker saw."

"If I see them again, I'll let you know," Luke said.

"Are they hostile?" Taalon asked.

Luke felt a tug at his heart. "No," he said. "No, no one I saw here was hostile." Not even Jacen, not any-more. He shook off the remembrance, even as he was forced to acknowledge that he did hope that one beloved face, at least, would again rise to the surface. He thought of the comfort Mara had provided the last few days, coming to him in dreams, that comforting female presence aboard the *Jade Shadow*.

Not even death could truly separate two so deeply bonded. Gently, he pushed thoughts of his late wife aside and focused on the present.

"It was there that I saw Abeloth," he said, pointing to the mists. "She was hovering there, wanting me to come to her. The Mists of Forgetfulness."

"You did not go to her then?" Khai asked.

"I was heading in that direction. I received many warnings not to. Warnings I'm glad I heeded."

Taalon regarded the mists steadily. "I see nothing there now."

"No," Luke agreed. "But simply because we do not see her doesn't mean she isn't there."

Faal said, "You wish to go to a place called the Mists of Forgetfulness?"

"If there are answers, I believe they will lie there," Luke said.

"In the Mists of Forgetfulness?" Faal asked, slightly incredulous. "The answers might be there, but how will you remember the question?"

Taalon shot her a look and Faal fell silent. "If you are certain, Master Skywalker, then let us go investigate." He smiled coldly. "Since you're familiar with this place, you may take the lead."

"Thanks," Luke said dryly, although he would have insisted on leading regardless. He trusted the Sith not to jump him from the rear—not when he was the only one who knew how to get them there. "The path is close to the shore and is shallow. Do not go too far out into the Lake. I don't know a lot about the Depths of Eternity, but I was informed that once you stumble into them, no one can pull you back. You'll be lost. Forever. It could be a lie; it could be true. I personally don't want to find out." He looked at each of them in turn, making sure they appreciated the direness of the situation.

"Now. Follow me, step where I step, and take your time to make sure your footing is secure."

He moved carefully into the cold water and moved toward the far end, testing each step carefully. At first the lake was utterly undisturbed by their passing. There were no splashes, not even ripples.

And then *they* came forth.

The faces of the dead began to emerge from the depths, floating upward but still lingering about a dozen centimeters below the surface, their eyes closed, their expressions tranquil. So many that Luke knew in life. He searched, but did not yet see the one face he had hoped to find. He was surprised at how bitter the disappointment was.

The Sith were too disciplined to gasp, of course. But they could not quite suppress their shock in the Force. He heard names—whispered, called out in surprise or in joy.

And the responses. Luke paused and turned back, listening to the conversations. He did not particularly want dead Sith imparting advice to the living, but on the other hand, he felt it was wrong to silence the communication. Such a chance was too rare not to be given, even to one's enemy.

He need not have worried. These were loved ones, not generals or military strategists. The slightly gurgling words were gentle and tender, farewells never made or vows of eternal love repeated one more time. He was uncomfortable, and it was clear the Sith, too, were torn between wanting these unlooked-for connections and maintaining their mystery and threat in Luke's eyes.

"These might be tricks," said Taalon, but his voice sounded oh-so-slightly uncertain.

"They might be," Luke said. "But I didn't find them to be." He turned around and moved forward. "We should not linger."

On they went, step by step. This time, unlike the previous attempt Luke and Ben had made to reach the mists, they made progress. Luke honestly hadn't expected this, but he felt hope rising within him. He didn't know what awaited him inside the shifting gray tendrils of mist, but he was ready to find out. More than ready.

He had not gotten this far the last time, and the path became trickier. He slowed his pace, stepping forward carefully—

The rock gave way and he started to fall forward. A strong hand closed far too tightly on his upper arm, yanking him to safety.

"Thank you," he said to Gavar Khai. Their eyes met, and Khai nodded.

"I would not lose our guide quite so soon," Khai said. "Besides . . . now the great Luke Skywalker owes the Khai family a debt."

"I would say rather that we are even now," Luke said, disengaging his arm from the durasteel grip of the Sith Saber. "I spared your daughter."

Khai's black brows drew together. "Only because you were tracking her," he snarled. "Only—"

"Khai!" snapped Taalon. "Later. We must find Abeloth before we settle scores."

Khai bridled, but fell silent. Luke turned to continue.

At that moment there was a sharp cry. Luke whirled to see Leeha Faal on her hands and knees in the water, and he and the other two exhaled in relief. Even Faal smiled shakily.

"I slipped," she said, embarrassed, and started to get to her feet. "I thought for sure I—"

The hand beneath the water that suddenly seized her wrist was pale purple. So, too, were the hands that shot out to grab her legs. She struggled, her eyes widening in surprise as her strong, slender body strained for the safety of the path.

"High Lord!" Faal cried. She got one hand free and reached out to him imploringly, unable to hide her terror. The water did not splash or churn as she fought desperately against the imperfectly glimpsed specters in the inky water.

"*Leeha!*" Taalon surged toward her. Gavar Khai snatched his arm just in time to prevent his commander from falling into the cold, black depths. "No, no, let me—"

Leeha's hand closed on a jutting rock and she tried to pull herself back to safety. But the dead things in the water would have her, and there was nothing living beings could do to stop it. Her hand slipped. She opened her mouth to shout. Water filled it, then closed over her perfect, purple face.

Taalon, still held by Gavar Khai, reached into the water after Leeha. Khai grabbed that arm, too, and pulled him back. "It's too late!" Khai shouted.

And it was. Leeha Faal was already beyond their reach. Luke stared at the sight of her lithe form, still struggling, being borne inexorably downward into an eternal darkness.

Aboard the *Winged Dagger*, Leeha Faal's body spasmed. Her vitals spiked and zigzagged crazily and the monitor was beeping wildly.

"What's going on?" one of her attendants cried, attempting to hold the flailing Keshiri down and trying to read the monitor at the same time.

"I don't know—I—"

Faal arched, every muscle in her body tight, and then

went limp. The jagged lines that had indicated her brain activity suddenly subsided to a flatline, although her heart continued to beat and her lungs to draw breath.

The two attendants stared at each other. Then one of them cleared her throat and pressed her comlink with steady fingers.

"Sumar to Captain Syndor. There has been an incident with Commander Faal. All brain activity has ceased. You are once again the commander of the *Winged Dagger*. Congratulations, Commander."

"Thank you," came Syndor's voice. He made no attempt to hide his pleasure. "Terminate life support and report back to your stations. We will await orders from High Lord Taalon."

"What happened?" Taalon demanded. He jerked his arm free from Khai and turned his fury upon Luke. "What have they done to her?"

"I don't know," Luke said.

"Liar!" Taalon spat. He pointed at the dark surface of the lake, as calm as if a few seconds ago there had been no life or death struggle. "Who was that? You said the apparitions were harmless!"

"I don't *know* who it was," Luke repeated, keeping his voice calm. "And I said that only the ones *I* encountered were harmless." It seemed as though the Depths of Eternity were populated by one's enemies. Sith though she was—and Luke knew of at least one despicable act she had committed—still Luke pitied her. He somehow intuited that her fate would be nothing as brief and merciful as drowning.

Taalon had seemed unduly upset by Faal's death, but now he was recovering. "Let us press on. The less time we spend here, the better I shall like it."

Luke couldn't have agreed more. He turned to continue, then he stopped.

It had been Mara who had warned him not to go to the mists.

*Forget her,* she had urged him. *She's one of the old ones. Leave her alone . . . trust me.*

*Mara . . .*

"What is it, Skywalker?" snapped Taalon. "I thought you said the answers were there, in the mists."

He hadn't seen her, and he had been looking. He had thought, after sensing her so strongly on the ship, that she would be waiting for him. He again looked into the water. He saw many beings, but none he recognized.

He had to talk to her. He trusted her, trusted her more than anyone he had ever known. She had insight now, insight that could help save him and Ben. Surely, she would give it.

"Mara?" he said quietly, knowing that in this place she would hear even a whisper.

At first, there was nothing. He did not repeat her name. She would either come, or not. And then, he saw her, a small shape in the water, floating up to him, her long red hair billowing about her like a cloud.

Despite everything, Luke smiled. "Mara," he said again. Her emerald eyes opened and she smiled.

"Skywalker," she said, her voice warm. "What are you doing here again?"

Luke squatted down. It made no sense, she wasn't physical, any more than he was—even less so—but he still wanted to be closer to her. "The woman in the mists," he said. "She's not there anymore. We've come for her, Mara. We've come to stop her."

Her red brows drew together in a frown. "I can tell whom you're keeping company with," she said. "They reek of dark-side energy."

He laughed softly. "That they do," he said, looking back over his shoulder. They were paying close attention. "And I'm sure they're highly complimented by that. But I'm comfortable in my choice, for now. It feels right, and so does going after Abeloth. Is there anything else you can tell me?"

"About her? Other than to warn you again to stay away from her? No." She shook her head, her hair swirling about her. "But since you've come back, I guess you're not going to listen to me." She softened the words with a gentle smile of resignation.

"No. I have to do this. Too much is at stake. I had thought this would be the most logical place to look for her."

"Not if she doesn't want to be found."

He nodded. "All right. Back to the old-fashioned way of tracking down an enemy."

"Sending in the Emperor's Hand?"

Luke actually laughed. "I do wish you were with me," he said, not caring that the Sith heard the love in his voice. Let them. Love was a powerful thing. It had built and shattered empires, shaped the history of billions, and of two. He was glad of how deeply he had loved, and did love.

"But then again, you have been," he amended. "It's meant so much to me. To see you in the dreams—to almost be able to roll over and touch you right before I wake up."

"Luke," Mara said gently.

He didn't want her to stop him, to tell him she needed to go, not before he had said what was in his heart. "And even when I am awake, I feel you with me. You even talk to me."

"*Luke.*" He fell silent, regarding her. She searched his eyes for a moment, then the specter of Mara Jade Skywalker said quietly, "Whomever you were with on the *Jade Shadow* . . . it wasn't me."

# Chapter Thirty-one

SHOCK EXPLODED THROUGH LUKE AND HE LITERALLY stumbled backward a step.

"W-what?"

He thought of the female presence aboard the *Jade Shadow,* slipping into his dreams and even those moments of borderline wakefulness. A body curved into, an arm draped over him . . . He had been so convinced it was Mara. It was her ship, she had been his wife. Why *wouldn't* it be Mara?

"What is it, Skywalker?" It was Gavar Khai, and his voice was concerned. No doubt he was thinking anything powerful enough to distress Luke was something they all needed to worry about. And maybe it was.

"It wasn't me," Mara repeated.

Who else could it—

And he knew. Horror and repugnance buffeted Luke. He tried to speak, but nothing came out. Luke forced back the shock and nausea. It would serve nothing now.

"No, it wasn't," he managed finally, his voice raw. "I should have known. I'm sorry."

Her brilliant green eyes were kind. She was beyond annoyance or jealousy. "You couldn't have. She is ancient, and powerful, and dangerous. *Very* dangerous. But you're onto her now. She is never what she appears. Remember that. And next time you feel a ghostly presence lying beside you—" She smiled, even as she began to drift downward, her face becoming a smaller oval in the dark water, her hair a fiery nimbus, "—make sure it's me."

Luke laughed, a sound that was almost a sob, and nodded.

"Skywalker, if you have anything to share with us that could help us, please do." It was Taalon's voice, cold and irritated.

Luke took a deep breath. "We need to return. Now."

Ben stifled a yawn. Sitting beside his father's body was every bit as boring as it had been back on Sinkhole Station—more so as there wasn't the fear of the unknown to keep him alert. Luke knew what he was doing, his body was safe, and Ben could still sense nothing of Abeloth.

"Why do you think she's hiding from us?" he asked Vestara.

"I wish I could say I think she was afraid," Vestara said. "But I think she's just playing with us."

"Do—do you think we can beat her?"

"I am Sith, Ben. I'm supposed to think Sith can beat anything in the known universe."

Her voice was serious, but when he glanced over at her she was smiling. It faded a moment later as she continued. "But she's ancient, and very powerful. The only way is if we can trick her, somehow."

"Trick? Dad wants to go up and start a conversation with her. I'm afraid I have to say I'm with Taalon on that. I don't think that will do much except get us killed."

"Yet you are prepared to back his attempt to do so."

"So are the Sith." He paused, peered at her. "Aren't they?"

Vestara's gaze slid away. "We'll do whatever is necessary to achieve our goal."

"And what is that?"

"I don't know everything, Ben, I'm just an apprentice," she snapped.

"Vestara," he said quietly, "don't you get tired of this? All the plotting, all the scheming, all the backstabbing? Wouldn't it be nice to just . . . trust somebody? To completely let go of your suspicions?"

She lifted her eyes to him again, and there was sorrow in their dark brown depths. "It sounds lovely, Ben. But that's not my world."

*It could be.*

The words were on Ben's lips, and he might have uttered them, had not Luke begun to stir. He turned his attention back to his father, checking the drip and making sure the transition back to his body would be an easy one.

And it was at that moment that Dyon bellowed, bolted upright, and sprang for the door.

"Vestara!" Ben cried. "Stop him!"

But the Sith girl actually took a step backward and permitted the Force-user to pass. Ben stared at her, anguished and infuriated, unable to leave his father until Luke had fully returned. Vestara turned back to Ben and folded her arms.

Luke's blue eyes snapped open and fixed on Ben's face. "What happened?"

"Dyon just bolted," Ben snarled. "And Vestara let him go."

Dyon couldn't believe it. Not-Vestara had kept her word, letting him pass freely, and perhaps stopping Not-Ben from coming after him. He hoped that no harm would befall her for helping him. He reached out into the Force, limited as his ability to do so was, and cried out to the being who had called him here.

*I come, I come!* he cried silently.

He edged carefully behind the *Jade Shadow* and turned to regard the plants crowding the bank. He had no weapon; but through them was the only way to get to Abeloth. He took a deep breath, his heart racing, and stepped forward.

The plants did nothing. He laughed, shakily, in relief. He took another step, then another, moving confidently now. They neither helped nor hindered him, behaving like ordinary plants on other worlds.

Dyon took it as a sign, and his spirits continued to lift. Upon reaching the top of the bank he looked over the beach, at the dozen or so frigates there, then up at the volcano. He sensed her there, waiting for him, and tears stung his eyes. Dyon knew he would have to be very careful. He could not allow his enemies to follow him. He believed Not-Vestara about the Not-Sith supporting Abeloth, but even so, he would not put his mistress in danger. It was possible the Not-Jedi might come out and see him.

Slowly, although he ached to break into a run, he cleared another rise and half walked, half slid down the other side.

"You what?" Luke was sitting up now, anger in his blue eyes.

"I let him go," Vestara said. "I convinced him that I was on his and Abeloth's side. He was aching to go to her, and he knew where to find her. While I was assuring him that the Sith were his and Abeloth's dear friends and supporters, I planted a tracking device on him." She fished in the pocket of her robe, held out a small piece of equipment, and wagged it at them, smiling a little. "And it's working beautifully. Did you get any insight Beyond Shadows?"

Ben let out a small laugh that sounded like a yelp. "You might have told us, you know."

She shrugged. "I didn't think you'd trust me."

"I don't," Luke said, "but right now, it really is the only lead we have. We lost Faal. The spirits in the Lake of Apparitions—apparently some old enemies had a grudge to settle. She fell into the water and they dragged her down."

Vestara shrugged again. "I never much cared for her anyway. I dare say she had accumulated quite a lot of old enemies with grudges."

"That's probably true of every Sith," Luke said. He turned to Ben. "I think we may have an edge we can use against Abeloth, though. She . . . seems to have a particular interest in me. I'm not sure why."

"In Jedi, or in you in particular?" Ben asked.

"Me in particular. She—have you felt any kind of a feminine presence on the ship, Ben?"

His son nodded. "Yeah . . . I thought it was Mom. This being her ship and all, and you and I the only ones on it for a long time. I kind of felt she was looking after us."

"I did, too," Luke said. "But I saw Mom in the Lake. And she said it wasn't her."

Ben gasped and drew back slightly. He didn't need confirmation on who it actually was. "That's . . . really creepy, Dad."

"I know," Luke said, and grimaced slightly. "But the good news is, we can use that against her."

"She did seem particularly interested in you," Vestara said. They both turned to look at her.

Ben let out an exasperated sound. "Again, Ves, why didn't you tell us?"

"I didn't think it was personal. I just thought she was gravitating toward power." Her voice was sincere, almost apologetic. "I am sorry. I should have said something earlier."

"Well, at least we know it's not our imaginations,"

Luke said. "Come on. Let's meet up with Taalon and the others and follow where Vestara's hound is leading us."

She was there, waiting for him. She stood outside the entrance to her cave, between the two large boulders on either side. Her dress clung to her tall, strongly muscled form, blown back against her by a gentle wind. It toyed with her thick dark hair, and as she turned to him, smiling widely, her gray eyes were alight with joy.

"Dyon," she said. "You've found me. You've come home."

He stood for a moment, trembling from the exertion, sweat gleaming on his brow, drinking her in.

He loved her. He felt her need of him, her wanting, her yearning—not passionate, but as sweet as it was intense. It was like a vine entwining about him, pulling him toward her. He was unable to resist it, but then, he did not try. He felt seen and known and cherished. Like a lost child who finally has found his way back to a loving mother, Dyon stumbled toward Abeloth.

Peace radiated through him as she caught his hands with her own. Peace, and certainty. She looked up at him, only a little way, for she was tall, and her gray eyes crinkled in a smile.

"I've been so alone," Dyon whispered.

"I know," she said, touching his cheek gently. "All that you have known, all that you have learned—these beings do not understand who we are, what we are. You have brothers and sisters, Dyon. Scattered everywhere. Once you were with me, here in the Maw. Once, you were all with me. Now you are apart, but one by one, you are all awakening. And once awake, you can hear my call, and come to me."

"I come," Dyon whispered. "This is where I belong. All my life, I've searched for a purpose."

"And now you know that purpose," Abeloth agreed,

closing what little space remained between them with a step. Only a few centimeters separated them now. They were so close he could feel and smell her breath, sweet as flowers, caressing his face. "To serve me. To be with me. Part of me. I need you, Dyon. I need you very much."

"I want to be with you, with my brothers and sisters," Dyon said. "I want to understand."

"You will," she assured him. "You will be with them . . . with me. As long as I live. And I," she whispered, reaching up to cup his cheeks with her strong, warm hands, "will live forever."

And that was when the torment started.

He stood frozen in place as securely as if his feet had rooted there. He couldn't move, couldn't pull back, couldn't cry out in pain or in warning, for now he suddenly realized that this being was not what he had thought, was not what she—was it even a she?—had pretended to be. The smile, so loving, grew cruel. It spread across her face, widening like a crack in the ground, the lips growing hideously full in that dreadful smile. Her eyes turned from gray to silver to white and grew smaller, seeming to recede into the suddenly black depths of her eye sockets like something falling into a well. Her hair sprouted, grew, undulating as it rippled to her feet, and the hands, the strong, human hands that had cupped his face so tenderly now became tiny, slimy tentacles that seemed to thrust into his skull, into his brain, and suck out what they found there.

A terrible heat, white hot, seared him there, and he smelled burning flesh. Then his heart spasmed in terror as she moved that hideous, huge mouth closer, closer, until it was touching his own.

She pulled back, and a glowing golden mist clung to her lips. The mist grew, mercifully obscuring her face as she extracted—

A deep, agonized groan was ripped from Dyon,

hauled from his innermost soul, floating on that golden mist. Every limb, every centimeter, every *cell* of him was coming under attack. It was not like the searing, focused pain in his temple; this pain was aching and deep. The pain at his temple changed from white-hot to icy cold, and it began to enter him. As Abeloth pulled forth something—

*Life energy, she's taking my life essence . . .*

—from his body, she gave in return a dreadful cold. A slithering, dark cold that wrapped around his throat, closing it, then his heart, then his entrails, then seeped implacably into the rest of him.

He could feel himself withering up, the desiccation turning him into a living corpse, dried and husklike, as if he had been buried in the sand for centuries.

Abeloth chuckled, a throaty, warm sound. "You have served me well, better than any have in a long time. Soon, we will become one, Dyon Stad. Soon, you will never leave me. And you will have enabled me to continue."

# Chapter Thirty-two

"The cave," said Vestara, peering at the tracking device. Sweat beaded her face, and tendrils of dark hair clung clammily to her cheeks and neck. They were all baking in the blue sunlight. Under other circumstances, Luke suspected that the Sith would waste the Force by creating cool breezes and lowering their body temperature. But not now, not here. There was no place for trivialities here. There were twenty of them who had fought their way through the voracious plant life lurking on the shores and in the red river itself.

Twenty of them left, anyway. The yellow water plants and the funnel-shaped trees claimed two Sith before they were finally beaten back. Blasted with Force energy, sliced by lightsabers of three different hues, and cut by glass parangs, the damaged foliage hung back almost sullenly as the group stood at the base of the cliff.

"It seems too obvious," Taalon said. He frowned as he regarded the small dark shape about a kilometer up the shoulder of the volcanic mountain. "Even if Abeloth is unaware that we placed a tracking device on Dyon, which I doubt, she knows that this is the place Vestara first encountered her. Why would she wait here to be attacked?"

"It could be more of a stronghold than Vestara realized," Luke said. His voice was doubtful. "This could be her ultimate seat of power, somehow." To Luke, this whole place reeked of the dark side. It was strong where the cave was, to be sure, but there were other places on this world where dark-side energy gathered just as strongly—even more so. "Or there could be a nice little trap waiting for us, which seems more likely."

"A trap is only a trap if it takes one by surprise," Gavar Khai said. "Otherwise, it is merely an obstacle to be overcome."

"On that, at least, we are agreed. Let's find out which."

They moved quickly despite the heat up the trail to the entrance to the cave, weapons in hand, senses alert.

It was no trap. It was no attack. Abeloth was not here, but her cat's-paw was.

Dyon lay on the floor of the cave, his face and arms pale and visible even in the dim lighting. A quick check, both with conventional tools and in the Force, revealed that he was alone, and Ben raced up to him.

"He's still alive," Ben said, "but only just."

Dyon opened his eyes. Luke expected him to struggle, but instead he reached out and clasped Ben's shoulder.

"Ben . . . so sorry . . ."

Ben and Luke exchanged glances. "You know me? You don't think I'm an imposter?"

"She—she's not what she seems," Dyon gasped. "She tricked me. You still seem—seem wrong to me but I know that's her influence. She tried to kill me. She sensed you coming and left me for dead."

"Let her fear us," Taalon said. "Hundreds of Sith, powerful in the Force, come to take her down. She *should* know fear."

"I believe that she left, but not because she was afraid," Luke said. He and Ben helped Dyon to his feet. Color was starting to return to his face. "You all right?"

"I am now. Good timing," he said, and gave Luke a weak grin. "She tried to—to drain my life energy some-how."

"Looks like once the contact is broken you're all right," Ben said. "Good thing to know if she tries that kind of attack on us." He smiled at Dyon, who seemed to grow stronger by the minute.

"Where did she go?" Luke asked.

Dyon pointed to the back of the cave. In the red glow of several lit lightsabers, everyone could easily see the mouth of a tunnel that opened onto utter blackness.

"There," Dyon said.

"Do you know where this tunnel leads?"

"I haven't the faintest idea."

Luke turned to the others. "I think she went through here to better her attack position, and it was a smart move. There could be all kinds of traps or dangers in that tunnel. She'll certainly be waiting to pounce the second we emerge on the other end."

"I cannot sense her in the Force," Taalon said, and the admission clearly pained him. "Now that Dyon is no longer with her, I think that this is, unfortunately, our only option."

Unease rippled through those assembled. Vestara took a step closer to her father, who reached out to squeeze her shoulder briefly. It was, Luke mused, likely certain death. Abeloth held every advantage now. But if they were slain, or taken, there were at least several hundred other Sith who would come. It was not an even fight, but it was a fairer one than he had had any right to expect.

"I think so, too," Luke said. "Ben and I can go first, and if it's safe, we can let the rest of you know."

Taalon flushed, his lavender cheeks turning dark purple. "Are you calling us cowards, Master Skywalker?"

"No," Luke said. "You're the one who used that term."

"I am not afraid, nor is anyone else here," Taalon growled.

"Then you're an idiot," Luke said. "You *should* be

afraid. Lack of fear makes one careless, and being care-less here will get you killed." He gave Dyon a comlink. "You stay here."

"I'd like to come with you," Dyon said.

"You've already helped a great deal," Luke said. "But I need someone here I can trust if this backfires and she comes back this way. Taalon, pick some of your people to stay here and give Dyon some backup support."

Taalon's eyes narrowed. Luke knew he was pushing the Keshiri by continuing to angle for control of the situation, but he also knew that showing anything that could be perceived as weakness to this Sith would be fatal. Luke was significant, in some way, to Abeloth, although that thought disgusted him. Taalon knew it. He might dislike Luke, might take joy in attacking him, but he would not until his own purposes had been achieved.

"It is wise to cover all avenues of her possible escape," Taalon said, instead of what he no doubt wished to say, and nodded to two others. "Let us know if you see anything out of the ordinary here," he told them, then turned back to Luke. He offered a completely false smile.

"Let us go to Abeloth then, Master Skywalker. And since this is again your plan . . ." He left the sentence unfinished, instead extending a hand mockingly toward the yawning black mouth of the tunnel.

Luke did not put walking through a dark, tight tunnel with several Sith behind him at the top of his list of high-lights of his life, but it was not as bad as he had feared.

The tunnel was clearly artificial. It was almost a per-fect circle, and was wide enough to permit everyone to walk erect, even to have some freedom of movement. It went slightly downward at first, leading them through the mountain. Roots, powerful on this world, had forced their way through the sheer stone in clumps, slicked with some kind of ooze that dissolved the corpses of the small animals clutched in their grip. Abeloth apparently had not had time to rig any elaborate traps for them. Nor did the tunnel suddenly abruptly collapse. The greatest threat came from the occasional root that came to life, pushing through the top of the packed soil passageway attempting to wrap around a throat, or from the bottom to seize an ankle. The ooze was not acidic, although it was likely toxic, and there were no injuries. The roots were quickly repelled with the glass parangs each Sith appeared to carry, or a quick, precise lightsaber stroke.

"It seems our luck is holding," Gavar Khai said.

"For now," Luke cautioned. He and Ben led the way, with Taalon, Vestara, and Khai behind them. "She may simply be conserving her strength."

"For a Jedi, who is supposed to be so positive, you are quite the pessimist," Khai said. Confidence radiated from him. Luke mentally shook his head. Khai was strong in the Force, as was his offspring. He was, Luke was certain, well trained in combat. But there was a naïveté about these Sith that confounded him. As if they were at once ancient and new. He hoped he'd live long enough to get to the bottom of it.

"A realist, Khai. I've seen quite a lot in my life. I know to expect the unexpected. Your Sith underestimated Abeloth once before. How many did you lose last time, Taalon?"

The Sith High Lord did not reply. The tension increased, and the rest of the way through the tunnel was spent in a silence that was broken only by the sound of errant roots being slashed.

Finally, Luke halted. "Extinguish lightsabers," he said.

"What?" exclaimed Taalon.

"Just do it," he said. There was some muttering, but one by one, the red lights went out.

And up ahead, they could all see the bright blue smudge of light that showed the end of the tunnel.

Luke extended his thoughts in the Force, but again, could sense nothing. He frowned, perplexed. He had no doubt that Abeloth knew exactly where they were. If she could reach his consciousness aboard the *Jade Shadow* in his sleep—a thought that still turned his stomach—surely she would know how to find them here, where her power was the strongest. He couldn't imagine she wouldn't be out there waiting for them, ready to pounce.

"Activate lightsabers," Luke said. "And be ready for anything."

There were several sounds of the *snap-hiss* of the lightsabers in the underground corridor that was no doubt about to deliver them right into Abeloth's hands—or tentacles. He held the lightsaber in his right hand and counted down: "three, two, one."

And then they rushed forward into the blue light of day.

Into the empty ruin of an old courtyard, overgrown with vines, tree ferns, and other plants. It was contained by steep walls on all sides. Pillars jutted up, blue-green with moss. In the center of the courtyard was the basin of a fountain. The sound of its bubbling floated to them on the still, hot air that stank of sulfur. And from the fountain, buffeting him in the Force as the sulfur was assaulting his physical senses, rose dark-side energy.

Luke knew the place at once. He had been here, Beyond Shadows. This was where he had seen Abeloth for the first time. Had seen her grotesque face in the dark cloud formed by the sulfur, had felt her tentacles wrapping around his leg, trying to wriggle their cold way inside of him. Whispering his name.

*Luke,* it had said.

*Come.*

He had refused her then. Mara had warned him not to continue pursuing her.

He couldn't see her, couldn't feel her, but he knew she had to be here.

"Abeloth," he called. "Abeloth, I'm here."

"So am I."

Luke whirled. As he turned to face her, out of the corner of his eye he saw his companions all stiffen suddenly, expressions of stark terror on their faces. But he had no time for them, not when she had finally appeared.

Standing before him was not the monstrous, hideous form he had seen Beyond Shadows. No being with long, strawlike blond hair, tiny eyes like deep-set stars, a too-wide mouth and arms that ended in writhing tentacles. No, this being did not present that form to his eyes.

She was tall, true, but looked human. She had long, curly dark hair, thick and heavy. Her eyes were gray, and crinkled in a smile. And then she shifted again, the hair shortening, becoming straight, the color of honey, the eyes turning a slightly silvery shade of gray.

"Luke," she said, stepping forward. Her eyes were bright with tears, and the arms that she extended to him trembled. "You've come for me. You've finally come for me. I knew you would. All this time, I had faith."

For the second time that day, Luke was sent reeling in shock. He stared at Abeloth, at this being that had done so much harm to so many. Who had driven young Jedi mad, who had taken so many lives. This ancient, evil being of whom even Mara Jade was afraid.

And he knew her.

He suddenly, sickly understood why it was she had been able to touch him so profoundly, so tenderly, aboard the *Jade Shadow.* Why it had been so easy for him to confuse that contact, which should have been so reprehensible, with that of the loving touch of his mate.

Because he had once loved her with his whole heart and being. Loved her more than anything in the universe. Had once intended to breathe his last breath in her arms.

"*Callista,*" he whispered.

# Chapter Thirty-three

"I KNEW YOU WOULD KNOW ME," THE CREATURE WHISpered. Her gray eyes were bright, bright as stars, and they glistened with tears of joy. "You have always been able to know me. You knew me when my very essence was part of a ship. You knew me when it was in a body that was not my own, and even now, even here, you know me."

Luke stared at her, his vision tunneling, blood thundering in his ears. Not since Darth Vader had uttered the terrible words, *I am your father,* had he been so shaken.

He couldn't help it. He extended a hand, clasped hers, and they met in the Force.

Time stopped.

This thing was indeed Abeloth. Was the being who had slithered into his son's mind when Ben was just a toddler. Was the instigator of mad Jedi, had turned plants to predators that attacked her enemies. Had destroyed Sinkhole Station and the hundreds of unfortunates who dwelt there. It was horrific, radiating darkside energy, fueled by hatred and evil, by fear and by need and by loneliness. It represented everything Luke had dedicated his life to fighting.

It was also, inconceivably, impossibly, Callista.

This was no trick, no act. This was no illusion, to make him think of his lost love, to soften him so she could strike when his guard was down. That would be difficult enough to have to witness. But this really *was* Callista.

He had fallen in love with her when, at the time of her body's death, her spirit had been woven into the dreadnought *Eye of Palpatine*. Callista's physical self had been destroyed, but she had used her Force skills to merge with the vessel. There, she had spoken with Luke, had shared visions of her life with him through the Force. He had had dreams of her then, as he had aboard the *Jade Shadow;* dreams of her lying beside and behind him, her long, strong body pressing comfortingly into his. He'd fallen truly and deeply in love with a spirit, a soul. Later, his student Cray Mingla, for personal reasons of her own, had chosen to give her body to Callista, so that she and Luke could finally be together.

Still dazed, he recalled the description that Vestara had given of Abeloth: sometimes she had dark, thick, curly hair, such as Callista had had in her first life; sometimes she appeared with the short, honey-gold, stylish locks that Cray Mingla had worn.

Tears stung his eyes and his heart swelled with a bittersweet aching. Oh, it was *her,* it was his Callie, and the love he had once felt for her was still there, still sweet and warm and true.

In becoming human once again, Callista had lost her connection to the Force. She had learned that she could only touch the dark side, and they had parted ways long ago as she embarked on a journey to recover her Force powers.

He felt Callista affirming his thoughts, her essence washing over and around and through him, her love bright and true and strong, and the tears began to pour down his face. Luke leaned forward, pressing his forehead to hers.

She had come here, seeking answers, and found only the lonely, needy monster imprisoned at the heart of the

Maw. The thing that had lured Jacen in, had damaged so many, had grown and fed and used Callista as it had used others before and since.

The warmth enveloping him chilled suddenly. He pulled back, just slightly, from her presence in the Force. Immediately, her longing for him became not sweet, but desperate, frightened, needy. He felt the tentacles slipping into the center of his being. She had him again after so long, too long. She had been a fool to have walked away from what they had had together. To have let him marry another, father a child not of her body. It had been wrong, and she would not make that mistake again, ever. They had found each other, she and Luke Skywalker, after so many wrong turns and bitter regrets. Her one true love. And they would now be together, forever.

No. That was not the way. Luke touched her cheek gently, and she leaned into his hand. Luke wanted to help her. He needed to take her away from here, find a way to separate that part of her that was warm, stubborn, brave, humorous Callista from the monster in the Maw capable of such vast evil and cruelty. It would be all right. It would all be all right. He could unravel the bright thread of Callista from the ugly tapestry of Abeloth and her darkness, he knew he could, if she would let him—

Let him? *Let* him? Let him take away the power she had discovered? Let herself become less than the magnificent being into which she had evolved? No, Luke had it all wrong, *she* would make him like *her*, would teach him to grow so far beyond himself that he would laugh at the small being he had once been, even as she now laughed gently at his misguided earnestness. This was why he had come. Luke's path had led him here, beyond any hope or dream or wish, to the Maw, to Callista's arms again, and now he would never leave.

They would be together.

The way she was, and the way she would make him.

For eternity.

Luke's heart broke, again, inside him.

Mara's words came back to him: *She is never what she seems to be.*

This being was not Callista. Oh, it wore parts of her like some obscene costume, real, true parts of her, parts that made him ache to behold, but it was not her. Callista had once vowed to never use the Force again, if the only way to do so was to touch the dark side. She had fought bravely in the Clone Wars, had sacrificed her life to save others. She was a Jedi. And he knew now that she was as dead as if he had seen her lifeless body.

The woman he had loved was gone. Abeloth had taken her, as she had already taken so much from so many. He wanted to reach Callista, to save her, but he realized sickly that there was not enough left *to* save.

*I'm sorry. I can't help you.*

Callista—no, it wasn't her, he needed to stop thinking of her as that—Abeloth dropped his hands and stepped back, shock on her face.

"After all this, after all we went through, together and apart . . . you would forsake me?" Tears filled the silver gray eyes, poured down her cheeks.

Luke swallowed, forcing calm alertness through his body. He dropped into a pre-fighting stance, balancing lightly on the balls of his feet, the lightsaber, still lit, in his hand.

"You might once have had part of Callista in you," he said quietly. "But whatever was good, and true, and right about her—that's all gone. You took it all and left only shards of her behind. Just like you tried to do with Dyon. For the love I once bore her, I again say, I am sorry, I cannot help you."

She continued to gaze at him, and the expression on

her face would have moved a harder heart than Luke's. But his was already broken with the knowledge of what had happened. That his Callie was gone, forever. He continued to regard her solemnly, and she fell to her knees, looking dazed. Sobs racked her frame and she lowered her head.

"Then you doom all you love, Luke Skywalker," said Abeloth. Three voices seemed to come from that throat.

She raised her head. Her face had changed, had become that ugly, tiny-eyed, wide-mouthed monster. Except the part of her that remained Callista. Luke wasn't sure which—the nose, the hair, but it was an obscene amalgam he knew was designed to torture him.

He had refused her, and she would destroy him.

Her eyes suddenly blinked quickly and she glanced upward. Luke could feel it now, too, a tingling of darkside energy overhead, but nothing of Abeloth's doing. Hope surged within him.

In her arrogance and her fixation on Luke, Abeloth had discounted the hundreds of Sith scattered over the area. She had focused on him to the exclusion of almost everyone else who was physically with him, and certainly those who were not. And thus ignored, the rest of the Sith had begun their weaving.

The Dathomiri Nightsisters used the Force to create a sort of net called a control web. Working together as a team, they wove tendrils of Force energy together and extended it over an area of ground. It felt as if a ball of yarn were being tossed from one to the other as strands of energy crisscrossed and interwove. Beasts beneath this net, this web, would obey the weavers. Luke, Ben, and Vestara had all been firsthand witnesses to this web weaving on Dathomir.

*Never let it be said,* Luke thought, *that the Sith did not learn quickly, nor that they did not know a good thing when they saw it.* It had been Vestara's suggestion to have those who were not directly involved in attacking Abeloth stand by and work together. The weaving was shaky, inexpert, but with so many strands from such powerful Force-users—hundreds as opposed to tens—even this beginner's web was enough to unsettle Abeloth as they had hoped it would.

She lowered her head, fixed him with anger and rage, and lifted her hands.

And suddenly Luke knew what she intended. Who she would attack.

It would not be him.

Luke charged.

It was out there. Jaina could feel it—Ship, the Sith training vessel Ben had once piloted, that he had found on Ziost and had awakened from its centuries of slumber. The vessel she, Jag, and Zekk had encountered not so long ago on Lumiya's asteroid—the vessel Zekk had sent away from Alema Rar, with instructions to find a better master. And it most certainly had—it had found the Lost Tribe.

And Jaina knew that if she could feel it, it could feel her.

*Oh well,* Jaina thought, shrugging mentally as she piloted her StealthX toward where she sensed the meditation sphere was lurking.

From what little the tight-lipped Sith girl had shared with Ben and Luke, and Luke had passed on to Jaina, Ship had been very chummy with the Lost Tribe Sith until Abeloth had called it to serve her. Vestara had said that Ship felt unhappy obeying Abeloth, but that could be Sith lies. Regardless, to Jedi, it was an enemy, whoever was controlling it, and she wanted to blast the cursed thing to tiny bits of . . . whatever it was made of.

She could sense it more clearly now. She had expected it to be in the atmosphere, probably already attacking the group assembled to harm its master. But it was in orbit about the planet, doing . . . nothing.

No, not nothing.

Waiting.

She could see it now, a tiny dot on her tactical display. "Rowdy, get me a better look at this thing."

WHY WOULD ANYONE WANT THAT? THOSE THINGS ARE UGLY.

Jaina smiled a little. "Agreed." She'd given the astromech a new name and a sort of personality, tinkering with it recently to upgrade it with a humor protocol. Despite its wisecrack, the droid, of course, obeyed, and Jaina got her first good look at the Sith meditation sphere.

She'd not seen it up close before, and it was even uglier than she had expected. It looked like a giant yellow-orange eye, covered with veins, with spikes on four sides and propelled by batlike wings. Jaina shook her head at the thought that it had been her cousin who had found this thing, who had gone inside it and made it obey him.

*I see you, Jedi Solo.*

*I see* you, *big ugly orange-red thing.*

Humor rolled off it, then she felt it . . . ignoring her. Her immediate reaction was irritation.

*You're working with Abeloth.*

*I am programmed to obey a strong will. The girl is strong, you are stronger, Sword of the Jedi, but neither of you can break the hold she has on me. She is older and more powerful than you can possibly imagine.*

*So powerful she has you just sitting there because she anticipates needing you, instead of letting you fight me, is that it?*

She felt stoic silence in the Force.

"Enough chitchat," she said to Rowdy. "Launch shadow bomb one."

She felt a gentle bump beneath her seat as the bomb

was forced from the tube. She reached out for it in the Force, her eyes fixed on Ship, directing the bomb directly toward it. It simply sat there. For a wild moment, Jaina wondered exactly how sentient it was. Why wasn't it attacking her, or moving out of the way? Was this thing choosing suicide by Jedi rather than continuing to help Abeloth against the Sith it had been designed to serve? Was it really going to—

And suddenly, as if someone had snatched something she was holding right out of her hand, she felt Ship commandeer the direction of the bomb and send it spiraling off harmlessly. It turned to "face" her now. And as Jaina watched, its surface seemed to shiver. Strange appendages began to form, and she realized Ship was making its own weapons and training them on her.

The battle was on.

Good.

Abeloth was raging. Ben felt buffeted by the sheer hatred roiling off her. Sweat sprung on his brow, beneath his arms, and a brush of what had terrified him so badly a few moments ago shuddered through him. She turned her tiny eyes upon him and he gripped his lightsaber. If this really was Callista—or rather, what the thing in the Maw had left of someone his father once loved—then he knew there was no better target to hurt Luke Skywalker than himself.

What could he do against her, really? But he had to try.

He took his cue from his father, who lifted his lightsaber and charged the creature. Taalon and Khai, too, rushed into the fray. Ben started to join them. Vestara was right by his side.

Abeloth was still staring at Ben, and as he raced toward her, she smiled, and flicked three of the tiny tentacles that served as fingers.

Beside Ben, Vestara's eyes flew wide as something seized her by the throat, lifted her two meters off the ground, and shook her. She dropped her lightsaber, one hand going to her throat attempting to pry off the invisible fingers, the other hand outstretched, fingers splayed hard. Blue force lightning shot from her palm to dance erratically in the air around her for a moment, not reaching its target. Then, inexorably, the blue lightning began to twist, like heated metal folding, to go back on its creator. At the same moment, a thick white root, tipped with finger-length barbs, shot out of the ground. The roots, capped with a thick green spike, twisted around Vestara, then reared back like a snake about to strike. Vestara's eyes darted to the spike and she yanked in her hand, folding her arm over her chest as the spikes struck home a second time.

"Vestara!" shrieked Ben. He sprang forward, slashing frantically at the vines, calling her name again and again. She dropped like a stone to the ground, landing hard on her arm, face twisted in agony, booted feet churning up the loose soil. Blood poured from several puncture wounds on her arm and chest, and there was something obviously wrong with her shoulder. Tears poured from her eyes, but she stayed silent, so silent—

*Vestara . . .*

He gathered her in his arms and raced away from Abeloth's fury, setting her down, away from the vegetation that even now struggled to crawl up on her. Her face was sweaty and her eyes rolled in her head.

Ben realized he was shaking as he cradled her. "It's okay, I've got you Ves, you're okay," he murmured over and over again. He forced his fingers to stop trembling as he tried to examine her injuries. There didn't seem to be anything life-threatening; it looked like the shoulder was dislocated. The puncture wounds were deep, but nothing had hit a vital organ or artery. Relief flooded over him. She was going to be all right. Ben gave her a quick smile and turned, started to rise.

Her hand, slick with warm blood, clamped down on his arm. She was shaking. "Don't leave me," she whispered. ". . . p-poison . . ."

Ben felt as though someone was squeezing his heart as he swore violently. He hadn't seen anything to indicate that the spikes on the roots were poisoned, but Vestara had been here before. If she thought the barbs were poisoned, Ben wasn't about to take a chance. He glanced over at his father even as he rifled through his pouch for something, anything, that would help.

Abeloth was surrounded by five powerful Force-users: Luke Skywalker, High Lord Taalon, Saber Gavar Khai, and two others Ben didn't know. It was almost like a dance, with the combatants leaping, somersaulting in midair, tumbling aside. The cries of curses in the musical Keshiri tongue, the unique sound of the sizzle of lightsabers batting back Force lightning, the smell of sulfur all combined to unsettle Ben.

And even as he watched, Abeloth suddenly was not there.

The ring of five enemies was now inadvertently battling one another. Gavar Khai grunted in annoyance as his red blade sliced cleanly through not the monstrous Abeloth, but one of his fellow Sith. Luke had to Force-leap straight up to avoid the blade's follow-through, landing lightly on his feet and looking about for their escaped enemy. Mocking laughter seemed to echo from all directions. They sprang apart, and then there she was again, at the far end of the courtyard, laughing as the four raced toward her. Their comrade lay dead and ignored, and as Ben watched, the vines reached to latch on to the corpse and started to pull away the pieces.

Again, the three Sith and Luke encircled Abeloth, and

this time they seemed to be wearing her down. Ben ached to help them, but Vestara—

Gavar Khai surged forward, bringing his lightsaber down on the whirling, dancing figure that was the laughing Abeloth. At the last moment, he diverted the blade, and Ben watched in horror as it swung, not to the agreed-upon common enemy, but at his father. At the same moment, he felt the net being woven high above them tighten.

The Sith had betrayed them.

Ship was good. It had taken Jaina two tries before she was able to prevent Ship from redirecting the shadow bombs she fired at it. In the meantime, she contented herself with laser cannons, smiling grimly as she simultaneously saw and felt the blasts strike the Sith vessel.

Its self-created weapons fired in return, steady and rapid. Jaina pulled back on the stick hard and was slammed back against her seat. Rowdy toodled in distress.

WHOSE SIDE ARE YOU ON?

Jaina didn't have breath to answer, taking the StealthX into a roll that brought it underneath the spherical vessel, where it didn't have suddenly sprouted cannons, and launching a volley of torpedos.

Except now it *did* have suddenly sprouted cannons there, and they were firing. Jaina's blast tinting darkened instantly and she hung on as her ship spiraled out of control, struggling to bring it back in line before it was too late.

"Dad!" Ben screamed. Luke heard him, and just in time got his own blade up. Red and green clashed, sizzling.

"Ben, please, I need—"

Ben shook off the clinging hand and gave Vestara a single scorching look of naked loathing before leaping into the fray to help his betrayed father. He Force-launched himself on Gavar Khai from behind, knocking the Sith off balance and then leaping free as Khai got to his feet.

Vestara had played him. And the bitter knowledge, the righteous fury of it all, lent Ben strength. Surprise and admiration flickered in Gavar Khai's dark eyes as Ben pressed the attack.

"You're good for a whelp," Khai said.

"Should have done this the first time I saw you," Ben snarled. He leaped backward, not quite in time, the red blade cutting a horizontal slash in his black tunic. He winced as it grazed the flesh beneath it. Khai feinted and then came at him again. Luke had returned his attention to Abeloth, and Ben was glad of it. He wanted Khai all to himself. He wanted to kill this piece of Sith spit, to cut him into sizzling chunks, for what he had made of Vestara.

In his anger he grew reckless, overextending his reach and having to again leap clear of Khai's return stroke. He landed on one knee, catching the blade with his own, then executing a roundhouse kick that almost caught Khai unaware.

"Better," Khai said. "Let the anger flow. Hate me all you like. It is what feeds the dark side within you."

It was the wrong thing to say. Ben had heard this song before, and he wasn't having any of it. The words had the opposite effect, calming the young Knight and clearing his head.

The Sith had betrayed them. Vestara had used her injury to try to play on his feelings for her, to keep him out of the way while her father attacked his. Out of the corner of his eye, he could see Taalon and the other remaining Sith using the Force net technique—the technique Vestara had suggested—not to try to stifle Abeloth's powers, but to try to trap the now seriously struggling

Abeloth, even as Luke was using his own mastery of the Force to destroy her. And it was with a fierce sense of pride and love that Ben realized that, despite the odds, his father was *winning*.

The net was working. It was starting to stifle her ability to use the Force. He could see it in the terror on Abeloth's face, feel it in the wild flickering of her Force aura. And Luke was fighting as Ben had never seen him before, pain and love and duty grim on his face, darting and leaping, moving his lightsaber so swiftly it was a blur. Ben let out a shout of delight and continued to press the attack on Gavar Khai, who no longer was smirking and gloating, but instead felt genuine concern that he might not make it out of this alive.

A sudden shock wave hurled Ben into the sky. He felt paralyzed for a second, unable to use the Force to direct his fall, and landed hard. He blacked out briefly, and when he came to, he heard shouting. Ben got to his feet, grabbing his lightsaber from where it had fallen.

Abeloth was gone. He realized, as everyone else did, what must have happened. She had gathered her strength to send out a powerful Force shock, to throw her attackers off her briefly, and disappeared.

"Where'd she go?" Ben cried, ignoring Khai for the moment.

Luke had recovered faster than he and didn't reply. Instead, he raced down the tunnel at full speed, even though Ben could see he had been at least slightly injured in the attack.

Their division among themselves forgotten, Ben and the Sith followed. Ben heard Vestara following him at a distance, could feel her pain and mingled regret and resolution in the Force. Wincing, he shut her out.

The three Sith that Taalon had left to aid Dyon had already been dispatched. There was no obvious damage to the corpses, but they all had looks of terror frozen on their faces. And now, Abeloth had returned to Dyon to finish the job she'd started earlier.

Dyon lay on his back, his face contorted in fear. Abeloth straddled him in a horrible parody of lovers, her tentacle fingers pressed to his face, her huge, grinning mouth a centimeter from his. Glowing golden energy wrapped about them. As Luke emerged from the cave, Abeloth hissed, sensing his presence, and turned to look at him.

Her features rippled, melted into those of Callista. She turned to Luke, hand outstretched, imploring.

"Luke—please. You don't understand. It really is me. It's Callie, your Callie. I love you. I've never stopped. Please—"

*She is never what she seems.*

And then Luke understood. She wasn't Callista.

She wasn't even Abeloth.

Trusting his feelings, as he had so many times before, Luke brought his lightsaber down.

On the writhing body of Dyon Stad.

"Abeloth" recoiled as the bright blade went straight through Dyon Stad's chest, through the stone floor of the cave. He arched his back and cried out, clawing frantically at Luke's face.

"Dad! What are you doing?" came Ben's voice. The Sith were shouting something, too. Luke ignored them all, his blue eyes peering into Dyon's.

The wide, imploring, human eyes of Dyon Stad changed. They became tiny, hard pinpricks of light, like stars in a dark well of nothingness. The hands clawing at him became tentacles, the mouth wide and gaping. Luke felt one more attack from her, a crashing wave of dark-side energy, and braced himself for the assault.

She died halfway through. He felt it. Felt her wink out of existence, strangely small in death. He moved off the body and sat on the floor for a long moment, catching his breath.

Ben was there. "Dad? You all right? Is she . . . ?"

Luke lifted his head. It felt like it weighed a kiloton. He smiled a little as he saw Dyon Stad lying to the side, unconscious, but breathing, and looked again at the monster that had worn first Callista's face and then Dyon's.

"Yes," said Luke. His throat was dry, the words a whisper. "She's dead."

# Chapter Thirty-four

*DIRECT HIT ON ENGINE NUMBER TWO,* Rowdy informed Jaina.

"Stang," Jaina swore. Ship was opening fire again. The vessel stopped its spiral and she was able to get it back under control just in time to veer out of the path of the next round of torpedos.

"Target Ship," she barked, juking and jinking to avoid the attack.

*Targeting array damaged.*

Another hit. The StealthX shuddered.

*Targeting display offline.*

Jaina pressed her lips together grimly. She still had the Force. Ship twirled, spinning around rapidly but in full control of itself, and she felt its dark gloating. It came to an immediate stop and seemed to be impaling her with its "eye."

*Ship has us target locked,* Rowdy informed her.

"I can see that," Jaina snapped. "Ready—"

She felt the oppressive attention vanish. And a second later, Ship was gone. It was moving, not down to the planet presumably to help Abeloth, but *away* from the planet, into space.

"What is it doing?" she asked aloud.

*RUNNING AWAY BECAUSE IT IS SO OBVI-
OUSLY OUTMATCHED PERHAPS.*

"I wish," Jaina said. With only three engines and a
useless targeting array, she had been at a serious disad-
vantage. No, something else had happened. She just
didn't know what. At least the vessel wasn't down there
firing on Luke and Ben.

"Okay, Rowdy," she said, "let's head back to the
*Rockhound* and see if there's any news."


ASYLYM BLOCK, JEDI TEMPLE, CORUSCANT

Cilghal's heart was heavy as she made her way to the asy-
lum block. As a healer, she mourned every loss of life, and
Kani's murder on the very steps of the Temple infuriated
and saddened her profoundly. It had been, as it had doubtless been calculated to be, a severe blow to the morale of
the besieged Jedi. There was still no luck in finding anything that could be utilized as an escape route, although
the Solos' ingenious idea to send in badly needed medication on vermin-back had helped lift spirits somewhat.

Still, small creatures could carry only small vials. They
had merely staved off the inevitable. The chrono was
ticking on the siege deadline. One way or another, something would shift.

Although the ysalamiri prevented usage of the Force
in close proximity of the patients, Cilghal used it now to
calm herself. It was time for another dose of the sedative; they would be alert and awake, and if they could
not sense her in the Force, there was still body language
and voice inflections. The calmer she was, the calmer
they would be.

There were three of them, now, Sothais Saar, Turi Altamik, and Kunor Bann. Each of them had his or her own
comfortable living area, the walls made of transparisteel,

with cams that were usually turned off in the more private areas, but could be activated if need be. When they were alert, Cilghal found Saar raging violently—he was the one most in need of the sedative—Altamik clawing at something, and Bann rocking back and forth with tears pouring down his face. She slowed and came to a full stop as they came into view.

Shul Vaal, her Twi'lek colleague, approached her. Normally tranquil, Vaal seemed to be suppressing excitement. "Master Cilghal," he began, "there's something—"

Cilghal lifted a hand and Vaal fell silent.

Sothais Saar was sitting calmly at the small table. Datapads and holovids had been provided to all the patients, but they seldom made use of them except to break them. Now the Chev's heavy-browed head was bent over the datapad, and he seemed to be, quite peacefully, engrossed in reading.

Turi Altamik was brushing her hair. Her expression was strained, tired, but reflected none of the madness that had turned her pert, pretty features into scowls or glowers. And Bann—he stood gazing out the transparisteel, hands clasped behind his back. As soon as he saw Cilghal and Vaal, he lifted his hand and waved, smiling uncertainly.

"I don't believe it," Cilghal said slowly. "It's not possible . . . is it?"

They looked . . . sane. All three of them.

"It could be a trick," Vaal said. "Seff Hellin tricked the Solos before. They could simply be pretending to be sane."

"All three of them? At once? They couldn't possibly have coordinated this, there's no way for them to communicate."

Hope rose within her, almost unbearably bright. She forced it down. She had no proof yet. She would not rejoice until she knew, for an absolute certainty, that all of them had returned to their normal selves.

And then . . . then she would have something that would lift the Jedi's spirits to the skies and beyond.

Armed with stun sticks and a tranquilizer pistol, they ascended to the catwalk on the upper level of the cell-block. Cilghal desperately wished that she had all the ill Jedi here now. It would be interesting to see if Valin Horn, the first one to display the madness, would also show these positive signs if he were not encased in carbonite. For now, though, she supposed she should be grateful she even had these three.

"Jedi Saar first," she told Vaal, who nodded thoughtfully. "He's been the most violent, and of the three, he's been ill the longest."

They paused in front of the door to the transparisteel cell. Vaal rapped gently. Saar turned and saw them. He smiled, a stiff, formal smile—completely typical for him—and rose.

"Sothais?" said Tekli. "We'd like to come in."

"I am so glad to see you," he said. "Please, please, do come in."

The two healers exchanged glances, then Cilghal entered the code. He made no rush to attack or escape, simply stood by the table, still holding the datapad. "I remember everything," he said. "I'm terribly embarrassed. I'm so sorry I attacked you, Master Cilghal. And I must apologize to Chief of Staff Dorvan as soon as possible."

"You . . . remember? You don't think we're imposters?" Cilghal asked.

Color rose in the Chev's cheeks. "I did, at one point. It seemed . . . right. I can't explain it better than that. Even when I knew what to look for—when it happened, it seemed completely believable."

Tekli gestured to the datapad. "What are you reading, Sothais?"

"Updates on my treatise," he said. "Apparently, there has been an uprising on Klatooine. I am most gratified and I hope this will inspire other oppressed beings to take their destinies into their own hands."

That certainly sounded like Saar. Cilghal made a decision. It was risky, but she was willing to chance it. "I'd like you to come with us to the infirmary. We'd like to run a few tests."

"Certainly." He did not move.

"Jedi Saar?"

"I assume you are going to secure me in some fashion," he said, slightly puzzled.

"No," Cilghal said. "Come along."

The center of her back itched, waiting for the blow.

Hamner was in his office. Normally, it was a tidy, orderly place, but now it was strewn with datapads and half-drunk, cold cups of caf. Hamner himself was unshaven and exhausted. He was poring over old blueprints of the Temple, and jotting notes about his conversation with Bwua'tu. If only the Bothan would act! Get Daala to call off this siege, this terrible siege that was causing them all so much harm.

His comm chimed. He clicked it. "Hamner."

"Master Hamner?" It was Cilghal. Her voice was higher pitched than usual.

"What is it? Is everything all right? Have you run out of sedatives?" He rubbed at his aching, gritty eyes.

"Everything is more than all right," said the Mon Calamari, her gravelly voice filled with pleasure. "I am . . . delighted beyond words to report that all three of the ill Jedi appear to have made a full recovery."

The exhaustion fled. "What? All of them? How?"

"I'm not sure, but it seemed to happen to all of them simultaneously. We've run test after test; all three of them seem to be back to their old selves. My best guess is that, somehow, Master Skywalker was successful in his quest to find the cause and effect a cure."

Hamner's throat closed up and he couldn't speak. He lifted a hand that trembled to his forehead for a moment.

"Master Hamner?"

"That's wonderful, wonderful news, Cilghal. News we sorely needed. News . . . *I* sorely needed. Thank you."

*So,* Ben thought, glancing at the several Sith who stood by, staring at the corpse of their mutual enemy. *What now?* He didn't turn off his lightsaber.

Luke got to his feet, and went to check on Dyon. "He should recover, but he needs care, right away. Ben, take him to the *Shadow.*"

"But—"

Luke shot him a look and Ben fell silent.

"My daughter is injured as well," said Gavar Khai, moving to Vestara's side and examining her injuries. Vestara was pale, but she was doing her best to show no weakness, even now. "I will take her back to my ship and—"

"I don't think we've decided what's going to happen yet, Khai." The words, unexpectedly, were spoken by Taalon. The Sith High Lord looked thoughtfully at Luke. "There's still the body to examine."

"And this place, and the others that I saw Beyond Shadows," said Luke, nodding. "And I'm certain you're every bit as interested as I am in learning what Abeloth was."

"Indeed," said Taalon. "It would seem that our alliance is not yet quite dissolved."

Ben sighed.

"Surely you don't need more than a thousand Sith hanging around with nothing to do but plot treachery among themselves," Luke said.

"You are afraid," Taalon said, smiling thinly.

"Actually, I'm not," said Luke. "But I think *you* are."

The smile vanished. Taalon's eyes flashed. "Manners, Skywalker, or I shall lose my temper, and you and your boy will die without having your questions answered."

"Send them away," Luke said. "I'll let Jaina and Lando go, too. Two Jedi, three Sith. The numbers do seem a bit unfair, I admit. For you."

Taalon and Khai exchanged glances, smiling ever so slightly. "I agree," said the High Lord.

"Good," Luke said. "Ben, take Vestara and Dyon back to the *Jade Shadow* and take care of them both. Contact Jaina and Lando, and tell them the terms we've agreed on."

Ben expected Khai or Taalon to protest. Instead, Khai looked to his leader, and Taalon said, "Yes, I am sure your sick bay is quite well stocked. Vestara deserves the best care. Do not let him out of your sight, child. Is that understood? We need you watching the boy."

Ben had to try really hard to not roll his eyes. His father had essentially reclaimed Vestara as a hostage, and here was Taalon, trying to make it look like Ben was the prisoner being watched over by the girl. It was all silly, pointless posturing as far as he was concerned. He knelt beside Dyon, lifted his friend as gently as possible, and glanced over at Vestara.

"Looks like you can walk okay," he said. He was still angry and hurt at the deception she'd perpetrated earlier. "Come on."

Taalon watched them go. He wondered if the boy, if Khai and Vestara and the others, had all been personally assaulted by Abeloth as he had been.

He knew it had been only a second that the creature who now lay dead at their feet had frozen him in order to attempt to seduce Skywalker. But it might as well have been an eternity. He had been unsettled enough by Faal's fate, though he would never admit that, and it was as if Abeloth knew it.

In that second that was a lifetime, a dozen lifetimes, she had looked inside him, violated him on a level even he, a Sith High Lord, had not imagined was possible, and beheld what it was that Sarasu Taalon feared most.

And called it forth.

He had been running, running on feet that were blistered and bleeding, running with labored breath and near-exploding heart. And *they* had been behind him.

All the beings whose lives he had taken, or broken, or twisted. All the friends he had betrayed, all the family members he had ordered slain, all the rivals whose loved ones he had tormented, and those loved ones as well who had not even known his face in life. As long as he succeeded, they would not touch him. As long as he won every battle, made no mistakes, spotted every foe, he would be all right.

But the minute his foot wavered—

His ankle betrayed him, and he fell, hitting the ground upon which he was running hard. Tears, shameful tears of abject terror poured down his purple face as he scrambled to rise.

They were upon him, ripping, tearing, biting; their touch freezing and burning. He realized they would not kill him, not at once. They were going to tear him apart piece by tiny piece. And even then the torment would not stop. Abeloth had shown him it wouldn't.

"High Lord?" It was Khai, looking at him searchingly.

Taalon's heart leapt within his chest. He couldn't falter. Not in front of this one. Not in front of Skywalker.

He couldn't falter, or fall, or be wrong, or make a single miscalculation.

Ever.

"Ben? Ben, are you all right? Is Luke okay?" Jaina waved away the droid that was trying to attend to a cut on her forehead. Ben's voice was being patched through the ship's intercom from the bridge.

"We're fine. We got her." Ben's voice was filled with

pride, and Jaina couldn't blame him. She listened to him recap the fight while the healing droid fussed over her. She hated to admit it, for a variety of reasons, but it did seem as though the Sith worked well together. It had been good for everyone—this time. And only this time.

"You guys have any trouble?" he asked when he was done.

"Not much. I had a little dogfight with a very ugly vessel named Ship." Now it was her turn to grin as Ben demanded the details. "Unfortunately, we had to call it a draw. He stopped firing at me abruptly and just took off. My StealthX was too beat-up to follow. Lando's going to help me repair it."

"It just left? Huh," Ben said. "I wonder . . ." His voice trailed off, and too late, Jaina realized that he was probably not alone. She was willing to bet the girl was with him.

"Anyway, I've got orders from Dad for you and Lando."

At that moment, the door opened and Lando entered. "Good timing," Jaina said. "Luke and Ben beat Abeloth, and Luke's got orders for us."

"Hi, Lando," Ben said. "Dad, me, Taalon, and Vestara and her dad are all going to stay behind and do some investigating. See if we can learn anything more about Abeloth. Part of the agreement is that Dad needs both you and Jaina to head home."

Jaina's jaw dropped. "He wants us to go? After we came all the way out here to help him, Luke wants us to go and leave him alone down there with the girl's dad and the High Lord?"

"That's what he said," came Ben's voice. Jaina stared at Lando, looking for a little help, but all Lando did was shrug.

"Don't look at me," he said. "I just came out here to tow debris."

"Jaina, you need to get *home*. So does Lando."

There was something in the way he said it that gave Jaina pause. She nodded to Lando to mute the communication. "Of course," she said. "Luke needs us to get out there with the news about Abeloth and the Lost Tribe. We've got a lot more information on them now, information the Jedi can use. Maybe we even have enough to take it to Daala." This last, though, she said with more doubt in her voice.

"Maybe," Lando said doubtfully. "I'll settle for letting the Jedi know that Luke's alive and Abeloth isn't." He thumbed a button on the intercom.

"You're right, Ben," Jaina said. "I do need to get home, and so does Lando. Tendra and Chance will be worried about him. I assume the Sith will depart, too?"

"All of them, except for the three staying behind," Ben assured her.

"Okay then. Take care of yourself, and your dad, too, all right?"

"Will do. Bye, Jaina."

"So," Lando said. "What are we really going to do?"

"I don't trust those Sith any farther than I can throw them."

"You're a Jedi, Jaina, you can throw them pretty far."

"You know what I mean."

"I do, and I agree. But your StealthX isn't good for much at the moment, and this ancient thing was never built for attacking. You might be better served by actually doing what Luke says."

She eyed him.

"For a change," he couldn't resist adding.

"Oh, shut up. Let's get back to Coruscant before I change my mind."

# Chapter Thirty-five

CHIEF OF STATE NATASI DAALA STOOD IN HER PRIVATE apartments, staring out the huge transparisteel window onto the nightscape of Coruscant as she sipped a cocktail. It was never dark or silent. Always, there were bright spots of color, the motion of vessels frenetically going about their business at any hour of the day or night. Other buildings towered around her own, many of their lights on. Some of them were apartments, like hers. Others were businesses. She knew down to a window who lived or rented what. She was one of the most powerful beings in the galaxy, and Wynn Dorvan had insisted that she know exactly who all of her "neighbors" were.

It was beautiful and comforting in its own way. The crowded city had a life, an edge to it, that Daala found energizing. She took another sip, the ice in her glass clinking. The décor in her own home, in contrast to the organized chaos that zipped past outside, was simple, almost stark. The main room had high ceilings and unfussy but comfortable furniture. There was art—small statues, a fountain in the corner, and framed, precise abstract paintings by Ku Chusar, one of the most famous artists of his time. Quiet instrumental music played unobtrusively in the background. All was orderly, with clean lines, a union of form and function. It was her personal refuge.

Her outfit, too, was orderly with clean lines. She wore a shimmersilk tunic and pants, with simple slippers. She was well aware that the green brought out her stunning eyes and red hair, but she was also able to move and relax in the outfit even as it flattered her. It did double duty, and was therefore efficient. Daala liked efficiency as much as she liked order.

When the door buzzed, she opted to greet her guest herself. Her chef's work was done and keeping warm. She had sent him home and had deactivated her droids for the night. Droids were useful things, and had prepared the apartment well, but she wanted to have true privacy for the conversation that was to ensue—for various reasons.

So she opened the door, smiling, to a slightly surprised Admiral Nek Bwua'tu.

"Answering the door yourself, Natasi?" he said, his voice warm with amused affection. "Next thing you'll tell me is you've cooked the dinner."

She laughed at that, waving him in and embracing him as he entered. "Never, Nek. I didn't claw my way up the ranks to prepare my own meals."

"I find it restful on occasion," Bwua'tu said. "But I imagine you didn't invite me here for my crowd-pleasing recipe for nerf steaks with gravy and mashed taku roots."

Daala smiled a little and moved to the bar. "I'm afraid not. Another time perhaps."

Nek sighed. "When we're both retired," he said. She shot him a smile over her shoulder.

"Maybe then," she agreed. She indicated the array of bottles. "The usual?"

The Bothan smiled. "Please," he said. Daala busied herself with the drink, then walked it over to him. Bwua'tu lifted the glass and clinked it lightly against hers. "To absent friends," he said, his voice far gentler than most had ever heard it.

She ought to have expected the toast, and yet her smile faltered. "To absent friends," Daala said, her voice not revealing the sudden quick pain. They drank, then she indicated the couch. He sat down, holding his glass, regarding her thoughtfully.

"Your uncle is causing me no end of trouble," Daala said. She sank down onto the sofa beside him, a nexu comfortable and at ease in her own den, her body language open.

Bwua'tu laughed. "Uncle Eramuth," he said. "I imagine he is. He's very good at what he does, you know. When he's able to do it."

"Hm," she agreed dryly, then inquired, "what do you mean, able to do it?"

"Uncle Eramuth is quite elderly by Bothan standards," Bwau'tu said. "And he's always been a bit eccentric. You've seen how he dresses."

Daala nodded. "I have," she said. "I always thought that was part of his strategy—to charm the jury with his slightly out-of-date, slightly odd mannerisms."

"Oh, I would never say that it wasn't calculated," Nek agreed. "But the lines between calculatedly offbeat and not exactly sane can blur from time to time."

"Really? I will keep that in mind, thank you."

"Don't dismiss him, either," Nek said. "I know that it sounds like a contradiction, but as I said—he is very, very good at what he does. Your open and shut case is likely not quite as open and shut as you think."

Daala sighed. She had been leaning toward him in an affectionate manner, but sorrow seemed to settle upon her fine features and she turned away slightly. Facing toward the window, the bright, multicolored lights dancing on her skin, she said quietly, "You spoke of absent friends, Nek. Gil was one of them. So was Cha Niathal. I know too many, now."

Understanding shone in his dark eyes. "Ah . . . I see. Well, we all do, Natasi. That's the price of growing old, I suppose."

"Speak for yourself," she said with forced lightness.

"I do. You, my dear, will never grow old. Ambition keeps you young." He lifted his glass in mock salute.

She smiled halfheartedly. "I'm not sure about that. The last few weeks have aged me quite a bit, I'm afraid."

"The situation with the Jedi, and the Mandos," Nek said knowingly.

She turned to him, an old friend and more than an old friend who, thank any deities there might and might not be, was not yet absent. Not yet.

"I feel no qualms about any decisions I've made in that area so far. I was right in how I handled Skywalker. And the mad Jedi. Still feel comfortable with what's going on there. But . . . these uprisings."

Her eyes were intense as she spoke. "These are fires, Nek. They're little fires right now, barely more than wisps of smoke on worlds that most people haven't even heard of, and if they *have* heard of them, they wouldn't care—at least, that's how it's been. Even Klatooine is far enough away so that it doesn't affect most peoples' day-to-day lives in the Galactic Alliance. They shouldn't care about what's going on. But now—"

"Needmo's little Devaronian girl is bringing them right into the living rooms."

Daala nodded. "That she is, and handily, too. Javis Tyrr, I could at least manipulate to an extent. Control some of what he did, what he learned and when he learned it."

"He was playing you," Nek pointed out.

"He's not anymore," Daala said simply.

Nek had to laugh. "Quite true. How did you muzzle the barking dog at last?"

"The invaluable Wynn Dorvan. He contacted Tyrr's cam operator, who had been his accomplice. She had all kinds of video documentation on what he'd been up to, and apparently Wynn used both the carrot and the stick to get her to cooperate. If she cooperated, her name would be unsullied. If she didn't, she'd be sharing the same cell as Tyrr."

"Elegant, simple, and effective. Perhaps I should borrow Dorvan from time to time."

"Only on his days off." She sighed. "So yes, I'm pleased Tyrr's no longer being a pest. But this Madhi Vaandt . . . she's out of my reach. And the story's too big. I can't silence the coverage."

His ears swiveled forward, catching the subtle nuance in how she said the word *coverage*. "What *can* you silence, then?"

She looked at him levelly. "The uprisings themselves. I can stop them. Frankly, I should have done this at the outset. Then Vaandt wouldn't have had anything *to* cover because it would have been all taken care of—quietly, behind the scenes, and beings could get on with their daily lives. Dorvan has been marvelous about sniffing out possible sites where there could be trouble. I can put Mandos there before things erupt. Lock it down."

"Natasi," Bwua'tu said slowly, considering every word before he spoke it, "it's possible that some of those uprisings need to happen. I doubt there are beings out there fomenting rebellion simply to ruin your day—even if that does happen to be the end result."

Few beings could have spoken to Daala like that and not roused her ire. Dorvan was one, Nek was the other. The rest were no longer counted among the living.

"One of the recurring themes I keep hearing about is how long the institution of slavery has persisted on many of these worlds. Frankly, if it's existed on these worlds for this long, it can wait a little longer. Wait until I've brought the Jedi to heel, wait until there's a little more stability. I'm not a dictator, Nek, you know that. But I can't lose control over this situation. I can't even be *perceived* as losing control."

Bwua'tu downed his drink and rose to prepare another. "Do you need a refill?" he asked as he went to the bar.

"I'm good, thanks," she said, "and you're delaying."

He chuckled as he poured. "Rather, I'm considering the best response." He turned to face her, swirling the liquid in his glass slightly. "I agree that you need a victory of sorts," he said. "But I'm not sure that stamping out legitimate forms of protest against a planet's government is the right way to be seen as keeping control over a situation. Especially not using the Mandos."

"They're not the GA," she said.

"Nor are they much liked, and your continued usage of them is not getting you what you are telling me you want. The current stalemate with the Jedi is a perfect example of that."

Daala sighed and rubbed at her eyes. "You sound like Dorvan."

"No, I'd need to be more monotone to sound like Dorvan."

That got a genuine chuckle out of her. Nek smiled and sat back down beside her, draping an arm supportively over her shoulders. She leaned into him. They were quiet for a long moment, and when Daala spoke, her voice was barely audible.

"I can't stop thinking about Cha Niathal."

"She made the decision to take her own life. That's not your respon—"

She waved impatiently and he fell silent. "No, I don't feel guilt over that. But what she said—she believed she had not made a mistake with Jacen, that it was not possible to anticipate what he would become, what he would do. And her suicide note—*This has been done with honor, without error, and by my choosing.*"

Daala looked up at him. "I've long since lost any fear of death. I don't think you can be career military and be afraid of dying. But I've been entrusted with the care and well-being of the Galactic Alliance. Every decision I make determines not only my own legacy, but the fate of billions of beings. I have to act like Niathal—with honor, without error, and by my own choosing. If I'm not firm *now,* if I don't crack down *now,* chaos will erupt, and everything we all want is going to be swept away by the onrushing tides."

His eyes were kind in the soft light as he regarded her. "We all do what we must," he said gently.

*We all do what we must.*

Admiral Nek Bwua'tu wasn't used to irony when it came to his own words, but now, at three-fourteen in the morning as he quietly let himself out of Daala's apartments, he found himself haunted by it.

He nodded to the security droid at the entrance to her gleaming apartment building. Normally, he would stay the night, and depart early in the morning in the same small speeder in which he had arrived. The droids were programmed to be discreet, and the living beings who sometimes operated security were paid to be so. But tonight—tonight he wanted to go back to his offices.

He needed to talk to Kenth Hamner.

The area was home to many of Coruscant's wealthy and powerful, and the neighborhood was quiet at this time of night. He transferred a discreet, handheld blaster from the inside of the well-tailored coat he wore to his right-hand pocket. Bwua'tu had not risen to the heights he presently enjoyed without preparing for all eventualities. He stepped forward into the night, eyes and nose alert, but overall relaxed.

His path was along one of the pleasant pedestrian walkways that helped keep those who could afford to live this high above the city streets from having to mingle with those who couldn't. Colored lights from the various vessels zooming along above him lit his path with rainbow hues. There were very few beings out at this hour, but that would change in a short while.

Daala was doing the wrong things for the right reasons. He cared for her, deeply, but he had sworn an oath of krevi, and his first and last allegiance was to the Galactic Alliance. And Daala, like a well-intentioned but misguided parent, was alienating her charge, and further, harming it with punishments that were intended to do the opposite.

He had come to her for several reasons tonight. First, because he enjoyed her company, always. Second, because he wanted to be a supportive listener. And third, because he had hoped to sound her out on the issue of the Jedi.

He hadn't even been able to get that far. He had known she would not listen to other viewpoints once she started voicing her opinions about Madhi Vaandt and the uprisings and the need to put them down before they got out of hand. She saw only the disorder and chaos that such things would cause; she could not, or would not, see what a policy such as the one she was advocating would do.

He kept up the brisk pace, thinking hard, and moved into an area on the walkway that was covered by transparisteel. There were a few such areas, where pedestrians could take refuge in case of inclement weather. The wind shifted, and he caught a faint whiff of the scent of human. He swiveled his ears behind him, his fur rippling with unease. The scent grew stronger.

Bwua'tu came to a halt, his hand gripping the hilt of the small blaster concealed in the pocket of his coat. He turned around slowly.

And saw no one.

Too late, he glanced upward. One was already dropping silently down. He heard at least one other scrambling up from where he had waited, concealed, beneath the walkway. Thugs, robbers, predators, lurking in hopes of preying upon the weak.

But Bwua'tu was a predator himself, in the prime of his years, with an extensive knowledge of hand-to-hand combat and a blaster in his pocket. He dove out of the way, not quite in time to avoid his legs being struck, but swiftly enough to land and leap back to his feet.

Yes, there were two of them. One of them wore street clothes. The other wore long brown-and-tan robes and—

There was a *snap-hiss* and a green lightsaber sprang to life. Bwua'tu stared, stunned.

"What have you done with Admiral Bwua'tu?"

They'd snapped. Both of them. Two Jedi, convinced he was a doppelgänger of the "real" Bwua'tu. There was no time for talk, not against insane Jedi Knights. He drew his blaster and fired repeatedly, while simultaneously reaching for an emergency signal in his vest pocket and diving for the railing.

Much more agile than humans, a Bothan as fit as Bwua'tu was able to safely drop down to another walkway and maneuver himself onto it.

So, too, it would seem, could Jedi.

The Jedi with the lightsaber batted back the blaster bolts like it was a sport. The other one sprang after Nek as he dove off the side. Bwau'tu reached out and caught the railing of the second walkway with one powerful hand, firing wildly with the other. His sharp ears heard a cry of pain and a thump above him as, grunting with the effort, he hauled himself up onto the walkway with one hand, then threw his other arm, still clutching the blaster, over the railing, hooking his elbow firmly. He heaved and tumbled over the rail to safety.

He heard noises behind him—the thump of landing feet and the whizzing, unique sound of a lightsaber. Guided by pure instinct, Bwua'tu sprang and rolled to the right. He could feel the heat and hear the sizzle of the durasteel as it melted, and kicked up hard.

The Jedi sprang away, snarling, but Bwa'tu's booted foot caught him behind the knee and he dropped, the knee buckling. The Bothan admiral lifted the hand with his blaster.

An instant later he found himself staring at what was left of his arm: a cauterized stump.

The Jedi brought the blade around for another blow. Bwua'tu twisted violently, striking out with his remaining arm to deflect the strike.

That he was able to do so shocked him. The still-lit lightsaber skittered along the walkway floor, the Jedi diving after it. Bwua'tu was on him in a second, getting him in a chokehold with his remaining good arm and sinking his teeth into the human's shoulder.

The man cried out, grasped the lightsaber, and struck back at Bwua'tu over his own shoulders as if he were performing some dark act of self-flagellation. White-hot pain sizzled along Buwa'tu's back and he roared in agony. He released the human's throat, going for the lightsaber arm instead, pinning it down and slamming it against the hard durasteel.

The man let go, but Nek had no time to savor the victory. A fierce punch landed against the side of his head and the world went white for a moment. He was dimly aware of his assailant scrambling out from under him, and the glow of the lightsaber.

Time stretched out like a thin, perfect line of ultimate

clarity to Buwa'tu. And in that moment, he knew two things with utter certainty. He had stared Death in the face before now, and knew that if he did not act quickly and correctly, Death would win this fight.

He also knew that the men who had attacked him were not Jedi. He should never have been able to hold his own for three minutes against them if they had been.

Which begged the question, *Who were they and who sent them?* But there was no time for that now.

Bwua'tu reached out with his good hand, grasped his own severed arm, wrapped his living index finger around the dead one, turned, and fired the blaster point blank into the fake Jedi's face.

Nek had only an instant's satisfaction of staring up into a face of blackened bone and melted flesh before the corpse fell atop him. The excruciating pain of the lightsaber, still lit in the deathgrip of the human, seared across his belly. Nek Bwua'tu spasmed, trying to thrust off the corpse, and knew no more.

# Chapter Thirty-six

"MAY IT PLEASE THE COURT, I HAVE NEW EVIDENCE TO introduce."

Tahiri stiffened. Beside her, Eramuth's ear twitched. "At this late hour?" he murmured, then rose. "Your Honor, the defense demands to know the nature and the source of this so-called new evidence."

"Approach the bench," Judge Zudan said, waving them both forward. The two obeyed, and three heads bent together. There were sharp, sibilant whispers for several moments.

Eramuth's ear twitched like mad. Tahiri felt her heart sink.

He returned, sat down beside her, and whispered in her ear, "It's a recording that was allegedly made of your, er . . . conversation with Gilad Pellaeon."

"What?" She yelped, she couldn't help it, and he placed a furred hand on her shoulder gently to quiet her.

"It's passed all tests, it appears to be genuine. I'll try to stop them from playing it right now but, if I cannot, I will have my *own* experts examine it. And trust me, I have quite expert experts."

He smiled, trying to bolster her. It was useless. She knew what she had said, what she had done, and her attorney's intense efforts to play on the jury's sympathy were about to be blasted to bits, and nothing that anyone could do or say would change their minds once this was heard.

Dekkon swept forward, his robes fluttering behind him, his voice almost, but not quite, as melodious as Eramuth's.

"Gentlebeings of the jury," he began. "I realize that it is late in the process, but what you are about to hear is information that is absolutely vital to your decision regarding Tahiri Veila's guilt or innocence. I am unable to reveal my sources, but I can assure you that before I decided to bring this evidence to light, I had it verified. What you are about to hear is the genuine article."

He paused, looked about with an imperious mien. "You are about to hear a murder, gentlebeings. The murder of a ninety-two-year-old, unarmed man at the hands of this woman!"

He pointed to Tahiri, extending a long blue finger accusatorily. She kept her face neutral somehow.

"The defense would like you to think that Tahiri was a poor, muddled, misguided, lovesick girl lured to the dark side—only temporarily, mind you—by an extremely powerful Sith Lord. My esteemed colleague would have you believe that she was merely following orders, that she is as much a victim as Admiral Gilad Pellaeon himself. What you are about to hear, gentlebeings, is the truth of the matter."

"Objection!" Eramuth was on his feet. "Your Honor, I request a twenty-four-hour delay to verify the accuracy of this so called 'true' recording before it is played before the jury."

"Objection overruled."

"But Your Honor! If it does transpire that the recording has been falsified or tampered with in any way, the jury will have already been swayed by it! It is hard to forget something once it has been heard, even if later one knows it is false."

Dekkon glared at him. "I hardly think the jury is so shallow as to believe something that is later proven to be a fake, Counselor Bwua'tu," Judge Zudan said. "If the evidence proves false, the jury will not consider it in their deliberation. And sit down before I hold you in contempt of court."

Eramuth stayed standing for a moment longer, then took his seat. "I have the utmost faith in the decency of juries," he said. "Rest assured, I will have this recording thoroughly analyzed."

Tahiri had a feeling that it would just be a waste of time and credits. She remembered that day with painful clarity, and she suspected that, somehow, someone had caught every word of those awful moments.

The recording began in a banal manner, as fateful things so often do, with the simple sound of a hatch opening and closing again, and a slight rustling, as if someone had removed the recording device from an article of clothing.

And then again, the hatch opening.

A female voice. Tahiri's.

"Sorry sir, but I had to speak to you."

Several heads turned to look at her. She fought to keep her face neutral. But she recognized her own voice. This was no fake.

"There's always knocking."

The dead were speaking. The voice was recognizable to almost everyone in the room. It had belonged to Admiral Gilad Pallaeon.

Every part of Tahiri's body suddenly sang with the surge of adrenaline. She was catapulted back in time to that moment, perhaps the single most pivotal of her life. All the sights and sounds and smells rushed back to her, all the certainty that she had to do what she was about to do. And juxtaposed along that vivid, almost cellular recollection, was the here and now. A courtroom. A judge who, if not exactly in Daala's pocket, was most assuredly on her side politically. Sul Dekkon, doing his best to conceal a smirk. And Eramuth, poor, dandy Eramuth, who had pulled out all the stops for her and had come *this* close to winning what would likely be his final case.

"Sir, there are lives on the line. If you let the GA tear itself apart, everyone loses." Her own voice again, cool, blunt, determined. Flat, Tahiri thought wildly. Lifeless in a way that Pallaeon's voice most assuredly was not, although he had been ninety-two at the time of his death—

—murder—

—and would within a handful of moments never speak again. Had Jacen really sucked that much out of her? She barely recognized herself.

"I'm not letting it do anything, Lieutenant. I'm giving practical support to an ally."

"If Colonel Solo is deposed, the GA will revert to its indecisive self and there'll be chaos."

Laughable, almost, to hear those words and look around at where she was now. There was nothing indecisive about the GA in the wake of Jacen Solo's death. Whatever else Daala had done, whatever threat she was to the Jedi, Luke Skywalker, or Tahiri herself, she'd brought calmness and order back. Chaos. The only chaos roiling right now was in Tahiri's heart and likely in the head of Eramuth Bwua'tu.

He was accomplished enough that he was able to keep a neutral expression, but his left ear twitched. Twice. Tahiri's heart sank. What would come next would doom her, and she did not think even the galaxy's most brilliant defense attorney would be able to save her once the jury had heard this with their own ears.

"I'm afraid I can't agree with you, my dear, but then I don't have to." The voice of the dead, speaking calmly and confidently. "Loyalty is a fine thing, don't think I don't respect that—but Jacen Solo's the chaos, not the cure." She hadn't realized it at the time, but Tahiri could now hear the amusement in his voice. She wondered how she had looked to him—probably painfully young and gullible and so completely and utterly in the wrong. "Is there anything else?"

"The Moffs will break it off if you tell them to. I witnessed the influence you wield. Moff Quille was ready to defy you, but you just put him back in his place. I can feel things in beings that even you can't see."

Quille. He had been in Jacen's pocket, just like she had been, and shortly after the events of the recording had assumed command of the *Bloodfin*. He'd never made it off that ship alive. He had been killed by the Mandos pouring onto the vessel, dying as violent a death as the man he betrayed had done.

"I've no reason to refuse Admiral Niathal's request. Subject closed."

Cha Niathal, dead, too, now. The ghosts were lively in this snippet of the past. The recorded Tahiri sighed softly, then there came another rustling sound.

"Please, Admiral, just do it." A click. The safety catch was now off. There were enough beings in the room who were familiar with blasters that a slight gasp rippled through the room as the sound was recognized. "Call off your fleet and give Jacen Solo a chance. He needs to win at Fondor."

"Win . . ."

"Destroy its capacity to threaten the GA again. It's a practical matter but it also shows the rest of the galaxy how high the stakes are for them."

Tahiri resisted the urge to bury her face in her hands. She'd forgotten just how it all sounded. At the time, it had made sense, but now—

The jury members were turning to look at her, not

bothering to hide their stares. Some of them had disgust and contempt on their faces. Others were confused. Still others looked betrayed, as if this was a personal attack. And Tahiri supposed it was. Eramuth had led the jury on a journey to get to know Tahiri. To sympathize with her, to see how step by step she had been ruthlessly broken and then just as brutally remade. But that flat voice spouting such things—

"No. I won't ignore a surrender, and I won't enable the bombardment of civilian centers afterward, and I will not lend the Empire to a petty despot."

How would it be possible for any jury to hear those words, and not feel sympathy and admiration for the one who uttered them? How would it be possible for them to then decide that the one who killed that man was not guilty of murder or treason?

"You know you're going to die."

Angry murmurs, now, and Tahiri closed her eyes. She did not want to see this anymore. Did not want to watch as a jury that had been growing increasingly sympathetic over the last several days lost that concern in a matter of minutes. Did not want to see Eramuth's ear twitching. Did not want to see the growing smirk of satisfaction on the prosecuting attorney's face.

She had not lied. Pellaeon was seconds away from his death—at her hands.

But she was going to die, too. She wondered if Pellaeon in some way understood and felt any satisfaction from beyond the grave. He and Natasi Daala, his old crony, would have the last laugh.

"I'm ninety-two years old. *Of course* I'm going to die, and quite soon, but it's *how* I die that matters to me. Please—get out of my cabin."

How he died. Tahiri suddenly and painfully thought of Anakin and how *he* had died. Making a difference. Sacrificing his bright, beautiful life for others. And she was going to die executed, for firing a blaster at a ninety-two-year-old unarmed man.

Jacen had lured her to the dark side with the temptation of love, of sweetness, of a last kiss. What bitter, brutal irony it was that that love, the love of a good and true young man, was the tool that man's own brother had used to turn Tahiri into someone capable of this.

Suddenly Tahiri was fiercely glad that Anakin Solo was dead—dead and where he could not see this.

She hoped.

She wished with all her being that she had just "gotten out of his cabin."

The recording continued mercilessly.

"Last chance. All you have to do is call a halt. The Moffs obey you."

There was a long, heavy silence. Then Pellaeon's voice.

"Pellaeon to Fleet. Fleet, this is Admiral Pellaeon. I *order* you to place your vessels at the complete disposal of Admiral Niathal, and take down Jacen Solo, for the honor of the Empire—"

The sound, the inevitable sound, of a blaster being fired, the slam of a body hitting the bulkhead. This time, the gasp was not a ripple throughout the courtroom. It was loud, sincere, accompanied by hands clapped to mouths and angry, wide stares. Then the sounds of shock were hushed, as all present strained to listen to the last words of a good man.

"So that's Jacen's new Sith Order." The strong voice had been replaced by a whisper, ragged, each word brought with pain. "Wiping out civilians . . . from a safe distance, and getting . . . a child to . . . kill an old man . . . just make sure . . . you can dismount from that . . . bloodfin of yours."

"I can save you, Admiral. It's not too late. The heart's a resilient muscle."

Tahiri couldn't help it. Now she did lean her face into her hands, but closing her eyes did nothing but replace the current scene of the courtroom with the image of a dying old man.

"Go . . . rot somewhere else . . . villip."

The sound of boots, as if someone were shifting uneasily.

"Is he gone?" asked one of the Moffs.

"Not yet." Quille, treacherous Quille, she had never liked him and he had gotten what he deserved. But then, many would argue, Tahiri Veila would soon get what she deserved as well. "I'm not going to touch him, so we're totally clean . . ."

A whisper from Pellaeon. "Quille."

And then Tahiri realized with a start that the admiral had known he was being recorded. Who was on the other end? Who had leaked this to the prosecution? She glanced up quickly and saw that, while Eramuth was leaning heavily on his cane, his face, too, was alert. If they could figure out where this came from, who might have an agenda—

But Eramuth would be hoping that at least part of the recording was falsified, and Tahiri knew sickly that the recording had not been tampered with.

There came the sound of the door closing, and then silence.

Dekkon strode over and pressed a button.

It was over.

It was all over.

Read on for an excerpt from
*Star Wars®: Fate of the Jedi: Vortex*
by Troy Denning
Published by Del Rey Books

BEYOND THE FORWARD VIEWPORT HUNG THE GOSSAMER veil of Ashteri's Cloud, a vast drift of ionized tuderium gas floating along one edge of the Kessel sector. Speckled with the blue halos of a thousand distant stars, its milky filaments were a sure sign that the *Rockhound* had finally escaped the sunless gloom of the Deep Maw. And after the jaw-clenching horror of jumping blind through a labyrinth of uncharted hyperspace lanes and hungry black holes, even that pale light was a welcome relief to Jaina Solo.

Or rather, it *would* have been, had the cloud been in the right place.

The *Rockhound* was bound for Coruscant, not Kessel, and *that* meant Ashteri's Cloud should have been forty degrees to port as they exited the Maw. It *should* have been a barely discernible smudge of light, shifted so far into the red that it looked like no more than a tiny flicker of flame, and Jaina could not quite grasp how they had gone astray.

She glanced over at the pilot's station—a mobile levchair surrounded by brass control panels and drop-down display screens—but found no answers in Lando Calrissian's furrowed brow. Dressed immaculately in a white shimmersilk tunic, lavender trousers, and a hip cape, he was perched on the edge of his huge nerf-leather seat, with his chin propped on his knuckles and his gaze fixed on the alabaster radiance outside.

In the three decades Jaina had known Lando, it was one of the rare moments when his life of long-odds gambles and all-or-nothing stakes actually seemed to have taken a toll on his con-artist good looks. It was also a testament to the strain and fear of the past few days—and, perhaps, to the hectic pace. Lando was as impeccably groomed as always, but even he had not found time to touch up the dye that kept his mustache and curly hair their usual deep, rich black.

After a few moments, he finally sighed and leaned back into his chair. "Go ahead, say it."

"Say what?" Jaina asked, wondering exactly what Lando expected her to say. After all, *he* was the one who had made the bad jump. "It's not my fault?"

A glimmer of irritation shot through Lando's weary eyes, but then he seemed to realize Jaina was only trying to lighten the mood. He chuckled and flashed her one of his nova-bright grins. "You're as bad as your old man. Can't you see this is no time to joke?"

Jaina cocked a brow. "So you *didn't* decide to swing past Kessel to say hello to the wife and son?"

"Good idea," Lando said, shaking his head. "But . . . *no*."

"Well, then . . ." Jaina activated the auxiliary pilot's station and waited as the long-range sensors spooled up. An old asteroid tug designed to be controlled by a single operator and a huge robotic crew, the *Rockhound* had no true co-pilot's station, and *that* meant the wait was going to be longer than Jaina would have liked. "What are we doing here?"

Lando's expression grew serious. "Good question." He turned toward the back of the *Rockhound*'s spacious flight deck, where the vessel's ancient bridge droid stood in front of an equally ancient nav computer. A Cybot

Galactica model RN8, the droid had a transparent head-globe, currently filled with the floating twinkles of a central processing unit running at high speed. Also inside the globe were three sapphire-blue photoreceptors, spaced at even intervals to give her full-perimeter vision. Her bronze body casing was etched with constellations, comets, and other celestial artwork. "I *know* I told Ornate to set a course for Coruscant."

RN8's head-globe spun just enough to fix one of her photoreceptors on Lando's face. "Yes, you did." Her voice was silky, deep, and chiding. "And then you countermanded that order with one directing us to our current destination."

Lando scowled. "You need to do a better job of maintaining your auditory systems," he said. "You're hearing things."

The twinkles inside RN8's head-globe dimmed as she redirected power to her diagnostic systems. Jaina turned her own attention back to the auxiliary display and saw that the long-range sensors had finally come online. Unfortunately, they were no help. The only thing that had changed inside its bronze frame was the color of the screen and a single symbol denoting the *Rockhound*'s own location in the exact center.

RN8's silky voice sounded from the back of the flight deck. "My auditory sensors are in optimum condition, Captain—as are my data storage and retrieval systems." Her words began to roll across the deck in a *very* familiar male baritone. "Redi*rect* to *desti*na*tion* Ashteri's Cloud, arri*val* time seven*teen* hours fif*teen*, Gala*c*tic Stan*dard*."

Lando's jaw dropped, and he sputtered, "Tha . . . that's not *me*!"

"Not quite," Jaina agreed. The emphasis was placed on the wrong syllable in several words; otherwise, the voice was identical. "But it's close enough to fool a droid."

Lando's eyes clouded with confusion. "Are you telling me what I *think* you're telling me?"

"Yes," Jaina said, glancing at her blank sensor display. "I don't quite know how, but someone impersonated you."

"Through the Force?"

Jaina shrugged and shot a meaningful glance toward a dark corner. While she knew of half a dozen Force powers that could have been used to defeat RN8's voice-recognition software, not one of those techniques had a range measured in light-years. She carefully began to expand her Force awareness, concentrating on the remote corners of the huge ship, and thirty standard seconds later was astonished to find nothing unusual. There were no lurking beings, no blank zones that might suggest an artificial void in the Force, not even any small vermin that might be a Force-wielder disguising his presence.

After a moment, she turned back to Lando. "They *must* be using the Force. There's no one aboard but us and the droids."

"I was afraid you'd say that." Lando paused for a moment, then asked, "Luke's friends?"

"I hate to jump to conclusions, but . . . who else?" Jaina replied. "First, Lost Tribe or not, they're *Sith*. Second, they already tried to double-cross us once."

"Which makes them as crazy as a rancor on the dancing deck," Lando said. "Abeloth was locked in a *black-hole prison* for twenty-five thousand years. What kind of maniacs would think it was a good idea to bust her out?"

"They're *Sith*," Jaina reminded him. "All that matters to them is power, and Abeloth had power like a nova has light—until Luke killed her."

Lando frowned in thought. "And if they're crazy enough to think they could take Abeloth home with them, they're probably crazy enough to think they could take the guy who killed her."

"Exactly," Jaina said. "Until a few weeks ago, no one even knew the Lost Tribe *existed*. That's changed, but they'll still want to keep what they can secret."

"So they'll try to take out Luke and Ben," Lando agreed. "And us, too. Contain the leak."

"That's my guess," Jaina said. "The Sith like secrecy, and secrecy means stopping us *now*. Once we're out of the Maw, they'll expect us to access the HoloNet and report."

Lando looked up and exhaled in frustration. "I told Luke he couldn't trust anyone who puts *High Lord* before his name." He had been even more forceful than Jaina in trying to argue Luke out of a second bargain with the Lost Tribe—a bargain that had left the Skywalkers and three Sith behind to explore Abeloth's savage homeworld together. "Maybe we should go back."

Jaina thought for only an instant, then shook her head. "No, Luke knew the bargain wouldn't last when he agreed to it," she said. "Sarasu Taalon has already betrayed his word once."

Lando scowled. "That doesn't mean Luke and Ben are safe."

"No," Jaina agreed. "But it *does* mean he's risking their lives to increase *our* chances of reporting to the Jedi Council. *That's* our mission."

"Technically, Luke doesn't get to *assign* missions right now," Lando pressed. "You wouldn't be violating orders if we—"

"Luke Skywalker is *still* the most powerful Jedi in the galaxy. I think we should assume he has a plan," Jaina said. A sudden tingle of danger sense raced down her spine, prompting her to hit the quick-release on her crash harness. "Besides, we need to start worrying about saving our *own* skins."

Lando began to look worried. "What are you saying?" he asked. "That you're sensing something?"

Jaina shook her head. "Not yet." She rose. "But I *will* be. Why do you suppose they sent us someplace easy to find?"

Lando scowled. "Oh . . ." He glanced up at a display, tapped some keys—no doubt trying to call up a tactical report—then slammed his fist against the edge of the brass console. "Are they *jamming* us?"

"That's difficult to know with the ship's sensor systems offline for degaussing," RN8 replied.

*"Offline?"* Lando shrieked. "Who authorized *that*?"

*"You* did, ninety-seven seconds ago," RN8 replied. "Would you like me to play it back?"

"No! Countermand it and bring all systems back up." Lando turned to Jaina and asked, "Any feel for how long we have until the shooting starts?"

Jaina closed her eyes and opened herself to the Force. She felt a mass of belligerent presences approaching from the direction of the Maw. She turned to RN8.

"How long until the sensor systems reboot?"

"Approximately three minutes and fifty-seven seconds," the droid reported. "I'm afraid Captain Calrissian also ordered a complete data consolidation."

Jaina winced and turned back to Lando. "In that case, I'd say we have less than three minutes and fifty-two seconds. There's someone hostile coming up behind us." She started toward the hatchway at the back of the cavernous bridge, her boots ringing on the old durasteel deck. "Why don't you see if you can put a stop to those false orders?"

"Sure, I'll just tell my crew to stop listening to me." Lando's voice was sarcastic. "Being droids, they'll know what I mean."

"You might try activating their standard verification routines," Jaina suggested.

"I *might,* if droid crews this old *had* standard verification routines." Lando turned and scowled at Jaina as she continued across the deck. "And you're going *where?*"

"You know where," Jaina said.

"To your StealthX?" Lando replied. "The one with only three engines? The one that lost its targeting array?"

"Yeah, that one," Jaina confirmed. "We need a set of eyes out there—and someone to fly cover."

"No way," Lando said. "If I let you go out to fight Sith in that thing, your dad will be feeding pieces of me to Amelia's nexu for the next ten years."

Jaina stopped and turned toward him, propping one hand on her hip. "Lando, did you just say *let?* Did you really say *no way* to me?"

Lando rolled his eyes, unintimidated. "You know I didn't mean it like that. But have you gone spacesick? With only three engines, that starfighter is going to be about as maneuverable as an escape pod!"

"Maybe, but it still beats sitting around like a blind bantha in this thing. Thanks for worrying, though." She shot Lando a sour smile. "It's so sweet when you old guys do that."

"*Old?*" Lando cried. After a moment, he seemed to recognize the mocking tone in Jaina's voice, and his chin dropped. "I deserved that, didn't I?"

"You *think?*" Jaina laughed to show there were no hard feelings, then added, "And you know what Tendra would do to *me* if I came back without Chance's father. So let's *both* be careful."

"Okay, deal." Lando waved her toward the hatchway. "Go. Blow things up. Have fun."

"Thanks." Jaina's tone grew more serious, and she added, "And I mean for *everything,* Lando. You didn't have to be here, and I'm grateful for the risks you're taking to help us. It means a lot to me—and to the whole Order."

Lando's Force aura grew cold, and he looked away in sudden discomfort. "Jaina, is there something you're not telling me?"

"About this situation?" Jaina asked, frowning at his strange reaction. "I don't think so. Why?"

Lando exhaled in relief. "Jaina, my dear, perhaps no one has mentioned this to you before . . ." His voice grew more solemn. "But when a Jedi starts talking about how much you mean to her, the future begins to look *very* scary."

"Oh . . . sorry." Jaina's cheeks warmed with embarrassment. "I didn't mean anything like *that*. Really. I was just trying to—"

"It's okay." Lando's voice was still a little shaky. "And if you *did* mean something—"

"I *didn't*," Jaina interrupted.

"I know," Lando said, raising a hand to stop her. "But if things start to go bad out there, just get back to Coruscant and report. I can take care of myself. Understand?"

"Sure, Lando, I understand." Jaina started toward the hatchway, silently adding, *But no way am I leaving you behind.*

"Good—and try to stick close. We won't be hanging around long." A low whir sounded from Lando's chair as he turned it to face RN8. "Ornate, prepare an emergency jump to our last coordinates."

"I'm afraid that's impossible, Captain Calrissian," the droid replied. "You gave standing orders to empty the nav computer's memory after each jump."

"*What?*" Lando's anger was edging toward panic now. "How many other orders—no, forget it. Just countermand my previous commands."

"*All* of them?"

"Yes!" Lando snapped. "No, wait . . ."

Jaina reached the hatchway and, not waiting to hear the rest of Lando's order, raced down the rivet-studded corridor beyond. She still had no idea what the Sith were planning, but she *was* going to stop them—and not only because the Jedi Council needed to know everything she and Lando could tell them about the Lost Tribe of the Sith. Over the years, Lando had been as loyal a friend to the Jedi Order as he had to her parents, time after time risking his life, fortune, and freedom to help them resolve whatever crisis happened to be threatening the peace of the galaxy at the moment. He always claimed he was just repaying a favor, or protecting an investment, or maintaining a good business environment, but Jaina knew better. He was looking out for his friends, doing everything he could to help them survive—no matter what mess they had gotten themselves into.

Jaina reached the forward hangar bay. As the hatch opened in front of her, she was surprised to find a bank of floodlights already illuminating her battered StealthX. At first, she assumed Lando had ordered the hangar droid to ready the *Rockhound*'s fighter complement for launch.

Then she saw what was missing from her starfighter.

There were no weapons barrels extending from the wingtips. In fact—on the side facing her, at least—the cannons themselves were gone. She was so shocked that she found herself waiting for the rest of the hangar lights to activate, having forgotten for the moment that the *Rockhound* did not have automatic illumination. The whir of a pneumatic wrench sounded from the far side of the StealthX, and beneath the starfighter's belly she noticed a cluster of telescoping droid legs straddling the actuator housing of a Taim & Bak KX12 laser cannon.

"What the . . . ?"

Jaina snapped the lightsaber off her belt, then crossed twenty meters of tarnished deck in three quick Force bounds and sprang onto the fuselage of her StealthX. She could hardly believe what she saw. At the far end of the wing stood a spider-shaped BY2B maintenance droid, her thick cargo pedipalps clamped around the starfighter's last laser cannon while her delicate tool arms released the mounting clips.

"ByTwoBee!" Jaina yelled. "What are you doing?"

The pneumatic wrench whined to a stop, and three of the droid's photoreceptors swiveled toward Jaina's face.

"I'm sorry, Jedi Solo. I thought you would know." Like all droids aboard the *Rockhound*, BY2B's voice was female and sultry. "I'm removing this laser cannon."

"I can see that," Jaina replied. "Why?"

"So I can take it to the maintenance shop," BY2B replied. "Captain Calrissian requested it. Since your starfighter is unflyable anyway, he thought it would be a good time to rebuild the weapons systems."

Jaina's heart sank, but she wasted no time trying to convince BY2B she had been fooled. "When Lando issued this order, did you actually *see* him?"

"Oh, I rarely *see* the captain. I'm not one of his favorites." BY2B swung her photoreceptors toward the hangar entrance, and a trio of red beams shot out to illuminate a grimy speaker hanging next to the hatchway. "The order came over the intercom."

"Of course it did." Jaina pointed her lightsaber at the nearly dismounted laser cannon. "Any chance you can reattach that and get it working in the next minute and a half?"

"No chance at all, Jedi Solo. Reattaching the power feeds alone would take ten times that long."

"How'd I know you were going to say that?" Jaina

growled. She turned away and hopped down onto the deck. "All right—finish removing it and prep the craft for launch."

"I'm sorry, that's impossible," BY2B replied. "Even if we had the necessary parts, I'm not qualified to make repairs. The specifications for this craft weren't included in my last service update."

"I flew it *in* here, didn't I?" Jaina retorted. "Just tell me you haven't been mucking around with the torpedo launchers, too."

"This craft has *torpedo launchers*?" BY2B asked. "I didn't see any."

Jaina rolled her eyes, wondering exactly when the droid's last service update had been, then rushed over to a small locker area at the edge of the hangar. She activated the lighting, flipped the toggle switch on the ancient intercom unit in the wall, and stepped into the StealthX flight suit she had left hanging at launch-ready.

A moment later Lando's voice crackled out of the tiny speaker. "Yes, *Jain*a? What can *I* do for *you*?"

Jaina frowned. The voice certainly *sounded* like Lando's. "How about a status report?" she asked, pushing her arms through the suit sleeves. "My StealthX is really messed up. No use taking it out."

"*My* that is *too* bad," Lando's voice said. "But don't be *con*cerned. Ar-en-eight has *near*ly sorted out the sys*tem* problems."

"Great." Jaina sealed the flight suit's front closure and stepped into her boots. "I'll head aft and check out the hyperdrive."

"Oh." Lando's voice seemed surprised. "That won't be *ne*cessary. Ar-en-eight is running diag*nos*tics now. I'm sure the Em-Nine-O and his crew can *han*dle any *neces*sary re*pairs*."

And *his* crew. If there had been any doubt before, now Jaina *knew* she was talking to an imposter. Not long

ago, Lando had confided to Jaina that the only way he
had survived all those solitary prospecting trips early in
his career was to close his eyes whenever one of the
*Rockhound* droids spoke and imagine she was a beautiful woman. He would never have referred to M-9EO as
a male.

Jaina grabbed her helmet and gloves out of the locker,
then said, "Okay. If you've got everything under control, I'm going to stop by my bunk and grab some shut-
eye before my shift comes up."

"Yes, why don't *you* do that?" The voice sounded
almost relieved. "I'll *wake* you if anything comes *up*."

"Sounds good. See you in four standard hours."

Jaina flicked off the intercom switch, then started
back toward her StealthX, securing her helmet and
glove seals as she walked. Gullible, no Force presence,
and a terrible liar—the Voice definitely belonged to a
stowaway droid, probably one sent by the Sith. That
made enough sense that Jaina felt vaguely guilty for not
anticipating the tactic in time to prevent the sabotage.
The only thing she *didn't* understand was why the Sith
hadn't just rigged the fusion core to blow. A *living* stowaway, they might have valued enough to work out an escape plan—but a *droid*? She could not imagine that any
Sith deserving of the name would give a second thought
to sacrificing a droid.

Jaina reached her StealthX and found BY2B standing
behind the far wing, holding the last laser cannon in her
heavy cargo arms. Jaina made a quick visual inspection
of the bedraggled starfighter, then asked, "Is she ready
to fly?"

"*Ready* would be an overstatement," BY2B answered. "But the craft is capable of launching. I *do* hope
you checked your flight suit for vacuum hardiness."

"No need—it's not *me* that will be going EV." Jaina
ascended the short access ladder and climbed into the

cockpit. As she buckled herself in, she asked, "ByTwo-Bee, have you seen any new droids around here lately?"

"No," the droid said. "Not since departing Klatooine."

*"Klatooine?"* Jaina's stomach began to grow cold and heavy. "Then you *did* see a new droid before we left for the Maw?"

"Indeed, I did," BY2B replied. "A Rebaxan MSE-Six."

"A *mouse* droid?" Jaina gasped. "And you didn't report it?"

"Of course not," BY2B said. "Captain Calrissian had warned me just a few minutes earlier to expect a courier shuttle carrying a new utility droid."

Jaina groaned and hit the preignition engine heaters, then asked, "And I suppose he told you this over your internal comlink?"

"Yes, as a matter of fact," BY2B replied. "How did you know?"

"Because that *wasn't* Lando you heard," Jaina said, speaking through clenched teeth. "It was a sabotage droid programmed with an impersonation protocol."

*"Sabotage?"* BY2B sounded skeptical. "Why would anyone bother? We don't even have an asteroid in tow."

"It's not an *asteroid* they're after." Jaina unfastened her flight suit just far enough to retrieve her comlink from her chest pocket, opened a secure channel to Lando, and demanded, "What was the last meal I ate before boarding the *Exquisite Death*?"

"You expect me to remember what you had for lunch thirteen years ago?" Lando replied, taking the verification query in stride. "But you didn't have time to finish it. I remember that much."

"Good enough," Jaina said, satisfied that she was talking to the man and not the mouse. The meal to which she was referring had taken place aboard Lando's yacht, the *Lady Luck,* shortly before he had tricked a Yuuzhan Vong boarding party into taking her and the rest of a Jedi strike team aboard their ship. "Did you buy an MSE-Six while we were back on Klatooine?"

"No . . . why?"

"Because ByTwoBee saw one come aboard," Jaina replied. "Apparently, you told her to expect it."

"*I* told her?" Lando fell silent while he digested Jaina's meaning, then said, "*Blast*! Those aren't Sith out there—they're pirates!"

Jaina was skeptical. "What makes you think so?"

"Slipping a stowaway aboard is an old pirate trick," Lando explained. "Only this time, they were creative, impersonating the captain instead of just blowing an air lock."

"Maybe," Jaina said, still not convinced. An alert tweetle sounded inside the cockpit, announcing that the StealthX was ready to launch. "Time to go. You handle the mouse, and I'll take care of . . . whoever sent it."

"Affirmative," Lando said. "I'll have ByTwoBee organize a hunt. Can you lend her your comlink?"

"Sure." Jaina passed the comlink out to the droid. "Lando has a job for you."

The droid extended one of her delicate tool arms to accept the comlink. "How do I know this is the *real* Captain Calrissian?"

"You'll have to trust me on that." Jaina closed her flight suit again, then added, "That's an order, by the way."

"Well . . ." A soft hydraulic hiss sounded beneath BY2B as she allowed her telescoping legs to compress. "If it's an *order.*"

Jaina lowered the canopy and fired the engines, then slipped through the containment field and swung toward the stern, hanging tight beneath the asteroid tug to avoid silhouetting herself against the milky glow of

Ashteri's Cloud. With the *Rockhound*'s sensor suite temporarily disabled, any worthy captain would maneuver around behind the huge tug, then launch a first salvo from as close as possible, straight down the thrust nozzles.

Even at full acceleration, clearing the *Rockhound* took longer than Jaina would have liked. The asteroid tug was nearly two kilometers long, with a white, carbon-scorched belly pocked by rows of bantha-sized tractor beam projection wells. Around the perimeter dangled dozens of telescoping stabilizer legs, two hundred meters long even fully retracted. The stern of the ship was obscured by the glow of an efflux trail so enormous and bright that Jaina felt like she was flying into a comet's tail.

Finally, the canopy's blast-tinting darkened. Jaina dropped the nose of the StealthX and shot away from the *Rockhound,* counting on the brilliance of the vessel's huge efflux spray to blind distant eyes to the silhouette of a departing starfighter.

"Okay, Rowdy," Jaina said, addressing her astromech droid by the new nickname she had given him. "Bring up the passive scanners and prep the shadow bombs."

A long whistle of inquiry filled the cockpit, and Jaina looked down to see a question scrolling across the primary display. SHADOW BOMBS? WHAT DID CAPTAIN CALRISSIAN *SAY* TO YOU?

"This is no time for jokes, Rowdy," Jaina said. "Besides, your humor protocol is lame. Who installed it, anyway?"

Rowdy replied with a mocking tweedle. I WILL NEVER TELL.

Jaina chuckled. It was already an old joke between them, since she herself was the one who had designed and installed the protocol. During a recent bout of melancholy over ending her engagement to Jagged Fel, she had decided to spend a little downtime pursuing what had been one of her favorite teenage passions: tinkering with stuff. The result had been a new humor routine for her astromech droid—and one that had the unexpected benefit of reversing the R9 series' tendency to self-enhance their preservation routines. The bolder version was a definite improvement, at least to Jaina's way of thinking. But she still had not decided whether the lame jokes were a reflection of her rusty programming skills, or a subconscious effort to echo the bad jokes her brother Jacen used to tell back on Yavin 4— before *he* became Darth Caedus and *she* became his executioner.

An alert chime sounded from the cockpit speakers, and another message rolled across the display screen. BOGEYS COMING FAST.

The screen switched to a tactical map showing three generic starcraft symbols speeding toward the *Rockhound*'s tail. A fourth symbol, hanging at the top of the display, was not approaching at all.

"*That* doesn't look like a turbolaser assault in the making," Jaina observed. "Rowdy, how sure are you of your sensors?"

ALL SENSORS ARE FUNCTIONAL AND CONCORDANT, the R9 reported. WE HAVE FOUR POTENTIAL TARGETS, AND WE HAVE ONLY FOUR REMAINING SHADOW BOMBS AND NO LASER CANNONS. IF THAT IS NOT CHALLENGE ENOUGH, I CAN ALWAYS SHUT DOWN ANOTHER ENGINE.

"Very funny." As Jaina spoke, she was watching data readouts appear beneath each of the symbols on the screen. "Didn't I just *say* this is no time for jokes?"

WHO IS JOKING?

Jaina was too busy studying tonnage estimates to respond. The three craft approaching the *Rockhound* were carrying far too much mass to be starfighters, while the vessel hanging back was only about half the mass of the ChaseMaster frigates the Sith were using. In fact, its thermal profile lacked the high-output signature of military-grade engines at all, and there were no energy concentrations large enough to suggest a turbolaser preparing to fire.

"Rowdy, give me more on those bogeys in the lead." As Jaina spoke, she began to ease back on the control stick, bringing the StealthX up and pointing its nose toward the trio of tiny blue flickers still closing on the *Rockhound*. "They can't be fighters, or they would have attacked by now."

A magnified enhancement of the lead bogey appeared on Jaina's display. The image suggested a blocky craft about twenty meters long, with a wedge-shaped bow and four undersized ion engines attached to the stern. Thermal imaging showed a main cabin packed with at least twenty beings, while a small energy concentration just beneath the roof seemed to suggest the presence of a cannon turret.

Jaina frowned. "Maybe Lando was right," she said. "That looks like an assault shuttle."

NEGATIVE. THE HULL ARMOR ON AN ASSAULT SHUTTLE WOULD DEFEAT OUR THERMAL IMAGING, Rowdy reported. IT IS SEVENTY-EIGHT PERCENT LIKELY THAT ALL THREE CRAFT ARE LIGHTLY MODIFIED BDY CREW SKIFFS.

"Okay . . . and I suppose the *lightly modified* means that cannon turret on the roof?" Jaina asked.

AFFIRMATIVE. BDY SKIFFS ARE NOT SOLD WITH ARMAMENT OPTIONS.

"And *that's* why pirates love them." As she spoke, Jaina was trying to recall the latest intelligence on the rash of pirate attacks that Jaden Korr was investigating. The last she'd heard, he was still focusing on the middle Hydian Way, which was a long way from the Maw. "Vessels without military-grade sensors usually can't see a small cannon turret, so they don't get too worried when they see a BDY skiff coming."

SO WE ARE NOT BEING ATTACKED BY SITH?

"Apparently not," Jaina said, feeling relieved. A Sith frigate would have been a problem. But three shuttle-loads of pirates? That, she could handle. "It looks like someone is trying to board us."

The display returned to tactical scale, and Rowdy added a designator label beneath the large vessel, still hanging back at the top of the screen. AND THIS DAMO-RIAN S18 LIGHT FREIGHTER IS THE MOTHER SHIP?

"That's right," Jaina said. "Classic pirate tactics—get close and send over some fast shuttles."

THEN THIS IS GOING TO BE MORE FUN THAN WE THOUGHT, Rowdy reported. A DAMORIAN S18 IS LARGE ENOUGH TO CARRY *SIX* BDY SKIFFS.

"*Now* you tell me."

Just because an S18 *could* carry six skiffs didn't mean it *was,* but Jaina had to assume the worst. She continued toward the approaching vessels, trying to think of a way to take out six shuttles and a mother ship with only four shadow bombs, and quickly realized there wasn't one. Those pirates were no idiots. The three shuttles were staying at least a kilometer apart—well beyond the blast radius of a shadow bomb—and they were approaching in a staggered line.

"Rowdy, arm bomb three," she said, designating number three because bomb racks one and two were empty. She continued to close on the lead shuttle until the tiny flicker of its efflux tail had stretched into a blue dagger as long as her arm, then ordered, "Activate our transceiver and open a hailing channel."

A bleep of protest sounded over the cockpit speaker, and Jaina glanced down to find a message on the dis-play. A STEALTHX EMITTING COMM WAVES IS NO LONGER

A STEALTHX. IT IS JUST A POORLY ARMED, LIGHTLY AR-
MORED X-WING SAYING *COME GET ME.*

"We're required to issue a warning before opening
fire," Jaina said. Her target was just visible to the naked
eye, a tiny durasteel box with a wedge-shaped head,
being pushed along by an efflux tail as long as a cannon
barrel. "And you know how I feel about breaking the
law."

THERE IS AN EXCEPTION FOR CLEAR INTENT, Rowdy
pointed out.

"Better safe than sorry," Jaina said. "Besides, I want
them thinking about *us,* not the *Rockhound.* Do I have
that channel yet?"

An affirming *twoweet* filled the cockpit and the transceiver touch pad on Jaina's control stick turned green.

I UNDERSTAND, Rowdy scrolled. YOU ARE JUST TRYING
TO MAKE THIS MISSION INTERESTING. COUNT ME IN.

"Glad you approve," Jaina said, wondering if the
droid might be getting a little *too* brave. "Launch bomb
three."

She felt a soft bump beneath her seat as a charge of
compressed air pushed the shadow bomb out of the torpedo tube. Reaching out in the Force, she began to guide
the bomb toward its target, then placed her thumb over
the transceiver touch pad.

"Attention, BDY crew skiffs: Turn away *now,*" she
transmitted. "This will be your only warning."

During the two full seconds of silence that followed,
the lead skiff swelled to the size of a bantha outside
Jaina's cockpit. She could see the flexible ring of a telescoping air lock affixed to the hull at the front of the
passenger cabin, the band of the transparent viewport
stretched across its wedge-shaped bow . . . and the flattened dome of a weapons turret, swinging its laser cannons in her direction.

A gravelly female voice came over the cockpit speaker. "Turn away or *what*, Jedi Solo? We know—"

The transmission dissolved into a stream of static as the shadow bomb detonated. Lacking any real shielding or armor, the shuttle's crew cabin simply vanished into the silver flash of the initial explosion. The stern and bow spun away trailing bright beads of superheated metal; then the StealthX's blast-tinting darkened, and all Jaina could see was a ball of white fire dead ahead. She pulled the stick back and rolled away, pointing her nose toward the hidden bulk of the mother ship.

A soft chill of danger sense tickled her between the shoulder blades. She slipped her thumb off the transceiver pad and went into an evasive climb, juking and jinking so hard she felt the craft vibrate as Rowdy slammed into the walls of his droid socket. The crimson streaks of cannon bolts began to brighten the void all around, flashing past a lot closer than she would have liked. Even without a comm signal for their targeting systems to lock onto, the pirate gunners were doing a good job of keeping her in their crossfire.

The gravelly voice came over the cockpit speaker again. "That wasn't much warning, Jedi Solo."

Instead of replying, Jaina ordered Rowdy, "Get me a location on that transmission. Is it coming from one of the skiffs or the mother ship?"

Before Rowdy could answer, the voice spoke again, "You didn't even give me time to issue a recall order."

Space outside turned crimson as a cannon bolt glanced off the StealthX's weak shields. Knowing the enemy would see the bolt's change of vector and realize exactly where she was, Jaina instantly rolled into a spiraling dive . . . and cringed as space again turned red. Half a heartbeat later another bolt struck, then blossomed into a golden spray of dissipation static.

An alert buzzer sounded inside the cockpit, and Jaina

glanced down to see a message flashing on her display: SHIELD OVERLOAD.

"No kidding." She pulled her nose up and corkscrewed back toward the two shuttles, and the stream of fire quickly drifted away from her StealthX. "What about that transmission source?"

THE SIGNAL ORIGINATED FROM THE MOTHER SHIP.

"Thought so." Jaina swung onto an interception course with the nearest shuttle, then said, "Arm bomb four."

She had barely spoken before cannon fire began to flash past again, turning the void as bright as a bonfire. She spun into an evasive helix and continued toward her target. The enemy continued to close in on her, the bolts streaking past so close that the canopy's blast-tinting went dark and stayed that way.

"Rowdy, are we still transmitting?" she asked.

A negative chirp came over the speaker.

"What about leaks?" Unable to see her target through the darkened canopy, Jaina dropped her gaze to her display and began to fly by instruments. "EM radiation? Fuel? Atmosphere?"

Again, a negative chirp.

"Keep checking," Jaina ordered. "They're tracking us *somehow*."

A message scrolled across her primary display. BY SIL-HOUETTE? ASHTERI'S CLOUD IS STILL BEHIND US.

"I don't think so," she said, fully aware of the difficulty of tracking a distant speck of darkness by sight alone—especially one that was spiraling toward its target at thousands of kilometers an hour, with the gunners blinded by the flashing of their own laser cannons. "Not without the Force."

A soft ding announced that they had closed to launching range of their second target. With the canopy still darkened by the constant barrage of cannon bolts, guiding the bomb to its destination by sight was out of the question. So Jaina expanded her Force awareness in the direction of the shuttle until she felt the living presences inside. She was not surprised to sense a heavy taint of darkness in them, but she *was* shocked by how calm they seemed, by how focused and disciplined they appeared to be.

Of course, that was about to change. "Launch bomb four."

Jaina felt the gentle bump of the shadow bomb being forced from the torpedo tube. She reached out for it in the Force—then grew distracted by the all-too-familiar *bang-screech* of a cannon hit. Alerts and alarms immediately filled her ears, and the StealthX went into an uncontrolled . . . *twirl*? It felt like she was in one of those thrill rides that spun around the central axis of the car, plastering their passengers against their seats. Jaina eased the stick in the opposite direction and slowly brought the starfighter back in line . . . then realized she had lost control of the shadow bomb, and her heart rose into her throat.

"Uh, Rowdy?"

YES?

"Any idea where number four went?"

IT DID NOT STRIKE THE TARGET, Rowdy reported. OR US . . . YET.

"Not funny," Jaina said. The extra velocity of the launch had probably carried the shadow bomb far enough away from the StealthX to avoid triggering the proximity fuse—but when it came to baradium warheads, *probably* wasn't much of a safety margin. "No joking when there's baradium involved."

YOU DID NOT WRITE THAT INTO THE APPROPRIATENESS ROUTINE, Rowdy complained.

"Consider it an addendum."

Noticing that the canopy's blast-tinting remained

dark, Jaina checked her tactical display and saw that she had overshot her target by only a couple of kilometers. Despite her erratic course, both shuttles still seemed to know where she was, more or less, and they continued to pour fire in her direction. She banked into a turn, starting back toward the nearest craft, and found her stick heavy and slow.

"Rowdy, what's our damage?" she asked. "I've got a sluggish stick."

THAT IS HARDLY SURPRISING, Rowdy replied. THE VECTOR-PLATE POWER ASSIST IS OUT, AND WE HAVE LOST THE END OF OUR UPPER RIGHT S-FOIL.

The attitude thrusters, of course, were located on the foil ends.

"*Great,*" Jaina said. She checked the tactical display and saw that the remaining skiffs had closed to within a dozen kilometers of the *Rockhound*. That left time for only one more pass before the pirates reached the tug and began boarding operations. "Adjust the power levels to compensate, and arm bomb five."

OUR MANEUVERABILITY IS LIMITED, Rowdy warned. AND THE SHIELDS HAVE NOT YET REGENERATED.

"No problem." Jaina assumed a course parallel to her targets and began to overtake them, trying to align her interception vector so the nearest skiff would be directly between her and the farthest. "I don't need shields to take down a bunch of pirates."

EXPERIENCE WOULD SUGGEST OTHERWISE.

"That was just a lucky hit," Jaina said. "Never happen twice."

Despite her words, the cannon bolts continued to come fast and close. Her blast-tinting was so constantly dark that the interior of the cockpit felt like a closet during a lightning storm, and she could not shake the feeling that those gunners were too *good* to be ordinary pirates. Maybe they were ex-military—something like retired Space Rangers or Balmorran void-jumpers, perhaps even a band of outlaw Noghri.

The interception vector on her display finally lined up with both shuttles, and the blast tinting grew semi-clear as the farthest stopped firing to avoid hitting the nearest. Jaina quickly swung in for a flank attack and accelerated, easing the stick this way and that, fighting to keep her interception vector aligned with both targets. As she drew near the first skiff, its cannon bolts grew brighter, longer, and closer, and again the canopy turned as dark as space itself.

Jaina reached out in the Force, focusing on the dark-tainted presences ahead, and said, "Launch bomb five."

Again came the gentle bump of a shadow bomb being forced from its tube. She caught hold of it in the Force—and felt the StealthX jump as cannon bolts started burning through its light armor.

"*Stang!*" she cursed. "Who *are* those guys?"

A cacophony of alerts and alarms filled the cockpit. Jaina shoved the stick forward, diving for safety beneath the shuttle's belly where, at such close range, the cannon barrel would not be able to depress far enough to target her.

And this time, she did not release the shadow bomb. She kept her attention focused on the sinister presences inside the shuttle, pushing the bomb toward them even as her StealthX spiraled out of control. Rowdy tweeted and whistled, trying to draw her attention to the urgent messages scrolling across the display, and the second shuttle resumed fire, stitching a line of holes down the fuselage.

Then a white brilliance filled the void, so bright and hot that it warmed Jaina even inside her vac suit, and she felt the searing rip of two dozen lives being torn from the Force.

Afterward, everything remained quiet and dark inside

the cockpit, and Jaina thought for an instant the detonation had taken *her.* Then her stomach grew queasy. The blazing blue of the *Rockhound*'s efflux tail flashed past above her, and she realized her shoulder was straining against her crash harness. Her ears were ringing with damage alerts and malfunction buzzers, and her throat was burning with the acrid fumes of system burnouts. She hit a chin toggle inside her helmet, then coughed into her faceplate as it slid down to seal her inside her vac suit.

"Activate suit support." She grabbed her stick and began to right her tumble, bringing the starfighter under control *gently,* in case the superstructure had suffered any damage. "Give me a damage assessment."

NOT AS BAD AS IT COULD BE, Rowdy reported. WE STILL HAVE TIME TO STOP THOSE LAST PIRATES—AS LONG AS WE SUFFER NO MORE LUCKY HITS.

Jaina surprised herself with a grin. "I like your style, Rowdy." She glanced down and found the last shuttle highlighted on her tactical display, less than a kilometer behind the *Rockhound* and already starting to climb toward its belly. "But I was wrong. Those *weren't* lucky hits."

An inquiring beep sounded inside Jaina's helmet.

"Their gunners have been using the Force." Jaina swung around and accelerated so hard that her battered StealthX began to wobble and pitch. "That's why they hit us every time I launch a shadow bomb—they can find me in the Force."

PIRATES HAVE THE FORCE?

"*These* pirates do," Jaina said. The last skiff came into view and began to swell, four tiny circles of blue arranged around a boxy gray stern. "Arm bomb six."

Rowdy emitted a confirming tweedle, then scrolled a message across the cockpit display. IT HAS BEEN NICE

FLYING WITH YOU, JEDI SOLO. THANK YOU FOR GIVING
ME A SENSE OF HUMOR SO I WILL FIND THIS AMUSING.

"Relax, will you?" The hair on Jaina's neck stood up,
and a stream of cannon bolts began to fly back over the
skiff's stern. "They have a blind spot."

Jaina pushed their nose down, and the stream began
to fly past dozens of meters overhead. A moment later
the skiff passed beneath the stern of the *Rockhound*
and, dwarfed by the tug's two-kilometer immensity, continued forward between the massive stabilizer legs.

Knowing what would happen the instant the gunners
felt her reach for their craft in the Force, Jaina hung
back half a kilometer, then said, "Launch bomb six."

When she felt the charge of compressed air shove the
shadow bomb free of its launch tube, she grasped it in
the Force and pulled up hard. As she had expected, the
skiff rolled on its back, trying to bring its weapons to
bear before the bomb struck home. Jaina was already
rising into its ion stream, nearly scraping her canopy on
the *Rockhound*'s belly as she guided the bomb toward
the four blue circles of the BDY's thrust nozzles.

Rowdy issued a shrill alarm tweedle, no doubt warning her about the dangers of remaining inside the skiff's
ion tail. The friction alone would be pushing the
StealthX's skin toward the combustion point, and Jaina
could feel for herself how the turbulence was straining
the starfighter's battered frame. Still, she remained inside the efflux, her attention fixed on the bright blue circles until they finally swelled into the silver flash of a
detonating shadow bomb.

Half a second later the StealthX hit the bomb's shock
wave and Jaina slammed against her crash harness. The
temperature inside her vac suit shot up so quickly, she
thought her hair would burst into flames. The spatter of
ricocheting debris rattled through the starfighter, and

then there was nothing ahead but the dark-pocked sky of the *Rockhound's* vast white belly.

Jaina brought the StealthX under control. The starfighter's superstructure was showing through the nose in a couple of places, and its fuselage was vibrating so badly that she feared it was coming apart around her. She began to ease away from the *Rockhound's* underside.

"Rowdy, how are you doing back there?" she asked. "Still with me?"

There followed a short silence, then a single fuzzy beep finally came over Jaina's helmet speakers.

"Glad you made it," she said. "What's that mother ship doing?"

A blurred message scrolled across the cockpit's main display. TO DETERMINE THAT, WE WOULD NEED A FUNCTIONING SENSOR ARRAY.

"Good point." Jaina could see that the forward array had been melted completely off, so it made sense that the aft equipment had suffered heat damage, as well. "Can you open a channel to Captain Calrissian for me?"

A scratchy beep sounded inside her helmet, and a moment later Lando's static-distorted voice asked, *"Jaina?"*

Jaina pressed a thumb to the transceiver pad on her stick. "In the flesh," she said. "Do you have that mouse problem under control yet?"

"Just blasted it myself," Lando replied proudly. "Ornate will plot new jump coordinates as soon as you're aboard."

"Tell her to start plotting *now*," Jaina replied. She could see the hangar mouth's dark rectangle only a few hundred meters ahead, and she wasn't planning on making a gentle approach. "Jump the second she has them."

*"Jump?"* Lando echoed. "No way, not until ByTwo-Bee tells me you're aboard and—"

"*Lando*! Just make sure the barrier field is off." The hangar mouth was starting to swell rapidly as Jaina approached, and Rowdy was filling her helmet with wave-off alarms and speed alerts. "If you wait for me to buckle down, the *Rockhound* will be taking cannon bolts up her thrust nozzle. The situation is worse than we thought. A *lot* worse."

"That's hard to believe, considering how bad it was to start with." Lando's voice faded as he issued orders to RN8, then asked, "Okay, Jaina, worse than we thought *how*?"

"Well, you were right—and so was I." As Jaina spoke, floodlights began to shine down from inside the hangar. Ignoring a cacophony of alerts from Rowdy, she brought up the nose of the StealthX and streaked toward its gaping mouth. "They *were* pirates. *Sith* pirates."

# STAR WARS®
# FATE OF THE JEDI

Join the classic characters of *STAR WARS*
and a new generation of heroes
in this epic saga spanning nine novels.

A long time ago in a galaxy far, far away. . . .

# STAR WARS

**JOIN UP!** Subscribe to our eNewsletter
at readstarwars.com or find us on social.

**f** StarWarsBooks

**🐦** @DelReyStarWars

**📷** @DelReyStarWars

**t** DelReyStarWars

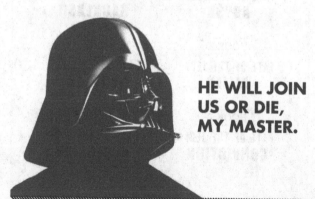

**HE WILL JOIN
US OR DIE,
MY MASTER.**

DEL REY

P.O. 0005513416 202